STEVE HEUZINKVELD

THE RAUDER BROTHERS

& THE LIZARDMEN'S PIT

For my wife, Hariezoy.

PROLOGUE

Gentle ocean waves lapped at the pearl white sand underneath the high midday sun. The azure blue water of the surrounding sea was a mirror image of the cloudless sky above. Far away from the prying eyes of the locals on the mainland, this lone tropical island's serene oval-shaped beach was virtually uninhabited – or so it seemed.

To the untrained eye, the sandy mound in the centre of the isolated haven was just an ordinary hillock. But for those who knew the island and its well-protected secrets, the camouflaged bunker served as a transport hub, one of the many hidden entry points into an underground network of tunnels that stretched across the entire world.

Yet despite the multitude of secret entrances into this subterranean labyrinth, this particular location was by far the most important; for beyond the northern end of the egg-shaped beach, where the fine grains of sand gave way to lush vegetation and dense jungle, laid a sprawling village. It was the last safe refuge for a race of forgotten people in an ever-expanding world, and for many of the *Kirzakai*, it was home.

Veiled by the thick foliage of palm leaves and mangrove trees, unblinking sentries scanned the surrounding shoreline for any signs of trespassing tourists and wayward fisherfolk alike. Stealth and seclusion were paramount to their species' survival.

One of the guards hissed in alarm – a sound that could easily have been mistaken as a mere rustle of leaves – as she spotted a solitary figure emerging from the sunken bunker.

It was Furesh, the Master of Combat and the Chieftain of the Ridgebacks; the last tribe to pledge their allegiance to Thorax. Furesh's terms had been simple: if Thorax could unite all of the tribes that had warred with each other for centuries – without bloodshed – he would have the undying loyalty of the Ridgebacks. In times past, too often had emissaries approached Furesh and his kin for military aid in dominating the other *Kirzakai* tribes, only to have their skulls added to his trophy collection. Thorax was different.

The battle-scarred seven-foot warrior strode towards the tree line, the trail of his clawed footprints concealed by his long powerful tail snaking through the sand in his wake. Twin scimitar swords dangled loosely on either flank from his scaly webbed hands as he crossed the threshold of jungle undergrowth. He stopped short of the wooden gate nestled deep within a shadowy grove of tangled trees.

Furesh tasted the air with a flicker of his forked tongue, his dark green eyes pinpointing each and every camouflaged sentry hiding within the dense tree line. His long snout curled into a faint smile at their fearful gazes, revealing a glint of the Lizardman's jagged teeth.

He was a menacing sight to behold. His eyes were sharp and stern, like those of an unforgiving instructor, as would befit the Master of Combat. A trio of short horns adorned the tip of his bony-plated wedged snout. His densely packed muscles bulged within his steely grey scales, and a row of spiked thorns protruded out of his spinal column like arrowheads, from the nape of his neck to the tip of his tail.

Still in awe at the sight of the revered Master of Combat, the chameleon guards slowly opened the gates of the palisade wall, bowing their hunched heads even farther to the ground as they granted him passage into the covert capital.

Sunlight filtered down through the thick foliage of mangrove trees to reveal the serene refuge. Steam rose from hot springs where young lizards splashed and played. Sandy paths formed over trodden vegetation snaked their way through the low mud-brick walls of the settlement.

Remaining motionless, Furesh stared open-mouthed at the peaceful village before him. Thorax had ruled them well. These *Kirzakai* seemed as though they had never seen a single raid. Brood mothers lazily watched their children frolicking free of fear in the shady hot springs. Fully grown males garbed in worn vests and loincloths – absent of any scars of war – trudged to and fro with woven baskets of freshly caught fish. One by one, their heads turned to see the lone figure standing at the open gates, their eyes focusing on the pair of scimitar swords held firmly in his sinewy hands.

Remembering why he was there, Furesh snapped his gaping mouth shut. He raised his powerful tail in the air and slammed it down on the ground behind him, sending an expanding oblong-shaped halo of sand flying from the earth-shaking impact.

Heeding their Chieftain's signal, the twoscore Ridgeback warriors lying in wait upon the beach rose from the shallows like their dim-witted flat-walking relatives discovering an innate ability to walk upright. Droplets of water fell from their thorny spines, coursing down their armoured scales in rivulets. Each of Furesh's highly-trained soldiers – his only type of soldiers – shook wet sand from the prongs of their tridents as they assembled into formation.

The five lines of eight marched with military discipline towards the gates. With the forty at his back, Furesh entered the village. Bewildered, the chameleon guards on their tree branch perches clumsily scrambled for their shortbows and javelins, even though none of the lowly sentries would dare challenge the Master of Combat.

Luckily for them, they would have no need for their weapons.

Unmet by any welcoming party, Furesh and his soldiers calmly strode past the pools of steamy hot springs. Lizard youths scurried out of his path, chattering in their own native tongues in the warriors' wake as hushed excitement rippled through the shady grove.

Furesh and his company emerged from the trees and stepped into an open field surrounded by jungle. The sunlit square was filled with *Kirzakai* of all different shapes and sizes sitting upon stone rocks around wooden tables. Former rivals mingled with their brethren as they feasted upon an array of fish and fruit in celebration of the long-desired peace among the tribes.

At one table, some Horntails were lecturing a pair of Frillnecks on defensive techniques as the latter feigned interest while gorging themselves on spiky fruit. At another, the normally aggressive Gravelhides had allowed the mulish Bluetongues to share their meat. Even the antisocial Blackbead chameleons hovering at the edges of the square did their best not to disappear into the trees as the ever-friendly Redcrowns approached to bring them plain wooden platters of crawling insects.

There was no sign of the scholarly Highbeaks; however their whereabouts had been unknown for hundreds of years, presumably wiped out in tribal conflicts, so Thorax could not be blamed for their absence.

One thick-set Horntail leapt up from his stone rock seat at the sight of Furesh. Like the Ridgebacks, Horntails, too, possessed thorns on their hide; although a Horntail's spikes grew not only along their spine, but also everywhere else. The Lizardman's leather brown chevron-patterned scales absorbed the sunlight as he angrily marched towards the new arrivals. Rearing up to his full height, he stood a head above Furesh.

"You and your warriors dare to bring weapons to this occasion!?" he boomed in a heavy tone, drawing attention from the feasting tribes. "Explain yourself, in common tongue!"

"Calm yourself, Boaresh," said Furesh, surveying the unarmed crowd. "You would know better than most that I am just as dangerous standing alone with naught but my tail."

"Watch your arrogance," Boaresh warned. "If it were not for your height, I would have mistaken you for Jawresh."

"And if it were not for your weight, I would have mistaken you for the Horntail Chieftain," Furesh threw back.

Boaresh shook with a series of low hisses, and onlookers from the crowd set their sights upon his uncertain Horntail followers rising to their feet, until the Chieftain erupted into brassy laughter. He held up his forearm, and he and Furesh knocked their elbows together in greeting.

"True!" Boaresh exclaimed, clapping a webbed hand on Furesh's shoulder as the forty Ridgeback soldiers dispersed to join the feast. "It has been many years since we have last met. This era of peace has drawn flab to my flanks. I find myself growing more Frillneck than Horntail with each passing day. I rue the day Thorax convinced us to join him."

"Yet it is for the good of our people," said Furesh.

"For the good of our people," Boaresh agreed. "Come! Give your respects to the *Kirzaka* who has united us!"

* * *

Seated on one side of the open field, the colossal red-eyed brute known as Jawresh watched the pair of Chieftains as they crossed the festive square. Tyrod – the impressionable adolescent brood son of Thorax – sat alongside the immense iron grey Gravelhide, sinking his teeth into the belly of a six-foot yellow-fin tuna.

"*Maxter of Combat*," Jawresh rasped scornfully. "If I had risen to power before your brood father came to my tribe, I would have xlaughtered that puny worm long ago."

Tyrod chortled, fish blood foaming from his snout. "You'll have your chance to prove yoursself againsst him." Hatched in the likeness of his brood father, Thorax, Tyrod's rear scales were coloured a walnut brown, splotched with small patterns of yellow to match his pale underbelly where his peppered brown scales became scarce in turn.

Tyrod was a member of the Bluetongues, commonly referred to as *The Builder Tribe* due to their passion for constructing walls and digging burrows, made possible by their long fingers and strong forearms. They could adapt to almost any diet and habitat, provided that there was a hot sun to bask under and a permanent source of water nearby. They possessed the ability to climb trees with their sharp claws to forage for food, or hunt for prey in the surrounding waters using their vertical blade-like tail to steer and propel themselves forward.

"Anyone can take on a xnake," said Jawresh, the shell of a crab crunching as he gnashed the crustacean whole within his massive maw, "Thix is no challenge. I crave for combat."

"Yess," said Tyrod, licking his lips with his blue tongue. "But *you* are the only one to have ever wresstled a *fully grown Colossiboa* into ssubmission."

"As far as we know…" a plump Lizardwoman wearing a purple robe over her orange hide said softly behind them. They turned to see the female Frillneck Chieftain, Kalarish, gouging at the innards of a juicy pineapple with her claws. "Only time will tell which of uz has the greatezt ztrength."

"Yess, time," said Tyrod. "The fasstesst contender to ssubdue a *Colossiboa* will become the new Champion of the Chieftains."

"And take charge of the Desert Complex, which is to be dedicated to learning," said Kalarish with a bitter tone of disgust. "Zuch a barbaric ritual to determine who is to become the teacher of the new generation of our unified *Kirzakai* tribes. What a wazte of a warrior, and a wazte of those who *can* teach."

"You xpeak as though your magic is xomething of value, *flesh tank*," said Jawresh. Then, with his red eyes burning brightly, "When the time comes for war, and it will come, what hope is there for the new generation, *if none of them can fight!?*"

* * *

Furesh and Boaresh approached the Council of Elders – wise, winged serpents with broad, triangular heads perched upon long slabs of intricately carved rock – each of them a treasure trove of knowledge with thoughts that could fill a library.

The colours of their hides ranged from dark orange to iron grey, but their bellies were pure white. The Elder Race rarely ever took flight, but when they did, they seemed like mere clouds passing high overhead. The only detail that one could hope to see from the ground was the puffy, jet black scales lining their throats.

Thorax humbly stood before the elders, with no ceremonial rock of his own, for though he matched them in wit and speech, he was not one of them. Some believed Thorax hailed from the Elder Race, though he was born in the body of a Bluetongue. Others believed he was born as a Bluetongue, with the mind of the Elder Race. Neither belief mattered, yet both garnered him a deep respect among all of the *Kirzakai*.

At the sight of Furesh and Boaresh, Thorax bowed from the Council to greet the pair warmly. "Furesh! Welcome to our village. I have heard rumour that no *Kirzaka* can defeat you. They shay you will become Champion of the Chieftains. Is thish true?"

"Nothing is certain, Thorax," said the battle-scarred warrior. "Only my presence here serves as testament that no *Kirzaka has* defeated me."

"Indeed, nothing is certain," said Boaresh. "I would not so easily be stripped of the title of champion, not even by the Master of Combat."

"Shuch worthy opponentsh!" Thorax exclaimed. "Let ush agree the title will be well-earned!"

* * *

Generations of *Kirzakai* had retold the tale of the *Colossiboas*. It was said that the Great Snakes had descended from the legendary Terrodrax himself, an enormous winged serpent of the Elder Race whose wings stretched across the sky. He gave his life to shield the world from a gigantic meteor, his gargantuan body the last defence against the planet's destruction. In his final death throes, he spilled his guts into the earth, which sprang to life as the *Colossiboas*.

The population of *Colossiboas* had long been managed by all of the *Kirzakai* tribes as a shared responsibility. A single venomous bite from a fully grown *Colossiboa* could reduce flesh and bone to a bubbling froth, as if one had fallen into a pit of lava. Yet their species still played a fundamental role in the lives of the Lizardmen.

As one of the rites of passage for groups of *Kirzakai* youths seeking to become warriors, they must collectively wrestle a juvenile *Colossiboa* – a Great Snake – into submission, allowing it to be harnessed, defanged, tamed, and used for transportation throughout the underground network of tunnels connecting the many different tribes spread out across the world.

On the east side of the settlement, a tangled mass of gigantic snakes twisted and coiled over itself within a dugout pit encaged in wrought iron bars. It was impossible to distinguish which head belonged to which tail as the writhing serpents competed with each other for the best vantage point of their kin being subjected to the Chieftains' contest.

The stooped Blackbead Chieftain, Teguresh, had perched atop a juvenile *Colossiboa's* head, his bandy legs locking him in place, ready to draw the leather harness over the serpent's muzzle. The Great Snake dipped its head and bucked back, sending the small Lizardman flying through the air and crashing through a wooden table laden with food to the crowd's rasping cheers. Before the dust settled, the chameleon *Kirzaka* had turned his scales to camouflage. No one was sure if Teguresh was still in the arena waiting for the right moment to strike, or if he had simply fled.

The huge scaly serpent coiled up into a defensive position with its head raised, poising to attack the next contender.

The Redcrowns serving platters of food to the roaring spectators looked imploringly at their leader, Savarish, to take up the challenge, perhaps to garner some respect for their peaceful tribe. The Redcrown Chieftain gracefully declined, having no interest in becoming the Champion of the Chieftains, reasoning that there were far better *Kirzakai* than her to take over stewardship of the Desert Complex. Some of the crowd however, inferred that she was too afraid of being thrown by the *Colossiboa* into the pack of Lizardmen ringed around the field, or locked within its deadly squeezing scales and requiring rescue.

"TREMBLE!!"

The *Colossiboa's* narrow eyes shrank in terror as Jawresh – a staggering nine feet of pure muscle, a titan amongst the *Kirzakai* – stepped forward. The Warrior Chieftain charged directly towards the coiled snake. Baring its deadly fangs, the *Colossiboa* lashed out at Jawresh. Without breaking stride, the Gravelhide dodged the strike, locked both of his massive fists together, and, with all of his raw strength, launched a bare-knuckled axe-swing into the giant serpent's head with enough force to rock it sideways.

The crowd rumbled as the dazed snake retreated. Jawresh drowned out their cheers with his own thunderous roar, parading around the field with his arms raised in an early victory. Tyrod was awestruck. Even Boaresh was impressed. Thorax laughed heartily and clapped his hands in applause. Only Furesh stood in silence, knowing that the battle had not yet been won. While everyone else focused on Jawresh's triumph, only Furesh noticed the *Colossiboa* shaking itself out of its stupor.

Still basking in the crowd's chorus, the Gravelhide Chieftain stooped to pick up the leather harness that Teguresh had dropped during his short flight. Jawresh approached the *Colossiboa*, its head lying upon the ground in feigned submission, both reptilian eyes fixed on the advancing brute.

As Jawresh shook out the harness to slide it over the snake's head, its giant tail rose almost imperceptibly, like a rock spire from an ebbing tide. Jawresh did not notice the tail's shadow until it engulfed him. The Great Snake slammed its tail into the Warrior Chieftain, sweeping him off his webbed feet, but instead of swatting him away, the immense serpent had knocked Jawresh into the heart of its coils.

A sudden hush fell over the crowd as the rest of them joined Furesh in his silence. Tyrod scrambled upon a table to watch as his idol struggled to free one of his arms from the Great Snake's embrace. Now the only applause came from the tangled mass of *Colossiboas* in the dugout pit, hissing in incomprehensible clicks and rattles as Jawresh was lost to sight in the folds of the huge serpent.

None of the other Chieftains rushed to his aid. Jawresh had long been their biggest threat; his unpredictability would not be missed. Not even the Gravelhides stirred themselves; if he could be defeated, he was not worthy of being Chieftain. The only noticeable change amongst the audience was from Kalarish and her Frillnecks, who had momentarily slowed their devouring of the unattended food on the surrounding tables with avid interest.

Thorax looked to the winged elders, who watched with indifference as Jawresh's grunts of exertion subsided, before signalling to his Bluetongue guards to intervene. Furesh's soldiers however, were the first to react, assembling into a crescent formation around the writhing beast with their tridents drawn, awaiting the Ridgeback Chieftain's orders.

"RAHAHAHAHA!!" an enraged bloodthirsty laugh erupted from the centre of the squirming snake's spiralled scales. Jawresh had managed to free an arm.

It was said that at birth, the Gravelhides wrestled with their freshly hatched brood siblings across rough terrain, rocks and grit embedding themselves into the newborns' skin until only one hatchling of the entire clutch remained alive. It seemed Jawresh had not forgotten his infancy, savagely wrestling with the Great Snake as it thrashed and coiled across the square, scattering spectators. Birds and bats took flight from the mangrove thickets as tables of food crunched like dead leaves under their combined weight.

Jawresh freed himself from the *Colossiboa's* coils, standing back to watch as the serpent writhed uncontrollably now, as if it were still grappling with a phantom opponent. Runnels of blood smeared across the ground as the pack of roaring spectators recognised Jawresh's handiwork. With his serrated teeth and claws, the raging Warrior Chieftain had torn open the snake's flesh in a dozen places.

Jawresh found the harness and brought it back to the convulsing serpent. He tossed the bridle's weighty bit inside the *Colossiboa's* mouth, its lower jaw opening and closing involuntarily in its death throes.

He was the first to complete the challenge.

Amidst the indecisive cheers of the crowd, Boaresh looked disapprovingly at the shuddering serpent that stared woefully back at him beneath the leather harness, half of its face coated in blood, leaking from one permanently-closed eye. As frightening as they appeared, the *Colossiboas* were still majestic creatures that were to be respected and embraced as part of the *Kirzakai* way of life. They were not beasts to be butchered for blood sport. At a nod from Thorax, Boaresh gave the order for the *Colossiboa* to be put down in order to ease its passing.

* * *

After the substantial body had been cleared, next up was Kalarish, facing off against a slightly smaller *Colossiboa*, yet no less dangerous. Due to her obvious lack of fighting prowess, the Chieftain of the Frillnecks had been advised against participating in the contest, yet she refused to heed the warnings.

Her tribe had never gained much respect. Commonly referred to as *flesh tanks* due to their gluttonous nature, their frilled necks originated from the excess folds of skin beneath their chins. To add insult, each of them possessed a comically small cluster of horns at the rear of their scaly skulls, resembling a tiny desert shrub clinging to life on an arid landscape. All of them shared the same simple and daft appearance, fuelled only by the desire for more food; yet they were sly and cunning creatures, patiently waiting for the opportunity to gain advantage.

For the longest time, the Frillneck Chieftain's strategy seemed to be merely staring the snake into submission with her amber orange eyes.

Snapping out of her entrancing gaze, the serpent side-winded itself across the square, but just as it launched to attack, Kalarish withdrew a large cloth from the folds of her purple robe and threw it over the snake's head. Blindly swaying, intoxicated by the fumes laced within the cloth, the *Colossiboa* fell to the ground.

If it had not been for her staring contest, Kalarish would have beaten Jawresh's time.

A fresh *Colossiboa* was coaxed out of the cage, Redcrown Lizardmen jabbing spears at its kin trying to follow in its wake. This one was an untamed, fully grown snake. Tyrod – having had a part in selecting the serpents – winked at Jawresh across the arena, confident that he would become the new champion.

Boaresh, the current champion, volunteered to take on the biggest challenge. The eight-foot tall Horntail squatting on his haunches in a ball of rugged thorns and thick muscle was a formidable sight. It was no wonder that he had reigned as champion in his youth.

The giant serpent slithered towards him, its forked tongue tasting the air before opening its cavernous mouth to reveal a pair of stalactite-like fangs.

Before it could come any closer, Thorax intervened with a flying front-kick to the side of the snake's head. The *Colossiboa* recoiled, its fierce eyes scanning the pair of *Kirzakai*. Disappointed murmurs fell upon the crowd.

"What is the meaning of this?" asked Boaresh, rising to his full height.

"Look closhely!" Thorax warned, loud enough for all to hear. He pointed at the snake's fangs.

Glistening in the sunlight, at the ends of the serpent's long poisonous barbs, small orbs of secreted venom had formed. The corrosive substance dripped across the sandy earth, melting small craters into the ground with wisps of acidic smoke.

"I do not wish to forfeit," said Boaresh, facing off against the snake again.

"Come now, old friend," said Thorax. "Thish is not a game of death. How the shnake's venom has been unnoticed for sho long is beyond me. We shall find another."

Boaresh had known Thorax long enough to know when to relent. Once a Bluetongue had reached a decision, they would stop at nothing until their will had been fulfilled, and they would walk their chosen path even if death was a certainty. Boaresh solemnly nodded his head, accepting Thorax's judgement.

Kalarish snickered, finding weakness in the gesture. Jawresh, his confidence in becoming the new champion now under threat, shot a glance at Tyrod, who shrugged his shoulders in uncertainty.

Savarish was ordering her Redcrowns to return the *Colossiboa* back to the snake pit, when a lone figure crossed her vision.

"Leave it to me," said Furesh.

The crowd surged with excitement as the Ridgeback Chieftain stepped into the arena. *Kirzakai* youths pushed to the front of the ring, their brood mothers too busy clutching at each other to grab at their children. With Furesh between them and the *Colossiboa* however, the youths were far removed from any danger.

Boaresh pulled Furesh aside, hurriedly whispering into his ear, "You realise this contest is merely a challenge to see who amongst the Chieftains could overthrow Thorax? By placing the victor in the Desert Complex on the other side of the world with such an important task is his way of distracting those who would threaten his plans for the future."

"Yes," said Furesh, his mantis green eyes glancing at Jawresh across the clearing, "But I have a reputation to keep."

Time slowed to a stop as Furesh squared off against the enormous serpent at the other end of the square. The crowd and the other Chieftains held their breath in silent anticipation. The noise of rolling waves and calling gulls no longer reached the makeshift arena, as if nature itself had muted the ambience in respect of the impending battle. Even the sun had paused in its descent to watch the fight.

Furesh clenched and unclenched the hilts of his curved swords, watching the *Colossiboa* intently. He smiled as it slowly snaked towards him, fatal venom splashing upon the earth with each twisting turn forward. The hungry serpent opened its immense mouth again as it reached striking distance. Furesh simply leaned back, his entire weight resting upon his powerful tail.

The crowd gasped in horror as the *Colossiboa* lunged forward; however, using his own tail as a spring, Furesh launched himself up out of the snake's reach. Rolling midair, he whipped the giant serpent unconscious with one deft stroke of his tail aimed precisely between its eyes. Then, landing upon his feet, Furesh curled the very tip of his tail around a strap of the leather harness, and in one fluid movement, flicked it over the snake's head.

The onlookers stared in shock and awe.

"Truly the Mashter of Combat!" Thorax proclaimed. He addressed Jawresh, "Although shtrength is a vital attribute of every warrior, the key to winning every battle is realising that control over yourshelf is more important than control over your opponent." Then, looking towards Furesh, he announced to the crowd, "Behold, your new champion!"

Boaresh led the applause amongst the crowd. Savarish and her Redcrowns joined him. Even Teguresh emerged from his hiding place to quietly praise Furesh in his victory. Kalarish snarled. Jawresh hurled his own tail at a nearby tree with enough force to uproot it and send it into one of the hot springs.

"Wait!" cried Tyrod. "He brought his sswords into the arena, he should be dissqualified!"

Tyrod's futile pleas for reconsideration on behalf of Jawresh were drowned out by the crowd's cheers for the new champion.

* * *

Feasting and revelry accompanied by grating hisses and raucous laughter continued throughout the rest of the day on the isolated island. As the sun touched the western horizon, igniting the sea with tides of crimson gold, Thorax held up his hands to lull the crowd.

"Too long has our great race been plagued by warfare, orphaned children being raised to continue to fight againsht each other, a fight which they do not undershtand. Too long have we held on to injushtices of the pasht to guide our actions for the future. Too long have we lived in the shadows, hiding ourshelves from the world in fear of the humans, and of one another. Today, we can shtrike one fear from our minds, our fear of one another. And tomorrow, we shall shtrike the other, our fear of the humans!"

Thunderous applause filled the darkening square. Torches were lit from campfires, their blazing flames dancing across the scaly faces of the *Kirzakai*. A low chorus for war against the humans rippled through the crowd.

"You sheek *war?*" asked Thorax, his reptilian eyes gazing at each of the Chieftains. "I shpeak of *peace!* Peace amongsht our brethren, and peace with the humans!"

Silent confusion descended upon the *Kirzakai*. Furesh and Boaresh exchanged a knowing glance as each tribe broke out into argument, some in support of Thorax, and others against him.

One booming voice deafened the divided crowd.

"Do you forget what they have done!?" Jawresh roared. "Now we are one, and as one, we can finally have our vengeanxe!"

His words were met with riotous approval from the pack.

"I HAVE NOT FORGOTTEN!!" Thorax silences the crowd. "Yet I have *forgiven*. Thish is the will of the Elders. Under their guidance shince my youth, I have worked to bring peace among the tribes. And under their guidance again, I will bring peace among the races."

"I shall accompany you, Thorax," Boaresh stepped forward.

"And you have my support, should you ask it of me," said Furesh, the new champion's Ridgeback soldiers following their Chieftain to Thorax's side.

"We leave tomorrow," said Thorax, one hand on Boaresh's shoulder. "Our diplomacy with the humans shall usher in a new era for our kind. One of proshperity and knowledge, but mosht importantly, one of peace. Trusht in me, brethren, as I trusht in our Elders."

None could argue with Thorax's call for peace, and for those who would, each trident borne by the Master of Combat's elite soldiers flanking either side of the trio of Chieftains served as a reason to hold their forked tongues.

* * *

Smouldering embers were all that remained of the bonfires. Many of the guests had retired for the night after a long day of festivities. Feral cats, rats and monkeys scoured the tables for scraps of food.

Tyrod waded through the moonlit water around the settlement, where the mud-covered palisade wall stood hidden behind the thick mangrove trees growing out of the shallows around the north end of the island, pondering his brood father's words.

Long ago, the humans had slaughtered thousands of the kind and welcoming *Kirzakai* out of fear, almost driving their entire race to extinction. Those who were lucky enough to escape with their lives sought new homes far away from humankind. War broke out amongst the tribes when they could not decide on a leader, splintering them further until each of them were as distrustful of one another as they were of the humans.

They had lived in solitude for centuries, disappearing from the wrathful humans' memories, and now, Thorax wished to expose their species again.

Tyrod jumped at a splash nearby.

Kalarish's tail swam lazily through the water as she lounged upon a low hanging branch, her purple robe drawn up from the water, revealing her plump scaly orange legs.

"A curiouz feeling, is it not?" she rasped, observing the young Blue-tongue, "When your brood father's ideals clash with your own."

"In the arena," Tyrod ignored her statement, curious about her fighting technique, "You hypnotised that ssnake. How did you do that?"

"Ahhhh," Kalarish exhaled. She glanced up at the palisade, checking to see whether anyone else could be listening in on their conversation. "That is the art of *conztriction.*"

"But that has been outlawed amongsst the tribes!"

"Not my tribe," said Kalarish, "It is a valuable tool which we will need when we go to war with the humans."

"But father ssays–"

"Please. It is a fool's fantazy to believe the humans will agree to peaze. War is inevitable."

"I trusst father's judgement," Tyrod lied.

"Then do not believe me, but zee for yourzelf," said Kalarish, withdrawing her tail from the water and gazing out into the night.

Tyrod looked through the trees to the distant lights of the shanty town on the mainland. As if on cue, the sound of an oar breaking the surface of the calm water reached his ears.

"We're getting close now," a man's voice said nearby. "There are people living on this island. I *know* it."

"Daddy, I'm scared," a young girl pleaded, "What if the ghosts eat us?"

"Hush now, princess. Ghosts can't light fires, can they?"

A wooden boat thudded into one of the outlying trees. Tyrod looked at Kalarish with uncertainty, thoughts racing through his mind. *Should I run? Should I try and talk to it? Or should I kill it and hide the evidence from my brood father, like all the others who have ventured too close to the island?*

Kalarish blinked back at him unfazed.

Tyrod froze in place as the man splashed into the shallows.

"Stay here, princess."

Tyrod's heart hammered in his chest as the human slogged through the water, the hidden existence of the *Kirzakai* under threat with each step forward. Then suddenly, the human's noisy approach stopped. Water swirled past Tyrod. His eyes slowly turned from Kalarish towards the man.

The human withdrew a small piece of metal from a strap around its waist. *Too small to be a spear. Too blunt to be a knife. Too hollow to be a club.* Tyrod stared at the hole in the end of the strange piece of metal pointed towards him with cautious curiosity.

The man's fleshy pink hand began to shake. He lifted another hand to double his grip on the odd-shaped contraption and took a wide stance, yet still, he trembled uncontrollably. The human raised its chin, determined not to succumb to its nerves. "Wh – Who… What are you?" it stammered, the thing in its hands rattling fiercely.

Before Tyrod could answer, Jawresh sailed over the palisade, splashing next to Tyrod and sending up a spray of seawater over the man's face. Momentarily blinded, the startled human summoned a deafening blast from the device in its hands.

Bats screeched as they took flight from the overhanging tree canopies. Jawresh snarled, looking down at the tiny bleeding hole in the meaty scales of his shoulder.

"Daddy? Are… are you okay?" the young girl's voice hesitantly called.

In a panic, the man pulled the device close to his chest to stop his shaking before taking aim at Tyrod. Before he could summon another blast, Jawresh's tail whipped up out of the water, curling around the man's hands. With one squeeze of his sinewy muscle, Jawresh crushed the human's bones and tendons until its fingers went limp, the device falling from its grip.

Before the piece of metal could pierce the water's surface, Kalarish caught it with her own tail, careful not to activate the device herself. She studied it closely before withdrawing a ceremonial dagger from her robe. She tossed the dagger to Tyrod.

"The humans wish to deztroy uz, it is in their nature," she said, before directing his attention towards the bumbling man with a stabbing gesture. "Zlay him, zlay the brood father who would bring death to uz all, and together, we will reign over the humans!"

Tyrod flickered his blue tongue, tasting the human's fear. Reaching a decision, he curled his long snout into a smile.

"Daddy, *I want to go home!*"

1 - IS THAT MY NAME?

"Bring him to safety and get that thing off his face, we'll hold them off!" Jacob Rauder turned away from his two sons to yell into the trees. "You won't take my boys!" He charged back towards the documentary crew's fight against their assailants.

The incapacitated young boy looked up at his older brother blinking back tears as he carried the boy over muddy ground under shady canopies of the thick swamp. His tears were not of sadness, but of anger. The boy knew that his brother was eager to join their father, who was bellowing in the distant muck and mire that lay behind them.

Shafts of light danced through the leafy branches overhead as they rushed to safety. Sharp and bitter aromas from the cloth tightly covering his nose and mouth began to overpower his senses. Coughing meekly, the skinny boy could not draw in breath without inhaling more of the noxious fumes filling his lungs.

His heart hammered in his ears, adrenaline coursing through him, yet his arms dangled lifelessly. His body was numb to his older brother's rough handling as he hastily ambled over gnarled tree roots and squelched through the soft earth of the swamp.

They stumbled into a clearing. His adolescent brother spun wildly, checking to see that they were out of sight. Without warning, he dropped the boy upon a patch of hard ground. The dull landing on his backside was the first touch he had felt since the onset of the attack.

His older brother propped him up between raised roots of a moss-covered tree, its crooked arms receiving him in a cold embrace. The odour from the mask was unbearable. The boy's vision obscured for a brief moment as his brother yanked the pungent rag upward from his mouth.

Gasping for air, he breathed in the stench of the swamp; sweet, at least compared to the cloth. His brother's determined face appeared before him, and then vanished with a blur, replaced by the receding outline of his backside as he sprinted back the way they had come. Heavy footfalls upon the damp earth quickly grew faint, until nothing stirred.

Their father's shouts had ceased in the distance. It was as if the swamp had swallowed the noise altogether. The boy's head lolled around, trying to make sense of his surroundings. It was all just bogs of murky water and mud-sodden earth. It was a wonder how his brother had managed to drop him on the only hard patch of ground in the swamp's clearing. His gaze fell upon the mask tossed on the ground at his feet. He could not even guess what poisons had been laced within its fabric.

For an instant, he thought that he saw their camper van parked in another clearing just beyond a thicket of bald cypresses, but then his vision spun and blurred, weaving the grey tree trunks together into an ever-changing tapestry of melting paint. His chin dropped to his chest, and his eyelids grew thick and heavy.

His name was Benjamin Rauder. His friends at school would have called him Ben, if he had any. He was the polar opposite of his older brother, Raymond, a superb athlete at whatever sport he played, with an uncanny ability to talk to girls, both of which he usually achieved without even breaking a sweat. Ben, on the other hand, often felt that he was just a dirty secret that his brother needed to hide.

Ben never really had a good relationship with their father either, when he was around. Both of the members of his family shared an unspoken grudge against Ben, distancing themselves away from him ever since he was a child. The guilt of their mother's death was forever a burden upon Ben. She had died during childbirth. Ben was saved, but she was not.

The Rauders' kind and understanding neighbours took him and his brother in whenever their father was away for work. His job as a documentarian required him to travel frequently. His research focused mainly on evolution and reptiles. On this trip however, their father had decided to take Ben and Ray along with the documentary crew.

It was a rare occasion, but their father had decided on short notice that they would be moving to a new house after they wrapped up the filming. Ray was furious; all of his friends, including his girlfriend, were there in their hometown. Ben, on the other hand, was elated at the prospect of having a fresh start.

They had spent a few hours travelling on the road, riding together with their father's close friend, Joshua, before they came to a small town, where reports of a mythical swamp creature had resurfaced. The locals called the monster *The Lizardman*. Deputy Sheriff Lee Sullivan, along with two residents living nearby the swamp, volunteered to help them with the investigation. They ventured into the far reaches of the swamp before the entire film crew was attacked.

They had been led straight into an ambush.

Ben sat with his back against the tree, his head still spinning. Though the distant noises of the fight between the documentary crew and their assailants had subsided, the sinister sound of something even more disturbing drew closer.

Twigs snapped and mud squelched beneath dragging feet from behind the tree where Ben was sprawled. In a sudden panic, he attempted to crawl away, but for all of his remaining conscious effort, he only managed to lurch over to one side. Lying as still as a mouse under the watchful gaze of a cat, Ben shifted his eyes upward in his sideways world to see what approached.

Ray staggered into view, wrenching at a second mask covering his face, tugging desperately as he stumbled about, gasping for air, only to inhale more of its toxic fumes. Ben watched as his older brother collapsed, succumbing to the mask's effects before he himself slipped from consciousness.

* * *

Ben woke up in a small room upon a musty thin mattress, his body thick with perspiration. The sweat was mingled with fear from the flashback, and the humidity clinging to his skin. It was as if he had been removed from the cool shady swamp and whisked away to an entirely different climate, although both were just as stifling.

Shallow breathing; not his own, but close by. Ben chanced a glance to the side of his prone body to see a cold stone wall. His mind raced with questions. *Where am I? Where's Ray? And Father?*

He might have pondered further, if only he knew the source of those light rhythmic breaths. And that smell, almost overpowering his nostrils. He noisily suppressed a gag in the dank atmosphere.

A creak from below. The shallow breathing paused, as if a predator was poising to strike. Without thinking, Ben sat up to throw himself against the wall, but instead, he thumped his newly-shaven head against the low ceiling. He reached up, running his fingers over his roughly hewn scalp. *When did that happen?*

Dazed, he looked around at the small room. His narrow cardboard-like mattress stretched its length. The bed sheets were stained yellow. A rather miniscule iron-barred window set in wood existed inches from the foot of his bed. Ben sat up again, slowly this time.

No, it wasn't a window at all. He had only seen the top of a door. He was elevated.

Another creak sounded from below. Whatever it was could pierce through his thin mattress at any moment.

Acting out of fear rather than instinct, Ben leapt across the tiny room, a beam of light flashing before his eyes. A hollow metallic rattle sounded as his left shoe sank into something soft, warm, wet.

A screech of laughter filled the small room. "'ad a fall did ya?" It was difficult for Ben to see the reedy-voiced speaker. A shaft of light from an iron-barred hole in the ceiling of the otherwise dark room cast a bright veil between them, illuminating a metal drain set within the stone floor, reflecting an aura of sorts into the surrounding shadows. The bed frame creaked again as the silhouette sat upright, "Name's Daniel. The ovva boys call me Little Danny."

Metal scraped across the stone floor as Ben stumped into the square patch of light. Looking down, he suppressed another gag. He almost kicked the bucket over as he jerked his freshly-stained brown sneaker out of the mess. It matched the dried mud strewn over the lower half of his grey trousers and the back of his black shirt.

"A welcoming gift, prepared by yours truly," Little Danny chirped, rising from underneath the shadowy bed frame with a peevish grin.

Wiping his soiled shoe against the drab stone floor, Ben looked Little Danny over. The boy was not much younger than himself, but he was indeed little, standing almost a foot shorter, garbed in an oversized green shirt and matching pants. His bright blue eyes looked up at Ben.

"Well, what's your name then?"

Ben took a moment to gather his words, looking down at his own feet again. A blinking red light emitted from a dirty metal bracelet around his left ankle. "Ben… Benjamin Rauder. Ben," he answered, glancing at an identical manacle around the other boy's left foot.

"Oooh, you got a last name! Lucky you, Benny," Little Danny stretched his sallow malnourished cheeks into a wide grin.

"Where are we?" asked Ben.

"'ave a look for yourself," he said, nodding towards the door before picking his nose.

Through the iron-barred window, Ben saw a cavernous square hall full of doors just like the one in their room. Before Ben could ask another question, keys jangled outside, locks turned and metal clanked. He caught a glimpse of a dirty blonde-haired man, his face bristling with facial hair like a lion's mane, before the hardwood door was flung inward, narrowly missing Ben as it slammed against the wall with a heavy thud.

"Time for work, Benny," said Little Danny, wiping his finger on the door as he led Ben out into the large room where other boys were gathering.

"*Work?*" Ben repeated, a combination of curiosity and confusion across his face.

* * *

Far away from Ben and the others, a flickering light beyond the veil of his eyelids drew the adolescent to consciousness. A faint pull on his numb hand caused him to stir. His head throbbed. *Have I been in an accident?* He could not remember.

A sly chuckle from nearby pierced his thoughts. "At least we won't have to shave this one's head," said the speaker.

A second voice, closer than the other, gave a devilish giggle.

The teenager felt his head being raised, none too gently. Small hands worked roughly around his neck as his head lolled. Something metallic coursed over his shoulders, and a small weight lifted from his chest. His eyelids snapped open as his head dropped back down upon a hard surface.

His eyesight was groggy, but he could clearly see a gold chain glittering across his vision. A pallid pointed face came into focus. A pair of small green eyes beamed up at the golden necklace as the strange man held it aloft, curiously peering at the gilded diamond-shaped pendant. The necklace was something of significance to the teenager; however the unfamiliar face standing above him was not. The man's skin was so ivory and pale, he would have appeared to be an albino if it was not for his greasy black hair.

A caged tungsten bulb hung from the ceiling, illuminating the small room intermittently as the light flickered on and off in a smoky haze.

The muscular adolescent's boots and jeans were caked with dried mud. He was lying upon a wooden workbench, the only furniture in the room other than a rusty metal minecart propped up on railings across from him. The rail tracks ran between two of the three closed doors set in the surrounding concrete walls.

This is definitely not a hospital room, he thought to himself.

"Sully said this one didn't go down so easy," came the first voice again, "Gave 'em some trouble. They left his snare on longer than they should'a."

The voice belonged to a spiky-haired leather-vested man. He took a puff of his cigarette, sending up another plume of smoke into the smoggy ceiling.

Both men wore batons in their belts, although neither of them would ever be confused with a police officer. They admired the golden piece of jewellery, a medallion engraved with intricate etchings; both of them unaware of the late teen's rousing.

Tingling sensations struck the adolescent as he attempted to regain control over his stubborn body. He willed his numb arm to move, making a grab for the necklace, yet he watched his hand drop out of sight over the side of the wooden bench.

"He's stirrin'," nodded the taller of the two men. With his sunglasses and leather-vest, he took another draw on his cigarette as his companion's green eyes flitted fearfully towards their rising captive. The short man squealed in surprise, taking a step backwards and shoving the necklace into his front pocket. "Get him in the cart," said the leather-vested man, pushing his accomplice forward.

"You trying to rob me?" said the adolescent as he swung his legs from the workbench down to the stone floor, steadying himself as a rush of dizziness came over him.

The pallid man saw his advantage. He pulled the baton from his belt and raised it above his head, preparing to strike. The soft whistle of the blunt object halted suddenly as the captive caught his attacker's wrist.

The dumbstruck man stood with his mouth agape as the teen's other arm shot up to clutch his throat. Now standing, with a relentless grip around his captor's neck, the prisoner twisted around and slammed the wide-eyed man onto the table.

The adolescent watched his would-be assailant's pointed face pathetically gasp for air before kicking the bench over, sending the stunned man toppling over with it.

Something flashed over his eyes, followed by the cold metal of another baton being pressed up against his own throat. The muscular teen twisted his torso and threw an elbow back, landing a blow into the taller man's ribs.

"Get up and help me!" the captor wheezed behind him, keeping a firm grip on his chokehold, the shock stick pressing even tighter, crushing his windpipe.

The green-eyed man rose, fuming. He stepped over the upended workbench and he advanced with a devilish grin, eager for a second swing.

The captive reached up to clutch the baton squeezing his throat. Using the bar for support, he jumped up to deliver a double-kick into the short man's chest, sending him tumbling backwards over the table again. The prisoner's weight however, was too much for the second attacker to hold. He dropped to the hard stone floor along with the baton.

The teen yelped as sharp pain shot up his spine. It was a pity that his body's numbness had worn off already. He broke off the fight for a brief moment to catch his breath and raise his lower back off the floor in an attempt to alleviate the agony.

It was all the time they needed. The short man behind the bench tossed his shock stick across the room to his companion. A click followed by a static charge sounded from above.

The prisoner lunged for the other baton on the floor, but it was too late. Regret of his moment's pause hit him twice with two swift blows across the back of his neck. The electrical current from the baton shook through his very bones as he writhed and convulsed upon the floor. They worked him over with their fists to make sure he was down for the count, although part of him sensed that they seemed to enjoy it.

The defeated teen stared up at the man standing over him, fixing his sunglasses. He could not help but notice the familiarity of the silver ring around the man's middle finger. In a daze, the prisoner pondered where he might have seen it before. He could not remember.

The two captors hauled him up and loaded him into the rectangular bucket of the minecart standing by on the metal tracks in the floor. The leather-vested man disappeared from view for a moment, and a door creaked open from behind the adolescent slumped in the cart. The tall man returned to the teen's sight again, gripping the minecart's handle.

With an annoyed grunt, the greasy-haired captor grabbed hold of the cart's handle, flitting his fierce green gaze between his companion and their prisoner.

"Fine," said the other man, stepping away from the minecart with indifference. "You can push him the whole way if it makes you happy."

The short man's lips curled into a malicious smile. He bent down over the prisoner, his pallid pointed face filling the teen's vision, but only for a fleeting moment. With an aggressive kick against the cart, he sent the adolescent hurtling through the open door. Sailing backwards on a steep descent, the minecart's ungreased metal wheels grinding along the rail track sounded like fingernails dragging across a chalkboard.

The brief ride ended with a resounding crash, throwing the prisoner's head back against the cart's frame. The pale captor squealed with high-pitched laughter. The two men stood at the top of a flight of stairs, the twin set of rail tracks running its course. The pair of captors made their way down the steps towards the minecart, exchanging and sheathing their batons.

Shaken, the prisoner tried to lift himself out of the metal cart, yet the only movements he could make were the involuntary twitches from the after-effects of the electrical shocks still pulsating throughout his body. He glanced down at his feet, his eyes drawn by a blinking red light emitting from a bracelet fitted around his left ankle.

The pallid-faced man turned the minecart in the direction of a narrow corridor to the prisoner's left. The other captor shimmied past the cart and rounded the corner, taking the lead through the passage. The metal cart scratched against the stone walls with each turn. It was a small yet strangely warm corridor. The slight smell of sulfur filled the adolescent's nostrils, the stinging aroma making his eyes water.

Thick wooden doors lined the left side of the hot corridor. A small square window with three vertical bars was set within each door, allowing for a view into the rooms beyond; but in the prisoner's seated position, he could see nothing but a faint red glow accompanying the heat emanating from each of the barred windows. Over the sounds of the trundling cart, he could just barely make out a series of rasping whispers coming from the other side of one of the doors.

Another door creaked open up ahead, its rusted hinges screeching in protest, and the men wheeled the cart into the centre of a passage smaller in length. With a door on their left and two on their right, the spiky-haired man held up a hand. Reaching into his vest, he withdrew a pack of cigarettes and a lighter. The short captor shifted with impatience as the other man lifted a butt up to his mouth, attempting to spark a flame.

One of the doors on their right swung open and a tangle-haired blonde girl dressed in a green shirt and matching trousers entered, closing the door softly behind her. Her strained eyes widened at the sight of the two men leering at her.

The prisoner opened his mouth to speak, but he could only manage a rough croak. His vocal chords were still traumatised from being choked by the baton. He was lucky his Adam's apple had not been crushed altogether.

The girl opened up the second door on the right, opposite from where she had come. The captive flailed an arm against the side of the minecart to call for her attention, in the hope that she could at least explain what was happening and who these men were.

Their eyes met for a brief moment; yet glancing up at the two men again, she quickly disappeared out of sight, hurriedly shutting the door behind her. A plume of smoke blew after her, and the man in the leather vest shot the prisoner a sly grin.

The minecart turned to the left, towards the only remaining door in the passage. Taking another drag of his cigarette, the tall man opened the door just a fraction, peering through the crack into the room beyond. Whatever was waiting for them on the other side, it made him thrust his hand with the silver ring into his front pocket.

* * *

The ceiling of the big square hall was almost double the height of the cell they had emerged from. Ben gazed around from the corner of the room. Three of the four walls were lined with cell doors. To his right, the dirty blonde bearded man continued to unlock other doors, kicking them open to allow more boys to shuffle into the cell house, forming a line. They all wore the same green uniform as Little Danny.

Another door slammed against the wall in the far left corner of the room, opposite from where Ben and the small crowd were gathering. Two men marched into the cell house with a rusty metal minecart in tow. That was the only wall without a row of cell doors. Instead, behind a rack of chains and just to the right of the open door, a flight of stairs led upwards to yet another wooden door. Ben surmised that these two doors were the most important in the cell house, because neither of them had an iron-barred window.

In fact, there were no windows at all to show the outside world. Only four spotlights suspended in each corner of the room, casting pools of glaring light upon the row of prisoners.

"New one, 'ey?" said a fourth man, standing in front of Ben. He wore a shirt that might have been white at one stage, but it had long since become a sweat-stained yellow. His round face cracked a mischievous smile, showing his crooked yellow teeth. "Be a good boy and line up wiv the rest." He turned to address the two men in the corner, his loud voice echoing throughout the room, "Spike, took your time mate! Day shift's about to start!"

"Just came to make a report from the outpost, Mac," answered the taller of the two, clad in a leather vest and sunglasses, "Got stuck bringing in the new inmates." He leaned against the minecart with one hand in his pocket, flicking ash from his cigarette.

"Aye, and y'had Gremlin for company, no wonder you're late," said Mac, approaching the pair of men. The short one, green-eyed with greasy black hair and a pallid pointed face grimaced at the sound of his name. He wore a long-sleeved black shirt, casting a stark contrast against the ivory white of his skin.

"Better do what 'e says," Little Danny murmured quietly, motioning for Ben to join the line-up.

Ben shuffled forward, joining the end of the row of uniformed teenage boys. All of them wore matching manacles around their left ankles, each blinking with the same red light. The only thing that separated Ben from the others was his clothes' distinct lack of green.

* * *

Still groggy in his seated position, the prisoner in the minecart could not see the source of the new voice over the rim of the cart, but he looked up to see who the speaker was referring to; the green-eyed man known as Gremlin, who was now fuming in silent anger.

"'ey, what's that?" the third man enquired menacingly. Spike stepped aside as footsteps approached the minecart, and a bald man with a mischievous look in his bright blue eyes came into view. "That's your name sunshine, don't like your name?" He grinned, revealing two rows of crooked yellow teeth to match his sweat-stained shirt.

Gremlin looked away sullenly.

"If y'don't like your name, just say someth–" he stopped ridiculing Gremlin, taking a sudden interest in the short man's front pocket. "What's this then, 'ey?"

The bald man snatched the gilded necklace hanging from Gremlin's trousers before he could react. Gremlin watched disdainfully as his prize was hung around someone else's neck. Mac held the necklace's shiny golden pendant up with dirty fingers to examine it, stroking his bald head as he admired his reflection.

He turned to Spike, "'ow's it look on me, mate?"

"Makes you look English," Spike smirked.

"We was made for each ovva then!" Mac exclaimed with a crude laugh. He turned to the adolescent staring blankly up at him from the minecart. "Don't mind, do ya?" he winked, "Already awake, 'ey? Gotta tell them ovva Watchers to up the dose on the venom snares!"

* * *

The prisoners watched the exchange between the three men in the far corner of the room, while the grizzled dirty blonde guard paced up and down the line of boys with dwindling patience. He was wearing a tattered and faded gold suit, with the sleeves cut at the elbow, exposing his hairy arms and chest, like some sort of movie super-villain who had lost all of his fortune and now had to work his way up from the bottom again.

Ben's eyes wandered towards the rack standing near the centre of the room. Long lengths of metal chains glittered underneath the glare of the four spotlights. To the left of the rack, another set of stairs led downwards to a room below.

"What is this place?" asked Ben. "What did you mean by *work?*"

"Don't wanna ruin the surprise, do I?" said Little Danny with a peevish grin.

Ben tried a different tact. "How did I get here? And where is my family?" Little Danny shrugged, turning his attention back to the three men surrounding the rusty minecart. Ben sighed in frustration, annoyed by his cellmate's lack of answers. "Who are all these people?" he asked, looking at the other boys in the line.

"Inmates," said Little Danny, finally offering some information. "Just like you and me."

Ben wondered what he could have done to deserve imprisonment. He remembered his flashback with a sudden realisation. *I've been kidnapped.*

* * *

"Hurry up," a gruff voice barked across the room. "I can hear the inmates from the morning shift already coming in downstairs!"

Sure enough, the captive slumped in the rusty barrow could hear shuffling noises and the voices of tired teenage boys rising up from a room somewhere below.

"Make yourself useful," Mac said to Gremlin, "Get 'im outta the cart and line 'im up wiv the rest ovvem."

Gremlin nodded begrudgingly, his green eyes lingering on the gold medallion. The pale man gave a grunt as he heaved against the metal cart, turning it on its side and spilling its contents out onto the floor.

* * *

Ben rubbed at his eyes. *How could this be?* He stared almost in disbelief at his older brother, Ray, as he lay sprawled on the ground.

"What a terrible start to the day," said Little Danny behind an impish smile. "Not even waking up in 'is own bed, and then 'aving to look at Gremlin first thing in the morning!"

Ray glanced around at the cell house, taking in his surroundings, sizing up the four men, and noting more guards descending the staircase along the plain wall behind him. He saw the owner of the gruff voice, a grizzled dirty blonde-haired man toying with the shock stick in his belt.

And then he saw them.

An entire row of other teenage boys and adolescents just like him. They stood at the far side of the room, all but one wearing the same green uniform that he had seen on the tangle-haired blonde girl in the small passage. Red lights blinked back at him from metal bracelets strapped around each of their ankles.

Ben stepped forward out of the line-up. Ray barely reacted at the sight of him. Ben knew that his brother had bad eyesight, even when they were young, but surely Ray could distinguish him from the other inmates. Maybe he could even shed some light on what was happening.

"Ray!" Ben called, moving to approach his brother, yet faltering at the sight of the bearded guard turning towards him, one hand on the baton in his belt.

Ray stared with curiosity at the one boy amongst them who was not clothed in green. The boy's black shirt and grey pants were stained with muck, identical to the dried mud that was caked on his own boots and jeans.

A pair of rough hands pulled the new prisoner to his feet and pushed him towards the others. He steadied himself and shoved Gremlin away.

With the guards watching his every step, and even more filing into the room behind him, he warily approached the line of inmates.

Ray. Is that my name? It sounds familiar enough.

Either way, the odd one out in the line-up was sure to have some answers.

2 - WELCOME TO PARADISE

Ray walked towards the line of inmates standing at the far wall of the cell house, but before he had the chance to speak to the only other boy not wearing the green uniform of the prison, the grizzled blonde-haired guard stepped between them.

"Get moving," he growled, shoving Ray towards the flight of stairs in the centre of the room leading down to the level below. "All of you, pick up the pace, we're already behind schedule!"

The line of inmates broke out into disarray as the larger teens jostled for position to be the first to reach the stairs. Ben joined the rush, trying to keep an eye fixed on his brother while avoiding the elbows of the other prisoners. Whether by disadvantage of his smaller stature, or by the seasoned inmates' prejudice against a newcomer advancing through the pack, Ben soon found himself at the back of the mob of teens, having lost sight of Ray in the process.

Ray, still worn out from the fight with the pair of guards earlier, halted at the top of the stairs. He decided to wait for the other inmates to cross the room, unsure of what awaited him down below. Gremlin seized advantage. With two quick steps towards his prey, the short man elbowed Ray in the back, sending him tumbling down the flight of stairs.

Stone steps and green uniforms and wooden tables filled his vision in a spinning blur. Catching himself before his face hit the ground, Ray looked up to see a queue of inmates inside what seemed to be the prison's cafeteria.

All of them were decked out in the same identical green uniforms as the boys climbing down the stairs after him. The only difference was that the clothes of the inmates in the cafeteria were dirty and soiled, and many of them were too hungry, thirsty, or just plain tired to notice him lying on the floor.

* * *

"Move aside, dreg," said a slick black-haired inmate as he kicked Ben out of the way.

Ben held up his hands in surrender, not wishing to fight, much to the amusement of the smug delinquent and the pig-eyed skinheaded goon standing beside him. Two more boys laughed with a delayed reaction, as if they were obliged to. One was horse-faced with a bent nose, and the other was covered in freckles. Chortling long after the other two had lost interest, they followed the pudgy goon as he shoved his way past other inmates down the stairs, with the snide and smirking teen kicking out at anyone who tried to fill the space behind their larger companion.

Mac, the bald-headed guard, sauntered towards Ben, hands on his hips with one finger toying with the hilt of his baton. "Don't expect any special treatment just 'cause it's your first day, sunshine," the guard said, his bright blue eyes twinkling with glee.

Ben nodded and quickly joined the straggling inmates milling about around the top of the stairs. Even though the remaining prisoners were smaller in size compared to the other boys, Ben still stood back as they pushed their way past.

* * *

"Wouldn't want to look like them after a day's work, would you?" came a smug voice from above.

Ray looked up from the floor to see a skinny boy with slick black hair standing over him, trying his best to put on a friendly face as he gestured at the weary prisoners sitting at the tables, hunched over their bowls of food. Standing next to the slick-haired boy, a chubby but muscular skinheaded inmate reached down to help Ray up to his feet.

"Sergei thinks you want an easy work, yes?" said the bull-necked prisoner in a thick Russian accent. He dusted Ray off. "Come, join Sergei and Levi."

"You'd be much better off with us than this rabble," said Levi, looking over his shoulder at the other inmates filing down the stairs.

Ray turned around, locking eyes with the boy who had called his name, standing at the top of the stairs behind the thronging teens.

* * *

Little Danny appeared next to Ben. "Better get used to being at the back of the line, Benny," he said. "You'll 'ave a chance to talk to your friend when we 'ave something to eat."

"He's not my friend. He's my brother," said Ben, catching sight of Ray at the bottom of the stairs, talking with the four inmates he'd had the misfortune of meeting only moments ago. Ben was relieved to see that his brother was barely paying attention to them, although they were just the type of people that Ray would normally have associated himself with back in their hometown.

There was a time when Ben had been knocked to the floor of a busy corridor at school, with his books scattered around him. Ray's best friend had walked by, and instead of helping Ben up to his feet, he kicked the books down the hallway, sending pages and notes flying everywhere. Ray had merely stood by when it happened.

Ben knew that this place, whatever its purpose, was very different from being in school. He just hoped that Ray would actually take on the role of an older brother this time around.

* * *

"I'll have to get back to you on that," said Ray, not even bothering to make eye contact with Levi.

"Offer won't last forever," Levi replied, clearly displeased by Ray's answer. He and Sergei joined the queue of inmates eagerly awaiting food and water.

"Wise choice," said the next inmate to join him at the bottom of the steps. His skin was thick and brown like tough leather. He laid a gorilla-like hand on his barrel chest and introduced himself. "My name is Rashad. What is your name?"

"Ray, apparently," he shrugged, still unsure of his own identity. "What makes my choice so wise?" Ray glanced at the two inmates ahead of them, only just now seeing another pair of prisoners shadowing Levi and Sergei, the two smaller boys standing nervous and uneasy.

"They work the minecarts," said Rashad, jerking his head towards the queue. Ray lined up alongside him as he explained, "Nobody respects those who work the minecarts. They take it easy while the rest of us slave under the hot sun. And in here, taking it easy is like painting a target on your back."

"Good to know," said Ray. "More importantly, maybe you can tell me what's going on?"

"Like the rest of us, you are here for manual labour," Rashad answered. Ray snorted. Rashad did not see the joke.

"What? You're serious!?" Ray exclaimed. Rashad nodded solemnly. "There's gotta be a mistake, I haven't done anything wrong! At least... not that I can *remember*."

* * *

Ben and Little Danny descended the steps as the inmates steadily joined a queue extending past the bottom of the staircase. The room was full of wooden tables, each surrounded by roughly hewn stone blocks that served as chairs. Other prisoners with soiled uniforms sat wearily upon the carved rocks, eating spoonfuls of thick mucus-like gruel.

Guards stood at the front of the room behind a stone bench, looking out over the crowd, and a tangle-haired blonde girl wearing the same green uniform of the prison ladled portions of the goopy porridge from a large cauldron into wooden bowls borne by each inmate.

"'ave a look at what I snagged off Gremlin, Leon," said Mac with a yellow-toothed grin, gloating to another Watcher as they descended the stairs behind the inmates. Ben saw that it was the same dirty blonde bearded guard from before.

"Be careful who sees that," Leon growled, glancing at the other guards standing at the front of the cafeteria, another Watcher already striding down the line of inmates towards them. "Don't you know what that means?" Leon jabbed a finger at the symbol in the centre of the gilded diamond-shaped medallion hanging from the golden chain around Mac's neck.

Ben's eyes widened at the sight of the intricate carvings. The fine etchings were divided across the four quarters of the pendant; one section with tiny coins upon balancing scales, another with a hammer driving a chisel into a pillar, the third with the flames of a fire, and the final section engraved with a sword and shield. He had never known what the symbol meant, but he knew that the medallion belonged to his father.

* * *

Rashad shushed Ray as a guard with a marine-style crew cut approached, his hawkish grey eyes at first enlarging at the sight of the new inmate, and then narrowing as if piercing through Ray as he strode past towards the back of the line.

"What is this place," asked Ray, "Some kind of juvenile detention centre?"

"Wishful thinking," said Rashad. "Can you remember anything prior to waking up?"

Ray thought hard for a moment. He shook his head.

"Do not worry, your memory will return in time," said Rashad. "But what you must know is: you have been kidnapped, and no one will be able to trace your disappearance. The world already believes that you are dead.

Do not give the guards a reason to make it become so."

"Kidnapped!? What would they want with us? They wouldn't be holding us for ransom if the world thinks we're dead."

"No," said Rashad. "They simply want us to work."

"There's gotta be a way outta here," said Ray, looking around the prison's cafeteria, as if he was the first prisoner to look for an escape route.

"Shhh, you will attract the Watchers' attention," said Rashad in a low tone, looking over his shoulder. "There is only one path out of here."

"Which way's that?" asked Ray.

"It is not a path you would wish to take," Rashad said flatly.

* * *

"What's that around your neck, Cormac?" came a stern voice as the pair of Watchers reached the bottom of the staircase.

Leon spat on the floor, with a sideways glance at the bald-headed guard.

Cormac's blissful smile quickly faded into a stony face of contempt. He whirled around to stand toe-to-toe with the speaker. "What's it to you, 'ey!?" he snapped.

The taller man slightly raised an eyebrow as he cocked his head to one side, silently demanding his question be answered. Their eyes locked, each trying to stare the other into submission. The guard drilled his hawkish eyes into Cormac's, unwavering. Cormac craned his head forward, holding the man's gaze.

"Finders keepers, Caleb, get your own," he spat before turning back to face Leon. He had half-formed words in his mouth when Caleb spoke again.

"Wager you for it," said Caleb. The inmates in the line shifted at his words.

Cormac narrowed his eyes, but this time he did not turn to face his challenger. "You're not usually a gambling man, Caleb. What've you got to offer me then, 'ey?" he asked, his eyes intently fixated on Leon, whose slight smile glinted through his bushy mane.

Caleb worked his jaw in contemplation, his cheekbones flexing as he bore his steely gaze into the back of Cormac's dome-like skull. "Keys to the pickup truck…" he answered, "For a week."

Leon let out a gruff chuckle. Cormac's ears prickled, a small smirk playing on his lips, but not enough to show his yellowed teeth as he turned to face Caleb again.

* * *

Murmuring erupted amongst the inmates behind them, and Ray turned back to see small groups huddling together in the line. Sets of two and three inmates sized each other up as the other groups formed. Their attention flitted between their fellow prisoners and a trio of Watchers standing at the back of the shifting queue.

"What's going on?" asked Ray.

"Whatever happens, keep your head down," said Rashad, turning to face Ray directly, spreading his feet in a wide, solid stance to lower his centre of gravity. His eyes slowly moved from side to side, scanning the groups of prisoners standing at their flanks.

Ray looked over the tops of the other inmates' heads to see Mac addressing the other Watcher who had passed them earlier. They appeared to be in the middle of a heated discussion. Mac nodded his bald head in Ray's direction.

From the corner of his eye, Rashad caught the same gesture. "Get ready," was all he said.

* * *

"I'll take the fresh ones," said Cormac, "That bigger one that just came in looks like 'e's got a bit of fight in 'im, gave Spike and Gremlin a bit of grief earlier," he nodded towards the front of the line. "Plus their new friends," he added on impulse more than anything, shoving Ben and Little Danny forward.

Caleb looked down at Ben, scrutinising the skinny boy with his flint grey stare. "I'll take Sergei and Levi," he said, pointing over Ben's shoulder at the two prisoners already eating, who seemed thrilled to hear their own names mentioned. "They never seem to disappoint. We'll round out the numbers with Cameron and Bryson." The horse-faced boy and the speckled inmate sitting with them reluctantly obliged.

* * *

As if in answer to Ray's confused expression, the guard standing with Mac pointed towards a nearby group of inmates who had just sat down with their bowls of porridge, or some ghastly abomination of the food.

Sergei, Levi, and their two shadows stared up at Ray and Rashad, the former already cracking their knuckles, and the latter incensed at the thought of having to leave their meals. The four inmates got to their feet.

Sergei extended his arms out wide, grinning at Ray. "Nothing personal!" he announced in his thick Russian accent.

Rashad raised his fists. Sergei's smile faded. He bent forward and charged at Rashad, catching him in the midsection between his blocky bull-neck and broad shoulder. Levi and the other two advanced towards Ray, but he was slow to react, still worn out from his previous fight with Spike and Gremlin.

"Don't fight back, and we'll let you join us," said Levi.

* * *

Cormac lowered his head between Ben and Little Danny, placing his grubby hands around their shoulders. His hot stinking breath whispered into their ears, "You boys win this for me, and I'll see to your rewards, 'ey?" He shoved them both forward.

The pack of inmates made way for them as they timidly advanced towards the fight, and then crowded around to form a circle. The other guards in the cafeteria jumped on top of the rock slab at the front of the room to get a better view, some of them placing their own bets.

Ray stood with his arms by his sides as Sergei and Rashad rolled on the ground. Smirking at Ray's lack of aggression, Levi directed the other two to help Sergei, and then prepared to deal with Ben and Little Danny.

Levi ran to meet them halfway, jumping up and kicking them both in the chest at the same time, sending them to the floor. He landed on his feet, sneering at them, to the general disappointment of the crowd. They had been hoping for more of a show.

Ray looked back towards Rashad. He did not appear to be struggling as he held back Sergei and the other two inmates with a pair of solid arms and a knee.

"Mercy!" yelled Rashad, despite his lack of need for it.

"No more!" Little Danny sobbed, covering his face and curling up into a ball.

Ben attempted to rise to his feet, but a hard kick to the ribs put him back on the floor.

"Welcome to Paradise!" said Levi. "Stay down, or me and Sergei will keep you down!"

Ray watched the other mud-stained newcomer squirming on the ground, his thin wiry arms shielding his face and chest as Levi aimed a volley of kicks at his torso, and an image of the same wide-eyed boy being thrown to the floor of a school hallway, his books scattering around him, flashed unbidden in Ray's mind.

Blinking hard, forcing his lost memories to stay buried for now, Ray tapped Levi on the back of his shoulder, interrupting the one-sided fight. Levi whirled around to face him, and with a flash of his arm, Ray sent a hard right fist into the bully's cheek. Levi crumpled to the ground like a house of cards, massaging his face with a whimper.

Ben wheezed as he tried to sit up. Little Danny, dry-eyed, sprang on top of the fallen Levi with an impish grin. He raised his scrawny fists in the air and rained them down on Levi's chest again and again and again like a manic drummer hammering out a drum solo.

Ray turned to deal with the other three, who now encircled him.

"So! You have made choice…" said Sergei, "Bad choice."

Before Ray could react, Sergei charged forward and caught him across the chin with an outstretched arm, clothes-lining him to the hard stone floor. The fight appeared to be over as the skinheaded goon kicked Little Danny off Levi, sending him sprawling as the other inmates around them began to chant.

"Bang on! Bang on! Bang on!" they pounded the tabletops, eager for more.

"ENOUGH!!" Leon barked, standing at the front of the cafeteria on top of the stone bench with the other Watchers. "Cormac, pay up. Caleb, get the last shift back in their cells!"

The gambling guards in the room made their exchanges. The prisoners in the queue shifted their attention back towards the pot of gruel, and the inmates at the tables filled their clenched fists with wooden spoons. Soon, the cafeteria returned to the sound of hungry boys eating.

Rashad sprang to his feet and helped Ray up. Sergei grinned at Ray as he and the other boys got back to their seats. Levi scowled as he massaged his cheek where Ray had clocked him.

Rashad led Ray over to a bench stacked with empty wooden bowls and spoons alongside the cauldron of gruel, first filling Ray's bowl with water from a tap set in the wall, and then his own.

Ray gulped the water down, and the tangle-haired blonde girl he had seen earlier ladled goopy porridge into his bowl before he could refill from the tap. He and Rashad found some empty seats fashioned from blocks of stone. Ray dropped down on the rigid surface without complaint.

* * *

Ben and Little Danny clambered to their feet. Cormac's reeking breath filled their nostrils as he drew close again.

"You boys cost me this pretty necklace," he said, savouring his final moments with the medallion as Caleb rallied the dirty and sweaty inmates from the previous shift up from their seats. "I think you'll be 'aving some special treatment on your first day after all, sunshine," Cormac winked at Ben.

Caleb strode back towards them, his steely eyes locked with Cormac's, expecting payment.

"It's too bad," said Cormac, "I woulda loved to get acquainted wivvat local bird you're seeing." He glanced down at the pendant still around his neck, then back at Caleb with a crude smile. "What say I give you a shiny gem from me collection instead, 'ey?"

"A bet is a bet, Cormac," said Caleb, his hand outstretched.

Cormac's smile vanished as he reluctantly lifted the medallion off his chest, throwing the necklace at Caleb's feet. "Oops, 'ow clumsy of me."

* * *

"You fought well," said Rashad, "Next time, try not to."

Ray cocked an eyebrow at him. "Is that what you meant by *keep your head down?*"

"You drew attention to yourself, but that could have happened to anyone," said Rashad. "Fights in the cafeteria, mostly over food, are frequent, and bets are placed between the Watchers over seized inmates' belongings." He indicated the stern Watcher, Caleb, donning the golden medallion he had won from Cormac as he monitored the inmates from the previous shift marching upstairs. "But you would still do well to keep your head down."

* * *

Ben and Little Danny shuffled forward in the queue, finally reaching a table stacked with empty bowls and spoons. Following the actions of the inmates who had been ahead of them in the line, Ben filled his bowl with water from a tap on the wall. He drank slowly, his ribs still aching from Levi's kicks.

The blonde girl working behind the gruel pot had to reach her entire arm down into the cauldron's mouth to scrape up what was left at the bottom. She heaped a spoonful of what appeared to be porridge into Ben's bowl. It smelled like spoiled fish. Little Danny smacked his lips.

Wrinkling his nose in disgust, Ben found Ray easily in the crowd of uniformed inmates, and they approached his table.

* * *

Ray lifted a spoonful of the goopy gruel to his mouth and spat it out immediately, the taste of cardboard and newspaper lingering on his tongue. He looked around at the surrounding inmates as they hungrily wolfed down the grey gravy.

"It is enough to fill our bellies, if you can manage to keep it down," said Rashad, swallowing with hardly a grimace. Clearly it was an acquired taste. "We have a long day ahead of us. You should eat."

"A long day of what?" asked Ray. "What's this manual labour you were talking about?"

"Ray," said a voice beside him, calling for his attention as he contemplated whether he would actually eat the foul porridge.

He turned to see the inmate he had saved from Levi, along with the scrawny one who had gone down beside him. The newcomer brushed off a dirty stone seat next to Ray before gingerly perching upon it.

"Who are you?" asked Ray.

The boy's eyes widened at the question. "Ray, it's me, Ben," he said. Ray stared at him blankly before deciding to give the sloppy gruel another chance. Ben tried again, "*Benjamin*. I'm your brother, don't you remember me?"

The name did not ring a bell. Ray pinched the bridge of his nose, trying to remember if this boy really was his brother. Flashbacks of the skinny boy being pushed back and forth in a school hallway entered his mind again. *Who is this kid?* He thought to himself. Definitely not his brother; Ray was not the type of person to let people treat his brother like that. Or maybe he was that type of person, and he just could not remember it yet.

Ray chewed the disgusting oatmeal in silence, staring at Ben.

Looking into his older brother's eyes, Ben could see that Ray was in another place entirely. *How can this be? How can he have suddenly forgotten who I am? Or maybe he's just playing another one of his mean jokes on me again, pretending we aren't actually brothers.* It would not have been the first time. However, it *was* the first time that Ray had defended Ben when he had knocked Levi to the floor.

The thickly-built inmate sitting across from the two brothers introduced himself as Rashad, shaking Ben's hand with a firm grip. "Your brother has lost his memory, for now. It is an occasional side effect of the venom snares they used to capture you."

Ray contemplated thoughtfully, cringing as he swallowed the cardboard-like gruel. Cormac had mentioned the "venom snares" earlier, although Ray had no recollection of what they were. He watched the scrawny inmate sitting beside Rashad gleefully lift a spoon full of porridge only to let it slop back into his bowl.

"Little Danny's me name, pleased ta meet ya!" the boy exclaimed in a reedy voice.

Ray ignored the boy, turning to Ben. "If you're my brother, then you should know how we got here."

"You don't remember?" asked Ben. "I thought you would know more than me. I was going to ask you what happened to our father!"

Leon cut across the chatter, standing at the back of the cafeteria alongside Cormac and a handful of other guards, clapping his hands and rousing the inmates' attention. "Time for work, ladies!" he barked. He spat to punctuate his words, his saliva arcing through the air and splashing into one unfortunate prisoner's half-eaten meal. "Day shift, on your feet!"

Rashad pushed aside his empty bowl. Little Danny hurriedly shovelled food into his mouth as others rose from their seats around them. Ray followed suit, eating the gruel, but he could not bear to finish it; just watching the scrawny kid devour the cardboard slop caused him to lose even his forced appetite. Ben attempted to eat some of the goopy porridge. He took one mouthful and cringed.

"Eat more," Rashad urged. "You will need your strength for today."

Ben took one more mouthful before pushing it away with a disgusted moan.

* * *

The Watchers marched the inmates through a door at the back of the cafeteria, across a wide corridor – flooded by daylight at one end, with a dark ramp leading upwards into an unseen room at the other end – and through another door opposite the cafeteria.

Shovels and mattocks lined the cinder block walls of the tool shed. Empty minecarts stood at the far end of the room, and a large metal drainage pipe ran the length of the ceiling, with small downpipes connected to it in evenly spaced intervals from the cells above. Everything in the room told its own unique history of wear and tear, with blunt-edged tools, rusted metal wagons, rotting wooden handles, and mould growing on the ceiling and the upper walls, no doubt as a result of water damage from leaky pipes.

"Come on, Benny," said Little Danny, leading Ben over to the rack of shovels. "Sergei and Levi would never let guys like *us* push the carts."

Ray started towards the mattocks, but Rashad caught him and pulled him in the direction of the shovels. "Do not take the easy work. But do not take the hard work either."

The Watchers ordered the inmates back out into the wide corridor, then they marched to the left and into the warmth of the brilliant daylight streaming in from outside. As the inmates filed out of the tool shed, Sergei and Levi cut across the brothers' path with a minecart, chuckling.

"Welcome to Paradise," Sergei grinned.

3 - BACK OF THE LINE

The crowd of inmates trudged outside and into the morning light. The sun cast its rays between a row of decaying stone columns, the weather-worn pillars supporting cells above the complex's entrance. Large storm drain outlets were set on either side of the exit. Mould from the sewerage runoff encrusted the foundations of the building. Small metal drainage grates lined the outdoor ceiling between the support pillars, with one grate for each cell.

Ray paused and waited for his eyes to adjust to the brilliant sunlight. He stood at the edge of a huge pit. He felt as though he was standing in the nosebleed section of a stadium, gazing down into an arena the size of a football field below. However, instead of lush green grass, the morning sun's beams were just beginning to cast light on the quarry's barren dirt floor. And instead of a stadium's bleachers, sheer cliff walls stretched high on all sides, the surrounding rock faces studded with large wooden pegs that held a tapestry of fishnet mesh in place.

"Keep moving," said Rashad, nudging Ray back towards the shuffling mob. "If one inmate stops, then all of us face the consequences."

Not wishing to make any more enemies out of his fellow inmates – at least not until he recovered his memory – Ray followed Rashad down a long dirt ramp set along the cliff wall to the right of the support pillars.

Ben, lagging behind the others, stopped in both fear and awe at the sight of the vast quarry. *To think, all this was done with shovels,* he mused. He did not realise that he was the last one in the pack, the crowd before him thinning out, until he was shoved forward.

"To you newcomers," Leon barked from behind, his gruff voice bouncing off the cliff walls, "My one rule is: put your back into it, *or I'll put you back into it!*"

Afraid of what might happen to him, Ben quickly moved to follow Ray, Rashad, and all of the other inmates down the ramp, descending the dirt path's sickle bend into the dry basin. Ben ran his hand over the loose fishnets draped across the rock face, until his forearm collided with one of the large wooden pegs jutting out from the wall.

"What are these for?" asked Ben, trying to keep his shovel off the ground while rubbing at the red mark on his arm.

"The pegs and fishnets are the quarry's makeshift retaining walls," said Rashad. "They help to prevent landslides in the rainy season."

"Does it work?" Ray asked with amused scepticism.

"Usually," said Little Danny appearing next to him, his lips curling into an impish grin.

The forced labourers reached the bottom of the dirt ramp and marched across the quarry floor to a rock shelf at the far end of the pit. Inmates carrying mattocks led the pack, striking their tools against the wall of rock while the others fell in behind.

Cormac and Leon climbed the rock shelf to the upper level of the pit, quickly crossing to a pair of lounge chairs that sat underneath a sun umbrella while the other Watchers took up guard positions. The two men sipped from their water canteens while a small electric fan blew the only breeze in the quarry to cool their faces. Next to them stood a floodlight, although Ben seemed to think they would have no need of it; the sun was already burning intensely overhead, and the day was only just getting started.

Inmates bearing shovels, including Ben, Ray, Little Danny and Rashad, lined up behind those with the mattocks. Sergei, Levi, Cameron and Bryson brought the minecarts to a halt behind the two rows of prisoners, standing in the shade with their arms crossed as the others went to work.

The two brothers followed the actions of the teens alongside them, plunging their shovels into piles of dirt building up around the feet of those in front with the mattocks, and tossing the broken rocks into the minecart. Tiny glittering gems sparkled in the clumps of earth as they flew into the metal wagon.

The rhythmic scrapes of metal against rock filled the quarry, coupled with the occasional grunt of an inmate ploughing through a particular dense patch of earth. Ray noticed a tan line on his thumb in the shape of a ring. He wondered whether he had lost the ring when he was captured, or if it had been stolen from him, just like the medallion.

At one point, Ben turned around to see Sergei glaring back with his arms folded. Ben quickly looked away, to the delight of both Sergei and Levi, who chuckled at how easily intimidated he was. Turning back to his work, Ben wondered if people purchasing jewellery ever stopped to think about where their prized possessions had originated from, but his musings came to an abrupt end when he felt his skin tear.

"Ouch!" he gasped in pain, jerking his hand away from the shovel's handle.

Ray glanced sideways to see his alleged brother turning his hand over, a blister already beginning to form on his soft palm. Ray did not need his memory to judge that Ben had never been conditioned for physical work in the past. He, on the other hand, was feeling fine.

Ben looked up at the sweltering morning sun, waiting for the day to end. His eyes widened with sudden clarity at the fishnets hanging from the cliff walls.

"Why hasn't anyone tried to scale the walls yet?" asked Ben, setting his shovel aside for a moment.

Rashad checked to make sure that no guards were within earshot before answering, "If your weight did not rip the wooden pegs out of the wall, the sparkers would surely bring you back down to earth."

"Even for me," Little Danny piped up on Ben's left, "That barbed wire fence at the top would be a bit ovva problem."

Ray shaded his eyes, straining his vision to focus on the top edge of the cliff walls. He could just barely make out the thin wire fence slightly swaying in the breeze on the surface, where it covered the entire circumference of the pit.

"Where are those sparkers you mentioned?" asked Ray, plunging his shovel into a steadily building pile of dirt as a guard passed by, "Are they on the fence as well?"

"You saw those chains hanging on that rack in the cell house?" asked Rashad. The two brothers nodded. "They were used once, back when they were effective, but they proved to be too troublesome during shift changes. We are now controlled by the manacles attached to all of our legs, which are able to emit electrical shocks. They are activated by a radio signal from the sparkers. If anyone acts out of line, the whole shift is sparked."

Ray glanced at the flashing red light on the metal bracelet around his ankle, wondering if the manacle could conduct the same amount of electrical voltage as the shock stick he had been beaten with. He supposed it did not matter if it was any lesser in intensity, as they could just hold down the button until the battery died.

"Each manacle is given a unique frequency according to their shift," Rashad continued. "Whenever a shift swap occurs, the sparkers are taken back to the Watcher barracks to be recharged, and the next set of guards bear fully-charged sparkers for the next shift."

"Never 'ave to worry about a flat battery when it comes to one ovvem!" Little Danny chirped like a proud child showing off one of his toys.

"How many shifts are there?" asked Ben, trying to determine when their shift would end.

"Three," said Rashad. "The left row of cells in the cell house works from midnight until morning. Our shift, the day shift, works from morning until afternoon, and the last row of cells works from afternoon until midnight.

Ben grasped his shovel with a pained sigh. It was still only morning.

* * *

The inmates' green uniforms were the only signs of life stirring within the bowels of the barren dustbowl. Ben had lost count of how many times the bludging boys behind them had pushed the minecarts up and down the dirt ramp, trundling the metal wagons to and fro with ease.

"How did they get such easy jobs?" he wondered aloud.

"Wait 'til the rainy season comes," Little Danny cackled, "Then they'll wanna swap!"

"When's that?" asked Ben, glancing up at the clear cobalt blue sky.

"Does it look like we have a calendar, Benji?" Ray said in exasperation, now remembering the annoyance of his little brother's incessant questioning and constant curiosity.

Wincing at his brother's harsh words, Ben cast his eyes upon the ground. *He did call me Benji though; at least he's making some progress.*

"I have been here for a few seasons," said Rashad. "All I know is, when the dark clouds come, the rain soon follows."

Sergei and Levi emerged from the shadows of the complex with a fresh minecart. Ray recalled his decision to side with Ben and the others in the cafeteria, feeling the bitter taste of regret in his mouth at the sight of their light work. Or, perhaps it was just remnants of the goopy gruel still lingering in his mouth.

"'ow'd you end up 'ere anyway, Benny?" asked Little Danny.

Ray's ears pricked up.

Flashes of his older brother carrying him through the muck and mire of the swamp entered Ben's mind. "Our father brought us to a swamp," he said. "He was – *is* – a documentarian."

"What's 'is name?" asked Little Danny. Other inmates nearby slowed their work, eager to hear the newcomers' story to make the day pass quicker.

"Jacob. Jacob Rauder," said Ben, looking sideways at Ray, hoping that their surname might have rung a bell. "We were investigating a reported sighting of a monster living in the swamp. It was us three and Uncle Joshua, plus the rest of the camera crew."

"Uncle Joshua?" Ray repeated, leaning slightly towards Ben.

"He's not *really* our uncle," said Ben. "He's one of our father's friends. Don't you remember him?"

Ray shook his head, deep in thought.

Ben told them about *The Lizardman* monster they were searching for. Rashad shifted at the words. Ben talked about how the Deputy Sheriff had led them through the swamp, straight into an ambush – a whole group of people appearing out of nowhere – and how their father had led them out of the immediate danger.

"After that, things get a little hazy," Ben finished.

"I know the feeling," said Ray. "So what happened to dad? Where'd he go? What happened to that guy, Joshua, and the rest of the camera crew?"

"I don't know," Ben shrugged. "You were the one who ran back to help them. Surely you remember something?"

He looked enquiringly at Ray, who was busy focusing his thoughts until his head throbbed, either from the heat of the quarry or from the strain on his mind; or, perhaps from seeing something he did not wish to remember.

* * *

The white light of the hot, midday sun glared down at them with a burning intensity the likes of which Ben had never seen before. He narrowed his eyes to protect his retinas. It even hurt to look down at the ground that was almost glowing, reflecting back the sun's brightness. Although he had never really spent much time outside if he could avoid it, he knew that this sun was not the same sun that they had at home.

We must be somewhere close to the equator, he thought to himself.

Ray spat on the ground as he shovelled, and Ben watched the parched earth embrace his saliva with a sizzling puff of smoke.

Sergei, Levi, Cameron and Bryson materialised out from the shadows of the complex, trundling back down the dirt ramp again with a pair of fresh minecarts; but this time, as they rattled down the slope, water sloshed over the sides of the wagons. The other inmates let out a collective sigh of relief and stabbed their tools into the ground, some removing their shirts and hanging their sweat-stained uniforms upon the tool hafts, others tying their soiled green shirts around their heads.

Ben left the others to approach the carts, eager to have a drink of water. He was one of the first in the queue forming, while most of the other inmates were busy tying off their shirts. The few labourers ahead of him were comparing hands, and Ben looked down at his own. The blisters that had formed on his palms from handling the shovel had already split open and begun to bleed. He could not wait to soak them in the water.

* * *

To combat the humidity, Ray decided to take off his own shirt too. He hung it on his shovel and then fell in line with Rashad behind the other inmates already queuing up. The teens ahead of them compared their hands against each other's. Ray looked at his own palms, seeing nothing of interest on his leathery skin.

"On the day shift," said Rashad, "Respect is earned by those with deeper and thicker calluses. That way, we can at least maintain some level of order."

At the front of the line, a muscular red-haired inmate stooped for the first drink of water. He cupped his hands and splashed it over himself, the water mingling with the sweat on his freckled face and back. He turned to walk down the length of the queue when he abruptly halted beside Ben, who had somehow gotten ahead of Ray and Rashad.

"Show hands," he said in an Irish accent, outing him for being one of the newcomers. Ben sheepishly turned his bleeding palms upwards. "Back of the line, dreg," he said, pushing Ben out of the line-up. "Water's dirty enough as it is."

Ben hung his head as he trudged towards the end of the queue, marching shame-faced past Ray and Rashad. Now it was their turn.

"Show hands, lads, give us a look!" the red-haired inmate approached them.

Ray followed Rashad's example, turning his hands over for inspection.

The Irish teen gave them his nod of approval and singled out another group of prisoners.

Ray splashed the cool water on his face and chest, and then cupped his hands to take a drink. He and Rashad stepped back before they overstayed their welcome, other inmates yearning to quench their thirst.

* * *

Little Danny greeted Ben at the back of the line. "Nice try, Benny!" Little Danny beamed up at him. "Nothing slips by Kenneth though."

Ben turned back to see Kenneth inspecting the rest of the queue, ejecting the other inmates with bleeding blisters. Each one plodded towards the back of the line, yet they pushed their way in front of Ben and Little Danny.

"Hey, that's not fair!" Ben croaked at the other inmates.

"I wouldn't if I was you," Little Danny warned. "If you cause too much trouble, you'll be drinking dregs at the back of the line for a lot longer, no matter 'ow good your 'ands look."

Ben heeded the boy's advice, wondering if Little Danny had once argued with the other inmates too much. Or maybe it was just that his malnourished and childlike stature could not earn him a better position in the queue other than at the back of the line.

After enduring what seemed like an eternity of thirst, Ben finally approached the minecarts. He looked grimly at the muddy sediment in the remaining water. He wanted to cry. He wanted to scream at the top of his dry lungs. He wanted to lash out at the other prisoners, but it would do him no good. Taking a deep breath, he decided against his thirst. He would wait until the shift was over. He could drink from the tap in the cafeteria instead.

Sighing, Ben walked back towards the rock shelf. He could feel the eyes of the minecart pushers upon him. The four of them casually flung rocks into the muddy carts from a seated position in the shade provided by one of the cliff walls, the midday sun having already passed. By the looks of their self-satisfied expressions, Ben would have bet that they had already indulged in the water before bringing it down into the pit for the other boys.

* * *

Cormac and Leon emerged from underneath the sun umbrella, another pair of Watchers immediately taking their place in the shade. Under the light of the sun, Cormac's dome-like head showed patches of different shades of skin, arranged in random splotches, like that of a leopard.

Ray thought that the guard's spotted scalp was probably the result of constant sunburns as the sun threw its glaring radiance onto every surface and into every crevice of the pit, cooking the pigmentation of Cormac's skin and marking him permanently. Glancing up at the cloudless sky, he returned to the sweaty shirt he had left hanging on his shovel, tying it around his own closely-shaven head to avoid the same fate as the guard.

As the other inmates returned to work, his eyes fell on the entrance to the prison. Just above the support pillars and the overhanging cells, he noticed a flag set on top of a wooden deck looking over the quarry, furling and flattening on the breeze. Ray squinted at the symbol on the flag. It almost resembled an image of the sun.

"Like an eye watching us all in our toil," said Rashad, catching his gaze.

* * *

Ben passed under the watchful glare of Leon, standing in his shorn and faded gold suit next to Cormac on the rock shelf. He wondered how the man could tolerate his shaggy facial hair in such hot weather. Ben assumed that the heat trapped under Leon's grizzled beard, hairy forearms and bushy chest hair sprouting up from the old suit's collar was the stem of his seemingly quick temper.

He picked up his shovel, his hands stinging in pain under the weight of the tool. He looked across at Ray and Rashad, both of them staring upwards at some obscure flag on top of the complex. He was trying to discern what the symbol was, when four silhouettes appeared on top of the wooden deck overlooking the quarry, their dark figures contrasting against the brilliance of the azure blue sky, one at least a head taller than the other three. They seemed to be staring down into the pit.

"Back to work," said Rashad, pulling his shovel out of the ground.

"Who are they?" asked Ben, trying to dig without tearing any more skin from his palms.

"The Warden," Little Danny answered in a jittery voice.

"And the other three?" asked Ray, indifferent as he lobbed a clump of earth into the minecart.

Rashad clucked his tongue, stooping to lift rocks from a mound of dirt.

* * *

The shift wore on. On many occasions, they saw glints of gold and other valuable gems among their toils. Ray picked up one of the golden nuggets, moving to stash it in the pocket of his jeans.

Rashad caught his hand. "What need would you have for it in here?"

"It's not worth what they do to ya," said Little Danny. "Trust me, I know."

At the disapproving glances of Ben and the other inmates nearby, Ray tossed the golden nugget over his shoulder, hearing a faint jolt of surprise from the minecart pushers lazing behind them.

The sun began to set in the mid-afternoon, the western cliff casting a shadow that stretched across the entire pit floor, touching the east wall. Rashad straightened up, letting his shovel hang by his side. Like a ripple effect, the rest of the inmates stopped working with a collective sigh of relief.

"See?" said Rashad, indicating the pit's floor almost fully covered in shadow now. Ray had not noticed the setting sun, but its beams still washed over the quarry's east wall with its radiance in the clear blue sky. "Our shift is over." Rashad stretched his muscle-bound limbs.

While the Watchers were not looking, Little Danny showered himself with a hail of dirt from his own shovel. He patted the soil into the folds of his uniform, other boys following suit while glancing warily at the guards. Ben moved to do the same.

"Not now," said Little Danny, looking pointedly at Cormac watching over them. "You'll get caught."

Cormac jumped down from the rock shelf and into the lower level of the pit, catching a stooping inmate from behind while he frantically worked to smother dirt on his own uniform.

"Oi!" Cormac yelled. "You better watch yourself, sunshine, or I'll punish your cellmate and 'ave 'im do you in while you sleep!"

All of the inmates were led back to the tool shed, where they hung up their shovels and mattocks on the racks before filing into the cafeteria. Ray was eager for a bowl of water and some food; thirst and hunger taking hold of him. He would even settle for a lukewarm bowl of the cardboard-like porridge, although he hoped *that* was not on the menu again.

Lagging behind, Ben hung his bloodstained shovel on the rack and followed the others into the cafeteria, hoping that his hands would be toughened by the rigours of daily work soon. His thirsty eyes caught sight of the water tap on the far wall of the cafeteria, and he licked his cracked lips with a dry tongue.

The guards lined the weary prisoners up along the back wall of the mess hall. Leon nodded approvingly at most of them, who let their shoulders fall as they lined up for the cauldron in the front corner of the room. Cormac sauntered over to the inmate that he had caught dirtying up his uniform, pulled the boy forward out of the line-up, and then yanked his cellmate along with him. Leon nodded at Ray and Rashad, who quickly joined the queue for the food. Ray looked back at Ben.

Ben's stomach rumbled. He could not wait to have a morsel of food in his mouth, no matter how bad it tasted. Most of the other inmates had already joined the queue. He did not care whether he was at the back of the line, as long as he had his fill. Leon approached Ben. At a wink from Cormac, the grizzled guard dragged him forward, without even looking him over.

Ben began to hyperventilate, looking left and right at the handful of boys standing on either side of him. They each shared the same sullen sombre expressions.

Cormac sidled up next to Ben. "Told you you'd be 'aving some special treatment on your first day, sunshine," he said, his hot breath permeating on the side of Ben's face.

Ray started towards his brother, but Rashad held him back. "What's happening to them?"

"If you do not work hard enough in the pit," Rashad answered, "They send you back in."

In his gruff voice, Leon barked out his one rule as a reminder: "put your back into it, *or I'll put you back into it!*"

4 - CLEAN SLATE

One of the prisoners along the back wall of the cafeteria – standing alongside Ben – protested against the Watchers placing him on a double shift.

"I'm done, I've finished my shift! I'm done!" he yelled, attempting to rejoin the other exhausted day shift inmates standing in the queue for the gruel pot.

Leon lunged at the prisoner, thrusting the tired teen back against the wall. "You don't rest until you earn it!" the Watcher roared, his bearded face coming within inches of the terrified inmate. The boy slid to the floor in a whimper, accepting his fate. "Get on your feet, mongrel," the grizzled guard growled, "Eat something and get back to work."

Ben stared open-mouthed at the exchange, wringing his hands together. He gasped in pain after tracing a thumb over one of his burst blisters.

"How do they know the difference?" asked Ray, standing in the queue, watching Ben blowing gently on his ruptured palms.

"The difference?" Rashad repeated.

"How do they know who's worked hard, and who hasn't?"

"By their uniform," said Rashad as they shuffled forward in the queue. "If an inmate is not dirty enough or sweaty enough, or even just for fun, a Watcher may decide to throw them back out to work again."

* * *

Cormac sidled up next to Ben, his hot foul breath blowing into Ben's ear. "Should've put up more of a fight earlier, sunshine," said the crude Watcher. "Maybe you wouldn't be working a double shift if you 'adn't lost me that shiny necklace."

Ben thought back to Levi knocking him to the floor before breakfast, resulting in Caleb winning his father's medallion from Cormac in the bet they had made.

"Little Danny went down in that fight too, why isn't he doing a double shift?" Ben blurted out before realising he was volunteering his cellmate to share his punishment.

"Aye, but at least 'e 'ad the guts to get back up again," said Cormac, eyeing Caleb who now descended the stairs into the cafeteria, ordering the night shift inmates to join the queue for the gruel pot. Ben's gaze fell upon his father's medallion as it hung from around the stern Watcher's neck, as if to mock the pair of newcomers.

Cormac stooped down, his stubby dirt-encrusted fingers roughly working around Ben's ankle. The Watcher's scalp shone between tufts of closely-shaven hair in the dim light of the cafeteria as he changed Ben's manacle over.

"Haven't I worked hard enough for one day?" Ben pleaded, holding out his hands as evidence, the broken blisters caked with dried blood and glistening with tender flesh.

Locking a new manacle into place, Cormac stood up, once again bringing his foul breath deep into Ben's personal space. "You might 'ave, but you didn't do it wiv a smile, did ya?" The bald-headed guard pierced him with his bright blue eyes. "Come on, let's 'ave a glance at that pretty smile of yours, 'ey?"

Ben turned his head away from him in disgust. He forced a fake smile, anything to get rid of the Watcher's stinking breath. Cormac screwed his face up into a crude grin, revealing his crooked yellow teeth. He lingered for a moment before moving on to the next inmate, leaving Ben feeling both violated and repulsed.

Embarrassed by his submission to the guard's degrading request, Ben looked around, checking to see whether anyone else had seen his lack of resistance, although it seemed that all of the other prisoners were either too hungry or too tired to care.

Ben tramped towards the queue for the gruel pot, his manacle now blinking with a yellow light in accordance with the night shift sparker remote's frequency, instead of the red light of the day shift. Other inmates selected for the double shift pushed past Ben, ensuring that he remained at the back of the line.

Cormac and Leon laughed derisively at him as they marched towards the other Watchers standing behind the stone bench at the front of the mess hall.

*　*　*

Standing in the queue of prisoners along the side of the cafeteria, Ray eyed the gilded diamond-shaped pendant hanging from Caleb's neck. He knew that the medallion held some significance to his family, but he could not recall what that significance was, let alone remember the other members of his family.

With his view of Ben now blocked by the night shift inmates between them, Ray looked to the front of the line to see the petite blonde girl serving up the goopy porridge again.

"I saw her outside the cell house just after I woke up," said Ray. "Who is she?"

"Just another prisoner," said Rashad. "The girls have access to other parts of the complex. Once, all of the inmates were treated equally, but many of the girls rarely lasted longer than the shift's water break when they were working under the hot sun, and so they were given other duties to help keep the prison running."

"Like what?"

"Like serving gruel," Rashad replied flatly.

They reached the side table with the empty bowls and spoons. Grabbing one of the wooden bowls and filling it with water, Ray brought the dish up to his mouth, the shirt still wrapped around his head almost unravelling and falling to the floor behind him as he tilted his head back, feeling the cool liquid wash down his gullet to revive his organs. He let the water spill down his chest, soothing his sun-browned skin.

Another inmate attempted to jostle for position in front of the tap while Ray was refilling his bowl. Instinctively, he knew that it was a power play; a test of what he would do next. He threw a blind elbow back at the unseen prisoner. Nonchalantly draining the second bowl, he looked to his side to see Levi clutching his chest, winded, with Sergei fuming behind him. Ray cocked an eyebrow, but neither of them made a move.

Rashad lingered by, warily watching the other inmates as the milky white-skinned girl filled Ray's bowl with the grey gravy. She looked about the same age as him. Ray introduced himself to her. She looked up and searched his face, her mildly baggy bloodshot eyes betraying the beauty of their hazel colour, and she gave him a weary smile, but she seemed at a loss for words.

"What's your name?" asked Ray.

"Ava," she replied.

"Thanks for the food," he said. "Be generous to my little brother. He's the only other guy not wearing green."

She leaned out to see Ben standing at the back of the line and nodded at Ray with a smile.

* * *

Ben stared down at his hands, wondering how he would be able to work a second shift, let alone grip the handle of a shovel. He had thought that his open blisters would be proof that he had worked hard enough to at least earn some privilege, yet everyone else seemed to consider it as a sign of weakness. He silently hoped that his blisters would form into calluses soon, as they seemed to be the only asset to an inmate in this prison.

Ray was already at the front of the queue. He was holding up the line, talking with the blonde-haired girl behind the gruel pot. Ben had always admired his brother's ability to talk to girls. Even without his memory, Ray's talent still came naturally. Ben, on the other hand, had always shied away from talking to girls. He had shied away from talking to everyone, for that matter.

A sudden thought occurred to him, an optimistic one, despite his rough day. This prison was his chance to start over with a clean slate. He could not think of a worse place to start over, but they would not be here forever. For now, this was his chance to earn his brother's respect, and respect from others, too. Ben shuffled forward in the line with a slight spring in his step, drawing closer to the front of the cafeteria.

* * *

"Keep the line moving!" Leon roared, making Ava jump with fright, the poor girl almost dropping the ladle into the cauldron of porridge.

Rashad shouldered past the fuming Sergei with a warning glare as he and Ray found a table. "Very smooth," Rashad said as they sat down to eat.

"Just trying to help out Benji," Ray shrugged, picking up his spoon. "I can't say for sure, but it doesn't look like he's used to working that hard."

Ray looked up at Ben, now standing at the back of the queue of inmates, even behind those from the night shift who had arrived later. He pitied Ben, but perhaps this would serve to toughen him up.

He dropped his spoon, and he held his throbbing head as the vision of the wide-eyed boy on the floor of a school corridor flashed into his mind again. He lay there, surrounded by his scattered books, with other boys and girls laughing around him.

One guy in particular, someone who Ray could only remember as The Berserker, kicked one of Ben's scattered books down the hallway as he passed by, hands in his pockets, smiling up at Ray. He remembered smiling back and thinking to himself, *this should toughen him up.* Ray watched his brother on the floor, waiting for him to get up and strike back at the bullies.

* * *

Cormac and Leon were talking with another pair of Watchers, pointing out which inmates had been selected to serve a double shift. Leon indicated the handful of prisoners standing near the back of the queue, poking a gnarled finger in Ben's direction. The other two guards were Caleb and a tall goateed black man wearing a plain brown shirt. Standing beside Caleb with his crew cut, they almost looked like a pair of army drill sergeants who had lost their hats. As if hearing Ben's thoughts, Caleb glared at him with his dark hawkish eyes.

Ben turned away from his stern gaze, glancing at the gruel pot again, quickly realising that he was the last boy left in the queue. He rushed over to the wooden table set against the wall, grabbed one of the remaining bowls and filled it from the tap. He gulped down the water, choking and coughing, and then filled the bowl and drained it again. And again. And again. Ava, the hazel-eyed blonde girl, watched him with a mixture of patience and pity.

Once he had drunk his fill of the water, Ben bore the bowl with his abraded hands to the gruel pot. He had expected that there would be scarcely any leftovers, but she ladled him extra porridge, filling his bowl to the brink with the goopy gruel. He thanked her profusely, thinking that perhaps the back of the line was not so bad after all; there was no limit on how much leftovers he could have.

With a light heart, Ben looked out over the tables of the cafeteria. Seeing Ray and Rashad seated together, he walked towards them.

Passing a table beside the staircase, he tripped, falling flat on his face, the bowl slipping out of his tender-fleshed hands and spilling out across the floor with a clatter. Ben looked around to see a shoe poking out from behind the table he had just passed.

Smirking, Levi withdrew his foot. Sergei, Cameron and Bryson chuckled. Little Danny sat at a table nearby. He quickly averted his gaze away from Ben, fearing what the four inmates might do to him if he helped Ben to his feet.

* * *

"Starting to remember?" Rashad's voice floated across to him from far away.

Ray opened his eyes, and he was brought back to reality. Staring down at the blurry-edged bowl of gruel in front of him, he picked up his spoon and wolfed the porridge down. In his craving for sustenance after the hard day's work, he completely disregarded the horrible taste, ravenously devouring every cardboard-like morsel.

"It's not much of a memory," Ray said out of the side of his mouth, still chewing. "But it's a start."

"Give it some time," said Rashad. "Your memory will return, eventually. Although I am not sure that it would be of any use to you in this place."

"Sure it would," said Ray, tightening his grip on the spoon. "If I could remember the faces of the people who attacked me, my dad and my brother at the swamp, I'd know who to pay a visit to once we get outta here."

Within a few moments, the entire bowl was empty. Ray swallowed the last mouthful of mystery sludge, settling his rumbling stomach.

Rashad knocked Ray's elbow with a heavy hand and pointed at something over his shoulder. Ray turned to see Ben lying on the floor next to the stairs just a few tables away, the porridge from his bowl spilled out across the dirt-tracked floor. All of the inmates turned their heads, some getting out of their seats, muttering.

"Bang on. Bang on. Bang on..."

Ray rose up from his own seat too, seeing the minecart pushers sitting near Ben. They laughed at him as he flailed around on the ground. Ray did not have to see what happened to know that they'd had something to do with it.

"Get up, Benji," Ray urged in a low tone, his voice mingling with the chants of the inmates. He clenched his fists, "Hit them. Just get up and hit them."

* * *

Ben felt a lump building in his throat. He glanced from his cellmate to Levi's smug smile to the spilled bowl of gruel. It was still standing upright, but only a quarter of his food was left.

With tears welling in his eyes, Ben looked back at Levi again. He felt a sudden rage take hold of him, urging him to wring Levi's neck. He wanted to. He wanted to see the smug teen's eyes bulge in surprise as he fought for breath. Ashamed of his own thoughts, Ben let his tears fall, to the bullies' delight. He turned back to the porridge splayed out across the floor, aware of every inmate watching and chanting over the top of their laughter.

"Bang on. Bang on. Bang on..."

Ben never was much of a fighter, not while he was at school, and certainly not now. He knew that others had always viewed this as a weakness, and continually sought to exploit it, but Ben felt that true strength was found in not sinking to their level, lowering himself to base violence and striking back. At least, that was what he told himself so that he could feel better about letting other people walk all over him.

He hoisted himself back upon his tired feet and gathered up his bowl and spoon without so much as a word, doggedly padding over towards Ray and Rashad's table with his head downcast. The chorus of the inmates died down with a note of disappointment as everyone turned back to their meals.

Ben sat next to Rashad and ate what remained of his bowl's contents in silence, tears streaming down his cheeks. *So much for starting over with a clean slate.*

* * *

Sergei looked over at Ray, the Russian skinhead shooting him a wink. Still on his feet with his fists clenched, Ray looked back at Ben, sobbing as he shovelled the pitiful remainder of his porridge with a sad hunger in his eyes. Rashad rested a heavy hand on Ben's shoulder, and then shook his head at Ray, cautioning him not to start trouble.

Ray refused to heed the warning though. He refused to sit down. He was not going to start trouble; he was going to add fuel to the fire. This was just another power play, after all. Retaliation for elbowing Levi in the line. That was their answer, now it was his turn.

Sergei and Levi looked as though they had already forgotten the incident, eating from their bowls, oblivious to Ray's approach as he marched up to their table. Neither one of them appeared to notice him. Cameron, seated at the corner of the table, looked up at Ray and choked in surprise. Ray grabbed him by his soiled shirt and threw the boy out of his seat, and then stood in front of the empty stone block chair.

They noticed.

* * *

Ben wiped the tears from his eyes, feeling better with each mouthful of the lumpy gruel. He had not realised how famished he was until they had returned to the cafeteria. With red-rimmed eyes, he looked back down at his bowl again to find that it was already empty.

"I told him to keep his head down," Rashad muttered under his breath, unintentionally squeezing Ben's shoulder.

Cringing in pain, Ben wriggled free of Rashad's grip and looked up to see his brother confronting Sergei and Levi. Cameron was spread-eagled on the floor, and Bryson was already backing away. Only a table stood in between Ray and the pair of bullies, but they remained seated.

All of the inmates drummed the tables in unison, their anticipation mounting again.

* * *

"He is little brother, yes?" asked Sergei.

"We heard you talking to Ava," said Levi, his upper lip curling in scorn.

"And you tripped him anyway?" Ray accused, his tone dripping with anger.

Levi smirked up at him, revealing a mouthful of gruel, the smug teen brimming with confidence while he had the pig-eyed Sergei sitting beside him.

The drumming on the tables picked up speed, growing louder as more inmates looked up from their meals and joined in. Kenneth, the fiery-haired freckled teen, seemed to be the loudest, wanting to see what Ray was made of. Watchers standing at the front of the room murmured to each other, already placing bets on the fight.

Ray grabbed the wooden table and thrust it forward, pushing Sergei and Levi backwards as it caught them in their stomachs, wedging them against the inmates behind them. Levi coughed up his mouthful of gruel.

Sergei rose to the challenge. The blocky inmate lifted the table and threw it to the side with ease, sending bowls and spoons flying, narrowly missing Cameron on the floor. He held his arms out wide, inviting Ray to hit him.

Ray accepted the invitation gladly, throwing a heavy right fist into his pudgy face. The blow seemed to glance off his chin as Sergei turned his head with the punch, simply snapping his gaze back towards Ray with a wide grin.

Levi kicked Ray in the side of his leg, just above his kneecap. Ray answered with another punch, but this time Sergei caught it.

"This is for your elbow to Levi," Sergei announced in his thick Russian accent. Still grinning with a vice-like grip on Ray's arm, the bull-necked inmate lunged forward, hurling a solid fist into Ray's chest.

Winded, Ray fell to his knees, fighting the urge to vomit. This was not the way he had planned for the fight to finish.

* * *

The other inmates crowded around the three fighters; even the guards had climbed up on top of the stone bench at the front of the cafeteria to watch their investments. Cameron and Bryson stood off to one side, not wishing to get involved if they could avoid it. Beside the cauldron in the corner of the room, Little Danny was using all of the excitement as a distraction to help himself to another serving of gruel.

Rashad moved past Ben to join the melee. His view blocked by the other inmates thronging in front of him, Ben wormed his way through the crowd of spectators.

"Oi! Watch whose shoe you're stepping on, dreg!"

"Sorry. Excuse me, sorry," said Ben, squeezing himself between a pair of thick-set inmates to glimpse Ray upon his knees.

* * *

Wheezing as he fought for breath, Ray stared up at Sergei towering over him, the skinheaded Russian winding his fist up for another punch, the surrounding pack of inmates cheering them on. Ray shut his eyes, bracing for impact.

Suddenly, a pair of large gorilla-like hands hauled him upright from behind. He turned to see Rashad's granite face.

The roar from the crowd was deafening as Rashad stepped into the fray, and Ben gave a small whoop of his own, glad that the huge prisoner was on their side.

Sergei squared his shoulders, rocking his head from side to side and cracking the vertebrae in his neck, getting ready for the new challenge. With a heavy arm, Rashad moved Ray behind him, away from danger.

The Watchers were bellowing at each other, demanding to change their bets.

Rashad turned back to Sergei, and just as the crowd's anticipation reached its peak, he uttered a single word over the top of the cheering inmates:

"*Mercy.*"

Ben was filled with awe for Rashad; his thick build was more than capable of taking on Sergei in a fair fight, perhaps even winning, yet he humbly declined his foe with one simple word.

"Hit him!" Levi screamed. "Hit him anyway!!"

Sergei looked around, savouring the moment, all of the prisoners clamouring to see the fight. Rashad was holding his hands up in surrender. Ignoring his gesture, the Russian skinhead cocked back a fist and plunged it into Rashad's gut.

With a delayed reaction, Rashad doubled over to absorb the blow, but again, he refrained from violence, holding up one hand as a sign of submission. *"Mercy,"* he repeated, although Ray noticed that there was no strain in his voice.

Sergei front-kicked Rashad in the shoulder, sending him down to his knees in an attempt to provoke the big barrel-chested prisoner.

Still wheezing for lungfuls of air, Ray moved to attack Sergei. Rashad blocked his attempt to get back into the fight, holding up a solid arm against Ray's waist.

Caleb, followed by the dark-skinned goateed guard, shoved past Ray. Sergei reared back to throw another fist at Rashad, but Caleb hooked his arm at the elbow. Reaching into his belt, the stern Watcher withdrew his shock stick.

Sergei's maniacal grin fell away from his face, realising that he had lost control of the fight. His pig-like eyes stared in horror as Caleb sparked up the shock stick and thrust it into the prisoner's throat. Sergei's body snapped as straight as a ruler. He frothed at the mouth before falling backwards. Caleb ensured that the surging baton stayed connected to his neck all the way down to the floor. Levi stood dumbstruck, helplessly watching his friend squirm under the electrical shock.

All of the inmates crowding around shared the same stunned silence. The only sound that could be heard was the volts of electricity crackling against Sergei's gurgling throat.

Caleb bore his steely grey stare into Sergei's panicked eyes. "When he says *mercy*, you show him mercy!" The stern Watcher pulled back the shock stick and looked over his shoulder to face Cormac and Leon. The pair of guards were grinning, apparently amused by Sergei's demise. "Send him to the Desert Complex, he seems ready enough."

Sergei's pitiful, pudgy face flushed pink with fear. He kicked and screamed like a pig being hauled to the slaughter. His thick Russian accent had been momentarily sapped by the shock stick, and the volts still lingering in his throat made it seem like he was speaking into an electric fan as he jolted out, "No! Not yet, please!"

As relieved as the brothers were by Caleb's decision to transfer the blocky skinhead elsewhere, they could not help but wonder what a big guy like Sergei could possibly be afraid of. Neither of them could imagine a place worse than this.

5 - SET IN STONE

Despite the mass of inmates of the day and night shifts presently gathered in the cafeteria, only one voice could be heard: Sergei's yells of fear and panic as he struggled with the concept of being transferred to the Desert Complex.

Rashad pulled Ray aside, as well as Ben, who had come closer to watch the fight that had broken out during the routine shift change. "Try to blend in," he said, before vanishing into the pack of inmates.

Following Rashad's lead, the brothers took off in different directions as Sergei continued to bargain, beg and bellow, his strained voice resounding throughout the mess hall. Cormac and Leon managed to catch Sergei's flailing legs, the pair of guards lugging the squirming inmate feet-first up the stairs.

Caleb, still holding the shock stick that he had used to pacify Sergei, turned to the dark-skinned Watcher scratching at his goatee beside him. "Evander, help them get the day shift back in their cells, I'll handle the rest."

The tall goateed Watcher and the rest of the day shift guards directed half of the prisoners in the cafeteria back up the stairs into the cell house. It was easy to distinguish who belonged to each shift, judging by the different coloured lights of their manacles, each corresponding to a different sparker remote's frequency. Ray, Rashad and Little Danny followed Evander with tired feet.

Ben, on the other hand, remained below in the cafeteria with the night shift inmates, about to commence his double shift. Caleb made his way through the crowd of teens, his shock stick still drawn and sparking with electricity. He opened the door at the back of the cafeteria, tapping his baton against the wall, wordlessly calling the inmates to work with a stony glare.

* * *

Ray fell in behind the other inmates from the day shift ascending the stairs, following Sergei's shouts through the cell house to the door in the far corner, the same door Ray himself had come through that morning.

As he reached the top of the steps, someone tapped him on the shoulder from behind. Still on edge from the fight, he whirled his entire body around to face the prodder, expecting to see Levi.

He came face to face with Kenneth, the red-haired freckled Irish teen from the water carts during their shift. "Good try, lad. I've not seen many go against Chubby Chekhov like that and walk away. Unless of course, your name's Rashad. Be a strange coincidence if it was. What set you off on those clowns anyway?"

"It's Ray," he replied. The pair of prisoners let the other inmates waiting patiently on the stairs behind them pass by, trudging back to their own cells. "That kid they tripped up before is my little brother, Benji."

"Well, now I feel bad about kickin' him outta the line-up for the water carts earlier," said Kenneth. Then, throwing up his hands in a mock surrender, he added, "Don't go throwin' a table at me now, boyo!" Ray snorted in amusement, and Kenneth dropped his hands. "How was your first day?"

"Looking forward to my last day," said Ray.

"Aren't we all?" asked a ropy fair-skinned inmate that had been lingering by the stairs, listening in on their conversation. If Ray had to guess, he was in his late teens, with an American accent, keen green eyes, and unruly black hair that was held at bay with a green sweatband tied around his forehead, no doubt fashioned from one of the uniforms.

"Meet Aiden," said Kenneth, "Me cellmate. Wouldn't've been me first choice, but I guess I'm stuck with the manky yankee, right?"

Aiden shrugged, exchanging a smirk with Ray, clearly perplexed by half the words that came out of the Irish inmate's mouth.

Kenneth caught the exchange. "Oh, go on you tools, have a gas at the Mick," he smiled at Ray. "If you had your own cell, I'd say you two Yanks are welcome to shack up together and leave me in blessed peace, but you don't, and I happen to appreciate the amenities in my presidential suite, so it looks like we're stuck."

"Alright everyone," said Evander, addressing the remaining inmates who were still milling about discussing Sergei's departure. The tall goateed Watcher stood halfway up the staircase leading up to the second closed door along the otherwise blank stone wall. The guards from the day shift had already left the room. "You all know the drill, back to your cells, and don't cause any trouble. I ain't got time to be messin' around."

Ray looked around, watching the other prisoners voluntarily returning to their cells, some even shutting their own cell doors for the guard. Levi and Bryson headed to one room, the former scowling back at Ray. Cameron, the skinny bent-nosed boy took another room, somewhat glad to have it all to himself in Sergei's absence. Ray looked back at the lone Watcher in the cell house, standing on the staircase with his hands on his hips.

"I know what you're thinking," said Aiden. "But that door at his back leads to the Watcher barracks, and it could open up at any second. Besides, we like Evander."

Ray shrugged. "I think I've been in enough fights for one day," he said as they headed towards the back row of cells. "Which one should I go in, then?"

"Looks like you had a bit of good luck to be windin' up in a cell with Rashad, he doesn't usually leave his door open," said Kenneth, nodding his head towards one of the middle cells. "Luck of the Irish windin' up here though."

* * *

Ben looked down at his hands while he shuffled along with the other meandering inmates. His blisters had dried up, but his palms were still swollen and puffy. His arms had begun to turn pink from the harsh sunlight during the day. With difficulty, he put the thought of itching his sunburn out of his mind.

They were herded like cows into the tool shed, the shock stick held in Caleb's hand like a cattle prod, ready to shepherd the prisoners back into line if one of the teens dawdled for too long.

Hoping to catch a break with some light duties, Ben passed by the racks of shovels and mattocks, tramping towards the minecarts at the back of the tool shed. Gingerly grasping the handle of one of the metal wagons with his tender hands, he tried to wheel the minecart out, only to come face to face with a pair of inmates, both of them glowering back at him.

"Where are you planning on taking that, dreg?" one of the boys asked, his arms folded across his chest. Ben released his grip on the minecart's handle.

"Sorry, I – I… it's my first day," he said, sheepishly picking up the same blood-stained shovel he had hung up after his last shift. *At least it isn't a mattock*, he thought to himself.

The inmates filed out of the tool shed and into the quarry. Water dripped down from the drainage grates in the ceiling and onto the dirt below, gathering around the foundations of the weathered support pillars.

The water must have come from inside the cells, as the sky was mostly clear. The setting sun had cast its shadow halfway up one of the pit's cliff walls. The few clouds that had formed in the sky during the shift change were turning orange in the fading afternoon light. Down below, the shadowed sun umbrella, the unlit floodlight and the idle electric fan in the barren basin resembled forgotten pieces of trash in an otherwise-empty junkyard.

A crackle of electricity accompanied by a shriek from one of the lagging inmates suddenly motivated all of the other teens to hurry down the dirt slope and into the quarry pit, lest they face the consequences.

* * *

Ray entered the small cell to find Rashad already clothed in a fresh green uniform, his hair wet and dripping onto his shirt. A puddle of water on the stone floor drained through a small metal grate in the centre of the room. A bunk bed with two thin mattresses and sweat-stained sheets occupied almost half of the cell. The fading afternoon sun filtered down through a tall square shaft in the ceiling with three iron bars set both at the top and at the bottom of the skylight; six in total. The wooden cell door slammed shut behind him, Evander turning the key.

"Your uniform," said Rashad, waving his hand at a bundle of green clothes stacked upon the thin mattress of the upper bunk.

Ray reached up and held the green shirt out in front of him with distaste. "Can't I just keep wearing my own clothes?"

"I will not stop you," said Rashad. Then, with a chuckle, he added, "You will get tired of the smell though. And then I will regret leaving my door open." Rashad gestured to a metal bucket on the floor, half-filled with water.

Ray got halfway across the cell in just one step. He stooped, putting his hands in the water.

"Do not drink it," said Rashad. Ray's hands were cupped halfway to his mouth. He looked up at Rashad, puzzled. "Do you see a toilet in here?" Rashad asked rhetorically.

Ray dropped the water in disgust, standing up so fast that he almost knocked the bucket over. "Could've told me that before!" he said, wiping his hands on the front of his jeans.

"It has been cleaned," Rashad laughed, "But the water is meant to be used for a shower." He settled onto the lower bunk, the bed frame creaking under his weight. "Relax, I am not going to look."

Ray took the shirt off his head. It reeked of his own musky sweat and was coated in dust from the quarry. He cast it into a corner of the cell. He thought it would be a punishment befitting this prison just to wear the shirt without it ever being washed again. Cormac's white turned yellow sweat-stained shirt came to mind. "So, how long have you been here?"

"Too long," said Rashad, facing the wall. "I do not count the months, but I have seen a few rainy seasons. My only hope is that *they* do not realise how long I have been here. I fear that I may soon receive Sergei's fate."

"What's happening to Sergei?" asked Ray, taking off his jeans.

"After an inmate has reached a certain level of muscular strength, they are transferred to the Desert Complex, where they are trained to become one of the Watchers."

Ray picked up the metal bucket and poured it over himself. The water felt good running over his sun-reddened skin. He felt it washing away the grime and sweat from the day's work, yet the tranquil feeling quickly dissipated, the last of the water sloshing over the stone floor and down through the metal drain. Almost instantly, the humidity of the air in the prison returned, clinging to his skin.

"Great, so Sergei will be back soon, *and* he'll be one of the guards?" Ray reached up to the top mattress for his uniform.

"Not for some time, but yes, we will see him again."

* * *

Ben took up position alongside the other shovel bearers, and those with mattocks began striking at the shelf of rock still jutting out at the bottom of the quarry.

Very soon, the rock shelf would be cleared away and the ground would be levelled out once again. Ben found himself wondering when additional fishnets would be hung from the wooden pegs in the dirt walls to cover the exposed cliff edges surrounding the deeper level of the pit.

One of the shovellers working nearby drew in a sharp breath upon his first scoop of dirt. Leaning the tool against his shoulder, he attempted to remove a splinter from his dark hand. The inmate to Ben's left – a stocky adolescent – also stopped working to address the paused digger.

"What happened, you break a nail?" he said in a jovial Australian accent. "Man up, buddy, we're just getting started!"

Before anyone could take notice of Ben's hesitation to start working, and seeking to at least make a good impression with this shift of inmates, Ben kicked his shovel into one of the mounds of dirt steadily piling up behind the inmates with the mattocks cutting away at the ledge. As he lifted the shovel to dump the load into the minecart behind them, he felt the skin of his hands tearing, and blood appeared on the handle again.

He grimaced with each impact tremor and lift of the shovel, again finding himself hoping that his calluses would form soon.

Evander appeared at the prison entrance. He made his way down the dirt ramp and climbed up onto the thin stretch of the remaining plateau to stand beside Caleb and the other Watchers looking out over the inmates. None of the guards seemed tempted to lounge in the pair of chairs beneath the sun umbrella – at least not while Caleb was present.

* * *

Ray donned the green uniform with difficulty. His body was sore, slightly from the day's work, but mostly from the fighting. The shirt was surprisingly airier than what he had thought, far more suitable for this sweltering environment than his woollen shirt and jeans had been. He looked up through the shaft in the ceiling. The sun had already set, and the purple sky was calling forth the evening.

Rashad, sensing that Ray was now fully dressed, turned to face him. He sat up on his mattress, stooping underneath the upper bunk. "Do not show your strength," he said. Ray cocked an eyebrow. "You brought too much attention to yourself in the cafeteria. You were lucky Sergei is strong, otherwise it would have been you that was sent to the Desert Complex."

"Is that why you called for mercy?" asked Ray. "You're big enough to knock him flat."

"Sergei would be waking up just now, if I had meant to fight. Yet I feel my own transfer is imminent, and I must keep my head down for as long as possible."

"What's so bad about this place that it has big tough guys like you and Sergei so afraid?"

Rashad watched a small green lizard – no bigger than a hand's span – scuttling down through the skylight. He produced a tiny lump of porridge that he had tucked behind his ear. "They twist your mind," he said. "They force you to become loyal to the Watchers. They force you to take pleasure in tormenting others. Those who return are never the same."

"Sergei's mind won't have to be twisted too much, then," said Ray.

"That may be so, and all the better for him," said Rashad, holding his hand out for the small lizard skittering down the wall. He smiled as it nibbled at the cold chunk of gruel. "But for you or I, how much pain would they inflict upon us before we would wish it upon others?"

As if comprehending his words, the lizard caught the rest of the oatmeal in its mouth like a chipmunk and scuttled back up the wall, across the ceiling and into the shaft of the skylight.

Ray sat down next to Rashad. "I don't even know what kind of person I was before all this," he said. "I could've been worse than Sergei for all I know."

"I do not believe it to be so. But if that is true, then consider this a second chance."

"Before, you said something about a *venom snare*," said Ray. "What is it, some kind of tranquillising dart? Is that why I can't remember anything prior to waking up here?"

Rashad nodded. "The mask they fire at your face causes you to sleep. If you are exposed for too long to the chemicals infused in the venom snare, you may experience temporary memory loss. It does not happen to everyone, but you must have put up quite a fight before you succumbed to the snare's effects. That is why you do not remember."

Ray got to his feet. "Will I ever remember who I was?"

"With time, your memory will return. Mine did."

* * *

Night had fallen. Ben tried to massage the back of his neck, his skin feeling raw after working under the glare of the sun all day. The sunburn was itchy, although each time he touched his tender neck for temporary relief, the itching sensation only returned worse. The blisters on his hands did not aid his attempts to soothe his skin. And then there were the mosquitoes, droning around the toiling prisoners like hungry patrons at an all-you-can-eat buffet. Oh, how he hated them.

He was not accustomed to being outside for such extended periods of time. While Ray had always been outside during their childhood, playing sports with his friends, Ben had always preferred to spend his time indoors, watching movies, playing video games and reading books.

In an effort to take his mind off his sunburnt neck, Ben looked up at the night sky to see hundreds of stars studding the clear evening. It was amazing to see so many stars at once. He had read about places such as this, in a book that drew comparisons between ancient times and the present. He always had a passion for the olden days. The future was uncertain and ever-changing, yet the past was forever set in stone.

The book discussed the effects of light pollution in the present day, which referred to the amount of lights in each city; headlights, street lamps and any other artificial light source brightening up the night sky too much for most stars to be visible. Even his peaceful hometown was too well-lit during the night. Only rural locations allowed such a multitude of stars to be seen.

"Oi mate, quit daydreaming and get back to work."

Ben looked away from the night sky, half expecting to see a Watcher beside him, but instead, it was another prisoner, the same stocky inmate who had mouthed off to the digger who had paused earlier. He was sun-bronzed and had stubble across the lower half of his face. Ben lowered his head and plunged his shovel into another mound of dirt.

The inmate clapped Ben on the back, "Just kidding, mate! We're pretty fresh to all this ourselves," he said, indicating the teenager beside him who had splintered his hand. "Where you from anyway?"

"A small town," Ben mumbled, "Just a few hours outside of New York."

"New York!" the Aussie exclaimed. "I flew up there to see the sights, didn't think I'd see a big pit!" he said with a wink. His friend beside him chuckled. "I was sitting at a train station when I got snatched up. Ethan here swears that he was there at the same time, but if he was, he must've been hiding in the shadows with his natural camouflage." The other inmate chortled at this. "Anyway, one minute I'm sitting there, waiting for the train, next minute, I'm sweating buckets in a cell!"

"Two guys," said Ethan, holding up his fingers. "It was two guys that shot Jack in the face with a mask. I heard them call it a *venom snare*. I ran over to help him, and then they turned around and shot me too, got me with the same type of mask." Ben remembered having his own face covered with a pungent cloth when he was captured, its odours desensitising his entire body.

"Too bad they couldn't leave the mask on," said Jack. "Now we're stuck with looking at your ugly mug."

"Sometimes I wonder why I even bothered trying to rescue you," said Ethan.

"Mate, some rescue," Jack scoffed. "And then, as if my day couldn't get any worse, right? I get paired up with him in a cell. The guy doesn't stop talking. He keeps me up all night asking things like *do you ride kangaroos in Australia?*"

"Do you?" asked Ben, having wondered this himself.

Jack rolled his eyes.

Ethan laughed, his big smile showing two rows of pearly white teeth. "I keep you awake so that everyone else can get some sleep," he said. "Your snoring's loud enough to keep the entire cell house awake at night!"

"Whatever mate," said Jack. "I'd be surprised if *anyone* could get some shut-eye with you flapping your gums." A few other inmates chuckled at the pair's exchange. Ben half-smiled at the two bantering back and forth, but he was far too weary to laugh along with them.

"Do either of you know where the nearest town might be?" Ben asked before Ethan could dish up his next insult. The snickering teens nearby fell silent.

"Thinking of getting out?" asked Jack.

"I like this guy already," said Ethan, looking around to make sure the Watchers were out of earshot.

Ben looked over his shoulder too. Caleb and Evander were at the other end of the pit.

"I noticed that when the manacles are changed for those working a double shift," said Ben, "The inmates are temporarily free from being sparked. It could give us a chance to strike before the next shift's manacle gets fitted."

The other prisoners' ears pricked up, and they slowed the pace of their work to listen in.

Suddenly, blinding light flooded the pit. Ben covered his eyes, feeling as though the sun had just knocked the night out of the sky. He hoped that none of the guards had overheard him.

* * *

For a while, it seemed as though the entire prison was quiet at night, but after Rashad had drifted off to sleep, Ray's ears scanned through the white noise, picking up the smaller, unnoticed sounds: the steady scrape of shovels into dirt, mattocks picking into the hard earth, the occasional grunts of exertion of inmates pushing a full minecart up the dirt ramp and the hollow trundle of an empty metal wagon going back down again.

Separate from the sounds of the quarry, he could hear a leaky tap dripping, guards laughing and throwing insults at each other, and the sounds of other boys in their cells, some talking, and some turning in their sleep with muffled sobs.

It reminded him of home, when he could hear Ben through the drywall, crying himself to sleep after a bad day at school, or if the silences between Ben and their father had been going on for longer than a few days at a time. There was always a degree of resent in their dad's eyes whenever he looked at Ben. With Ray, their father was more relaxed, but Ben always seemed to be a constant reminder of something. Something that Ray could not remember, or perhaps something he had never known.

Ray looked up through the skylight again. Night had completely fallen, and dozens of stars filled the small square patch of visible sky through the shaft in the ceiling. Even though he had lost most of his memory, he was sure that he had never seen so many stars. Confined within the bounds of his small window, the cluster of distant light outnumbered what he would have normally seen across the entire stretch of sky in his hometown, wherever that might have been.

As his sight adjusted to the darkness, Ray noticed the little green lizard clinging to the wall on one side of the vertical shaft, blinking back at him with its tiny yellow eyes, taking shelter from the large bats swooping by overhead, flapping their wings and screeching in search of prey. Oddly, the lizard reminded him of Ben as well, and he wondered how his little brother was holding up on his double shift. Surely he must have been worn out by now.

A door creaked open somewhere in the cell house. Ray looked through the cell door's window, another small square with three vertical iron bars set within. A figure with short dark hair emerged through the doorway in the corner of the cell house and into the light cast by the big glaring lamps suspended from the four corners of the roof.

Clad in the same green uniform as he now wore, it was definitely an inmate, and from what Ray could see, the inmate must have been a girl. Though he could not clearly see her face, she was too skinny to be one of the guys working down below, and too tall to be just a boy. He watched as the inmate walked between the stairs and the chains rack, entering one of the empty cells on the right hand side of the room. He glanced at the doorway she had come through, yet no one followed. He wondered how she was able to roam around the prison, unsupervised by any of the guards.

She emerged from the cell, carrying a chamber pot and heading back in the direction of the open door on the left of the stairs. He called for her attention in a whispered shout. She stopped next to the chains rack, looking around, and he called out again.

The prisoner ventured towards the back row of cells, and by the looks of her leg, she was not wearing a manacle either. Her face began to materialise as if from a blank slate as she approached. She wore her hair in a knot at the top of her head, keeping it from falling into the chamber pot in her hands. Her eyebrows were thin and arching, and her nose was pierced with a metal stud that glinted in the spotlights' glare.

"Can you help us get outta here?" asked Ray, indicating himself and Rashad, who now lay awake on his bunk bed, already knowing the answer she would give him.

She drew even closer, holding the chamber pot at a noticeable distance away from her body. Ray slowed his breathing as he smelled the reeking odour wafting into the cell, and he retreated back half a step. The foul stench escaped through the cell's skylight, probably giving the small lizard enough reason to evacuate the building and take its chances with the bats soaring above.

"You must be new here," she said. Ray nodded, but still eyed her intently. She looked over her shoulder and whispered, "I would, but I can't. They only open up the cells that are empty so that I can clean out the chamber pots. They don't give me the keys."

Ray let out a sigh and slumped against the wall. She lingered for a moment, waiting for him to say something else before grunting with impatience and getting on with her work.

"Mara seems to be in a good mood today," said Rashad, sitting up with an amused smile. "I remember the time when Kenneth tried to talk to her, and he received the contents of a chamber pot flung through his cell window."

"You could've given me a heads-up," Ray exclaimed, "She was carrying one just now!"

* * *

Before the flash of light, Ben had barely noticed that they had been working in the dark. Allowing his eyes to adapt to the intense brightness, he lowered his hand from his face. While the inmates had been busy talking, the Watchers had moved the floodlight to the top of the rock ledge and switched it on. Dust motes kicked up from their work swirled and eddied in the blazing lamp's glow.

Jack lowered his voice to speak. "You know, the spotlights in the cell house, the green uniforms, and all of the mattocks and shovels and fishnets… They all must've come from somewhere. I reckon there'd be a town nearby."

"I'm sure they wouldn't be asking too many questions either," said Ethan, "As long as they're getting paid."

"Who knows how far away it is though," said Jack. "The food in the cafeteria isn't exactly fresh."

The inmates fell into silent contemplation. The only noises in the pit were the sounds of the mattocks cutting into the rock shelf, piles of earth crumbling around their feet, shovel blades scraping into the dirt mounds and the clumps of rock being tossed into the minecarts behind them.

The brilliant light illuminating the worksite was like a magnet to the nocturnal wildlife from the surface. Flying insects began floating down from above, buzzing around the glaring orb of the floodlight.

Small green lizards scaled down the light-bathed quarry wall, the tiny critters flitting in and out of the fishnet mesh. Large screeching bats circled overhead, beating their leathery wings in ever-descending wheels and turns, each member of the tropical ecosystem following their prey into the pit.

A mosquito droned past Ben's ear, landing on the back of his raw neck. Without thinking, he clapped a hand over his shoulder, immediately gasping in pain from the slap on his sunburnt skin. He arched his upper back and craned his head towards the sky; it was as if someone had thrown ice down the back of his shirt and then scalded him with boiling water.

Ben felt the shovel slip from his grasp, the wooden handle stained red. He stared down at his hands, blood glistening from his broken blisters under the harsh beam of the floodlight. His throat was dry. He was transfixed by the sight of his bleeding hands, almost paralysed. More mosquitoes flocked towards him, his hands outstretched as if in offering to the insects. He fell backwards.

"Water!" yelled Jack. "He needs water!"

Ethan dropped his own shovel and knelt beside Ben, gripping him by the shoulders and attempting to shake him out of his stupor. Ben's vision began to blur. Ethan's face disappeared and Jack's voice faded.

He felt himself being lifted up, as if he was levitating a few feet above the ground. The stars of the night sky merged together in his cloudy vision, forming a white ceiling with varying degrees of intensity. Only the glossy black wings of the bats flying overhead broke the dazzling fluorescence as he floated upwards.

Then, everything vanished. Ben's heavy eyelids drooped as footsteps echoed through vast empty chambers. He smiled to himself as he hung limp in mid-air, still floating upwards; the prison, the quarry, it was all just a bad dream.

Very soon, he would wake up in his own bed, far away from this place, from the heat, the guards, and the inmates. He would start his day off with reading a book over breakfast – anything but porridge. He would tell his father that it would be a bad idea for them to explore the swamp for the fabled *Lizardman*. He would tell them about his terrible premonition. He would tell all of them; his father, Ray, Uncle Joshua, even the camera crew if they cared to listen.

Ben urged himself to wake up. *Wake up, and leave this nightmare.*

6 - FURESH

Ssssssssssssssssssssssssss…

His mantis green eyes snapped open at the sound, surveying his surroundings with keen scrutiny. His subterranean chamber was bare, save for the stone chair he sat upon and the basin of water mounted atop a small stand by his side; yet he scanned the corners of his room nonetheless. The flames burning in the torches set on either side of the long narrow corridor leading out from his chamber cast dancing shadows across the mud-brick walls and ceiling. He searched the sand – which coated every surface of the entire complex – for signs of footprints, seeing none save his own.

The Master of Combat relaxed his grip on the hilts of the two scimitar swords laid across his scaly battle-scarred chest. The Ridgeback Chieftain had no doubt in his guards' ability to subdue any warrior attempting to gain access to his chamber without his summons, yet a stealthy assassin from the camouflaged Blackbead Tribe was a different foe altogether. It would not have been the first cowardly attempt on his life. It had been years since the last time he knew peace.

Sssssssssssssssssssssssssss…

Furesh lifted himself from his chair, the column of spiny thorns running down his rear scratching against the groove carved in the centre of the stone seat's backrest. A chunk of stone had also been removed from beneath one of the armrests to accommodate his powerful steel grey tail.

Momentarily ignoring the hissing sound stemming from the small room behind his chamber, Furesh moved to the water basin and, seizing a wooden cup with his thumb and forefinger, he took care not to slice himself with his own sword as he drank. The basin refilled itself through a pipe embedded in the smooth sand-covered wall, discreetly linked to a nearby oasis.

Furesh had awoken with even less sleep than usual. Two Watchers had come during the night, carrying a fat little flesh tank of a prisoner between them. The pudgy boy had screamed at the sight of the *Kirzakai*, on and on until his voice had broken, and after that, he had kept half the complex awake with his incessant whimpering.

Sssssssssssssssssssssssss...!

Exhaling abidingly, Furesh dropped the cup back into the basin with a hollow *plop* and strode around his chair into the next room, his tail sweeping sand into the corners of his chamber.

He came face to face with a large hooded snake extending its head through a hole in the wall. Its silver-scaled hide shimmered in the dim torchlight glowing from the other room, giving it a sleek sheen over the top of its cream-coloured belly.

Its fierce black eyes considered him for a moment, seething at his delay. Furesh stared back at the bewitched serpent with equal intolerance, raising a scimitar as if to lop off the snake's head. The cobra relented, its black eyes rolling back into its skull as the serpent unhinged its jaw to regurgitate its message. A green orb rolled forth from its inky gullet, the snake catching the sphere between its twin fangs and narrow forked tongue.

The metallic green *Kemuri* smoke inside the sphere poured over itself like rolling storm clouds until a face materialised within the orb: Kalarish. The years had not been kind to her physical appearance; a just reward for her actions. She had grown as plump as ever. The tiny cluster of horns crowning the back of her head did nothing to draw attention away from her bulky figure. Even the smoke's clashing green shades could not hide her sagging jowls as she scowled at him from halfway across the world, yet Furesh did not need a full spectrum of colours to detect the sly deception that twinkled behind her amber orange eyes.

"Speak, witch," he said sharply.

"Greetings, *Champion of the Chieftains*," she mocked. "Did I dizturb your zlumber? I had forgotten how far behind you are… the hour of your dawn, that is."

"Cut to the point," Furesh rumbled.

"As you wish," she said, her jagged teeth protruding from her snout as she curled her lips into a wicked smile. "We are near on locating one of the Faction ztrongholds. I have zeen it in a vision. A great battle is coming, Furesh. How goes the training of the latezt batch of Frillneck warriors?"

For years, the other tribes had been sending their soldiers to receive training from the Ridgebacks, supplying food to the barren Desert Complex in exchange.

Warriors, she says, Furesh suppressed a snort, "Veterans, all of them. Better than my own soldiers."

"Lying is not an honourable virtue, Furesh…" Kalarish rasped.

"DO NOT PREACH TO ME OF HONOUR!!" Furesh bellowed, shaking sand from the ceiling. The snake bearing the orb retreated as far back into the hole as its open jaws would allow, the back of its skull ramming against the niche's rim.

He heard his soldiers stir from their slumber in the barracks nearby. They plucked their tridents from the weapon racks with hisses and grunts, assembling into formation in the hall outside his corridor with startling efficiency.

"Temper, temper," Kalarish clucked her tongue. "I had only meant to make zertain that the Frillneck Tribe is given the highezt rankz among the *Kirzakai* army."

"Hag, your flesh tanks are unworthy of holding a blade, save those forged for slicing food. What makes you think I would grant an officer's title to *any* of your craven tribe?"

"A good queztion…" said Kalarish, shutting her wicked eyes for a brief moment to pluck a ploy from her palette of plots. "Perhapz it is time for you to pledge zome of *your* warriors to Tyrax's zervitude, as a show of loyalty. *You know how he doubtz you.* Yet ztill, members of your tribe are always welcome in the Command Complex."

Furesh dreaded the thought. He recalled the tropical island, a beautiful place full of so much promise and potential for the *Kirzakai*… until Tyrax came to power. Now, the minds of all who set foot inside those walls were twisted, *constricted*, bent to Tyrax's will, and to those who whispered in his ears.

"You will never have power over the Ridgebacks, witch," Furesh fired back. "It will take an entire army to force even *one* of my tribe to join you… An army the likes of which we alone have the power to raise."

"Let uz be rational, Furesh. An attack on your tribe would be unthinkable. But… if your zupply tunnel were to collapze… how long would your ztockpile of food lazt? The desert above you is a barren wazteland, void of any nourishing wildlife. What would you do, forage for fruit? Venture too near to the humans and expose yourzelves? No… you would fall upon one another, juzt as the Gravelhides cleanse themzelves of their weak. And then, not even one of your tribe would join uz, *for not one of you would remain.*"

Furesh's spines bristled. His tail thumped the ground and he clenched his curved swords still tighter in his scaly hands. *Every army requires food,* he knew. His gaze pierced the orb, silently vowing that she would never have another opportunity to make this threat again. "You shall have your officers, hag," he relented. "And woe to the true warriors they lead."

"I knew we would come to terms, Furesh. Have fun playing in the zand."

Kalarish's derisive cackle continued even as the silver snake swallowed the sphere, her rasping laughter reverberating up from the bewitched serpent's gullet until it snapped its jaws shut and eyed Furesh again. With a final flicker of its forked tongue, the cobra receded into the obsidian darkness of the wall's niche, leaving Furesh alone in the fading torchlight.

The seven-foot tall Master of Combat strode out from his chambers and into the sand-filled hall. The two chamber guards had already fallen into the troop's formation: ten lines of eight. His warriors stood tall, snout up, chest out, eyes front, the butts of their tridents buried in the sand next to their clawed feet. Behind the eighty statuesque Ridgebacks was the entrance into the arena, where a golden beam of dawn light was just beginning to shine down through the hole in the roof of the vast underground cavern.

Sharisse, his stalwart captain, greeted him in the hall. "We stand ready, Chieftain. What is your will?"

His eyes traced over her. Half his age and half a foot shorter than he, Sharisse's maple brown scales were still smooth and tight around her muscles. She bore a single scar over her left shoulder, one that only Furesh himself could have inflicted, when she had duelled for her captaincy. Their fight had lasted near over an hour before blood was shed. She had been his finest student, surpassing warriors greater in strength, size and years. Her emerald green eyes awaited his orders.

"How fare the Frillnecks in combat, Sharisse?"

"Ripe for the slaughter," she answered. Furesh's elite soldiers allowed themselves a snort. "They lounge in the shade while the others train. They use the Redcrowns and the humans alike as food servants. The flesh tanks are too lazy to pick up their own food, let alone pick up a weapon."

"Good," said Furesh. "Grant them all titles of note and send them back to the Command Complex. I'll not have them disgrace my arena with their presence any longer." *Once they clash with the Faction, only those worthy of rank will survive,* he thought to himself. He turned on his heel, yet halted mid-step, "And Sharisse..." he studied his soldiers, "Assign half-rations for all food supplies henceforth."

"Your will, Chieftain," Sharisse bowed unquestioningly.

Dismissing the assembly to run drills with the students of the remaining tribes, Furesh marched to his left, through the Ridgebacks' private dining area – comprised of simple spartanesque wooden tables and benches – and around the corner into the shrine room.

Morning sunlight filtered down through the sand-covered mesh draped across a small hole in the ceiling, casting its rays against the wall. By midday, the enormous golden statue standing in the centre of the room would bathe the chamber in its pale yellow light.

The shrine of solid gold had been forged in the likeness of the Redcrown Lizardwoman, Raptrish, one of the first Chieftains. It had been gifted as a sign of peace after many who had flocked to the Desert Complex following Thorax's death believed that Furesh, as Champion of the Chieftains, should lead the *Kirzakai*.

It was Tyrax's folly to believe that Furesh's honour could be bought by a simple trinket, although he did find solace beneath the gaze of the Redcrown Chieftain, standing proud beside her long gilded spear.

Furesh settled into a cross-legged position, closing his eyes in thought. Many had doubted Tyrax's claim that his brood father, Thorax, had been killed by the humans during his peaceful mission to reveal the existence of the *Kirzakai* and establish diplomatic relations between the races. When his body had been brought back as proof, it did not take a Highbeak to recognise that he had died of multiple spear wounds in his back.

He still remembered the day that he had offered to accompany Thorax with an armed escort of Ridgebacks, but the Bluetongue Chieftain had refused, reasoning that a mission for peace could not begin with implements of war. He deferred to Thorax's judgement. After all, it was he who had brought peace to the warring tribes. Yet on the day he had witnessed Thorax's lifeless body, and on countless sleepless nights since, Furesh still wondered what would have happened if he had insisted on guarding the Chieftain of Chieftains.

Representatives from each tribe had beseeched Furesh to challenge Tyrax, but he was too preoccupied, intent on discovering irrefutable evidence concerning the truth behind Thorax's death. Boaresh, the Horntail Chieftain who had accompanied Thorax on his mission, was the only one who he could trust to verify the claim. Furesh had searched far and wide throughout the subterranean network of tunnels for the Horntail Chieftain, following a trail of dried blood as far as The Swamp, where the tracks were obscured by the murky waters.

Some believed that Boaresh, overcome with shame for his inability to protect Thorax – the greatest leader of their time – imposed an exile upon himself, cursed to live out the rest of his days in solitude. In their absence,

Tyrax, Jawresh and Kalarish were all too quick to manipulate the angry *Kirzakai* into adopting a militant approach to reclaiming their right to live freely amongst the humans, or rather, *above* the humans.

Once enough of the *Kirzakai* had rallied behind the three bloodthirsty Chieftains, any who opposed them were captured and subjected to *constriction*; the elimination of free will, crushing them into weak-minded beings. *Constriction* was only ever intended to tame the *Colossiboas*, to allow transport throughout the vast network of tunnels connecting the tribes. For as long as any *Kirzaka* could remember, the techniques were deemed highly invasive and without honour, and therefore prohibited for use upon any other creature.

Unbeknownst to any outside her tribe, Kalarish, the scheming hag, had been practising the art of *constriction* all along. The few Blackbeads who had managed to escape her clutches with their minds intact had informed Furesh that some kind of craven spell had fallen upon the Command Complex, testing the will of all who entered its domain.

He knew that a full frontal assault was out of the question. The Ridgebacks would not even earn a warrior's death; they would live out the rest of their years as slaves. *If only Boaresh was still with us*, he thought to himself. *The Horntail Chieftain would know all of the island's defensive shortcomings.*

He still visited The Swamp from time to time, hoping to discover Boaresh in his solitude, one of his visits just as recently as a few days ago, yet that had only resulted in the capture of three humans. Two had been sent to the Quarry Complex, and the third – older than the pair of boys – had been *constricted* by the Frillnecks and trained by the Ridgebacks. They had sent the man off with the other pair of Watchers last night.

7 - THE NEW WATCHER

Ben woke up, eager to find himself in his own bed, far away from the elaborate yet horrible dream. He attempted to sit upright, expecting to see his bedroom again – his shelves full of alphabetically-arranged books, his spotless desk underneath a reading lamp, and his school uniform folded in a neat pile on top of his dresser – yet instead, he bumped his head on the low stone ceiling of his cell.

With a taste of copper in his mouth, he fell back upon his mouldy sweat-stained mattress, sending dust motes drifting up into the dank air.

The dank stone walls of his small cell were illuminated by the beams of the spotlights shining in from the room beyond through the door's barred window. The skylight's shaft in the ceiling reflected the morning sun's rays down into the cell, casting a square patch of light upon the stone floor, yet sunlight was the last thing Ben wanted to see; his skin had been burnt bright red from all of his hard labour in the hot sun yesterday.

He groaned at the thought of another day in this nightmarish prison. His body screamed in torment, traumatised by the monotonous *dig, throw, repeat.* Not once in his entire life had he ever dreamed of straining himself past the point of exhaustion. He thought that if he just lay perfectly still, he could sleep forever.

Sensing a bump forming on his forehead, Ben reached up to check whether he was bleeding, yet before his hand was even halfway to his head, the torn muscle fibres of his skinny biceps grated against each other, shooting agonising needles of pain up his arm. His hand jerked up to his shoulder involuntarily, lighting all those needles of pain on fire. He yelped and writhed and twisted his body in anguish, setting off a chain reaction of other muscle spasms. Through all of his squirming, his sunburn flared up as well, his raw skin's nerve endings alternating between itchiness and agony.

Little Danny stirred at the sound of his cellmate's pained whimpering. "Good morning, Benny," his reedy voice chirped up happily from below. "And a very fine morning it is!"

"How did I get back in the cell?" Ben moaned after he had forced his aching arm straight again. The last thing he could remember was Jack calling for water.

"That blackie, Evander, 'e brought you in. 'e said you fainted. Is that true? You faint?"

Ben thought to lecture him on his racial slur; however he did not wish to create another enemy, no less out of his own cellmate. "What happened to Sergei after he was dragged out of the cafeteria?" he asked instead, avoiding confrontation.

"'e got transferred to the Desert Complex," said Little Danny. "I've 'eard they play games wiv your 'ead, and then you become a Watcher."

Ben's stomach turned at the thought of Sergei returning as one of the guards, or maybe it was his hunger. He had barely eaten anything yesterday.

* * *

In an identical cell a few doors away from Ben's, Ray yawned, stretching and flexing his stiff muscles. His body was sore, not so much from the digging, but from all of the fighting. Despite the dull aches, he was still able to rouse himself out of bed, as if his body was already conditioned for such physical strain. He thanked himself for whatever past life he had led prior to this place.

Climbing down from his thin mattress on the top bunk, his lower back sent a sharp pain through his midsection as his feet hit the floor, a memento of his fight with Spike and Gremlin, when he had fallen on his tailbone.

Ray took off the shirt of his green uniform to check whether the sun had damaged his skin yesterday. Splotched bruises had formed over his slightly reddened skin. Across some of his contusions, he found a clearly defined purple indent in the shape of a thin band. Someone must have been wearing a ring when they fought, though most likely it had been left by one of the Watchers, since the inmates would have been robbed of anything of value.

He looked down at the tan line encircling his thumb, which also appeared to have been left behind by the shape of a ring, roughly the same size. *I'll get it back*, he thought to himself, also remembering the medallion hanging from around Caleb's neck. He made a mental note to ask Ben about where the pendant had come from the next time they saw each other.

Ray attempted to stretch to his full height in the cell, yet his hands brushed the roof before he could fully extend himself. He reached up through the skylight instead and gripped the bottom set of iron bars. Lifting his feet off the floor, he let gravity stretch out the rest of his sore body.

His bones cracked, relieving the pressure in his joints. By sudden impulse, he began performing pull-ups, as if his muscles had some stored memory of the movement. It was one of the few memories that had come naturally to him prior to being captured.

Rashad awakened at the sounds of Ray's grunts of exertion. He rolled out of bed and caught himself upon the ground, pumping out push-ups. After some time, Ray dropped down from the skylight and they rotated exercises.

Cormac's face appeared in the door window. "'ello sweet'earts, looks like you're about ready for another nice 'ot day in the sun, then!" he said as he unlocked the door. With a mischievous wink, he added, "Don't wear yourselves out before you even start, 'ey?"

Ray stood upright and Rashad let go of the skylight bars, the pair of inmates facing the Watcher. Their muscles were inflated from the exercise routine. Cormac's yellow-toothed grin snapped shut, and he drew his shock stick.

"You ever *really* wanna feel the burn, you just let me know, 'ey?" he thumbed the baton's switch, flicking the electrical volts on and off, his piercing blue eyes flitting between the pair of prisoners. "I'd be 'appy to give you two a good working over." His eyes settled on Ray's bruises. "Nice beauty marks you've got on ya. Not a scratch on Sergei, mind you. Wait until 'e comes back a Watcher."

At their silence, Cormac shot them another crude grin and moved on to the next cell. Ray put his green shirt back on before they walked out to join the line-up of other inmates already gathered in the cell house.

* * *

"Up!" Leon barked as he unlocked the cell door. Ben rolled over on his mattress to be as close to the wall as possible, loathing the idea of working another day in the pit. The grizzled guard entered the cell in one stride. "I heard Evander carried you back to your cell last night while you slept like a young pup," he growled. "If you want to act like a young pup again on my watch, I'll be sure to let you dig holes in the dirt using just your little paws!"

Ben reluctantly moved to the other side of his stale yellow mattress, flailed his legs out and collapsed onto the floor below.

"Put on your uniform," Leon spat on the floor next to their chamber pot, indicating a pile of green clothes at the end of Ben's bed. Eyeing them both, the Watcher took leave of their cell with disgust.

Little Danny giggled in his wake.

"*Young pup*, ha!" he echoed, planting his feet on the floor beside Ben. "'e's always a laugh, 'e is!"

Little Danny left the door open as he exited the room to join the other inmates lined up in the cell house. All of the prisoners standing outside had their backs turned to the row of cells, and the Watchers were busy making sure that they stayed in line.

Ben stumbled across the cell on sore legs and shut the door so that he could change into his uniform in privacy, muttering under his breath. *"Young pup,* yourself." Even Little Danny had joined in on teasing him. *Surely he doesn't know any better,* Ben thought to himself. *He barely even looks eight years old.*

* * *

Ray looked up and down the line. He saw Levi, his eyes nervously darting left and right, feeling out of place without Sergei beside him. Ray figured that Levi had made a lot of enemies while he could count on Sergei's protection, and now he stood vulnerable amongst his past victims. Bryson and Cameron stood alongside Levi, more out of habit than anything else.

Looking past the other boys, Ray caught sight of Little Danny exiting the last cell on the left. "Where's Benji?" he mouthed with a frown.

"Putting on 'is new clothes!" Little Danny's reedy voice carried over the chatter of the other inmates.

He must have been too exhausted to change into his uniform after his double shift, Ray thought to himself. *Benji never did take too well to physical activity.* His head throbbed as another memory flashed through his mind of Ben reading a book on the couch while Ray and his friends were working on their football tackles in the yard. A few girls were watching them practice, but his attention had been drawn to a brunette girl with dimpled cheeks.

Someone tapped him on the shoulder, ripping him out of the memory. Ray blinked hard, and he saw Kenneth and Aiden beside him.

"Nice shirt you got there," the Irish teen grinned. "Is there a sale on that I should know about?" Ray looked down at their identical clothes, and Kenneth slapped him on the arm with a meaty palm, stinging his mild sunburn. "Just joshin' ya lad," then, turning to the group, he announced boisterously, "Come on boyos, breakfast's on me today! What's the hold up?"

* * *

Ben pulled his dirty black shirt off with difficulty, taking care not to exacerbate the pain in his muscles, or allow his soiled garment to scrape over the itchy red sunburnt skin on his arms, face and neck. He resisted the urge to itch at the damaged skin, knowing that it would only get worse.

He would have traded one of his blistered hands for some aloe vera lotion, or at least some sunscreen to stop his sunburnt skin from turning tomato. Blotches of dead skin had already begun to peel away, and angry red dots had risen on the raw pink flesh beneath.

Ben cast his old shirt aside, odours of sweat and grime travelling with it. His shoulders ached and his skin rubbed raw on the back of his neck as he reached up to grab the green shirt lying upon the upper bunk. He wondered who could have left it there for him.

He slipped the new shirt on with the same awkward difficulty, his sunburn stinging despite his caution. The fabric felt smooth and crisp, almost as if it were made of silk, if he had known what silk felt like.

Three wood-splintering bangs against the cell door startled him, Leon's face appearing on the other side. "HURRY UP!!" the grizzled guard roared at the timid teen.

"Let's get a move on, 'ey sunshine!?" Cormac's crude voice followed from behind. "Y'know what? For every second you're late, everyone else loses a minute of chow time!" As Cormac started counting the seconds, the other inmates began shouting their indignation. Cormac held up his hands with a mischievous yellow smile, "Well, the show must go on, innit!"

Worried that the other inmates would look down on him yet again, Ben quickly changed out of his dirty grey trousers and slipped on the green pants, ignoring his sore body's painful protests.

Everyone's eyes were already on Ben before he even swung his door open, slamming it against the wall as he burst into the cell house. Full of apologies, his face was red with a mix of agitation and embarrassment, but mostly sunburn. The bright red of his skin contrasted with the green hue of his new uniform; the Christmas colours making him look like one of Santa's elves.

"About time, young pup," Leon growled, shoving Ben forward.

"Come sweet'earts, time for the morning newspaper!" said Cormac, leading the inmates towards the cafeteria stairs with a slight spring in his step.

"Don't remind me," Ray muttered to nobody in particular. He dreaded the thought of the gruel's wet cardboard-like taste.

All of the inmates in the line-up glared at Ben for costing them precious time at breakfast. Levi smirked at him amongst the crowd. Averting their gazes, Ben lined up at the rear with his head downcast, and the prisoners trudged down the stairs into the cafeteria.

* * *

The inmates from the morning shift were already seated, the sounds of their chatter and their spoons scraping the wooden bowls filling the mess hall. Gremlin stood by the stone bench at the front of the room with the other Watchers, his pale pointed face craned forward like a gargoyle as he wordlessly singled out the inmates who had been selected to work a double shift.

Ray stood near the front of the queue, filling his bowl from the water tap. The water spilled out from the sides of his mouth as he drank. He allowed Rashad and a few other inmates to pass by him in the queue while he quenched his thirst. The other boys must have grown accustomed to malnutrition and dehydration, as they only filled their bowls once.

Having slaked his thirst, he rejoined the queue, finding himself standing behind Levi, who nervously glanced over his shoulder at Ray, fear flickering in his eyes. Levi approached the gruel pot, and Ava spooned him a ladle of the sickening porridge while Cormac monitored them nearby.

"Oi, Levi," the guard muttered with a crude grin. "If you keep a close eye on the ovva inmates for us, we'll let you rejoin Sergei in the Desert Complex. 'ow's that sound, 'ey?"

Levi swelled his chest and turned away from the gruel pot, smugly looking down his nose at the other inmates in the queue as he passed by. Leon chuckled at Cormac's false promise as Ava filled Ray's bowl with the goopy gruel. Ray searched for Rashad's hulking figure and moved to sit beside him.

* * *

Once again, Ben found himself at the back of the queue for the gruel pot. Even Little Danny stood ahead of him.

"I see you've learnt me trick, Benny!" his malnourished cellmate said over his bony shoulder. "Staying 'ere at the back means there's no one left to push you around, so you can drink all the water you want!"

"Good idea," said Ben, although it meant that he would always be seen as the boy at the back of the line.

"You keep that between us though!" Little Danny exclaimed, his sky blue eyes suddenly flashing with an icy glare, realising that he had just betrayed his own secret.

Ben let a few feet of distance grow between him and his cellmate, the impulsive outburst unsettling, especially for one so small. He soon picked up an empty bowl, filled it with water and drained it several times over before receiving a serving of the grey gravy.

* * *

Ray and Rashad looked up as Ben and Little Danny joined them, the latter squatting on top of one of the stone seats beside Ben like a frog. Ray studied his brother's sunburnt skin, his bright red face lined with dirt and grime.

"Didn't you even shower?" asked Ray.

Ben looked up, his eyes wide in astonishment. "There's a shower here? Where?"

Rashad choked on his oatmeal.

Ray shot Little Danny a glare. "Didn't you leave any water in the chamber pot for Benji to clean himself with?"

"I was 'oping they'd refill it when 'e came back," Little Danny lied, failing to stifle an impish grin. Ben – instead of confronting his cellmate – lowered his eyes and pushed his food around his bowl.

Ray lowered his voice an octave. "Have you heard about the Desert Complex? That place where Sergei got sent to yesterday."

Ben nodded, "That's where they turn the inmates into Watchers, right?"

"Right," said Ray. "Rashad said he might be getting sent off soon, too." Rashad ate his food in silent contemplation. Ray leaned across the table. "We need to come up with a plan to get outta here. *Fast.* I'm thinking we could start a brawl as a distraction in the tool shed, or down in the pit. While the guards are busy making their bets, we could flip the fight on them and start a riot. We can use the shovels and mattocks as weapons."

Rashad shook his head disapprovingly. "If the manacles are sparked, the riot would be over as quickly as it began."

Ray glanced down at the small metal bracelet with the blinking red light around his ankle. "It couldn't hurt that much, could it?" he asked. "I doubt they could get enough volts through this thing to actually make a difference."

"Are you 'aving a laugh, mate?" Little Danny piped up. "It 'urts an awful lot!"

Ray looked him up and down, thinking that it would not take much for the scrawny kid to burst into tears at the first sign of pain.

Ben looked down at his own ankle flashing with the red light, thinking that Evander must have switched his manacle before carrying him back to his cell. Suddenly, he sat up, his eyes lit with excitement.

"Last night when I worked the double shift," said Ben. "My manacle was changed to match the sparker frequency of the night shift. But in that brief moment, when the manacles were being changed over, I was immune to the threat of the sparkers. Maybe we could riot here in the cafeteria?" Ben beamed broadly at Ray, proud of his own suggestion, expecting his brother to embrace the idea.

"It's useless to fight without weapons," said Ray, shattering his brother's short-lived confidence. "Plus, we'd have to deal with double the guards." He glanced pointedly towards the front of the cafeteria where the Watchers of the morning and day shifts congregated.

"We'd have double the inmates fighting on our side though," said Ben, hoping that Ray would not completely disregard his idea, or at least be willing to hear another suggestion.

Rashad pushed aside his empty bowl. "Perhaps we can convince the minecart pushers to steal some tools on their way to the treasury."

Ben's face screwed up, and it was not because of the gruel's newspaper-like taste.

Ray looked over at Levi, still wearing his smug grin from Cormac's promise, and he shook his head at the idea, much to Ben's satisfaction. Even if they could manage to convince Cameron and Bryson to help them, he did not want to take the chance that Levi would report them all as soon as the snivelling weasel suspected something was off.

"Even if one of *us* could steal some tools instead," said Ben. "I think there would be too few tools that we could take without their absence going unnoticed. Especially while all of the other mattocks and shovels are being used in the quarry."

"Not to mention, getting caught stealing," Little Danny chimed in around a mouthful of gruel.

"Maybe…" said Ben, "We could use a fight between two inmates as a distraction for some of us to get into the tool shed unnoticed."

"Let us assume we can reach the surface," said Rashad. "Where do we go from there?"

"While I was working on the night shift," said Ben, "I met two inmates named Jack and Ethan. They said that the uniforms and spotlights must have come from some town on the surface. We couldn't guess at how far away it might be, or which direction, but at least it's a start."

Ray straightened up in his seat with a realisation, "The spotlights in the cell house. There must be power lines nearby to provide electricity. We can follow the power lines back to civilisation."

"Or…" said Rashad, "The lights in the prison could be running on diesel generators."

Ray grunted, fed up with the amount of pessimism being passed around the table. "We're just gonna have to take the chance that there's somewhere we can escape to."

"At the very least," said Ben, "We should focus on getting up to the surface in the first place. Then we can decide which way to run."

The brothers' eyes met. Ray was grateful that at least one of them shared his enthusiasm to escape.

Little Danny perked up, noticing something over Ray's shoulder. "Hm. 'e's new, 'aven't seen 'im before," he said, pointing to the front of the cafeteria.

Ray turned around to see a man standing out of place amongst the guards behind the stone bench. Straining his eyes, he could not distinguish any of the man's facial features. He began to think that there was a problem with his eyesight.

Ben finished chewing his mouthful before looking down Little Danny's reed-like arm. His eyes widened in surprise. He dropped his spoon at the sight of the new Watcher. After what seemed like an age of staring across the cafeteria, fumbling for words, he finally summoned his voice. "Uncle Joshua?"

8 - WITHOUT STRUGGLE

The brothers and their cellmates stared across the room at Joshua as he stood at the front of the cafeteria with the other Watchers, sizing up each guard and all of the prisoners with an uninspired expression. With his close-cropped hair, blue polo shirt and khaki shorts, the lean thirty-something-year-old man seemed like he was just returning from a golf course. He hunched over his folded arms, as if freezing in the humid prison, sombrely surveying his surroundings. He must have been overwhelmed by it all, as he was barely paying attention to Caleb's instructions while the stern Watcher gave him a rundown of the prison.

"That's dad's friend, right?" asked Ray.

"Yes, he must have been captured at the swamp, too," answered Ben. "Do you remember him now?"

"I remember you talking about him yesterday," Ray replied. "What's he doing here? He doesn't look like an inmate."

Already knowing the answer, Rashad cleared his throat, peeling their gazes away from Joshua. "If he is not one of us, then he is one of them," he said solemnly, focusing on Ben. "That is not the same man you once knew."

"Maybe he *is* an inmate," said Ben, refusing to lose hope. "We didn't receive *our* uniforms until after the first day."

Ben's excited smile faded as he noticed the shock stick holstered in Joshua's brown belt. They watched Caleb lead Joshua towards the back of the cafeteria with a few of the day shift guards trailing behind, catching a snippet of the Watchers' conversation.

"You'll work your first shift alongside Cormac and Leon…" said Caleb as they reached the door leading out to the corridor.

Leon cut across their eavesdropping, turning towards the inmates with a gruff roar, "Rise and shine, you lazy mongrels, time for work!"

Ben slumped over the table at the thought of entering the pit for another long hot day. Even if he *was* willing to get up, his aching body would not move from his seat. The rest of the inmates from the day shift were reluctant to move too, their meal time shortened by Ben's delay in the cell house earlier.

Cormac reached into his pocket and gave Leon a wink. He withdrew a small black box – the size of a TV remote – with a big red button in the centre.

Ray eyed the Watcher coldly, waiting to see what would happen, when Rashad grabbed his arm. *"Sparker!"* he exclaimed, shooting off his stone block seat and pulling Ray up with him. He reached across the table, gesturing for Ben and Little Danny to stand, yet withdrew his arm with a wince.

Pulses of electricity flowed up from Ben's ankle, and his knee launched into the bottom of the table. He fell off his seat in his throes of pain alongside Little Danny. Rashad soon dropped to the floor beside them. Ben looked up at Cormac, mashing the red button in the centre of his black remote and smiling with glee at the writhing inmates.

Ray grimaced, swaying on his feet as his manacle emitted a burning sensation, the electrical shock coursing through his ankle and up his leg. In defiance, he attempted to bear the pain for as long as possible. Out of all the other inmates of the day shift, Ray was the only one left standing. Again, Rashad grabbed him by the arm, this time pulling Ray to the floor.

While the other prisoners' teeth chattered around them, Rashad appeared calm and unaffected by the manacle's burning volts. *"Do not show your strength,"* he reminded Ray.

"*Enough,*" Caleb said sternly, after all of the day shift inmates had been subdued.

Roaring with laughter, Cormac let up on the sparker remote. The pain stopped, yet the inmates still groaned as they convulsed uncontrollably in the after-effects, their legs shaking and twitching from the lingering volts.

"Do we 'ave your attention now, sweet'earts?" asked Cormac, still brandishing the remote.

"Get up," barked Leon. "Into the tool shed, now!"

The morning shift inmates looked on in pity from their seats as the day shift filed towards the back of the cafeteria, some youths limping, others leaning on each other for support. All of them glared at Cormac bragging to the new Watcher about his privilege to use the sparker.

"Only a chosen few of us get to carry these around," said Cormac, waving the remote in Joshua's face. "Tell you what. I'll let you 'ave a play around wiv it if you like. It's your first day, after all."

Joshua turned away from Cormac's hot reeking breath.

"Cormac," Caleb warned in a testy tone. "Do I need to remind you that the sparkers are not a toy?" His dark hawkish eyes narrowed at the crude guard. "If I catch wind of you *playing around*, you will be stripped of your privilege to carry the sparker. Are we clear?"

"Clear as me shiny white teeth, Caleb!" Cormac mocked him with a sarcastic yellow grin.

* * *

Ray unhooked a shovel from the rack on the left wall of the tool shed. He looked over at Levi, who stood alone with his hands on a minecart. Another inmate attempted to take the cart away from him, yet he lashed out wildly, desperately defending his position. Cameron and Bryson, on the other cart, did not move to help.

Levi managed to wrestle the rusty metal wagon away from the other inmate by himself, and then pulled Bryson from Cameron's cart so that he would not need to push it alone.

Sidling up next to his brother, Ben removed a shovel from the rack, his hands clasping the handle causing slight pain to his blistered palms, yet the handle felt more inviting than it had seemed yesterday. He turned around to see Joshua watching the inmates through a pair of sunken bloodshot eyes. Ben's mind swam with questions about what had happened to their father, yet when he locked eyes with the new Watcher, Joshua seemed as though he was staring straight through him.

Ray entered the quarry alongside the other inmates, passing through the weathered support pillars and out from under the shadow of the overhanging cells above. The light of the sun warmed his skin, although his arms were still slightly red from the previous day. He walked down the slope with a light heart. The stale humidity inside the prison without the warmth of the sun had felt stifling and unnatural. He savoured the fresh air before their work would fill the pit with dust again.

Ben shaded his eyes, peering up at the cloudless blue sky. He could feel the morning sun beating down upon the back of his crisp neck as they trudged down the dirt ramp, his reddened skin already sizzling under the fiery glow. Breaking out into a sweat before they even reached the bottom of the ramp, he drew his green shirt up as high as he could, letting it hang from his ears.

Aiden, the ropy teen with the green sweatband around his forehead, stooped down to coat his fair skin with dirt before they started the shift, giving him an additional layer of protection from the sun. Ben considered trying it himself, but he decided against irritating his raw skin any further.

The quarry floor was completely flat now, or as level as it could have been with the handheld tools. It felt as though they were standing at the bottom of a giant barrel. The rock shelf that they had been working on yesterday had been cleared away from the opposite end of the pit. The lowest edges of the surrounding cliff faces were still bare. The wooden pegs jutting out of the walls looked naked without the fishnets draped over them.

Cormac, Leon, Joshua and the other Watchers reached the bottom of the quarry ramp behind the inmates.

"Looks like the morning shift cleaned up the last ovvit," said Cormac.

"And now you lot 'ave the pleasure of cutting down to the next level."

"And rightly so," said Leon. "There's no way you mangy curs could've finished off a level by yourselves!"

Kenneth was the first to march out across the pit. Picking a random place to start digging, he swung his mattock down hard against the flat earth. Following his lead, the other inmates scattered out into the dustbowl, digging into the ground wherever they pleased, although most of them chose to dig nearby the minecarts.

Ben eagerly followed Ray, Little Danny and Rashad to the foot of a cliff still wreathed in shadow from the morning sun. Cormac and Leon instructed Joshua and the other Watchers to move the sun umbrella and the floodlight away from where the majority of the prisoners were working before they settled into the pair of chairs.

* * *

Holes of varying sizes were spread haphazardly across the shaded area of the pit floor, which gradually shrank as the morning wore on and the sun steadily climbed higher into the clear blue sky.

After digging a few feet into the bedrock, Ben's shovel thudded against something wooden. He bent down to pick up the object, just as Ray uncovered a rusty broken sword from his own hole, snapped halfway down the blade.

"There must have been some ancient battle here," said Ben, shaking an old wooden buckler free of dirt. Arrowheads were studded across the shield's face.

Idling nearby, Levi caught the dull gleam of the broken sword. Before Ray could stoop to pick up the weapon, Levi dove for the sword and snatched it away from his grasp. He brought the broken blade to the Watchers, who at first reached for their shock sticks, yet the opportunistic inmate presented it to them with his head bowed solemnly like a humble servant trying to gain favour.

Leon seized the sword, erupting in a gruff laugh once the weapon was in his hands. "We aren't looking for antiques, Levi," the grizzled guard growled, settling back into his chair under the sun umbrella.

"Might 'ave a bit of value if we was looking to sell it to a museum," Cormac said speculatively.

"You don't think they'd get curious about where it came from?" asked Leon, slamming the hilt of the sword into a nearby guard's stomach. "Get rid of this junk." He turned to face Joshua, "You, go fetch whatever else they've found."

Joshua obediently followed Levi to the brothers' holes.

Ray glanced at the old shield still in Ben's hand. "The arrows," he whispered urgently. "We can use them as weapons."

Ben remained motionless, frozen like a deer caught in the headlights as Joshua approached with his shock stick drawn. Rashad walked across the new Watcher's line of sight, inconspicuously plucking one of the arrowheads from the wooden buckler.

"Hand it over, inmate," said Joshua in the same taut nasal voice that Ben had known for years.

Rashad clenched the arrow's metal barb in his fist, snapping off what remained of the carved sprig of wood with his thumb and flicking the shaft at Joshua's feet. Joshua sparked up the electrical current on his baton.

Ben could not believe what he was seeing. Even though they were not related, Joshua had always seemed like he was part of the family. Each time Ben had called him *Uncle Joshua*, he silently wished that it was true. That way, he would have had at least one family member who did not seem to resent his existence. He shuddered to think of what might have happened to Joshua in the Desert Complex that would have prompted such a change.

Tension was mounting in the pit. Most of the other inmates had never seen Rashad openly defy the Watchers before. Trying to read his cellmate's intentions, Ray prepared to blindside Joshua with the flat of his shovel. Family friend or not, he was still one of the guards.

Just as Cormac began fumbling in his pocket for the sparker remote again, Rashad calmly tossed the arrowhead at Joshua's feet.

"Levi, grab the shield," said Joshua, eyeing the four inmates icily, the blue arc of electricity still crackling from the end of his shock stick.

Ben did not realise that he was still holding the old wooden buckler until Levi yanked it from his grasp, along with all of the arrows embedded in its surface.

As Levi and Joshua rejoined the other Watchers, Ray cocked an eyebrow at Ben. "Still think he's one of us?"

"It could be an act," said Ben, averting his brother's gaze and plunging his shovel into the ground.

"The arrowhead was blunt," Rashad said under his breath as they turned back to their empty holes. "The only weapons we will find here are the ones which we hold now."

"We need to find a way to fight with the tools without being sparked," said Ben.

Little Danny, who had been listening silently up until that point, shaded his eyes against the radiance of the sun spilling into the quarry and pointed up at the prison entrance, "'ave a look up there, Caleb and Evander's coming down."

Ray strained his eyes, seeing the pair of Watchers pass through the support pillars wheeling a laden minecart down the dirt ramp, followed by a bunch of other prisoners. The sun's glare cast a veil over their faces. Ray could only just discern the striding silhouettes of Caleb and Evander, the golden medallion around Caleb's neck reflecting the sunlight, along with the green uniforms of inmates trailing behind. He again began to think that he might have a problem with his eyesight.

Ben stared past the two guards at the crowd of female inmates following them down the slope. He could not guess where they could have come from, as he had only ever seen the one blonde girl who served gruel at the start and end of each shift.

The group of inmates was halfway down the ramp by the time Ray could see their faces clearly enough. He saw the ebony-skinned Mara and the tangle-haired blonde girl, Ava, among them. All of the other inmates had stopped their work to gawk at the girls entering the pit, including his own brother. Ray caught Ben staring with his mouth open as if it was the first time he had ever seen a girl.

Amongst the new crowd of inmates, Ben saw a slender doe-eyed brunette girl. Her hair was long and straight, flowing over her shoulders like strands of silk, and she sported a light tan upon her face, neck and arms. She made eye contact with him, and he suddenly became aware of his open mouth.

"Wipe the drool off your face, Benji," Ray chuckled at him nearby.

Ben blushed through his sunburnt cheeks and his eyes darted upwards, all of a sudden interested in the sky, the cliff walls, and anywhere else he could avert his gaze to.

Caleb and Evander brought the minecart full of fishnets to a stop at the far end of the quarry. Caleb marched over to the sun umbrella, issuing a firm warning to all of the Watchers gathered there before he and Evander headed back up the slope.

Cormac and Leon crept out of their chairs, ogling at the female inmates as they busied themselves with the fishnets from the minecart. Cormac drew closer to them, advancing like a hungry animal stalking its prey.

Caleb and Evander halted halfway up the dirt ramp. "CORMAC!!" Caleb boomed, his sharp voice bouncing off the cliff walls and echoing up into the sky. "What did I *just* say!?"

Cormac straightened up with a snarl, cursing under his breath at Caleb. The stern Watcher signalled to Evander, who turned back down the slope and joined Leon underneath the sun umbrella. Evander took a seat in the shade, leaving Cormac's spotted scalp out in the bright morning sun, the girls now fully aware of his lurking presence. The crude Watcher grumbled, his piercing blue eyes roving from the alert female inmates to his occupied seat in the shade.

Mara, Ava, and the other female prisoners spread the fishnets across the ground before draping them over the large wooden pegs jutting out of the bare cliff faces, tying them off with rope. The fishnets would serve as the only barrier to any mudslides in the quarry once the rainy season arrived.

Ben watched as Levi, Cameron and Bryson took hammers and bundles of wooden pegs from the minecart of fishnets. Levi stopped to talk to the silky-haired brunette girl, and for a moment, Ben was filled with a deep envy of his position. To his relief though, she turned away from Levi, who sent a cloud of dust into the air as he kicked a rock on his way to a bare section of the cliff wall.

Cormac, his face livid with anger at Evander's presence during the day shift, soon turned his attention to the male prisoners. He ordered the staring teens to get back to work, unsheathing his shock stick and stomping a warpath through the scattered holes in the pit, looking for any excuse to beat an inmate.

"Benji," Ray called, breaking his wandering thoughts as they returned to digging, "The medallion that Caleb's got around his neck, that was mine, wasn't it?"

"It was our father's," said Ben, remembering the intricately carved golden necklace.

"What do those symbols on the pendant mean?" asked Ray.

"Father never told me," Ben answered. "Now that you mention it, he only gave it to you when we were ambushed in the swamp. He told you to keep it out of their hands because he wasn't sure if we'd all make it out of there together."

"He had that right," said Ray.

Ben stopped digging, turning a thought over in his head. "Do you think father knew about these people? This place?"

"Doubt it," said Ray, lobbing dirt over his shoulder.

"But what if he did?" asked Ben. "What if something important is in the ground here? Something that was meant to be kept hidden. *Think about it.* The sword, the arrows..."

Ray straightened up with an exasperated sigh before looking over at Ben, scepticism written plainly across his face, "Benji, what could be more valuable than the sparkling rocks we've been throwing into those carts?"

* * *

Once the female inmates finished hanging the fishnets across the cliff walls, Evander saw them back inside to whatever part of the prison they resided in. Levi, Bryson and Cameron wheeled out fresh minecarts full of water for the thirsty inmates. Cameron, by himself, struggled to keep his cart from careening over the side of the dirt ramp. It marked the halfway point of the shift, and everyone climbed out of the holes they had dug themselves into.

Ray presented his hands to Kenneth, who nodded and moved on down the line of inmates. He guzzled the fresh water, splashing his face with it and feeling its coolness soothe his skin. Having drunk his fill, he dipped his hands into the water once more and wandered off a short distance, rubbing them together to cleanse himself of the dirt and grime that had built up between his calluses and underneath his fingernails.

While the other inmates lined up for water, Ray took a seat at the edge of the hole he had dug, absentmindedly stroking the tan-line encircling his thumb. He stared at it fixedly, and soon, his vision began to lose focus.

Suddenly, he was sitting in the back row of a classroom, unable to distinguish the words on the board written by his teacher. He copied the notes from the student sitting next to him.

Peaches. That's what she smelled like. Her wavy almond brown hair fell behind her ears, revealing her dimpled cheeks. She wore an identical ring to his on her middle finger. He remembered the embarrassed smile she had given him when she had overestimated his finger's size for the ring, sliding it onto his thumb instead. It was a promise ring; a promise that he would come back for her, after they had settled down wherever his dad had planned on taking them after the swamp.

"Dana…" Ray muttered to himself.

* * *

Ben looked down at the palms of his hands and sighed. The new patches of skin that had formed over his blisters during the night had burst open again. He took his place at the back of the queue of inmates forming.

115

Waiting patiently in the line, he glanced up at the cruel midday sun, bathing the quarry's basin in its fiery glow. His reddened skin could no longer find shelter from the sun's harsh glare. His shirt could only cover so much of his body. If he drew his shirt up to cover his neck, his pale upper arms were exposed; if he tugged his sleeves down, his neck would burn.

His differing ailments screamed for his attention. His muscles ached, his papery skin was sweating out what little moisture remained in his body, and his parched throat almost strangled him with each breath of dust-filled air.

Ben approached the water carts to find only the dregs, yet again. He could not go any further without hydrating himself. He hated to think of what Cormac and Leon would do if he fainted on this shift. Leaning down, he closed his eyes, pretending that he was at the foot of some fresh mountain spring, and he drank greedily without reserve.

He drained the water cart down to its muddy sediment, then, remembering Aiden's trick at the start of the shift, he splashed the mud onto his skin to protect him from the sun's glare. Levi and the other minecart pushers sniggered at the sight of Ben covered in mud, but they quickly fell silent when a few of the other boys came back to the water carts for some makeshift sunscreen.

Trudging over to where Ray was sitting at the edge of his hole with his head in his hands, Ben glanced up at the thin streaks of cloud in the brilliant blue sky, wondering when the rainy season would come. His eyes widened at the sight of something flying high above the quarry.

Ray drifted out of his flashback and his eyes snapped back into focus as the inmates were called back to work. He saw Ben standing beside him, gazing up at the sky. Ray got to his feet and looked up too, and at the sound of the droning buzz descending from high above, the other inmates and even the guards paused to crane their necks skyward in a mixture of surprise and fascination.

Little Danny appeared next to them, staring up in wonder. "What sort of bird is that?" he asked in his reedy voice, "I 'aven't seen one ovvem before."

"It is a plane," Rashad answered, narrowing his eyes at the dot moving across the sky. "That is the first time I have ever seen a plane pass over the quarry."

"There must be an air-field nearby," said Ben, his eyes tracing its easterly flight path as if hypnotised.

Ray was the first to tear his gaze from the sky. He turned to the others, waiting for each of them to snap out of the trance they were in. "When we reach the surface, we're heading for that air-field."

* * *

The rest of the shift passed by uneventfully, and before any of them realised, the entire floor of the pit was covered in shadow. The inmates breathed a collective sigh of relief, and they plodded back up the dirt ramp in the last beams of the sun's waning light.

As he hung up his shovel in the tool shed, Ray tried to remember more about Dana, the girl who had given him his ring. But before he could evoke another memory of her, Joshua shoved him towards the cafeteria from behind.

Ben's hammering pulse subsided as Leon and Cormac passed by, selecting others along the back wall of the cafeteria for double shifts. The brothers and their cellmates sat down together with their bowls of horrid sustenance.

As the night shift queued up for the gruel pot at the other end of the room, the shiny metal drain set in the floor of Ben's cell flashed in his mind, and he looked up with a burst of inspiration.

"That drainage pipe in the tool shed, above the mattocks," Ben started, almost unable to contain himself.

Ray, too tired to guess at what his little brother was so excited about, looked up from his bowl. He cocked an eyebrow at Ben, "Yeah, what about it?"

"That must be where the rainwater from the night shift's cells drains into," said Ben. "If we can take out the drainage pipe, maybe the ceiling and the cells above will crumble."

"And get squashed like a bug?" asked Little Danny. "What good would come ovvat, Benny?"

"Well, it's worth the risk," said Ben. "If the inmates from the night shift drop down and fight alongside us, we could still have double the numbers against the Watchers."

"And they would be immune to the day shift sparker's frequency," said Rashad, nodding his approval.

"Exactly!" Ben exclaimed, calming himself down before he drew too much attention. "The night shift sparker will be recharging up in the Watcher barracks."

Ray gave a small grunt of endorsement. "So all we have to do is knock out the pipe and sit back while the night shift takes care of the rest?" he asked, already won over by being able to use the tools as weapons.

Ben smiled widely, glad that they were all in agreement with his plan. *His* plan.

A pair of prisoners bickered in a playful argument as they settled into stone seats alongside Ben. While they exchanged insults with each other, Ben introduced the two inmates he had met during his double shift; Jack, a stocky sun-bronzed adolescent with a rough yet cheerful Australian accent, and Ethan, a tall dark teen from New York, whose pearly white teeth shone each time he spoke.

Never before in his life had Ben spoken to more than three people at a time, and it showed. His pulse quickened, his chest tightened, and he stammered his words. However, despite his nervous jitters, Ben brought them in on the plan to stage a rebellion in the tool shed.

"You can count on us," said Ethan. "Just tell us when, and the boys'll be ready."

"Or you can knock the floor out from underneath us whenever you feel like it," Jack winked. "We'll just act surprised."

"We should tell Kenneth," said Rashad, looking across the cafeteria at the Irish inmate. "The other prisoners respect him. Without his leadership, they would not dare to strike against the Watchers, and the support of the night shift will count for nothing."

Ray rose out of his seat just as Leon ordered the day shift inmates to get back to their cells, and his path to Kenneth was blocked by the mass of weary prisoners thronging around the stairs, eager to rest from the day's work. Bringing Kenneth and Aiden in on the plan would have to wait until tomorrow.

* * *

Back in his cell, Ray poured water from the chamber pot over himself, and then put on a fresh set of green clothes. He kicked off his boots, dirt and pebbles showering the floor. A stone the size of a hockey puck rolled across the floor. Somehow, during the shift, it had managed to embed itself in his boot's tread. Ray stooped to pick it up, and with it, he notched two small lines in the wall above his mattress, recording his days spent in the prison so far.

He lay flat on the thin musty mattress, staring up at the low ceiling as Rashad showered himself off.

"How'd you end up here anyway?" asked Ray.

Rashad grunted, setting down the empty chamber pot. "After the success of my businesses in Sri Lanka, I wished to travel for a while. I visited many places, and met many people. But when they captured me, I was alone."

"Where did they get you?"

"It was near a great tourist attraction, unlike any other in the world; a concave waterfall, which cascades down on three sides into a river gorge. I was hiking up the mountain to one of the viewing decks early in the morning when I had caught sight of something strange, a flash of green in the jungle, and I strayed from the walking track."

"Sure that flash of green wasn't just a tree moving with the wind?" Ray chuckled.

"Perhaps," said Rashad, the lower bunk creaking under his weight, "At first, I assumed that it may have been the light reflecting from the waterfall, yet I felt a strong desire to be sure. Unfortunately, I could not find anything at the site where I had seen it. However, when I attempted to turn back, I realised I had ventured too far into the jungle. I was shot with a venom snare before I could return to the walking track. I could not see my attackers, so I ran for as long as I could. The next thing I knew, the *only* thing I knew, I was in this cell."

"How long did it take for your memories to come back?" asked Ray.

"In the first few days, only flashes of my past life returned to me. They were strange memories, things that I had never thought about before I was captured. I remembered that amongst my friends, I was named *Mi Haraka*, the water buffalo, of which they believed I share the same traits."

"Were you a fat kid?" Ray asked, a smile tugging at the corners of his mouth as he stared up at the ceiling.

Rashad rumbled with a deep slow laugh that echoed almost hauntingly in the small cell. "After I had spent some time focusing on why they named me so, my memories returned all at once. I remembered the hardship of my childhood, living in an area ravaged by the civil war of my country. As a child, I worked my way up out of poverty through hard labour, and with my earnings, I opened the first of my businesses. As time passed, I earned enough income to afford a new home, a good education, and the ability to travel around the world. My friends named me so, not only for my size and strength, but also for my ability to thrive even in the poorest of environments, just like *Mi Haraka*."

Ray pondered in silence. Although he could not remember his past, he was sure that his childhood had been far more privileged than Rashad's.

Rashad sensed his admiration. "Whatever challenge you face, you must be brave. *Without struggle, you can never be strong.* I am the man I am today because of what I have faced in the past."

"You think you could help me remember my own past?" Ray asked after some time.

"Of course," Rashad replied, "But first, you must focus on the things which you do remember, in order to remember that which you do not."

Ray shut his eyes. He visualised the face of Joshua, the new Watcher.

He bent his mind on the image, and the man's sombre facial expression twisted into one of panic.

He was back in the swamp. A fight was raging on all around him, yet he was drawn to a pair of intertwined mangrove trees. He stared through a gap between their trunks to see a small boat out on the watery marsh, full of people garbed in red uniforms, rowing through the murky depths towards the muddy shore.

"It makes no sense!" he grunted in frustration, his eyes snapping open to stare at the low ceiling again.

"Focus, you must *focus!*"

***

Ben squatted on the wet floor of his cell, peering down through the drainage grate to see a pair of inmates from the night shift passing underneath, trundling into the complex with a loaded minecart, and then wheeling out a fresh wagon between the support pillars and down into the quarry.

With slight resentment, he looked over at Little Danny, who had flopped onto his bed after his shower and instantly fell asleep before his hair had even dried.

As soon as they had entered their cell, the door slamming shut behind them, Ben had looked down at the chamber pot with surprise. The metal bucket had been cleaned out and filled with water. Ben darted towards it, almost knocking his cellmate over in his thirst.

Little Danny had stepped back, giggling as he took his shirt off. "Dare you to drink the water," he said in his reedy voice.

Ben had glanced back at him, puzzled and suspicious, before taking a closer inspection of the water inside the chamber pot. It was oily, and remnants of foamy bubbles lined the edges. He drew back, realising that this was the water intended for use as a shower, as Ray had mentioned earlier.

Ben had whimpered as he slowly pulled his own shirt over his head, flakes of tender sunburnt skin peeling away with the muddy sweat-stained uniform. He emerged to see Little Danny beaming in front of him, holding the chamber pot. The scrawny kid splashed Ben in the face with the soapy water, stinging his eyes as it washed down his pale skinny chest.

"I wasn't ready!" Ben exclaimed.

Little Danny grinned as he poured the remaining water over his own head, far more than what Ben had received. "Better than nothing, 'ey?"

Ben grumbled to himself, but it was true. It had been his first shower since he had been captured at the swamp, and there was no use in arguing about it now. The water was already gone. He gently rubbed away at the grime on his skin and the mud encrusted on his face, but he stayed well clear of his tender neck and arms.

With the setting sun giving way to twilight, glimpsed only through the iron-barred shaft in the ceiling, the small room's main source of illumination came from the spotlights in the cell house.

Slipping into the fresh clothes left on the end of his mattress, Ben went to the door's window, seeing two figures sweeping the floor around the rack of chains – from the early days of the quarry's formation – near the stairs to the Watcher barracks.

One had fair white skin contrasted with long coal black hair, and the other, when she turned, was the same doe-eyed brunette girl he had seen down in the quarry. He admired her grace from behind the bars, but he was too afraid to call out to her to catch her attention, just in case she would shun him in the same way she had avoided Levi earlier in the pit. Besides, he would not even know what to say.

She looked up from her work, and Ben's heart skipped a beat. He shrank away from the door, looking around his cell instead. He observed the many etchings made by previous inmates; day recordings, signatures, and what could only be abstract imaginations of the mind of an inmate driven to madness.

Ben would have scratched in a recording of the days himself, if he could find a place in the walls unmarred by the previous tenants, and if he had something to mark the walls with. He looked up at the scratches in the ceiling around the cell's skylight, which were most likely failed attempts to escape, until something else caught his eye.

A folded piece of paper was precariously balanced upon the middle bar of the skylight, gently rising and falling with the wind passing by overhead. He wondered how long it could have been up there. Taking the note down and ducking out of view of the cell house, he read the familiar thin, slanted handwriting underneath the skylight:

I wish to bring all of my loved ones to a better place, some day. For now, I can only hope that Raymond is able to look after Benjamin, though they are only separated by a few years in age, whilst my work is continued. Some day, I shall explain why all this has been necessary.

On the back of the note, in different handwriting, read: 'DON'T BE AFRAID'. Ben flipped the note back to the main passage. It was his father's handwriting, but the edges of the paper were torn. Someone must have found his father's journal when they were captured. *But who?*

* * *

Ray tossed and turned upon the top bunk's mattress after a lengthy session of attempting to recover his memory. His head was still pounding with throbbing pain when a woman's scream from somewhere in the prison roused him from his troubled sleep.

His eyelids snapped open. He clenched his fists, the thought of Cormac's yellow-toothed grin and Leon's derisive chuckle springing to mind. He wondered which direction the female cell house lay in.

"I have heard these screams before," said Rashad, sensing that Ray was awake. "We will all be free of this place soon, but first, we must ensure that our plan works."

Wide awake in the darkness of the night, Ray turned his head to the side, staring at the two notches in the wall marking his day count. He hoped that the tally would not grow.

124

9 - BOUND TO BREAK

Keys jangled, locks turned, and doors flew open with a *bang* as all of the prisoners were ordered out of their cells. The teens from the day shift lined up as per normal, but they quickly realised that today was no normal day. The entire prison's population was assembled in the cell house.

Inmates from the morning and night shifts joined the crowd forming, along with roughly twenty female prisoners huddling together tightly in the centre of the room next to the chains rack. The guards lined the far side of the room, gathered around the foot of the staircase that led up to the Watcher barracks.

Ben rubbed at his weary eyes, still half-asleep as he and Little Danny made their way through the crowd to stand alongside Ray and Rashad, who were both wide awake.

Rampant rumours rippled from inmate to inmate. At the far side of the cell house, a sweaty balding pot-bellied man stood on top of the staircase's platform, but he was not the object of everyone's attention. Even with his bad eyesight, Ray could spot Joshua's lean figure amongst the other Watchers, the new guard looking more sombre than usual with his right eye swollen purple.

"Check out that shiner," said Ray. "Looks like somebody got the drop on him."

"I'd 'ate to be the guy what done it," said Little Danny. *"Somebody* is gonna get a lot worse!"

"Is that why everyone's here?" asked Ben.

"Be patient," said Rashad. "The Warden will explain why we have been assembled."

The portly puffy-cheeked man on top of the stairs above the Watchers raised his hands to silence the inmates' faint murmuring. He was dressed in a Hawaiian shirt, although he looked like a man who was far from being on a tropical holiday, mopping his sweaty forehead with a handkerchief, his hands fidgeting all the while, clearly overwhelmed at the prospect of speaking in public.

Caleb and Evander stood closest to the Warden halfway up the stairs. Caleb wore a grey shirt and matching grey army pants, while Evander wore a plain brown shirt and black cargo trousers, like a pair of hired mercenaries. The two of them stared out over the crowd of prisoners still whispering amongst themselves.

Impatient, Leon stepped forward, filling the cell house with his gruff roar, "SHUT IT!!" The grizzled guard advanced to the nearest prisoner and cracked the unsuspecting teen's skull with his shock stick, the boy crumpling to the floor. He glowered over the fallen inmate and barked loud enough for all to hear, *"Don't even whimper!"*

Only nervous breathing was audible in the shaky silence that followed, Leon's victim managing to stifle his moans.

The Warden shuffled his weight on the platform. "Ahem! Yes, if I may please have your attention for a moment…"

Ray cocked an eyebrow at his courteousness; *this is the man in charge of the Watchers?* Ben shared his brother's surprise. The prison's Warden was the polar opposite of its guards. They both exchanged glances as the portly man continued.

"Something of *extreme* importance has been misplaced overnight, and I cannot seem to locate it anywhere. This leads me to believe that my key-ring has been in fact, stolen, and anyone with information in regards to its whereabouts is encouraged to come forth now, lest they receive harsh p-p-punishment, with all due swiftness." To make his point understood, he waggled a stubby finger at the inmate lying at Leon's feet as an example.

All of the prisoners glanced at one another, each teen looking just as confused as the next. They wondered who could have had access to the Watcher barracks overnight, let alone have the nerve to steal the Warden's key-ring. The guards looked out over the mob of inmates, searching the prisoners for a guilty face.

Cormac jabbed a finger at the tightly packed crowd of female inmates. All of the girls instinctively shuffled away from where the crude Watcher was pointing. Ben stood on the balls of his feet, trying to discern who the alleged culprit was. The crowd parted for a brief moment, revealing the same doe-eyed brunette girl he had seen yesterday, pointing at herself with a look of bewilderment.

With a mischievous smile tugging at his lips, Cormac nodded in answer to her puzzled expression. Ben's heart skipped a beat. "Sarah cleaned the barracks last night," Cormac said over his shoulder to the Warden, keeping his piercing blue eyes locked on the quavering girl. "If anyone 'ad a chance to snatch that key-ring, it'd be 'er!"

"I don't know anything about a key-ring!" Sarah shrieked amid outrage from the other prisoners who jeered at his accusation. "Amelia was with me the whole time, she'll tell you!"

The Asian girl's coal black hair bounced up and down as she nodded furiously in agreement, holding Sarah's shaking arms. Mara and Ava made their way through the crowd to their defence.

Cormac shook his head in mocking doubt before puffing up his chest and striding into the pack of prisoners, Leon and Gremlin following his lead.

Sarah shrank back into the close-knit group of girls, attempting to lose herself in the crowd, yet the three guards drew their shock sticks. The female inmates begrudgingly cleared a path before the trio of Watchers, knowing that the three vile men would not discriminate against gender when it came to beating a prisoner. They would probably enjoy it.

Sarah threw up her arms to protect herself, and Cormac seized her by the wrists with his grubby unwashed hands. His fingers were short and stubby, yet his grasp was firm, too strong for Sarah to break free from.

The other girls backed away in fear of the Watchers as Mara, Ava and Amelia held on to Sarah by her midsection, they and Cormac tugging at Sarah in opposing directions. Gremlin was the first to swing his shock stick at the girls, bringing it down upon Mara, who quickly released her grip on Sarah to defend herself, yet she was struck on her shoulder before she could catch the short man's blow. Next, he plunged the baton into Amelia's navel, sending her to the floor, convulsing from the electrical current.

Sarah's futile struggle forced Ben to move against his own will, and he inched closer through the crowd of yelling inmates. Rage built up inside him as Cormac parted her hands, blowing his hot breath into her horrified upturned face.

"Tell me where its 'idden," he hissed, "Or I'll take you to a nice quiet place and I'll *make* you tell me where it's 'idden!" He leaned in closer, baring his jagged yellow teeth in a callous smile, "Personally, I prefers if you don't tell me, so's we can 'ave our fun."

"Cormac," the Warden called out above the crowd's jeers, "I request that you bring Sarah here immediately."

The patchy-scalped Watcher reluctantly tore his gaze from her, acknowledging the Warden's command. Gritting his teeth against Sarah's struggle, Cormac let go of one of her wrists to draw his shock stick again, ready to strike down any inmate that came between him and the stairs.

Still clinging to Sarah's side as they were both dragged along, Ava chopped at Cormac's elbow with her hand, breaking his grip on Sarah, and together they ran towards the nearest group of inmates.

Leon shot out an arm, catching Sarah by the hair and wrenching her backwards. Tears welled in her eyes, and she cried out as he jerked her towards the stairs with the force of a feudal farmer tugging along a stubborn mule.

Chaos and anarchy swept the entire cell house at the sight of Sarah being savagely hauled by her hair. To the inmates, she represented the only purity and innocence within the wretched walls of the prison, and now her virtue was being twisted and torn by her hair before their very eyes.

Female inmates shrieked furious profanities at the three men, and the boys of the prison muscled their way through to the perimeter of inmates surrounding the Watchers' triangular formation, each of them clamouring and searching for a weakness in the guards' defensive retreat.

"Looks like the new guy isn't gonna be the only guard with a black eye!" Jack yelled, he and Ethan cracking their knuckles.

Ben found himself at the front of the crowd with clear open space between him and the three Watchers. The guards were busy clearing their way through the pack, pushing back the inmates and waving their shock sticks aloft in warning.

Fuelled by the adrenaline surging within him, Ben bounded forward between Cormac and Gremlin – who were distracted by prisoners on either side – and, side-stepping around Sarah, he caught Leon off-guard, landing a hard punch in the man's ribs and sending a shockwave of pain up his own arm.

Leon grimaced, but his grip did not falter. He snarled at Ben as the skinny teen staggered back, his wrist aching from the blow. "Looks like the young pup's grown some claws!" he growled.

* * *

Having lost sight of Ben in the unruly crowd, Ray looked to Rashad, "This would be the perfect time to start a riot."

"We must wait," said Rashad. "Not all of the inmates have yet been informed of the plan."

"Maybe it's time that we tell them," said Ray, and together they searched the angry mob for Kenneth and Aiden, who stood near the front, cheering at some inmate who had caught Leon by surprise.

Ray and Rashad shouldered their way through to the front of the crowd, coming alongside Kenneth. Rashad grabbed Ray's arm with a heavy hand and pointed at Ben standing inside the Watcher triangle, massaging his wrist. He was the last person Ray had expected to fight against the guards.

Gremlin whirled upon Ben, thrusting his shock stick into the skinny teen's side. Ben's legs turned to jelly as the electricity pulsed through his torso, and he dropped to the floor. Sarah watched with a mixture of surprise and sadness at Ben shaking on the ground before Leon resumed dragging her. Gremlin lashed out at Jack and Ethan and a few more advancing prisoners, clearing some distance from the crowd before turning back to Ben with a devilish giggle, eager for the opportunity to inflict more pain.

Without thinking, Ray ripped his arm out of Rashad's grasp and launched himself at Cormac with an elbow, sending him stumbling backwards. Ray darted to Ben's side as he lay on his back, Gremlin standing over him with his shock stick raised, his small green eyes lit with malice.

Ray charged forward, hurling a wild fist at Gremlin's pointed face. The force of the impact threw the short man off his feet, and he careened over Ben's body, falling back into Joshua's arms as the other Watchers came to the three guards' aid. Ben was thankful to see that his older brother had once again come to his rescue.

Ray helped Ben to his feet. Ben shivered with the volts of electricity still coursing through him. He leaned on his older brother for support, helplessly watching Leon shove Sarah up the stairs. The other Watchers maintained a rigid line across their side of the room, with both Caleb and Evander standing like mighty sentinels, foreboding any attempt to climb the stairs. The cell house fell silent as Sarah was brought before the Warden.

"Calm now, Sarah, calm," the Warden said gently, comforting her. "You have my word that you shall not be harmed if you simply reveal the whereabouts of my key-ring, and how you had come by it."

Sarah shook her head sadly, tears falling from her cheeks. "I swear..." she mumbled, "I don't even know what it looks like."

The Warden sighed with a doleful expression before gesturing for one of the Watchers to take her away. Cormac laughed merrily, awaiting her with open arms at the bottom of the stairs.

The inmates erupted in outrage again, and Ava shrieked, *"Evander!!"*

over the uproar. Jeers formed into a chant as other prisoners called out his name, seeking justice. Other guards grumbled with disdain for the kind Watcher. Evander glanced sidelong at Caleb, who looked out over the mob of angry inmates on the verge of swarming the Watchers.

Cormac climbed the stairs towards Sarah, who was trembling with fear. Sensing a riot brewing, Caleb bounded up the steps and cut across Cormac's path, placing himself in front of the callous man. The cell house quieted down.

"Warden," said Caleb. "I recall seeing you still carrying your key-ring *after* the two girls had finished cleaning the barracks and returned to their cells." The Warden frowned, pensively licking his lips, trying to retrace his steps from last night. Caleb added, "But I will search their cells for good measure."

The Warden considered Caleb for a moment, dabbing at his own sweaty forehead with his handkerchief. "Yes, yes, so be it," he said finally.

All of the inmates breathed a sigh of relief.

"Aye, aye," Leon growled, "And who will search *her*?" he gestured at Sarah's slender figure, sharing a crude smile with Cormac.

The inmates reissued their idle threats as other Watchers cracked their knuckles and flexed their fingers, eyeing Sarah with foul smirks and vile grins. Ben cringed at the thought of their hands upon her.

"Lygia!" Caleb yelled, calling forth a sickly green-skinned female Watcher for the task before anyone else could volunteer, somewhat keeping the peace within the cell house. The inmates' relief soon turned to revulsion as the skeletal-faced guard took great pleasure in frisking Sarah for any trace of the Warden's key-ring.

Ben gritted his teeth as fresh tears tracked down Sarah's cheeks. The poor girl had been accused of stealing, dragged by her hair and almost indecently inspected for the entire prison to see.

"What about Amelia!?" Levi shouted as soon as Lygia was done.

"There's no point," Cormac chuckled, "Not if Lygia's to 'ave all the fun!"

Sarah was released back into the crowd, the Watchers laughing cruelly in her wake as she marched with her head downcast, shaking from the traumatising ordeal. Ava and Amelia embraced her, the other female inmates huddling around, staring daggers at the wicked Watchers. Mara spat at the guards, and Leon spat back with a mocking smile. The Warden issued a final warning that harsh punishment would follow for the person responsible if the key-ring was not recovered soon.

"I've seen your key-ring," Kenneth yelled. "It's up your arse, you fat walrus!"

His insult was left unanswered. The inmates were already on the brink of a riot. Instead, the Watchers set about ordering the prisoners from the morning and night shifts back to their cells, who only complied under threat of the shock sticks.

The female inmates swore curses at Cormac, Leon and Gremlin as they filed towards the door in the corner, Sarah sobbing at the heart of their pack. Ava reluctantly left her side to tend to the cafeteria.

***

The brothers and their cellmates were led downstairs alongside the others from the day shift. With all of the inmates still brooding from Sarah's mistreatment in the assembly, Ray pulled Rashad aside, lingering by the stairs.

"We should talk to Kenneth now, while everyone's still heated," said Ray.

"Talk to Kenneth about what?" asked Levi, turning back in the line to listen in on their conversation. Ray and Rashad ignored the snivelling weasel of an inmate. Levi sauntered towards them, acting as though he was already a Watcher. "If I catch either of you two causing any trouble, I'll report you straight to the guards, and *then* we'll see who gets heated."

Ray folded his arms. "What are you talking about?"

"You heard me," said Levi, glancing at Rashad. "You'll go straight to the steam rooms if you're not careful." Rashad raised his chin at Levi, who slightly quavered under his gaze.

Ray grabbed Levi by his shirt and threw him up against the flight of stairs. "Listen here, you little runt: you threaten either one of us again, and I'll break your nose. Understand? I'll go to these *steam rooms* with your blood all over my knuckles."

Bryson and Cameron silently watched the exchange with Ray's back to them. They showed no signs of aggression, but Rashad stepped in their way all the same. Ray released his grip on Levi, and the three inmates meekly rejoined the queue, remembering that Sergei was no longer there to protect them.

* * *

Guards from the morning and day shifts took up their positions behind the stone bench at the front of the cafeteria. Although the prisoners from the morning shift were already back in their cells, the Watchers were not taking any chances with all of the inmates' heightened emotions.

Ben was surprised to find himself at the front of the queue. Cormac, Leon and Gremlin – still chuckling to themselves about the assembly – watched as Ben approached.

"Time's a'wasting, sunshine" Cormac said with a grin. "Better eat up while you still can, may 'ave to ask you to do some overtime again tonight after what you done to Leon," he cracked up laughing.

Leon snorted his approval before spitting at Ben's shirt. Gremlin squealed with wicked delight.

"Shut your gob, Gremlin," said Cormac, wanting to rile up the unpredictable guard.

The short man turned away, disgruntled.

As Ben outstretched his hands, waiting for Ava to fill his empty bowl, Gremlin made a fake lunge at Ben with his shock stick at an alarming speed. Ben jumped with fright, almost dropping his bowl into the gruel pot.

Cormac and Leon burst out into laughter again, slapping Gremlin hard on the back. His pallid pointed face gleamed with pride, feeling respected again by his larger companions.

Leon caught hold of Ava's arm before she could serve Ben with a ladle of gruel, the grizzled guard's eyes hardening at him. "You watch yourself, young pup," he said. "Or I'll make sure your food dish stays empty." He released the girl's arm, and Ben gladly whirled away from the Watchers with a full bowl.

* * *

After the inmates' frustration and anger dissipated and the reality of another shift in the quarry set in, everyone sat down to eat their gruel in silence.

In all of the excitement upstairs, Ben had nearly forgotten the message he had received. He looked around to see if any of the Watchers were looking in their direction before beckoning the others to huddle closer. He withdrew the note from his trousers waistband, laying it on the table in front of Ray, Little Danny and Rashad.

"I found this on top of one of the bars in our cell's skylight last night," he said.

Little Danny snatched up the scrap of paper as though it had been meant for him. His face twisted at the words, and he thrust the note out in distaste. "What sort of drawing is this?"

Rashad took it from him, glancing over his shoulder at the guards at the far end of the cafeteria. He smoothed out the creases on the note and read softly:

> *I wish to bring all of my loved ones to a better place, some day. For now, I can only hope that Raymond is able to look after Benjamin, though they are only separated by a few years in age, whilst my work is continued. Some day, I shall explain why all this has been necessary.*

"What's that on the back?" asked Ray.

Rashad flipped the note over to reveal the larger handwriting, 'DON'T BE AFRAID'.

"*A better place*, 'e says, ha!" Little Danny scoffed. "What joker wrote that?"

Ray shot him a glare. "Our dad," he said icily, recognising their father's thin slanted handwriting. He turned to Ben, "You think he's still alive?"

"I think the note was ripped from his journal," Ben said sadly. "But I think *someone* is trying to help us. Maybe it was from Uncle Joshua – or – maybe I should just call him *Joshua* now…"

Solemnly, Rashad folded the note, thinking back to the assembly. "After seeing his black eye, I found it strange that no punishment was given to the inmates."

"Maybe they were too busy looking for that stupid key-ring," Ben said bitterly, remembering the tears on Sarah's face.

"Or, maybe the inmates had nothing to do with his black eye," said Ray. "He must have done someth–"

"Oi! What's that in your hand?" Leon barked, stalking over from the front of the cafeteria with Cormac trailing in his wake, both Watchers laying a hand on their shock sticks.

Little Danny ripped the note out of Rashad's hand. He scrunched it into a ball and shoved it into his mouth along with a spoonful of gruel to help force it down.

"What was that, sunshine?" Cormac clutched Little Danny's scrawny shoulder, squeezing hard. The impish boy wilted under the crushing grip, his head involuntarily tilting towards the Watcher's hand.

Little Danny gulped loudly, "What's what?" he asked in his reedy voice, looking up at them with a peevish grin. The guards exchanged a glance.

"He might know where the Warden's key-ring is," Leon ventured. "Let's see if the steam rooms can make him talk."

Cormac flashed his yellow teeth in a cruel smile. Little Danny's expression of feigned innocence turned to indignation as the crude Watcher hauled him off his stone block seat.

The steam rooms, Ben thought to himself. *How could they be any worse compared to a long hot day working in the quarry?* He could scarcely imagine what his cellmate would suffer as punishment for his insolence.

Ray flashed back to being carted through a hot corridor after waking up in the prison, past the eerie red glowing chambers emanating warmth, and that one door from which he had heard a series of rasping whispers.

Caleb and Evander descended the stairs into the cafeteria just as Little Danny shouted with both hands behind his back, his cheek pressed firmly upon the table. "At least let me finish me meal!" he squawked, before bursting into mad laughter.

"You've already 'ad your fill of paper, sunshine!" Cormac knocked Little Danny's half-empty bowl of gruel off the table, its contents splashing out across the stone floor with a wooden clatter.

Little Danny kicked and laughed and squealed, "At least it tasted better than that slop!"

Caleb approached while the other inmates in the cafeteria watched Cormac drag Little Danny up the stairs to the cell house, the boy continuing his deranged giggling with a mad gleam in his eyes.

"Warden wanted to know whether the inmates are back under control," said Caleb.

Angered by Caleb's condescending tone, Leon whirled around, mustering his reply with sarcastic grace. "Well, the Warden would be delighted to hear that one of our residents is now being punished due to his destruction of possible evidence pertaining to the whereabouts of a certain key-ring." Straightening up with scornful refinement, Leon eyed Caleb coldly before hawking phlegm at his feet.

"You never struck me as a man with such an extensive vocabulary, Leon," said Caleb.

"Full of saliva *and* surprises, it seems," Evander remarked from the foot of the stairs.

Leon's beard shifted, the grizzled guard grimacing at the pair of Watchers.

Caleb turned to face Ray, Ben and Rashad. "Let me handle their punishments. One of them is bound to break."

10 - DON'T MAKE ME ASK AGAIN

In the wake of Little Danny being dragged away to the steam rooms for his refusal to convey what was written on the note Ben had received, the entire cafeteria sat in silence. Not one inmate lifted a spoon to scrape their bowl. Everyone was too anxious to hear the consequences that awaited Ray, Ben and Rashad.

The message had restored some hope for the brothers, but it had also caught the Watchers' attention, believing the note to have held some information about the current location of the Warden's stolen key-ring. They could not acquit themselves of the accusation without alerting the guards to the presence of the mysterious person trying to help them.

Caleb frostily glowered at the three inmates before singling out Ben and calling over his shoulder to Evander, "Cuff this one to the chains rack, I'll question him later." The stern Watcher looked down at Ben, sizing him up and adding, "It shouldn't take much to break him."

Leon let out a gruff chuckle. "I'd make the young pup howl if it wasn't my shift." The grizzled guard raised his arm, indicating the side of his chest and reminding Ben of his strike against the Watcher's ribs. "Teach the mongrel some respect while you're at it, Caleb."

Evander approached, lifting Ben out of his seat. Ray's fists clenched beneath the table as the goateed Watcher led his younger brother up the stairs into the cell house. Before he allowed his anger to make the situation any worse though, he followed Rashad's example, folding his hands over each other upon the table next to his empty bowl.

Rashad's eyes were downcast, his forehead slick with sweat.

This could be the day that he gets sent to the Desert Complex, Ray thought to himself.

Caleb turned to Leon. "Assign Rashad to the mattocks," he said, met by an audible sigh of relief from the big barrel-chested inmate. "And place the other on the minecarts."

"The minecarts are only earned by *good* behaviour," Leon snapped. "You know that, Caleb!"

The shrewd Watcher pierced Leon with his dark eyes, as if attempting to intimidate a disobedient dog, yet the grizzled guard held his ground. "Precisely," said Caleb. "This new inmate's lighter duties will make his cellmate condemn him after having been given a heavier burden, along with the rest of the prisoners yearning to fill Sergei's old position."

Behind his bushy beard, Leon cracked a toothy grin.

* * *

The cell house seemed abandoned, the exact opposite of how it had appeared during the assembly earlier that morning. The middle row of cell doors on the other side of the room were all flung open, the inhabitants downstairs in the cafeteria. The sound of inmates taking their short-lived showers, holding hushed conversations or snoring deeply arose from the locked cells on either side of the cell house. It was hard to believe that Sarah had suffered in front of so many people in this same room no more than fifteen minutes ago.

With a guiding hand on the inmate's shoulder, Evander led Ben over to the hardwood rack littered with metal chains in the centre of the cell house.

As the guard tugged on one of the chains, testing its strength, Ben turned around to face the dark-skinned Watcher. "Little Danny told me what happened on my first day during my double shift," said Ben. "I just wanted to thank you for carrying me back to my cell after I collapsed."

"I remember when I was an inmate," Evander said with a kind smile. "It's tough out there in the pit."

"You're not like the other Watchers, you're much nicer," said Ben.

"Having compassion for other human beings is a choice," Evander replied. "Not everyone loses their minds in the Desert Complex. But you gotta play by their rules if you wanna keep it that way."

Ben lowered his voice, "*Whose* rules? Why are you working here? Why not just leave?"

Evander's smile faded. "No choice," he answered stiffly as he secured cuffs onto the inmate's wrists.

Ben had struck a chord. He decided to push his luck a little further. "But you have the keys, don't you? You, Ray, Little Danny, Rashad, and I, we can all leave together." He was careful not to mention Joshua's name.

"It ain't that simple," Evander locked eyes with Ben, considering him for a moment before checking the inquisitive prisoner's restraints. "Listen, kid, you got off easy. Don't act up again."

Before Ben could ask any more of the good Watcher, Evander took his leave of the cell house without a backwards glance, ascending the staircase and entering the barracks. For a brief moment, Ben glimpsed gleaming whitewashed concrete walls beyond the doorway, a stark contrast to the dull grey of the rest of the prison, before Evander shut the thick wooden door behind him.

Left to himself, he strained at his shackles, the soft clinking of his metal chains echoing in the silent cell house. There was no use though. He was locked securely in place. Resigning himself to his restraints, he slumped against the wooden rack, looking down at his bound hands. The blisters on his palms had crusted over, and new patches of skin were forming. He smiled meekly to himself.

* * *

Ray, Rashad and the other inmates were marched into the tool shed. Out of habit, both of them approached the racks of shovels. Ray reached for one of the tools.

"Don't try to get cute with me, inmate," Leon growled from behind, spitting on the shovel's handle before Ray's outstretched hand could grasp it. The phlegm oozed down the wooden haft, running the length of the tool's handle.

Rashad about-faced to the racks of mattocks lining the opposite wall – underneath the rusty drainage pipe running the length of the ceiling – and Ray moved towards the back of the tool shed, where the minecarts awaited. Begrudgingly, he took his place on a metal rust-bucket alongside Cameron, who nervously smiled at him, his bent nose pointing even further to the left.

Levi beamed at Ray. "Told you you'd be far better off with us than with that rabble," he said, snobbishly indicating the grumbling prisoners taking tools from the racks before them. Ray could already feel the resentment glaring from the eyes of the other teens. His assignment to lighter duties was undeserved after both his behaviour and short length of labour.

"Listen, Levi, there is no *us*," said Ray. He shifted his gaze to Bryson, Levi's speckled cellmate, then to Cameron. "The same goes for the two of you. You stay on your side of the handlebar, I'll stay on mine. We're *not* together."

"Nonsense," Levi said with an overfriendly smile. "We were meant to be together ever since you started here, you just didn't know it. I know we didn't get along at first, but I'm really glad you made your decision to take us up on our offer. Sergei's absence has made pushing the carts a lot harder for poor Cameron, but with your assistance, we should all be able to take it easy while those chumps do all the hard work out there."

Rashad overheard the snide inmate, but said nothing.

They wheeled the minecarts out of the tool shed, Ray believing that if he held his tongue, Levi would eventually fall silent. The slick-haired youth's overzealous attempt to befriend him was more unsettling than the lump of gruel currently churning in his stomach. It was as if they had already forgotten that he had threatened to break Levi's nose just before breakfast.

They passed through the exit to the outside, the sun washing the barren quarry with its morning radiance, the spotless sky wearing its usual bright blue.

"Another day in paradise," Ray muttered under his breath as they descended the slope into the pit with Levi happily prattling on behind him.

After the shifts overnight and in the early morning, the scattered holes they had dug yesterday had now formed into one giant trench. Kenneth, Aiden and Rashad led the inmates towards the wall of rock waiting to be cleared. The inmates hewed and dug at the dirt, shovelling clods of earth into the carts as Ray and the other minecart pushers idly stood by.

Ray felt out of place, loitering under the shade thrown by the cliffs while everyone else around them laboured in the early humidity. He wondered how long Ben would have on the chains rack before Caleb worked him over for answers.

"… If you think about it," he tuned in to Levi's rambling, "Sergei has been promoted. Soon, he'll come back here, and then it'll be my turn to become a Watcher." The other boys shovelling dirt and gems into the carts gave them odd glances.

Ray groaned at Levi's enthusiasm to work for their captors.

"If you follow my lead," Levi said with eerie glee, "The three of you could become Watchers too, just like them!" he pointed over to where Cormac rejoined Leon underneath the sun umbrella, having delivered Little Danny to the steam rooms.

Having heard enough of his misplaced praise, Ray elbowed Levi in the chin, shutting the overly ambitious inmate's mouth for him. Levi held his chin in wide-eyed shock, and Ray let out a long sigh at the sound of his stifled sobs. The sulky boy retreated towards another section of the pit that was not yet underneath the morning sun, with Bryson soon heading over to console him.

Rashad swung his mattock with the rhythm of a metronome, and Ray decided that he would sooner swing a mattock alongside his cellmate rather than relax with these bludging boys. He looked over at Levi, who now sat with his head in his hands, eyeing the other prisoners with a sullen scowl.

* * *

Soon after Gremlin, the woman known as Lygia, and all the other guards from the morning shift climbed up the cafeteria stairs and returned to the barracks to pass around pale brown bottles of ale, the cavernous room had fallen back to its eerie silence.

Ben watched a lone female inmate – not wearing a manacle – enter the cell house through the door in the corner near the barracks stairs. She was one of the girls who had tried to hold Sarah from falling into the Watchers' clutches during the assembly. Her hair was tied up in a topknot, and she had slight muscles bulging within her ebony skin. Her dark eyes appeared empty and mournful as she walked past the chains rack and out of sight towards the empty row of cells behind him.

She returned back to his field of view holding a chamber pot at a distance from her face. He looked up at the closed door to the barracks, and then he scanned the room, ensuring that the cell house was otherwise empty before whispering to her, beckoning her to come closer.

She glanced at him, raising a thin eyebrow. A metal stud on the side of her nose glinted underneath the spotlights suspended in the four corners of the ceiling. She stared at him impatiently for a moment before grunting and walking back towards the door she had come through.

"Help me," Ben murmured, holding up his cuffs, the chains pulling taut as they ran their length from the rack behind him. His plea appeared to have fallen upon deaf ears, as she continued to walk out of the room. Ben raised his voice to a whispered shout, "Hey!"

She turned around with a bitter expression. "Shut. Up." And with that, she left the room.

Some of the inmates in the surrounding cells laughed at the exchange.

"Don't mess with Mara while she's got a full chamber pot," one prisoner yelled, "She's just waiting for a good excuse to not walk so far to empty it!"

Other girls – all of them wearing the green prison uniforms, but not the manacles – entered the cell house and disappeared into the empty row of cells. They reappeared, carrying bundles of dirty laundry, and left as quickly as they had come.

Ben slumped against the chains rack, wondering if all girls were like Mara. The girls at his school certainly treated him in the same manner. He had always admired his older brother's natural ability to talk to them. Ben, on the other hand, was generally too shy to offer more than a greeting, let alone last a full conversation without breaking out into a nervous sweat.

Mara returned again and again, fetching one chamber pot at a time and returning them filled with soapy water. None of the other girls assisted her, although who could blame them?

* * *

One of the minecarts was now filled with dirt, and Ray and Cameron pushed it towards the bottom of the slope. Levi and Bryson watched them from their narrow strip of shade, the midday sun almost reaching its peak. He and Cameron heaved their weight against the wagon, the rusty wheels whining as they rolled up the dirt ramp.

Ray admitted to himself that pushing the cart was much easier compared to shovelling dirt and rocks into the carts, although he could feel the jealous eyes of the inmates toiling away in the barren basin below. He realised now just how vulnerable Caleb had made him. Nobody liked the minecart pushers, not even him. Now, other than his brother, his only allies were the friends they had made over the past three days, which was not exactly a long enough time to build up a level of trust.

The strange flag upon the viewing deck overlooking the quarry fluttered in the wind. It did not appear to belong to any country that Ray knew of. All he could see was an image of a bright yellow sun.

"Thanks," said Cameron, breathing heavily as they reached the top of the slope. "Yesterday was tough by myself, but it sure beat having to deal with Sergei."

"He was your cellmate, wasn't he?" asked Ray. "I thought he would've done all the hard work for you guys, how was yesterday better without him?"

"I never liked him," Cameron answered, his eyes downcast. "Once, he… he broke my nose for snoring too loudly. I don't think it ever healed right. I'm glad he's gone. Bryson is, too."

"Not Levi though, I take it?" said Ray.

Cameron shook his head. "He's only being nice now because he wants you to protect him. He thinks if he can win you over, he can go back to treating everyone else like trash."

"Like that's ever gonna happen," Ray's sarcasm was thick enough to choke on.

"I understand if you don't want to be friends with us. Me and Bryson, I mean. We're not bad guys. We just ended up with the wrong cellmates."

Ray grunted, not fully convinced.

As they passed through the weathered support pillars and into the cool shade offered by the overhanging row of cells above, Ray glanced through the open door into the tool shed, glimpsing a few mattocks still hooked on the racks underneath the drainage pipe.

He thought that maybe if he was alone, he could stash a few tools somewhere hidden and close at hand, or he could at least weaken the overhead pipe with a few good swings. Just as he was thinking of a way to send Cameron along to take the full cart by himself, Ray was shoved in the back.

"Stop dawdling, sunshine, day's wasting," said Cormac, having followed them up from the pit. Ray and Cameron resumed pushing the cart up the corridor, the floor now slanting up on an incline. Cormac closed the door to the tool shed with a wary glance at Ray. "Don't get your knickers in a twist. You'll get your chance to 'ave a play wiv the mattocks, soon as the blackie does you in overnight for all 'is backbreaking work today while you was messin' about wiv your new best mate."

They entered the treasury. A dozen guards gathered around filled minecarts at the far end of the room, greedily shoving glittering gems into their pockets as they sifted through the dirt, scooping out fruitless clods of earth into another empty wagon behind them. To the inmates' left, lumps of golden nuggets gleamed from atop a workbench, surrounded by cloths and brushes. The bench stood between a hardwood door and a fiery red metal grate set in the wall. On their right were a leaking water tap and an elevator platform that led up to a big square-cut hole in the ceiling to the prison's barracks.

Gremlin and the other Watchers were too busy squabbling over gemstones to notice the arrival of the fresh minecart. The gargoyle-like guard clutched at a sparkling blue pebble, snarling at anyone who tried to wrestle it away from him. The gemstones seemed to be for whoever claimed them first among the Watchers, yet any pieces of gold were set aside on the wooden bench, off limits to the guards' pockets.

Cormac approached the other Watchers and pulled Gremlin away from the laden barrows. "Get the dirt carts ready for dumping," he said, taking Gremlin's place, scraping through the soil for gems and shoving the other guards away from his claims.

Seeing the Watchers squabble over the precious stones, Ray was reminded of the brawls that broke out between inmates in the cafeteria.

Without turning, Cormac absentmindedly gestured to Ray and Cameron to take another empty cart that was standing next to the hardwood door. Gremlin rejoined the Watchers rifling for valuables, unnoticed by Cormac, who was too busy pocketing some dirt-covered jewel with a yellow-toothed grin.

None of the guards seemed to be paying attention to the pair of inmates, consumed by their own greed and lust for riches. Even Cameron stood hypnotised by the glittering gems. Ray saw his opportunity to escape. He moved towards the door.

"No," Cameron whispered, snapping out of the spell with a great urgency in his eyes. He held Ray by the back of his shirt, "You'll get in trouble if you go that way."

Ray glanced from Cameron, to the Watchers, to the door. He shrugged off Cameron's hand, having already made up his mind, yet at that very moment, the door swung open, and a group of blue-uniformed men shuffled into the treasury.

At the centre of the pack stood a chubby bespectacled man clad in a white long-sleeved collared shirt. Embroidered twin patterns of thin golden thread snaked down on either side of his shirt's column of buttons. His eyes traced over the room as he stroked the bristles of his chevron moustache. His pale skin contrasted with the caramel hues of his men.

The local authorities must have discovered the illegal operations of this prison, Ray thought to himself. "Help!" he yelled, advancing towards his saviours. "They've got us here working as slaves. There's dozens more of us up in the cell house and out in the pit!" he jabbed a thumb over his shoulder to the corridor leading down to the quarry.

The Watchers woke up from their treasure-filled trance at Ray's outburst, finally noticing the inmates and the new group of men among them. For some odd reason, Cameron took a step away from Ray, busying himself with the empty minecart.

The moustached man laughed, his subordinates following suit with a delayed reaction. Saved at last, Ray began to form a smile too, until his teeth began chattering involuntarily. His legs gave way. He fell to his hands and knees. Gremlin stood above him with a shock stick, electricity crackling in a blue arc at its tip.

"Mayor Gaspar," said Cormac, bowing his head and revealing his spotted scalp, "Pleased to 'ave you wiv us." He roughly shoved the other Watchers away from the minecarts, and then with what little grace he could muster, Cormac invited the moustached man over to peruse the gems.

Mayor Gaspar dismissed the sight of Ray twitching on the ground with a half-amused smile, his beady eyes lighting up with avarice through his glasses at the sparkling jewels embedded in the dirt of the carts.

Another man wearing a black button-up shirt and cowboy hat sauntered into the treasury behind Gaspar's guards. He chuckled at the sight of Ray upon the ground. The man swaggered over, squatting down beside the fallen inmate and addressed him in a southern drawl, "Well, ain't 'at a familiar sight?"

Ray still involuntarily shook and convulsed, as if having a silent coughing fit. Gremlin had shoved the shock stick into the nerve endings of his back.

The stranger tipped his wide-brimmed hat. "Well, tell me now, boy, how's your stay been so far?"

A look of confusion drew across the inmate's face. *How could this man know that I'm new to the prison?* As far as Ray knew, he had never seen this man before.

The man raised his eyebrows and his face wrinkled into a wide grin. "You don't remember me, do ya, boy?" he stood with his hands on his hips, declaring proudly, "Deputy Sheriff Lee Sullivan, at your service. Y'can call me Sheriff though, everyone else does. *Hot damn!* 'n' here I was thinkin' you woulda jumped at the chance to get at me!"

Mayor Gaspar took in a sharp breath from nearby. He was already cradling armfuls of valuable gemstones, the dirt soiling his white shirt, yet his lusty gaze had fallen upon the chunks of gold set aside on the workbench.

Sheriff Sullivan held up a hand to Ray, still intermittently jolting on the floor. "Excuse me," he said before turning to Mayor Gaspar, who was inching closer to the bench. "Now Mayor, may I remind you we got an agreement, 'at gold is not to be touched. 'sides, I think you got about as much as y'can carry here."

Mayor Gaspar tore his eyes away from the yellow glow of the gold and glanced back down at the jewels in his arms with surprise, as if he had already forgotten that he was holding them.

"Yes, yes…" he stammered before recomposing himself. "We will come to collect again next week." One of Gaspar's guards shook the Sheriff's hand on behalf of the Mayor, who was too preoccupied with ogling his bundle of gems to offer any civil gestures himself.

Sheriff Sullivan reopened the hardwood door in the corner, allowing Mayor Gaspar and his guards to pass first. Cormac and the other Watchers returned to rifling through the gems with greedy haste, annoyed by the interruption. No one else saw the Sheriff pocketing a nugget of gold from the bench. He winked at Ray.

"Be seein' ya, boy," the Sheriff tipped his hat and shut the door behind him.

At the sound of Levi and Bryson trundling up the corridor with their own minecart, Gremlin hauled Ray up by his shirt and onto his feet, shoving him in Cameron's direction. The sheepish inmate stood along the opposite wall, quietly filling up the empty cart with water from the tap. Ray clumsily found his balance, catching hold of the minecart's handle to steady himself.

"Told you you'd get in trouble," Cameron mumbled, breaking the uneasy silence.

Ray clenched his jaw. The ache in the lower half of his body was too much for him to form a reply.

* * *

Ben stood against the rack for an indeterminable amount of time, not knowing how many minutes or hours had passed without knowing the position of the sun, although his reprieve from the sun's burning glare had its advantages too. Even though the metal shackles had rubbed his wrists raw, he was still grateful for the chance for his sun-damaged skin to heal.

His train of thought eventually turned towards how they had first come to be captured. He tried to piece it all together, although the finer details were still sketchy at best.

Their father had invited Ray and him along for a documentary trip. Usually, they did not accompany their father for his work, but he had told them that they would be moving out of town for a while after the film was wrapped. Ben was excited to move schools, a chance for a fresh start, but Ray was argumentative. His older brother was very attached to their hometown, certainly more attached than Ben, at least.

They had met with the local Deputy Sheriff, Lee Sullivan, new to his position, who would act as their guide through the swamp. The Deputy Sheriff's holstered modified pistol flashed across Ben's memory, and he recalled feeling relieved, especially if there really was a monster – or

Lizardman, as the townsfolk had called it – lurking in the swamp.

They had met a few local rednecks, a man and his wife, along with their adult children, living in the backwater swamplands. At first, they seemed apprehensive at the idea of having the film crew intruding into their territory, but with the presence of the Deputy Sheriff, they gave their consent. It was not like they owned the entire swamp anyway, just a small portion of it.

Soon after wading through the muck and mire, they had come upon a group of people in a boat, all dressed in red, dumping waste into the murky depths of the swamp. The Deputy Sheriff withdrew his pistol, yet to all of their surprise, the barrel was pointed at Ben's face. Before anyone could react, they were attacked from behind by the family of rednecks, and Ben was hit with the venom snare.

Ray and their father took him through the trees as the people in the boat rowed ashore, yet beyond that, he could not remember. He still wondered what had become of their father.

His thoughts were interrupted by the door next to the stairs creaking open. He looked up to see a female inmate entering the cell house. He half-expected it to be Mara again, but it was the Asian girl, Amelia, with Sarah following behind her, gracing the room with her kind face and silky chestnut brown hair. Their eyes met, yet Ben soon looked down at the ground, shying away from her gaze.

He felt small at the thought of talking to her, fearing that she might be just like Mara, and would ignore him if he attempted to engage her in conversation. He kept his silence, even as the pair of girls drew nearer to him.

They set down brushes and buckets full of soapy water and fell to their knees at the foot of the barracks stairs. Ben could not help but stare as Sarah scrubbed the first few steps. As if sensing his eyes upon her, she glanced over her shoulder, and their eyes met again. Butterflies within his stomach almost flew out of his mouth, and he took a sudden interest in the room's architecture, glancing at everything and anything in the cell house but her.

Amelia gave Sarah a wry smile, and prompted her to make the first move.

"Thank you," Sarah said in a tender voice, waiting for him to look back at her again, "For trying to help me get away from those Watchers during the assembly."

Ben shrugged, the chains rattling behind him. He summoned his voice. "Someone had to do something… I – I didn't do much good though." His eyes fell to the floor again as he remembered that his surprise attack on Leon had accomplished little more than interrupting the procession for a fleeting moment before he had been struck down from behind.

"But I appreciate it, all the same," she said softly. "I'm Sarah. Sarah Dawson. What's your name?"

"Ben," he replied, growing a little bigger with each word he spoke to her. "Are – are you okay, after what happened, when…?" his voice trailed off.

Her lightly tanned cheeks flushed, yet she nodded with a smile. "Ava, my cellmate, she knew exactly what to say to make me feel better. You might have met her already. She's the blonde girl who works in the cafeteria." Studying him with a kind smile, Sarah picked up her bucket and brush and set them down next to the chains rack, cleaning the floor around its base. Amelia stayed on the barracks stairs, allowing them some distance, but still listening in.

"Does it happen often?" he asked, "The way they treat the girls here?"

Sarah looked up at him, and Ben's butterflies melted inside him at the sight of her gentle doe eyes. "Not so much, although I wouldn't like to think about how things would be here without Evander. He makes sure we're treated properly."

The door in the corner flew open, and Caleb swept into the cell house. The girls bowed their heads, scrubbing at the floor. The stern guard glowered at Ben with a promise of later questioning before climbing the stairs towards the barracks.

As the door shut behind him, Sarah lowered her voice to barely a whisper. "We overheard him arguing with the new Watcher last night. I think he was trying to convince Caleb to join him for something."

Uncle Joshua, Ben thought to himself, *what's he up to?* His binding chains clinked as he tried to move closer, curiosity upon his face. "Something like what?" he asked, forgetting his nervousness. "And what was Caleb's reply?"

"You saw his black eye this morning, didn't you?" Amelia said quietly from the stairs, "That seemed like a clear enough reply to me."

Sarah stood to clean the rack behind him, "Whatever the new Watcher had asked him to do, Caleb threatened to throw the man off the roof if he ever crossed him again. After that, the new guard said that there is much more to discover downstairs than there is outside in the pit."

"Downstairs, as in… *the cafeteria?*" asked Ben, his curious face now drawn with confusion.

Sarah returned his confused expression. "Of course not, this place is much bigger than –" her reply was cut short as the entrance to the barracks opened again.

Joshua emerged, slamming the door shut behind him as he raced down the stairs. He paused mid-flight, noticing the trio of inmates staring back at him. It was difficult for Ben and the two girls to peel their gazes away. His right eye was still swollen purple. His one good eye flicked between each of them for a moment before widening.

"This place won't clean itself!" he yelled.

Picking up her bucket, Sarah glanced at Ben with a small innocent smile before lowering her head as she descended the flight of stairs into the cafeteria with Amelia in tow. Joshua raised an eyebrow at Ben with a slight wince before pacing towards the door in the corner, leaving the inmate to his own thoughts.

Maybe not all girls are bad after all, Ben thought to himself. He felt exhilarated, even though she had left him sweating and out of breath. He swelled his skinny chest and looked triumphantly at the occupied rows of cells on either side. The other inmates had probably not caught their exchange, but they definitely were not laughing at him now.

He suddenly felt a pang of pity at how Sarah could smile so sweetly after the way they had treated her, and all for some key-ring. *What does it matter anyway?* The Watchers were still able to open and close all of the cells, unless there were other doors in the prison that could only be unlocked using the Warden's key-ring.

* * *

The water sloshed over the sides of the minecarts as they walked down the ramp into the corridor, Ray struggling to restore his balance and coordination. He scooped some water into his mouth and splashed his face as Levi and Bryson drank their fill from the second wagon behind them.

Cameron explained that each week, Mayor Gaspar and his guards would visit the treasury to receive valuable gems as bribes for their continued cooperation in keeping the way to the quarry off limits to the locals and other government bodies alike.

"Politicians…" Ray muttered.

The four inmates exited the corridor, moving out from underneath the shade offered by the cells above and into the glare of the midday sun that was burning brightly overhead, filling every nook and cranny of the quarry with eye-straining light.

Ray and Cameron wheeled the minecart down the slope into the pit, losing a third of the water in their trundling descent. He realised that keeping the cart full was not as easy as he had thought.

All of the weary prisoners breathed a collective sigh of relief at the sight of the water carts. Leon emerged from underneath the sun umbrella, refilling his water canteen before retreating back to the only shade left in the quarry.

As Kenneth called for the inmates to form a line, Rashad pulled Ray aside. Ray winced as he left the support of the minecart's handle, electricity still pinching the nerves at the base of his spine. Kenneth soon joined them.

"It's a good thin' you got a way to get us outta here, lad," said the Irish prisoner, "Or the boys woulda made sure there was another spot open on the minecarts." Ray looked over at the other inmates, seeing resentment still burning in their eyes over his sudden elevation to lighter duties.

"We are lucky," said Rashad. "Kenneth and Aiden have agreed to spread the word among those who we can trust. The rebellion is coming."

* * *

Time almost seemed to be running backwards until a troupe of female inmates bearing neatly folded piles of green uniforms entered the cell house through the door in the corner, with Joshua appearing behind them. Ben was still unsure whether it was Joshua who had dropped the note into his cell.

"*Pssst*," Ben called. Joshua paused at the top of the stairs leading down into the cafeteria, and he turned around to watch the girls exit the cell house, hands on his hips. Once they were alone, Joshua approached the chains rack. "What's going on, Uncle Joshua?" Ben chanced to ask. "Why are you one of the Watchers?"

"Don't worry," Joshua said in a hushed voice, his face coming alive from his dour mask. "I was too strong to fall under their influence in the Desert Complex, but I still have a lot of work to do here." Joshua drew closer. "We've always known about this place."

"Who's *we*?" asked Ben, forgetting to lower his voice in his curiosity.

"That doesn't matter right now. We have a few people on our side in Lungsod, the fishing village nearby. You've been there before, back when you were a kid." Ben searched his memory, but he shook his head. Joshua continued, "Again, doesn't matter. There's a small motorboat waiting for us at the docks. The local who runs the hardware store has it in his possession, and he'll serve as our guide. There's a woman, too –"

"What happened at the swamp?" Ben interrupted, his thoughts of what had become of his father weighing heavily upon his mind.

Joshua swallowed, his sombre face returning as he chose his words carefully. "I knew we were outmatched, but Jacob *insisted* on fighting them. You, Ray and I were captured. Sadly, Jacob and the rest of our crew weren't given the same mercy."

Ben looked away sullenly, all hopes of his father still being alive forever cast aside. He slumped against the chains rack, wishing that they had never gone to the swamp, hunting some monster that was probably just as realistic as *Bigfoot*.

"Can I have his journal?" asked Ben, swallowing his grief. "We never really spent that much time together, and… and maybe it could make up for –"

"Your father's journal is here?" asked Joshua, surprised. "I haven't seen it yet, but I'll look for that too."

"Then who dropped the note into my cell last night?" Ben thought aloud.

The barracks door slammed open, and Caleb descended the stairs slowly, the golden medallion hanging around his neck, beneath his shirt. Joshua cast the gaze of his good eye downward and backed away from Ben. He retreated down the stairs to the cafeteria with a fleeting look of apology as the stern guard approached the chains rack.

"What did he say to you?" Caleb asked sharply.

Ben turned away from the Watcher.

Caleb punched the inmate in the stomach, taking the wind out of him and sending stars of pain dancing across his eyes. Ben breathed in a lungful of air to try to counteract the new indent in his diaphragm. He had taken bullies' punches before.

"No matter," said Caleb. "I can just ask him later. I'm sure he doesn't want another black eye to match. Now, what was on the note that Leon saw you passing to each other in the cafeteria?"

Ben thought of what Ray would have done if he was in this situation. "It was the breakfast menu," he said, exhaling slowly with a smile.

Caleb punched him in the stomach again, harder this time. Ben's saliva seeped out of his mouth as the dark-eyed Watcher drew his shock stick.

"Don't make me ask again."

The note was dropped into my cell's skylight," Ben spat, stretching as far forward as the chains would allow and staring up at him, "It said not to be afraid of people like you."

Caleb clicked on the shock stick's electrical current.

"I swear! It said 'don't be afraid'!" Ben exclaimed, his defiance deflating as his eyes widened at the blue arc crackling at the tip of the baton.

"Hmm, easier broken than I had imagined," Caleb said with a tone of disappointment. He sheathed his shock stick back into his belt. "Very well. Chow time."

11 - WHISPERS

The sounds of the boys from the day shift gathering into the cafeteria rose up from below as Caleb set about releasing Ben from the chains rack.

Other guards entered the cell house from the barracks. Caleb turned and instructed Evander to release the night shift inmates from their cells. The goateed Watcher obeyed, opening each door with a jingle of his keys.

Caleb unlocked the shackles from around Ben's wrists, and the prisoner teetered on his feet. His legs were stiff and sore from standing in the same position for so long. Before he had a chance to stretch, Caleb grabbed him by the upper arm and pulled him towards the stairs, his joints creaking and popping as he was half-led, half-dragged along.

"Line up with the others," said the stern Watcher. "You're lucky that you answered my question. Cooperation is rewarded. If you hadn't, you'd be working double shifts from now on."

* * *

Ray and the other inmates lined up along the back wall of the cafeteria as Cormac and Leon examined them. After a few unlucky inmates were selected for a double shift, they fell in line for the gruel pot.

Joshua stood at the front of the cafeteria amongst the other Watchers, surveying the crowd of hungry prisoners with his one good eye. His right eye was still swollen purple.

"Looks like he pissed someone off pretty bad," said Ray, turning to Rashad. "You think he had something to do with that note Ben found?"

Rashad shrugged. "Fighting among the Watchers occurs as often as it does between inmates," he said, "Although they make an effort not to fight in front of the prisoners."

Ray was inclined to agree after having seen the Watchers squabbling in the treasury. *There isn't much else that a new guard could've been punched for though*, he thought to himself. After all, Ben had said that Joshua was a family friend. He might indeed be trying to help them.

The inmates from the night shift descended the stairs to queue up behind the prisoners returning from the pit, adding to the noise in the cafeteria. Ray and Rashad moved up in the line, coming closer to the gruel pot.

Ray picked up a bowl and spoon, deep in thought. "I know you said they twist your mind in the Desert Complex," said Ray, "But I've been thinking… What are the chances of a person resisting whatever goes on over there?" Rashad cocked his head, confused. "What if a person could *act* as though they were loyal to the Watchers?" Ray glanced pointedly at Joshua.

"All of the people whom I have seen transferred have always returned corrupted and cruel," Rashad answered. "My previous cellmate, he is not the same man that I once knew." He nodded towards one of the guards standing with Cormac and Leon beside the gruel pot.

"*Gremlin!?*" Ray exclaimed. Wiping the shock off his face, he said, "You must be joking," with a half-smile, waiting for a punch line that never came.

Rashad shook his head sadly. "Before he was taken, *Gregory* was kind and compassionate. Do you recall the small green lizard you saw living in our cell's skylight? No matter how hungry Gregory was, he would always save some food for the tiny creature."

Ray stared at Gremlin in a new light, his quick green eyes, part fierce, part fearful, darting amongst the inmates and Watchers alike for any signs of danger. Ray turned away from the piteous wretch the man had become.

"What about Evander then?" asked Ray.

Rashad considered this for a moment. "Perhaps it is possible for one to resist becoming like the other guards," he said, before posing a question of his own, "But how long can a good man last among so many who are not?"

"That's why we need to move quickly," said Ray. He opened his mouth to continue, but Rashad shushed him as Caleb and Evander passed by to join the other guards at the front of the cafeteria. Joshua looked away sullenly as the two Watchers joined their ranks. Ava ladled gruel into Ray's bowl, and he dropped the subject with Rashad. "How's Sarah doing now?"

"She was shaken up before," said Ava. "But she went back to work soon after the whole incident."

"Good to hear," said Ray.

Cormac, the closest of the guards, leaned towards Ava. "And 'ow long would it take for you to get back to work, 'ey?" he winked at her lasciviously.

Ray clenched a fist, challenging the Watcher. "You really wanna try that again!?" he shouted, the inmates shifting in the line behind him.

Cormac raised his eyebrows in amusement, his piercing blue eyes twinkling as he withdrew the sparker remote from his pocket. Gremlin, Caleb and Evander tightened their grips on their batons, anticipating a fight.

Leon stepped in, barking at Ava, "He means *get back to work!*" he turned his gaze upon Ray, "And *you*, unless you want a double shift, get moving, you're holding up the line!"

Rashad placed a prudent hand on his shoulder. Ray took a moment to size up the situation. He straightened up, unclenched his fist and even mocked up a fake smile for the Watchers before turning to find an empty seat at the back of the cafeteria, away from the guards' prying ears. Rashad joined him soon after.

"Joshua's still got some traces of good left in him," Ray said knowingly.

"How can you be so sure?" asked Rashad.

"While everyone else had their attention on me and Cormac, Joshua was shaking his head. We need to make our plan happen before somebody else picks up on his act."

"I fear that somebody else has already noticed," said Rashad, their thoughts returning to Joshua's black eye.

* * *

Ben descended the stairs along with the rest of the pack of thronging teens coming down from the cell house. He massaged his wrists where the cuffs had rubbed his skin raw, as if they were not already red with his sunburn.

Someone nudged him from behind mid-flight, almost sending him off balance and down the remaining steps. *What was I thinking? I'm just a dreg. I should be at the back of the line.* He turned around to apologise, only to see Jack and Ethan behind him, in the midst of all the other prisoners preparing for the night shift.

"Saw you chatting up Sarah before," Jack said with a cheeky grin.

Ben blushed and turned away. Ethan slapped him on the back, and he flinched as his shirt tugged at the skin of his sunburnt neck.

"Come on, buddy," Ethan smiled widely, revealing his rows of pearly white teeth. "We didn't mean to embarrass you."

"Better move quick though, mate," said Jack. "I think that snot-faced weasel, what's his name? This idiot," he pointed towards Levi, who was licking his palm and flattening his hair a few places in front of Ben. "I reckon he's got the hots for her."

Ben looked down at his feet in disappointment. All of the girls he had ever taken an interest in had always ended up with some other guy. Ethan patted him on the shoulder reassuringly, Ben wincing at the pain of his sunburnt neck again.

"Levi ain't that much competition," said Ethan. "Take a look."

He looked up again to see Levi testing his breath, then crinkling his own nose in disgust. Ethan let out a giggle, and Jack burst with jovial laughter. Ben could not resist the urge to join in. This was the first time he had laughed since he was captured, and even before that too, as far back as he could remember.

Their laughter died down after the inmates around them exchanged odd glances at their sudden outburst. Levi glowered back at them, oblivious, before he refocused on appearing presentable for Ava.

Ethan turned to Ben. "You must be upset after what happened to Sarah earlier," he said. Ben gritted his teeth on impulse, and he shot a glare at Cormac, Leon and Gremlin, the three of them standing with the other Watchers at the front of the cafeteria. "Did she seem okay when you talked to her?"

Ethan's question brought Ben back down to earth, his tight jaw slackening. "Yeah," said Ben, "She seemed to be back to normal after the whole ordeal. Although, I've never actually spoken to her before today, so I wouldn't *really* be able to sense any change."

"What a way to meet though, hey? All chained up like that," said Jack. He looked around, "Oi, where's that little Pommy kid anyway? I thought you two were mates."

"Little Danny? He got sent to the steam rooms," said Ben, almost having forgotten about his cellmate.

"The steam rooms, what for?" asked Ethan.

"Steam rooms are no fun," said Jack.

"What are these *steam rooms*, exactly?" asked Ben.

"They're rooms that are connected to the sides of a natural heat vent," said Ethan. "A lot of the guys here think that we must be close to a volcano."

"Yeah, they're not cold," said Jack. "Looks like you're up, mate."

Ben turned around to find that he was next in line. He picked up a bowl and spoon, and before he could drink any water, a spoonful of gruel was hurriedly splashed into his bowl from Ava's shaking hand, Cormac and Leon scrutinising her from a few feet away.

Ava seemed to be shrinking into the wall, trembling under their gaze. *She must think that she might be next to get accused of stealing the Warden's key-ring*, Ben guessed, but he took some comfort in Joshua and the kind-hearted Evander standing among the other Watchers nearby.

He looked out across the room to find Ray and Rashad, who were seated at the far side of the cafeteria, both of them speaking gravely across the table.

Ray looked up to see Ben approaching.

"Good news," said Ray. "It looks like there really is a town nearby." Ben sat down next to Rashad, sore from his time on the chains rack but still intrigued. "Bad news is it looks like the local officials are on the payroll." Ray told them about seeing Mayor Gaspar in the treasury, and the weekly bribes he took in exchange for preventing the locals from venturing too close to the quarry. He turned to Rashad, "There you go, Mr. Optimistic, you and your *electricity could be coming from backup generators.*" Rashad grunted while chewing his porridge.

Between mouthfuls of gruel, Ben told them what had happened while he was on the chains rack; how Joshua had been posing as a Watcher, how he had mentioned their trip to *Lungsod*, the fishing village nearby, as children – although Ray could not remember – and how Joshua was working towards *something* in the prison, but Ben had not thought to ask about that.

"What else did he say?" asked Ray. "Does he know what happened to dad?"

Ben closed his eyes ruefully, fighting a sob rising up in his throat. "He said our father didn't survive."

They both looked down at their bowls. Ray was grateful that he could not remember much about their father at present.

Ben forced more gruel down, trying to swallow his sob along with it as he thought of another topic. "Joshua also said something else. If we escape –"

"*When* we escape, Benji," Ray corrected him.

"When we escape," Ben echoed, "We should make our way to the village's hardware store. He said that the owner of that shop is on our side, and he can guide us to safety on his motorboat."

"Why did he say *our side?*" asked Rashad. "Do all of the villagers know about this place?"

"I'm not sure," said Ben. "But he did say that there were a few other people that could help us in Lungsod. I'm beginning to think that our father wasn't being entirely honest with us when he said that he was a documentarian."

"What makes you say that?" asked Ray.

"That's something that Joshua didn't say," said Ben. "But we should aim to get to the hardware store when we get out of here, not the airfield."

"Sure," said Ray. "We'll just stop and ask for directions to the nearest hardware store in our inmate uniforms. That'll go down well. Benji, we don't even know if any of the locals here speak English."

"Actually," Rashad interjected, "English is quite widespread. Even without any education as a child, I had learnt it in Sri Lanka while growing up, along with our own dialect. Besides, we cannot hope to arrive at the airfield either without asking for directions."

Ray grunted, shovelling some food into his mouth, although with his lack of physical strain earlier in the pit, he found that he had no desire for the goopy gruel.

Ben looked back at the guards standing at the front of the cafeteria, and he recalled his brief conversation with Evander. "I don't think the Watchers are here by choice," he said.

Ray swallowed his porridge with a disgusted wince before he chuckled, "They seemed happy enough when they were shoving their pockets full of jewels in the treasury."

"While Evander was cuffing me to the chains rack," said Ben, "He said that they had been given no choice but to work as Watchers."

Rashad stroked his chin. "I agree that they are not here by choice... But then why would they be rewarded with gemstones?"

"Exactly," said Ray. "*We're* not here by choice, so where's our sparkling rocks?"

"That's not all," said Ben. "I think someone else is trying to help us."

"Yep, that'd be Joshua," said Ray. "Did you forget what he said about Lungsod? And I thought *I* was the one with the bad memory here."

"But Joshua couldn't have been the person who gave me the note from our father's journal," said Ben. "When I asked for the journal, he said that he didn't even know it was here."

"It could be the guards playing a sadistic joke," Rashad mused. "The

Watchers like to toy with the new prisoners by giving them a false sense of hope."

Ray nodded in agreement, "Maybe Evander's just leading you on then, Benji. Maybe he isn't as good as we thought. But then, if Joshua didn't have anything to do with the note, why's he walking around with a black eye now?"

Ben checked over his shoulder before answering in a low tone, "I think he has the Warden's key-ring. When Sarah and Amelia were cleaning the cell house, they told me that they had overheard a conversation in the barracks last night. Joshua was trying to convince Caleb to join him for something, and he was punched in the face for it."

"This could be good, or it could be very bad," Rashad said while massaging his temples. "Joshua may have a plan of his own to break us out, perhaps attempting to use profit as an incentive for Caleb, but if Caleb tells the other Watchers, then Joshua's plan could end prematurely."

"Well, just in case that happens," said Ray. "We should continue with our own plan."

"There's something I can't work out," said Ben. "Why wouldn't Caleb immediately report where the Warden's key-ring was if he knew that Joshua had it, instead of letting Sarah get accused in front of the whole prison?"

"Maybe Caleb's keeping his options open," said Ray. "It'd be the smart thing to do. I saw a lot of gold set aside in the treasury, and it seemed like none of the guards were allowed to touch it."

Their whispered conversation was broken by Kenneth, announcing himself by clacking his wooden bowl on the table. "So, what's the plan boyos?" he asked, sitting down next to Ray.

Ben's mouth opened in surprise, fearing that they might have been talking too loud, but judging by the faces of the other two, he quickly assumed that they must have brought him in on the escape plan already.

"It must occur in the tool shed," said Rashad, "So that we have weapons. Then, we must break the drainage pipe to release the night shift inmates from their cells above."

"That's what we talked about in the pit," the Irish teen reminded him with a touch of impatience. "What's new?"

"It should happen before the day shift starts," said Ben, "So that all of us are rested."

"Smart," said Kenneth. He took a spoonful of gruel before talking out of the side of his mouth, "How soon did you want this to happen?"

"We'll let you know," said Ray. "Just be ready to strike."

Kenneth swallowed his gruel, clapped Ray on the back and got to his feet. "I'll spread the word. Keep me in the loop, lads," he said, signalling to Aiden before he shifted to another packed table, huddling the inmates close for a hushed conversation.

The brothers and Rashad finished their meals in silence, watching Kenneth and Aiden move around the room from table to table.

"Time for work," Caleb's sharp voice boomed. "Get up!"

The night shift inmates finished their mouthfuls and marched out to the corridor. Jack winked at Ray, Ben and Rashad as he passed by, and Ethan gave them the thumbs up.

The brothers thought that by now, the entire night shift must have known the plan for the coming rebellion, and it was only a matter of time before Kenneth and Aiden would make the whole day shift aware too, with the exception of the minecart pushers, of course. The boys from the morning shift would simply be in for a pleasant surprise.

Ray, Ben and Rashad were led back to their cells where they fell asleep, waiting for the next day to come.

* * *

Ray saw his father in his dreams. He did not smile. The last time Ray had seen his father smile was when he was just a boy. Since then, his face was always lined with determination.

They were driving through a small village at the edge of the sea along with Ben. They were both very young. Then they were standing outside a tropical beach house made of hollow-bricks and decorative bamboo.

164

Palm trees swayed with the wind in the lush green rainforest behind the native house.

Then they were inside, and their father was arguing with a woman. The woman's hair was long, straight and brown. *Ma?* Ray heard himself say. Their mother was a brunette too. No. She could not have been his mother. She had died while giving birth to Ben.

He could not see.

The woman was replaced by a man wearing a black cowboy hat. *Deputy Sheriff Lee Sullivan, at your service.* The hollow-brick walls descended into the earth around them, as if they were surrounded by a pit of quicksand, and the tropical paradise fell away into a murky swamp. Grey mangrove trees blotted out the sun.

Local rednecks among other dark figures clad in red surrounded his father and Joshua, who refused to kneel alongside the rest of the documentary crew. The Sheriff pointed the barrel of his modified pistol at Ray and fired, yet only a small net issued forth.

He could not see.

Ray stumbled over gnarled twisted roots in the mud-sodden earth, wrenching at the mask over his face wreathed with foul smelling odours. *Where's Ben?* He choked on his own words.

He could not see.

The sound of a clatter of stone on stone startled him awake. Ray opened his eyes. He could see again, yet his sight was no better than the dream. He looked over the side of his bunk. Rashad was standing in the centre of the cell inspecting a small rock.

Seeing that his cellmate was awake, Rashad handed the stone up to him. "This fell from above while I was exercising," he said, brushing dirt off his shoulder. "I did not see who dropped it."

Ray got out of bed to examine the rock underneath the skylight. It was engraved with capital letters, *TODAY*.

"Good job bringing Kenneth and Aiden on board," said Ray, "Looks like they're eager."

"How could an inmate climb to the top of the cell house?" Rashad wondered aloud. "Or maybe it was from Joshua. Perhaps we should coordinate our plan so that it does not conflict with his."

"Maybe one of the girls is cleaning up there and they're just passing on the message," Ray shrugged. "Either way, we're getting outta here. Today."

The rock was flat enough to fit into Ray's waistband without drawing attention. He slipped it into his trousers, intending to use it as a backup weapon. He looked up at his day count – three scratches on the wall beside his pillow. He decided not to etch in a fourth line, thinking that it would be bad luck for the rebellion if he was to continue recording their days spent in the prison. He hoped to never see the inside of this cell ever again.

* * *

Ben woke up, covered in sweat. He had not yet grown accustomed to the humid heat. He leaned over the side of his thin mattress to check the lower bunk for his cellmate. *Still empty.* He lay back on his bed, hoping that Little Danny was at least being brought water. He could not imagine how hot the steam rooms were, especially if they were set alongside a volcanic heat vent, but surely after such a long period of exposure, his already-malnourished cellmate could not last much longer.

"He's just a kid…" Ben thought aloud.

A soft tapping at his cell door window shifted his attention to a set of slender fingers reaching through the bars. He bumped his head on the low ceiling as he jumped down from the top bunk. Rubbing his throbbing scalp, he looked through the window to see Sarah. Her gentle brown eyes seemed to brighten up as he came to the door. Ben could already feel the butterflies stretching their wings in his stomach.

"Ava told me that you're leaving today," she said.

His eyes widened, slightly taken aback at how fast Kenneth and Aiden had spread word of the brewing rebellion, but *today? Maybe in all the excitement of the rumour passing between the inmates, they must have put a date on their escape*, he thought to himself.

Sarah stared at him through the barred window, waiting for his response.

Ben's fingers fidgeted out of her view. He breathed slowly, attempting to retake control of his hammering heartbeat so that he could avoid making a shaky reply. "We do have a plan," he said, "Although I'm not quite sure whether it will be *today*."

"If you do go," she said, looking at him with pleading eyes, "Could you take us with you? Please don't leave us behind."

His fidgeting ceased, and on sudden impulse, he took hold of her slender hand through the bars. His butterflies fluttered up from his stomach and thudded into the inner walls of his chest, his heart pumping nervous tension throughout his entire body. This was the first time he had ever held a girl's hand.

"Of course, I'll make sure we do. I promise," he said reassuringly, despite fighting an inner struggle to hyperventilate at her touch, speaking the words a little louder than he had intended.

Sarah blushed, withdrawing her hand. "Thank you," she said. "I should get back to my duties now. The Watchers should be here any minute. Your shift is going to start soon." She thanked him again with another smile before disappearing from the window.

Ben breathed out a long wind. It felt as though his lungs had been inflated up to his throat in her presence. His cheeks were throbbing. He reached up to massage his face, wondering how long he had been wearing his foolish grin.

* * *

Keys jangled in the cell house as the doors were unbolted and kicked open to commence the next shift. Ray, Ben and Rashad lined up together and were led down into the cafeteria. Excitement filled the muggy air. All of the inmates – excluding Levi, Bryson and Cameron – carried themselves with renewed spirits.

The Watchers were oblivious to the reason behind Ava's cheerfulness as she smiled at each one of the prisoners, heaping large spoonfuls of gruel into their bowls.

Kenneth passed by the brothers' table as they sat down to eat. "Ready to strike, lads," he said, winking. "Let me know when." The fiery-haired inmate sat down with Aiden and some of the other mattock workers nearby.

Ray leaned across the table, "So, today then?"

Ben's foolish grin returned as he shrugged in agreement.

Suddenly, a panting ragdoll of a child flopped down into the seat beside Ben, half his bowl's contents spilling across the table. Little Danny used his scrawny hands to mop up the gruel, licking the moisture from his fingers with his dry swollen tongue. His hair was crisp and his lips were cracked from the heat of the steam rooms.

Ben, having fallen sideways off his stone block with fright, climbed back onto his seat and watched with pity as his cellmate scraped at the table with feeble fingers, sluggishly attempting to salvage his meal, popping lumps of porridge into his parched mouth. Ben could feel the heat emanating from the red glow of the wiry boy's skin, as if he had come fresh out of an oven.

Little Danny cupped his bowl with shaky hands, drinking the remainder of its chunky contents. With pity, Rashad pushed his own bowl towards him, and the boy greedily wolfed down the offering before groaning and holding his throbbing head with both hands.

"Are you okay?" asked Ben, a question that needed no answer.

"I 'eard something in there," Little Danny rasped in a hoarse whisper. "Strange 'isses. They was talking funny." His small fingers started to scratch at his dry scalp, suffering from an insatiable itch.

Ben and Rashad exchanged concerned expressions, but Ray remembered the strange whispers that he himself had heard coming from one of the red-glowing rooms upon his arrival at the prison.

"Are you sure it wasn't just the sound of the heat sizzling and crackling?" asked Ben. "Maybe you mistook it for a voice."

"You may have experienced a heat-induced hallucination," said Rashad. "I have witnessed many inmates suffer heatstroke in the pit."

Little Danny moaned piteously, lurching forward over the table. "It wasn't in me 'ead… I 'eard it," he panted between shallow breaths. He scowled up at Rashad, "You know what I'm talking about. They came from under where I was. There's a metal grate attached to the 'eat vent, see? That's why they call them the *steam rooms*. I almost burnt me ear off trying to 'ave a look down below. I couldn't see their faces."

Ray remembered the three silhouettes standing on the viewing deck alongside the Warden during their first shift. He glanced sidelong at Rashad, who was avoiding the subject, taking turns with Ben trying to give some reassurance to Little Danny. *There's something about this place they haven't been telling us*, he thought to himself.

"It's okay," said Ben, "We have an escape plan. Kenneth, Aiden, Jack and Ethan are going to help us get out of here."

Their encouragement went unheeded, apparently falling on deaf ears as Little Danny blankly stared down at the table with his sky blue eyes, rocking himself from side to side on his seat. Rashad and the two brothers glanced at each other, silently hoping that their plan would succeed, if only for Little Danny's sake. He looked as though he would not last longer than an hour in the quarry if they were to fail.

Leon clapped his hands unceremoniously, marching up and down the rows of tables, rousing everyone to work. The brothers and their cellmates stood, Ben supporting Little Danny. Kenneth and the other inmates practically leapt out of their seats, the Irish prisoner shooting them a grin.

Cormac, Leon and the other guards marched the day shift inmates out into the corridor. The boys from the morning shift watched them file out of the cafeteria with eyes full of hope. It seemed that the entire inmate population knew that today was the day.

As the prisoners waited with bated breaths for Cormac to unlock the door to the tool shed, Little Danny shrugged off Ben's arm and scampered up the corridor towards the treasury.

"He must be going for the water tap in there," Levi sniggered.

"Oi!" Cormac bellowed, kicking the tool shed's rusty-hinged door open with a screech before chasing after Little Danny.

"Not now… not now," Rashad softly murmured under his breath.

"Cormac has the sparker," said Ben, "We can use this to our advantage."

Ray, Ben and Rashad gathered around the entrance to the tool shed inconspicuously, trudging forward with glum expressions as if it was just another day in the quarry, trying not to draw too much attention too soon, yet Kenneth, Aiden and all of the other inmates muscled their way into the room, eager to kick off the rebellion.

12 - IT'S ABOUT TIME

The thronging mass of inmates shoving their way through the entrance to the tool shed made it impossible for the Watchers to follow them inside. Rashad, Kenneth and Aiden headed straight for the mattocks, throwing the tools to other inmates. The prisoners were unable to contain their excitement, giving up a cheer as they passed their all too familiar weapons around.

Outside in the corridor, Ben was separated from Ray and the others as more inmates surged into the tool shed. The Watchers exiting the cafeteria behind them were at first speechless at the level of motivation that the forced labourers were displaying. *The guards still don't have a clue.* Ben grinned widely as the inmates inside the room erupted with excited yells.

"That's more like it!" one of the Watchers roared with laughter.

Leon however, was not so easily fooled. He knew something was wrong. The grizzled guard held up a cautioning hand to the other Watchers. Withdrawing his shock stick, he advanced upon the smiling Ben, the volatile man's eyes twinkling with grim accusation behind his bushy mane.

"What are you up to, young pup?" he growled, menacing Ben like a wild beast stalking its prey.

Ben's smile vanished. Wide-eyed and flushed with fear, he shrank back against the wall, cowering at the sight of the crackling baton pointed directly at his face.

* * *

Ray made a dash for a minecart at the far end of the tool shed, wheeling it underneath the rusty drainage pipe and upending the metal wagon to Levi's dismay, who had just realised that today was not an average day.

Silencing Levi's wailing with a quick right hook to his face, Ray jumped upon the overturned cart and Rashad threw him a mattock. Kenneth kicked over some more carts from the back wall, crashing them into each other underneath the overhead pipe.

Levi held his gushing nose while standing next to the few minecarts as yet untouched by the rebellion, shrilly trying to restore order amongst the rampaging inmates. Prisoners bearing shovels cut the Watchers off from the entrance, buying time for those with the mattocks. Cameron and Bryson crouched in a corner, waiting to see which side would prevail.

* * *

Leon drew in a sharp breath, preparing to strike at Ben, when a wave of inmates charged out from the tool shed armed with shovels. All of the Watchers fell back in surprise, some dropping their shock sticks upon the floor as their startled fingers fumbled for the batons on their belts.

Aiden distributed tools at the doorway, tossing shovels to those who had remained outside in the corridor. Ben caught a shovel with shaky hands. Only half a dozen guards stood ready to repel the attack.

* * *

Ray took the first swing at the drainage pipe as others climbed on top of the overturned minecarts. The first crash against the pipe pierced the rusty metal, and the ruddy water from within splashed down on his face. He paused for a moment to wipe away the muck.

Cracks in the drainage pipe grew with each hollow metal clang as the other inmates put the mattocks to work. Cheers descended from the cells above as the night shift inmates prepared to take part in the rebellion.

"*BANG ON!!*" Kenneth roared, climbing on top of another minecart to strike at the pipe.

* * *

"CORMAC! THE SPARKER!!" Leon howled, spittle flying as he glanced up the empty passageway to the treasury, then, seeing that they were outnumbered, he grabbed the nearest Watcher by the scruff of his shirt and growled, "Get everyone from the barracks down here, *now!*"

The Watcher fled into the cafeteria, only to be greeted by more riotous inmates from the morning shift. The prisoners leapt up from their seats, hurling their bowls, the tables, and themselves at the guards present in the mess hall before they could send for reinforcements. Revolution was sweeping across the prison like a wild bushfire in a dry forest.

Leon slammed the cafeteria door with a pained snarl. "Hold your ground!" he barked at the handful of Watchers recoiling from the long-reaching weapons of the rebellious inmates. Dodging the wide swinging arcs of the shovel blades, Leon thrust forward, shocking an inmate in his throat so that he collapsed to the floor, gurgling in voiceless agony.

* * *

"Bring the roof down before they use the sparker!" Ray yelled.

The drainage pipe began to give way, the twisting metal mass wrenching from its suspending downpipes. Jagged cracks formed across the stone roof like a spider's web, clouds of dust and debris raining down from the ceiling's fissures.

"Put your backs into it!" Kenneth shouted, "We're almost free!"

The inmates smashed the metal pipe, bolts and shrapnel exploding with each strike. Rashad steadily grunted with exertion, hammering away at the pipe with the paced rhythm of a metronome.

Ray tightened his grip on the wooden handle before putting all his weight into a swing at the pipe, sinking his mattock's fang deep into the metal, the tool's head punching straight through and protruding from the other side.

Just as he was struggling to rip the mattock free of the rusty metal, Ray felt a sharp pain in his leg. Other inmates fell off the minecarts around him, clutching at their ankles.

"Sparker!!" Kenneth yelled, "Keep going boyos, we need the night shift down here, *now!*"

* * *

"Oi! Calm yourselves down a bit!" Cormac yelled, advancing down the ramp from the treasury, wielding his baton in one hand and mashing the sparker remote in the other.

Ben felt electric pain coursing through his shackled ankle, setting the nerve endings in his leg on fire. He fell to one knee, succumbing to the burning volts of the manacle.

Leon wreaked the most havoc upon the inmates, deftly dodging each shovel, jabbing his baton at the unruly prisoners and retreating before they could retaliate. Ben thought that if he could just overcome the pain in his ankle, he could strike at Leon with a jab of his shovel, and maybe turn the tide of the battle.

* * *

His weapon stuck in the pipe and his leg searing with volts of electricity, Ray gripped the tool's handle and leapt from the cart, using his weight as an anchor on the rusty pipe instead.

An ear-splitting screech of metal like fingernails on a chalkboard pierced their ears. Ray fell to the floor and rolled away as the drainage pipe collapsed, resounding in a tremendous crash reverberating around the dust-filled tool shed.

* * *

The heavy metallic clang echoed like a gong ringing through the walls of the prison. A cloud of dust billowed forth from the tool shed's entrance, obscuring the entire corridor in a thick shroud. Ben coughed and spluttered, holding his shovel up in a desperate defence against the encroaching silhouettes.

The Watchers used the screen of smoke to their advantage, getting inside the inmates' longer reach as they flailed their weapons blindly in the dark. One by one, the rioters fell, the guards quickly overpowering those who were not already on the floor choking on the cloud of dust or writhing in agony from the pulsating manacles.

Leon's shaggy blonde hair materialised out of the haze as he grabbed the scoop of Ben's shovel, wrenching the tool from his grasp. "Rib for a rib, young pup!" he growled with a wry smile before ramming Ben in the chest with his own shovel's handle.

Winded and weaponless, Ben lost his passion for the fight, choosing instead to contend with the pain of his manacle. He attempted to pry it off his ankle with his bare hands, but each time he made contact with the electrified shackle, the searing volts travelled from his fingertips up his arms to his shoulders, forcing him to let go. He kicked at the manacle with his free leg in an attempt to disrupt the sparker's signal, but to no avail.

* * *

Ray covered his head and peered up through the haze. The roof was crumbling, rocks and rubble were showering the floor, yet the ceiling had not fully collapsed. Inmates groaned in agony all around him.

"Bring me a shovel!" Rashad yelled above the confusion, "I need a shovel!"

Despite the sparking manacle sending spasms through his ankle, Ray scrambled to his feet, limping blindly over debris and fallen inmates alike to the shovel racks. He felt along the wall, groping in the darkness brought on by the cloud of dust, until he grasped the handle of a shovel.

"Heads up!" Ray shouted through the haze, throwing the shovel across the room to the lone silhouette of Rashad, who still stood upright on one of the carts. Soon, sounds of the shovel's head clashing against the stone roof could be heard.

Ray attempted to cross the distance to help Rashad, when a pair of hands clasped his good foot. His weight fell on his other leg, yet the pain from the manacle had rendered it numb, and he keeled over onto his hands and knees. He turned around to see Levi holding him back. Blood was still oozing out of the panicked prisoner's nose.

* * *

As the smoke in the corridor wafted outside to the quarry, the passageway became clear enough just in time for Ben to see Caleb, Evander, and a slew of other Watchers charging down the treasury ramp.

The cafeteria's door swung open, slamming against the wall. Ben's flicker of hope that the morning shift inmates had fared better was instantly crushed when Gremlin's pointed face appeared at the entrance, brandishing his shock stick with a devilish grin.

The skeletal-faced woman known as Lygia, along with a few other guards, pushed past Gremlin, the Watchers uniting in the corridor and storming into the tool shed.

* * *

"Help me," Levi panted, his face contorted from the manacle's torment. "Help me stop them!"

"Get off me!" Ray yelled, aiming a kick at the other inmate's already bloodied face, yet his convulsing leg involuntarily sailed off course.

"They'll make us Watchers in no time if we can stop this rabble!" Levi pleaded with wide eyes.

Ray flailed his electrified leg at Levi in answer, so that his manacle rested between the misguided teen's neck and shoulder. Levi yelped, releasing his grip on Ray as the burning volts bit at his neck. Ray let his foot linger for good measure as he peered through the cloud of dust.

Before Ray could get his bearings, Rashad broke through a load-bearing slab in the roof, and then, all at once, a fissure split down the centre of the ceiling with a thunderous crack, plunging inmates and bed frames and all manner of rubble down into the tool shed.

* * *

Another wave of smog blew out into the corridor, coupled with the sounds of rocks crumbling and clattering upon the tool shed's floor. Ben was relieved to know that the night shift inmates had joined the fight.

Gremlin and a handful of guards remained outside in the corridor. The greasy black-haired man patrolled up and down the cluster of fallen inmates with a vicious gleam in his green eyes, searching – almost hoping – for any more signs of trouble.

* * *

With the thick fog of dust redoubled in the tool shed, even the shafts of light filtering down from the ruined cells above could not pierce the dark shroud. Shadows of the boys from the night shift stumbled through the haze, coughing and spluttering in the confusion.

"*Watchers!* They're everywhe–" a whistling blunt object cut the unlucky prisoner short with a thud. The guards had breached the entrance. There was no telling how many there were.

"I don't know who I'm hitting!" Jack shouted in the confusion. A man's garbled yelp of pain gave him his response.

"Weapons, *where are the weapons!?*" another inmate cried.

"Ray, come now, let us make our stand!" Rashad bellowed from the rear of the tool shed.

Ray covered his mouth to avoid choking on the smog. He struggled to his feet, dragging his left leg over fallen rubble and debris towards the sound of Rashad's voice as the fight raged on. He staggered through the dark, kicking a fallen chamber pot and heaving aside a bed frame as he made his way closer to his cellmate's straining grunts.

* * *

Ben sat defeated with his back against the wall, his leg numb to the pain, yet still floundering on the floor like a fish out of water. Only now did he realise the fatal flaws in executing their plan as he heard the inmates' panicked yells from inside the tool shed. They were supposed to have been rioting while the manacles were being changed over for those who were to work a double shift. In all of the excitement of planning, they had forgotten this one crucial detail, and so the sparkers had brought them all to ground.

Then, they had failed to consider that the night shift inmates would be unarmed when they dropped down from their cells, and they had not anticipated that the clouds of dust from the collapsed ceiling would make it difficult for them to search for other weapons underneath all the rubble.

One inmate surged out of the tool shed, shouldering past the Watchers posted at the entrance. Stooping to pick up a shovel from one of the convulsing prisoners, he looked up to see Gremlin's ivory face in front of him, the short man's green eyes lit with wicked malice.

It was Ethan, covered in a grey film of dust and caught like a fly in a web. Before he could even raise the shovel to swing, Gremlin knocked his lights out with a flash of the shock stick. Ethan crumpled to the floor next to Ben, where he lay unconscious.

* * *

The haze thinned out to reveal three guards surrounding Rashad, harassing him with shock sticks. The resilient inmate was still on his feet, swinging his solid fists like a pair of wrecking balls, his shovel and mattock both lost in the chaos.

Ray grabbed the nearest Watcher from behind, wrapping an arm around the man's neck and pulling him backwards so that they both crashed down upon the rubble-strewn floor, strangling him in a chokehold. He locked his manacled foot around the Watcher's leg so that he, too, could feel the sparker's searing pain.

Rashad held his own against the two remaining guards attempting to subdue him. His resistance was unprecedented, his elbows and fists deadlier than their shock sticks. From the floor, Ray admired his cellmate's high threshold for pain. He seemed impervious to their electrical shocks.

Eventually, Cormac joined the pair of Watchers, and together the three of them beat Rashad to the floor. Ray peered through the veil of dust, wondering where all the other inmates were. Surely the Watchers could not have brought all of them down.

The dust settled and the smoke began to clear. Ray found that he had Evander within his chokehold, the dark features of the man's face now turning purple, and veins protruding from his forehead from the lack of oxygen. He felt a pang of guilt, remembering the compassion that Evander had shown to the other inmates, especially to his younger brother. He relented on his grip.

Evander hurled himself to one side, wheezing in lungfuls of air and choking on the dust. One of the Watchers standing above Rashad – Caleb – turned around to find Ray and Evander upon the floor. As Evander struggled to his feet, massaging his throat, Caleb swiftly plunged his shock stick into Ray's chest, taking the remaining fight out of him, along with the wind in his lungs.

Gasping for air, Ray rolled over to see all of the other inmates face down upon the floor, some trapped underneath stones fallen from the gaping hole in the ceiling, others lying beneath entire bed frames from the cells above. Aiden had been knocked unconscious by a fallen rock, the green sweatband tied around his forehead red with blood.

Cameron and Bryson had chosen not to involve themselves in the fight. Ray caught sight of them still cowering in a corner, too afraid to raise a hand to the Watchers lest they lose their precious positions pushing the minecarts. Levi sat scowling off to the side, tilting his head back and pinching the bridge of his broken nose, trying to stem the flow of blood.

Nearby, Jack was pinned to the floor by an obese Watcher sitting on top of him, who taunted the inmate with a shock stick.

Kenneth had the worst of it though. He was draped over one of the upturned carts, also unconscious, with one of his legs wedged between the minecart and the collapsed drainage pipe, his other leg bouncing involuntarily with the pulses of his manacle. *The luck of the Irish*, Ray reflected darkly.

* * *

The portly Warden ambled down the treasury ramp to investigate the crash and the sounds of the brawl in the tool shed. As he passed by, Ben could clearly see the man's puffy red cheeks and sweat patches, even through the haze. To him, the Warden did not fit the profile of the head of such an operation. He was more like a humble supervisor. Ben wondered if the Warden had been forced into his position, much like Evander had claimed that the Watchers had not freely chosen to live within the confines of the prison.

With the sounds of rebellion dying down, Leon emerged from the tool shed, brushing out the dust and spittle that had taken hold in his shaggy beard. He made his report to the Warden. "Inmates staged a riot. We stopped it. Tool shed needs fixing." He refrained from spitting.

The Warden looked through the doorway, dropping his jaw in shock at the destruction wrought by the inmates. He withdrew a handkerchief from his pocket to cover his mouth as he glanced back at Leon. "Bring all those responsible into the tool shed, I shall address them shortly."

Leon growled his compliance, combed his beard, and then stooped to grab hold of Ben's foot. Ben instinctively pulled his leg towards his chest, throwing the grizzled guard off balance. Leon quickly recovered his footing and kicked Ben in the stomach before roughly dragging him inside the tool shed, over the bodies of the other fallen inmates still twitching from the ongoing volts of the manacles. The shaggy-haired guard barked orders at Gremlin and the other Watchers to bring the rest of the inmates inside.

Ben looked around the tool shed, it was almost unrecognisable. Shafts of light from the cells above pierced the wisps of the settling dust. Rubble and debris covered the room's floor. Scattered throughout the wreckage were subdued inmates and shovels and mattocks and minecarts and bed frames.

He stared up at the ruptured ceiling. Although there was a gaping hole in the roof, not many cells had fallen through, maybe two or three. Perhaps if more inmates from the night shift had dropped down into the fight, they would have had a better chance.

The most notable damage though, was the broken drainage pipe, which now rested on an angle from the storm drain outlet in the outer wall down to the floor, its midsection propped up on some unfortunate inmate's leg that was sprawled on top of an overturned cart, although Ben could not see who it was.

* * *

The puffy-cheeked Warden stood at the entrance of the tool shed, surveying the remnants of the battle with a handkerchief over his mouth. Ray could not help but smile at the portly man's bemused expression.

The Warden shuffled into the room so that other inmates could be hauled in behind him. The chubby man, wearing his out-of-place Hawaiian shirt, pensively licked his lips, thinking of how best to commence his lecture when an alarm signal sounded off, blaring around the prison.

If only the Watchers had the same reaction time as the security system, Ray thought bitterly.

"It's about time!" Leon spat.

The Warden stared at Leon's saliva on the floor with disgust, as if the Watcher had just ruined the rubble-strewn floor. "Go and investigate, take

Gregory with you," he said. "Cormac, switch off the sparker, if you please."

The inmates breathed a collective sigh of relief as the manacles ceased to emit electrical shocks. Ray felt a loosening of the tension in his ankle, although the muscle fibres in his leg continued to contract of their own accord in the after-effects of the volts that had coursed through him.

* * *

Ben almost did not feel the cessation of the manacle's electricity. His leg was still numb from the searing pain. Dully tracing his eyes over the floor, he saw Aiden knocked out, breathing in shallow swirls of dust motes, his green sweatband stained red. Ben examined the fallen rock that was edged with the unlucky inmate's blood. It was intricately engraved with a familiar mark.

Catching Ben's gaze, Cormac snatched the stone from the floor with his stubby fingers.

"Oi! What's this, 'ey!?" Cormac yelled, agitatedly shoving the rock in front of Caleb, who had marched over from the far end of the tool shed.

Curious, the Warden reached for the stone. Cormac released the rock into his outstretched hand while staring daggers at Caleb with his piercing blue eyes.

The portly man examined the stone before waving it aloft for all to see. Ben saw that the carving on the rock held the same symbol as the cover of his father's journal, the very same one etched into his father's medallion, which still hung from around Caleb's neck underneath his grey shirt.

The Warden removed the handkerchief from his mouth to address the inmates. "Who is responsible for this insignia? Who is responsible?" he enquired, his pig-like eyes glaring at the crestfallen inmates, slowly scanning across the room.

* * *

Ray massaged some feeling back into his ankle before crawling over to where Rashad was lying, breathing shallow after his beating from the trio of guards. The Watchers flocked to the Warden at the front of the room, Evander glaring back at Ray.

"Hey, you okay?" asked Ray. With his eyes screwed shut, Rashad gritted his teeth and managed to nod. Ray peered around the tool shed as the other inmates began to recover. He looked back at Rashad, "Now that we can see what's going on, you think we might be able to go another round with the Watchers?"

Rashad cringed at the suggestion. "The punishments for this attack alone will be severe."

Ray saw Jack amongst the other inmates scrambling up to seated positions to listen in on the Warden's speech. "Come on," said Ray, "We still outnumber them. They don't have the sparker for the night shift either. If we just fight a little while longer, we can overwhelm the guards."

"Look at me," Rashad wheezed, turning his head with difficulty to face Ray. "I cannot continue. *We* cannot continue. They will surely defeat us."

Ray glanced at the other inmates again. Most of them were groaning and tending to their wounds, overcome by pain and exhaustion. Aiden and Ethan lay unmoving near the entrance with Ben. Kenneth was still out cold, sprawled over the upturned cart and trapped underneath what was left of the dripping drainage pipe.

Rashad was right.

* * *

The Warden still held the carved rock up high in the hushed silence. Eventually, his stare came to rest upon Ben, who met the round man's gaze.

"Whoever it may be," said the Warden, mopping his sweaty brow, "Know this: these people cannot help you. But I... I can help you! With time, you will learn this yourselves, each and every one of you," he said, pausing dramatically before straightening up to recompose himself. "I know that the majority of you did not *volunteer* to reside in our institution. I, myself, grew up in a peaceful farming community, with a beautiful stream flowing through the centre of our village. That is, until *they* came. They showed me, through hard work and perspiration, that I could prosper in this harsh environment. And so I did. And now, nothing looks more beautiful than the riches we procure from the earth."

An inmate coughed in the silence that followed, and Gremlin and Leon entered the tool shed. Gremlin was visibly shaken, and he hastily immersed himself in the pack of guards as Leon muttered something in the Warden's ear that made his eyes grow wide, nervously fidgeting with the small rock in his hands.

The sight of the Warden toying with the stone reminded Ray of his own rock marked with *TODAY* still stashed in the waistband of his trousers. He decided to keep it there. Perhaps it would be of use later.

Still watching the Warden, Ray was unsure whether the man was to be feared or pitied, although he did recall what Ben had said about the guards not being there of their own choice. *Who were* they *that took the Warden from his farm?*

Ben had similar questions running through his mind. *Are the Warden and the Watchers prisoners too, just as much as the inmates?* He knew that this portly man who was now gingerly pocketing the carved rock could not have been the same person who had masterminded the prison's operations. Ben wondered who was really responsible, but he need not have wondered for long.

Leon mentioned something that struck a chord with the Warden, causing the sweaty man to break off their whispered conversation and glance over his shoulder to the corridor outside.

The Warden licked his lips, deep in thought, before facing the crowd of inmates. "We have been very kind to you," he said. "Almost t-t-too kind, and you have taken this for granted. P-p-perhaps now it is time that you m-m-meet those whom you *really* serve."

All of the inmates gave a cry of shock and horror at what entered the tool shed next.

13 - THE KIRZAKAI

Icy terror seized Ben's insides. He scrambled backwards over fallen debris and the other inmates who were too slow to react, staring up at the strange beast stooping in through the doorway of the ruined tool shed. It walked like a man, but it was far from human. Ben almost did not notice the limp form of Joshua being dragged by the scruff of his shirt in the monstrous amphibian's webbed hand. He was not sure if Joshua was still alive, but he did not dare to approach to investigate further.

Ray rubbed his eyes, although his poor eyesight could not have deteriorated to such a degree for this chilling creature to have appeared in his vision. It was like something out of a bad dream, yet all of the inmates were fully conscious in this waking nightmare – with the exception of those who had been knocked out during the rebellion, of course.

It looked like an alligator standing up on its hind legs, roughly seven feet tall. Leathery smoky grey scales armoured the creature's muscular limbs. Draped over its shoulders was an open blue vest revealing a dark yellow belly through the opening of its garment along with a ragged blue loincloth. Jagged rows of teeth lined the sides of its long snout, with thin reptilian pupils set upon either side, matching the dark yellow of its belly.

Scanning the room with its narrow cold-blooded eyes, the beast hurled the unconscious Joshua like a ragdoll across the rubble-strewn floor, briefly flashing four razor-like claws. Spread-eagled upon the ground, Joshua did not stir. A long tail snaked out from behind the monster, sweeping aside debris as it slithered towards his motionless body. Attached to the end of its winding tail was an iron barb, now lifted and poised menacingly above Joshua's throat, threatening to slice it open at a moment's notice.

Rashad thrust his arms upward beside Ray, trying to propel himself off the ground for a better view of the giant reptile. Ray grabbed one of his cellmate's thick arms and pulled him upright.

"That green flash I saw in the jungle…" Rashad muttered. "There must be more of them."

The creature's tail swept back and forth of its own accord as it held Joshua at its mercy. Ethan groaned next to Ben at the front of the room, awoken by the shift in debris underneath him. Gazing up at the monstrosity from his backside, Ethan practically leapt one foot into the air before hurtling backwards into the farther reaches of the tool shed until he found himself sitting at Jack's side, trampling over rubble and the other wide-eyed inmates as they stared up at the reptilian horror.

The Warden edgily cleared his throat, snapping the prisoners out of their terrified daze. "Gentlemen, I present to you, Pythrisse! She is the faithful and graceful guardian of those who have dwelt within these walls since the Quarry Complex's formation."

Pythrisse swelled at her introduction, hissing her forked tongue at the inmates. Some of the Watchers uneasily reached for their shock sticks on instinct, as if they had any chance of inflicting harm against something so powerful.

"It really does exist," Ben murmured, almost in a trance, *"The Lizardman of the Swamp."*

From the back of the tool shed, Ray could not tell whether she was smiling, or if her jagged teeth naturally protruded from the sides of her snout. *If this is just the guardian*, he thought to himself, *then who does she guard?*

As if on cue, another scaly black-eyed monster entered through the doorway, a bony old reptile, immediately scuttling behind Pythrisse's great bulk, intimidated by the number of humans gathered before them.

"Ophidirick!" the Warden announced, "Revered sage of our residence."

Blinking his wide eyes curiously over the top of his snub nose, Ophidirick peered out from behind Pythrisse, who stood proudly in front of her master. The colour of his scales seemed to change under different angles of the light filtering down from the broken cells above, casting a motley array of moss green shades over his body, although splotches of brown scattered here and there appeared to remain the same, as if his age had affected his ability to adopt a uniform colour.

Ray and a few other brave inmates chuckled at the spindly hunchbacked creature hiding behind Pythrisse, this new arrival appearing to be no threat in comparison. Ophidirick turned back towards the entrance, his tail emerging on Pythrisse's other side, curling up in a big spiralling loop. He clasped his webbed hands together, expectantly bowing his head towards the doorway, the rear of his elongated skull still jutting out over the top of his slumped shoulders like a cyclist's aerodynamic helmet.

"And of course –" the Warden started to say, gulping as a third giant lizard entered the ruined tool shed. He mopped at his sweaty brow as he hailed her in a quavering voice, "Kalarish, Matron of the *Kirzakai!*"

Kalarish was a plump bipedal reptile, no taller than an average man. Patches of her orange hide and light yellow underbelly flashed from beneath the folds of her purple robe draped around her shoulders, covering the excess sagging flesh hanging from her neck. A small cluster of horns adorned the rear of her scaly skull like some tiny desert shrub.

"Do you still believe that we can fight them?" Rashad murmured to Ray rhetorically.

"If it wasn't for that Pythrisse," said Ray, "I think we'd still have a fair chance."

Her bulky figure supported by a wooden staff, Kalarish hobbled towards the Warden. She took no notice – or interest – of the inmates staring up at her in disbelief.

The Lizardwoman withdrew a clutter of jingling metal from the folds of her robe, a plain set of keys, all attached around a central octagonal ring. She held it outstretched to the Warden, who hesitated to take hold.

Another shock fell upon the gasping inmates as her soft wicked rasp filled the entire room, "We found the Watcher in our quarters bearing your key-ring. How did it come to thiz warm-blooded wretch?" She indicated Joshua's limp body, still held at the mercy of Pythrisse's tail barb. Without waiting for an answer, Kalarish looked around at the destruction in the ruined tool shed, as if just noticing the subdued inmates and debris scattered across the floor for the first time. "You allow thiz to happen? Tyrax will not be pleased."

The Warden lowered his head, revealing beads of sweat across his receding hairline as he reached for the octagonal key-ring. Kalarish glared scornfully through the thin reptilian slits of her amber orange eyes at the pathetic man meekly holding out his hand to accept her bestowal. Still waiting for his answer, she dropped the set of keys upon the rubble-strewn floor.

The red-cheeked man stooped to retrieve his key-ring. "P-p-punishments will be administered," he stammered, averting her gaze. "You have my word, Matron."

All of the Watchers stood by as their boss mumbled his submission to the cold-blooded creature.

"You are lucky you have zerved at length without inzident," Kalarish rasped. "Tyrax dezides your fate now." With that, she ambled out of the tool shed with a flurry of her purple robe, Ophidirick silently following in her wake.

Pythrisse snarled at the speechless onlookers, withdrawing her tail barb from Joshua's throat. Turning to leave, she whipped up rubble and debris at the inmates and Watchers alike with a single flick of her powerful tail.

A heavy silence fell as everyone slowly came back to their senses, as if recovering from some collective hallucination. The inmates looked at each other, exchanging bewildered expressions, almost in disbelief at what they had seen.

The Warden called Caleb to his side. "Caleb, kindly discover the residents responsible for this, this, this –" he was at a loss for words, his eyes blankly falling upon Joshua, who was still unconscious on the floor. Everyone took notice of the portly man's hands trembling at his sides.

"Insolence, sir?" said Caleb, bringing back the Warden's attention.

"Yes, this insolence! Find them out and punish them at once!"

Levi clambered up from his position in the corner of the tool shed, his dusty green shirt stained red, with a streak of dried blood trailing up to his nose where it had begun to crust. He held his nose with one hand, the other pointing silently at Ray and Rashad.

Jack turned around and saw the smug weasel proudly sticking out his chest as if he had been declared victorious. "What happened to you, mate? Pick your nose too deep?" he asked.

Ray, Rashad, Ethan and the surrounding inmates burst with laughter as Levi wavered with a bemused stare. Cameron and Bryson struggled to keep a straight face; Cameron especially, with his bent nose.

Caleb motioned for Levi to come forward to reveal the schemers behind the riot when Cormac interrupted, his blue eyes sparkling with glee, "No need for any ovvat!" The yellow-toothed Watcher climbed over the wreckage in the front portion of the tool shed and poked his head out through the doorway, "Danny, come 'ere!"

Small wet footsteps pattered down the corridor. Little Danny's scrawny face appeared at the entrance, his soaked clothes hanging from his malnourished body, wet from the treasury's water tap. Neither scratch nor bruise could be seen upon him.

"Tell 'em what you told me, Danny!" Cormac said with a mischievous grin.

Little Danny's sky blue eyes looked out over each of the inmates still sitting in shock upon the tool shed floor. "There!" the skinny waif croaked, jabbing a finger at Jack and Ethan. "There!" he declared with twisted eagerness, stepping into the room and pointing at Kenneth who was just now stirring, his leg still trapped between the overturned cart and the fallen drainage pipe. He continued pointing fingers; at Aiden's limp body, then Ray, Rashad, and lastly, Ben.

"What does he think he's doing?" Ray asked as Cormac patted Little

Danny on the head.

"If he did not break," said Rashad, "Levi would have told them."

"*Break!?* I'll break him in a minute, that little snitch!" Ray said through clenched teeth.

Seated in disappointment, Ben shook his head at his cellmate as Cormac ruffled his crisp hair. *But then again*, Ben thought, *if he was threatened with another day in the steam rooms, the poor boy might not have survived.*

Cormac raised his chin high, resting a hand on Little Danny's shoulder as he looked out over the inmates. Savouring his time in the spotlight, the crude guard waved towards the back of the tool shed. "Warden, I want to name our next *volunteer* to be sent over to the Desert Complex: that big gorilla up the back!" Everyone turned to see him gesturing at Rashad. "That one took on three Watchers at a time, even Caleb and Evander couldn't stop 'im!" he exclaimed proudly. "If it wasn't for me stepping in, those useless guards would be on the ground next to the inmates!"

Caleb stepped between Cormac and the Warden, cutting across his gloating. "I will see to the punishments of the inmates," the stern guard said. He ordered Evander, Gremlin and another Watcher to assist him with bringing Ray, Ethan, Jack and Kenneth to the steam rooms. "Cormac, you can take Rashad down to the tunnels, since *you're* the only one who can handle him."

Cormac cursed at him under his breath before calling Leon over to lend a hand. As the Watchers carried out Caleb's commands, Ben looked up at Little Danny, his cellmate still standing beside the doorway.

"*Why?*" asked Ben. "I thought we were friends."

"Well, I 'ad to tell 'im the truth," said Little Danny, "'e's me Pop, after all!" his indignant face curled into an impish grin. His sky blue eyes twinkled mischievously before turning away from the dumbfounded Ben to watch the guards carry out their duties.

As Rashad was brought to his feet, bound for the Desert Complex, Ray lunged for Cormac's leg. He was swiftly beaten back by Leon's shock stick.

Rashad smiled down at Ray. "Do not fear. Wherever they take me, *Mi Haraka* can only thrive," he said, allowing the guards to take him away.

Kenneth yelled in agony as Gremlin jumped up and down upon the fallen drainage pipe, dancing like an Old Western prospector who had just struck gold, taunting the inmate before lifting it from his leg. Caleb and another Watcher pulled Jack and Ethan to their feet, marching them out of the tool shed. Rashad was led by Cormac with Leon close behind, holding a shock stick at the back of the big inmate's neck, just waiting for a reason to strike.

"Good luck, Ben," said Rashad as they passed by. "I will see you again, someday. Stay strong."

Ben watched Cormac lead the barrel-chested inmate out through the doorway. Two more Watchers trailed behind Leon, just to be on the safe side. Little Danny leaned against the wall by the entrance, smiling at the procession. Ben could not believe that they had been deceived by Cormac's son.

Levi stooped next to Ray as he watched his cellmate depart. "You missed your chance to have a perfect record like me," he said in a nasal voice. "You'll be an inmate forever after what you did to me. I'll make certain of it, when I become a Watcher."

Ray was hauled roughly to his feet by Evander, the kindness having left the eyes of the good Watcher. Ray snorted at Levi's haughtiness despite the red track of dried blood running down from his nose.

"I told you I'd break your nose if you got in our way again," said Ray. "Here, have something to wipe your face with." He kicked up rubble at the smug opportunist, showering him with dust.

Evander pushed Ray towards the doorway where Little Danny stood grinning at the punishments being carried out. His sky blue eyes lit up as he watched Ray being manhandled across the ruined tool shed.

Ray felt a wave of fresh anger wash over him. He charged at Little Danny and bashed his knee into the little imp's gut. The scrawny boy collapsed to the floor, clutching at his midsection, reeling and gasping for air. Evander swiftly came up from behind and shoved Ray out into the corridor before he could do any more damage.

14 - WE'RE ALL PRISONERS HERE

Ray was thrown upon the floor of the steam room, which was no more than a few feet across. A large metal grate glowed a fiery red on the opposite wall, radiating light and warmth into the concrete cell. A slightly sulfurous smell filled the tiny room.

A thick hardwood door thudded shut behind him, the lock turning. He scrambled to his feet to face Evander through the three iron bars set in the door's window. Evander – with the swollen imprints of Ray's hands still around his neck – gave the inmate an icy glare before exiting the hot corridor.

Jack and Ethan were hauled past Ray's cell, wrenching and struggling with the Watchers. Caleb threw open the door of the adjacent steam room, yet Jack resisted, planting his feet firmly on either side of the doorway.

"You're gonna have to earn it, Caleb!" he half-yelled, half-laughed through grinning clenched teeth.

Caleb grunted with exertion as he tried to force the stubborn inmate inside the hotbox. Another door slammed and a bolt slid into place around the corner as Ethan was secured. The other Watcher reappeared in their section of the passage, sparking up his shock stick and rushing over to lend assistance. "Back off!" Caleb snapped at the guard.

"That's more like it, Caleb," Jack taunted, "You've gotta do this for yourself!" he thrust his feet into the wall, extending his legs farther and crushing the stern Watcher against the other side of the corridor.

Caleb's hawkish eyes widened in the physical contest. Using the wall as a support, he pushed back with all his raw strength against the inmate. Veins bulged forth from his sinewy muscle and his stony face cracked as he gritted his teeth in strain.

"Come on Jack, throw him back!" Ray shouted encouragement as the Aussie prisoner began to inch forward.

Jack screwed his eyes shut, roaring in defiance like a lion being forced into a cage, Caleb steadily pushing him forward. Jack's feet slipped down, but he caught the doorway with his hands.

Caleb's arms were now fully extended. Ray moved closer to the iron bars in his cell window to gain a better vantage point. The metal bars glowed with warmth, and he had to hold his face a fraction away to avoid burning his cheek. He and the second guard watched as Caleb lifted up his foot and planted it in Jack's backside, using the combined strength of his arms and leg to force the prisoner inside.

Jack's grip on the doorway faltered, and he hurtled forward, disappearing from view. A metallic clang and a scalding hiss sounded from the adjacent steam room. Caleb slammed the door shut behind him.

A slow clap applauded from inside Jack's cell. "Well done, Caleb," he mocked. "You deserve a pat on the back for that one. I wasn't really trying, just so you know. Didn't wanna embarrass you in front of your mate." Ethan laughed from around the corner.

"You're getting stronger, Jack," Caleb answered, breathing hard. "I may have to send *you* to the Desert Complex next time."

"How 'bout you send us *all* over there?" Ray asked, daring to push the Watcher even further. "I'm sure Rashad could use the company."

Catching his breath, Caleb reached an arm through Ray's window and pulled him by the collar of his shirt. Ray pressed his hands against the door, tilting his head back to stay away from the iron bars emanating heat.

"What, do you miss him already, inmate?" Caleb said with a stony glare. "How about Sergei, do you miss him too? After what you've done, you may see him sooner than you think. *But*, if you truly believe you're strong enough, I'll arrange your transfer now." As Ray's shirt began to tear, Caleb put another hand through the window, reaching around the back of the inmate's head and pulling him closer. "I'll make you a deal: if your face doesn't burn, then you can stay with Sergei and Rashad instead."

* * *

Ben grimaced as the sickly green-skinned Watcher woman cuffed his wrists to the chains rack in the cell house. Clothed in layers upon layers of black rags, Lygia's stringy black hair streaked with grey resembled a cobweb in some shadowy corner, like those behind the ever-shining spotlights in the ceiling, and her blackened teeth made her mouth seem like a gaping hole as she sneered at him.

"TWICE ON THE CHAINS RACK, *SSOMEONE'S A LUCKY BOY!*" she shrieked, pinching his cheek none too gently with long bony fingers, her nails filed into claws. The tip of her tongue was forked, perhaps in honour of the Lizardmen, although it had left her with a lisp.

Ben turned away from the bulging bug eyes set in her unsightly skeletal face as she drew closer into his personal space. His binding chains rattled, restricting his movement.

"You're a little *troublemaker*, aren't you? AREN'T YOU!?" she screamed shrilly, nodding in earnest at her own question, "Yess – oh yess you are! I shall have to keep an eye on you!" she stroked his head with a pasty white hand.

Ben writhed on the chains rack, twisting his body this way and that, trying to escape her gnarled fingers in futility.

"Pity we only have four ssteam rooms," she moaned, mocking him. "You could have sstayed with your FRIENDS otherwise!"

"Leave me alone, please!" Ben cried, repulsed.

Lygia patted his cheek and stroked it tenderly. "Please, oh please! Pretty little boy, aren't you?" she gripped one of his ears. "PRETTY! LITTLE! BOY!" Ben yelped as she yanked his earlobe down. Then, as if struck by a sudden thought, she pulled away from him. "You know, I'm *awfully* tired after my shift. I'll grant you a moment'ss peace *for now*, you lucky, lucky boy," she set her foot on the barracks staircase, turning back at him with a sultry gaze. "Don't go anywhere, handssome. I'll be back right after I've had my beauty ssleep."

She threw her head back and laughed in a high-pitched cackle, her black teeth glistening in the spotlights' glare before she danced away up the steps and through the door to the barracks.

Ben's ear throbbed. He struggled with his bindings for a moment, not trying to escape, but in an attempt to shake off the taint of Lygia's touch. He shivered, his chains clinking, as another screeching laugh pierced through the hardwood door of the Watcher barracks.

Just as her gleeful wail died down, a pair of footsteps shuffled up the staircase to his left from the cafeteria. A tuft of red hair appeared from the flight of steps, and Kenneth slowly limped up into the cell house.

Loud and aggressive grunts emitted from behind him, and an impatient-looking Gremlin came into view, thrusting his shock stick into the Irish teen's back, trying to propel the wounded inmate up the stairs faster.

Kenneth stumbled and tripped on the last step, clutching at his leg in agony. Gremlin hissed in exasperation before raining down swift strokes with his shock stick upon the prisoner, who could do nothing but hold up his forearms in defence. Ben was even less useful from where he stood. He screwed his eyes shut as the beating continued.

The inmates watching from the barred windows around the cell house jeered at the guard's cruelty. Gremlin paused for a moment at the noise. He looked up and gave them all a devilish giggle.

Kenneth seized advantage of Gremlin's boastful distraction, kicking the Watcher back down the cafeteria's staircase with his good leg. The inmates cheered as the fiery-haired prisoner hoisted himself up using the stairs' handrail.

Ben opened his eyes just in time to see the door in the corner opening, Evander emerging. "Kenneth!" Ben yelled, "Watch out behind you!!"

The dark Watcher crossed the distance in an instant, clothes-lining Kenneth to the ground just as he turned around. Gremlin ascended the flight of steps and looked down at the groggy inmate. He raised his shock stick again with renewed malice in his wicked green eyes, yet Evander caught his hand, burning his gaze into the short man's face.

"Was *bring him to the steam rooms* too hard for you to understand, Gremlin?" his voice was choked, probably due to the marks around his throat.

Gremlin lowered his shock stick, his pallid pointed face blushing red, as if he had just been caught with his hand in the cookie jar. He shook his head.

"Then bring him to the steam room," said Evander, "*Without beating him to death.*"

Gremlin grabbed Kenneth by the scruff of his shirt, dragging his limp body towards the door in the corner, glaring at Evander like a spoiled child who had been sent to his room. Evander stood with his hands on his hips, watching him haul the inmate out of the cell house.

Mara entered through the same door, standing to one side to let Gremlin and Kenneth pass. She started towards the empty row of cells at the opposite end of the room. For her, it was just another normal day working in the prison. The day shift had simply started later than usual. Only one cell door was closed to her: Kenneth and Aiden's. Aiden had not awoken from his head wound, no matter how hard he was shaken. The Warden had ordered that he remain in his room until he recovered, or otherwise.

Mara threw a bitter expression at Ben and the damaged cells above the tool shed as she passed by. Evander returned her stare, and she quickened her pace.

"Evander," Ben ventured. "Where did those Lizardmen come from?"

The kind Watcher's features softened as he turned to address Ben with a shrug. "Beats me," he started up the barracks staircase. "Like I said, we're all prisoners here, some more than others." And with that, he left the room.

Mara reappeared next to Ben with a chamber pot. "Hey, your name's *Ben*, right?" she asked, locking her eyes with his. He nodded nervously, suspicious of her slight smirk. Without breaking eye contact, she emptied the chamber pot at his feet, its steaming stench pervading his nostrils.

"Oops," she said, her voice dripping with sarcasm as she headed for the exit.

***

Ray stared at the outline of the golden medallion underneath Caleb's grey shirt drawing nearer and nearer as his face came dangerously close to the hot iron bars. He screwed his eyes shut and turned his head to one side, lifting his knees against the door.

Caleb's force was too strong for him to resist further. With the side of his face only half an inch away from the centre bar, Ray could almost feel his ear burning. Pushing the thought out of his mind, he heaved against the door with all of his remaining strength.

The door to the corridor's entrance suddenly flung against the wall. Ray snapped his eyes open to see Gremlin dragging Kenneth up the passage. Caleb relented on his grip to stand aside and let them through.

Ray fell backwards into the steam room, thudding against the burning metal grate behind him. Sharp sizzling pain seared through his backside and he hurled himself upon the floor.

His ears prickled at the sound of something crackling, and he turned to see that the back of his shirt had caught fire on the red-glowing grate. In a rush of cold adrenaline, he quickly pulled off his shirt and threw it into a corner of the room, where it erupted in a fiery blaze.

Caleb knocked on the door, tearing Ray's attention away from the small bonfire. "You got lucky this time, inmate. Challenge me again, and we'll see what happens."

The fourth steam room door was sealed and locked around the corner. Caleb, Gremlin and the other Watcher exited the corridor.

His back still stinging, Ray looked out through the wire mesh of the hot grill. He could dimly see two more glowing grills set along the left wall of the square stone shaft, where Ethan and Kenneth were. To his immediate left and out of his line of sight must have been where Jack was. Vague images of other rooms existed above and below their level, although in the shimmering heat radiating from the mesh screen, it was difficult to tell.

"Alright guys, you know the drill," said Ethan, "The more clothes on, the better."

Ray peeled his gaze away from the fiery furnace and glanced at what remained of his once green shirt, now a smouldering bundle of threads in the corner. "Why's that?" he asked.

"Think of it like a sauna," said Jack. "Don't strip, don't move, and you won't end up looking like Little Danny did this morning."

"What's the deal with that kid anyway?" asked Ethan. "Why'd he rat us out for?"

"Didn't you hear?" Jack replied. "He said he's Cormac's son."

Ray clenched his fists, knowing that Little Danny had shared a cell with his brother. The selfish runt had taken Ben's share of shower water after a double shift on his first day, and even then, they had trusted him. Rashad offered him food out of his own bowl when the scrawny little urchin came out of the steam room. *How long did Cormac* really *keep him in the hotbox for?* He wondered to himself.

"I feel sorry for the mother," said Ethan.

"Mate, I feel sorry for the family photographer, that'd be an ugly picture," said Jack. "Who would wanna get with Cormac anyway? Reckon it was Lygia?"

"Talk about bad images," Ethan snickered, "How 'bout the family dentist?"

"Hah, no wonder they're working here," Jack laughed. "They'd *need* diamonds to pay off that dental bill!"

Ray's fists unwound as he chuckled along with the other two inmates. He found himself thinking this punishment was not as bad as it seemed. It sure beat working in the hot sun all day.

A groan issued from the farthest steam room.

"Hey, Kenneth, you alright?" asked Ray, getting to his feet and looking through the hot wire mesh.

The fiery-haired inmate's silhouette appeared at his grill as he sat up.

"Yeah, no thanks to you," he said.

"What's that supposed to mean?" asked Ray.

"We wouldn't be in this mess if it wasn't for you," said the Irish teen.

"Hey man, that ain't fair," said Ethan, "Him and his brother gave us all a fair chance to get outta here."

"Yeah," said Ray. "Maybe if you didn't get yourself stuck underneath that pipe, we would've had an even *better* chance."

Jack snorted, listening to the others argue.

"Screw you and your brother, Ray," said Kenneth. "My leg's busted, and Aiden's worse off. Whose idea was it to pull the bloody roof down?"

"Hey, bright side, guys," said Jack, "At least we don't have to work today."

Ray silently flipped the bird in Kenneth's direction before settling down with his back against the cell door, stretching his legs out across the hearth of the furnace. *If only Kenneth had been sent to the Desert Complex instead of Rashad*, he thought to himself. *At least Rashad knows how to keep a cool head.*

"So, *Kirzakai*," said Ethan, trying to break the uneasy silence. "Where do you think they came from? What do you think they've got us digging in the pit for?"

"What, do you think I know?" Kenneth asked flatly in his singsong Irish accent. "*Gee*, excuse me while I gaze into me magic crystal ball for a moment. What's it matter? The answers won't help the situation we currently find ourselves in."

"Whatever they're looking for, we'll be the first to find it," said Jack, "No idea how the crocs started walking and talking though."

"Ray, what do you think?" asked Ethan, "Evolution, mutation… aliens, maybe? Ray?"

Ray quietly stared at the tan-line around his thumb. It was still lighter in colour against his browning skin, although it had gradually been fading with each day he spent in the quarry underneath the harsh glare of the sun.

Rashad's voice echoed in his ears. *"You must focus on the things which you do remember, in order to remember that which you do not."*

He looked up from his tan-line, gazing into the red grill. An image of the fierce hot sun embroidered on the flag on top of the viewing deck outside sailed into his mind. The flag erupted in flame, burning from the centre outwards, bright light forcing his eyes shut.

The sun lingered in his vision, as if it was burnt into his retina. It soared high above him across a clear blue sky. Ray looked away from its brilliance. He was sitting in the stands of a stadium. It was filled with other students around him for the school athletics day, a day dedicated to track and field events.

He and his best friend, Robert Zerka, sat side by side, resting up before the javelin throw. They were competing for medals; Zerka was ahead by one. Higher up in the stands, Ben was sitting in the cool shade by himself, his face buried in a book.

Ray turned back to the track to see a girl approaching, her almond brown hair waving in the sun. From their distance, he could not see her face, yet he knew exactly what she looked like. Every feature and physical trait he had memorised over the years fell into place one by one as she drew closer. Her lithe curves, her dimpled cheeks, and her soft brown eyes that always seemed to lull him into a deep sense of calm whenever he stared into them.

Dana. The girl who had given him the silver promise ring to wear around his thumb. She ran up to greet them after the hurdle race, her olive skin glistening with sweat, her perspiring fragrance giving off a hint of peaches.

"It's about time you came back," said Zerka.

Dana flipped him off with a smile, revealing the same silver ring around her middle finger. "Looks like we're even now, Robbie," she said, tossing her gold medal into Ray's collection.

Ray clasped his hands behind his head and leaned back with a smile, the sun smiling back at him.

* * *

Gagging and reeling in disgust at the upturned chamber pot's reeking contents, Ben backed up against the wooden pillar. He danced from one foot to the other, his chains rattling as he desperately tried to avoid touching the oozing pool of filth with his shoes.

Caleb, Gremlin and another Watcher emerged from the door in the corner, having already secured Ray and the others in the steam rooms. Caleb directed the other two guards up the barracks staircase without so much as a glance at Ben. Not even the reeking pile of waste at the inmate's feet could deter the dark-eyed Watcher's focus as he descended into the cafeteria to properly assess the damage in the tool shed.

The barracks door creaked open before Gremlin and the other guard could reach the handle. Dreading the thought of Lygia returning, Ben was relieved to see the back of a leather-vested man with spiky black hair hauling someone through the doorway; another prisoner it seemed, not yet clothed in the green uniform of the Quarry Complex.

The Watcher turned, minding his step down the stairs. It was the same man with dark sunglasses who had brought in Ray on their first day in the prison, except now, he was bringing in some new victim who had been caught exploring somewhere he did not belong.

Ben stole a glance of the boy as they passed by the chains rack. He was no older than Ben. He was wearing a tattered brown shirt, ripped jeans and a pair of flip flops on his feet beneath the blinking red light of the day shift manacle. His facial features were well-defined, and his muscles were lean and compact beneath his brown-hued skin.

As they moved beyond his vision, Little Danny's reedy voice carried up from the cafeteria. "... and I want a new cell, all to meself." Ben looked over at the traitorous imp climbing up the stairs. "And an extra chamber pot for me showers."

Cormac followed him up into the cell house. "Don't you worry your little 'ead, son, I'll make sure of it!"

Little Danny paused at the top of the stairs, staring at Ben in surprise. His eyes dropped to the floor, and his childlike giggle filled the cell house. "Hahaha! Look, Pop, look at what 'e's gone and done to 'imself!"

"It's not mine..." Ben mumbled, looking down at the filth at his feet.

"Course it's not," Cormac chuckled. "Someone else what was standing in your place must've done it, 'ey sunshine?" They both laughed as Cormac led Little Danny across the room to an empty cell above the tool shed – one of the many cells that were still intact.

A door slammed shut from the far end of the cell house, somewhere behind Ben. Cormac jumped and placed a hand on his shock stick. His face curled into a crude grin as he addressed the other Watcher.

"Spike! What brings you 'ere?"

"Here on business, Mac. We caught one of the villagers wanderin' too far up the road."

"Risky business, that," Cormac warned, as if he could ever presume to be the voice of reason. "Soon we'll 'ave all of Lungsod after 'im."

Spike shrugged as he returned to Ben's field of view, venturing back up the barracks staircase. "Good thing we've got the Mayor on the payroll, then."

"True!" Cormac laughed. "That greedy gasbag'll give up the 'ole town for a fistful of rocks. Say, we're 'aving a game of poker up on the rooftop tonight, what say you join us, 'ey?"

"I'll think about it," said Spike, taking a few more steps up the stairs.

"Come on," said Cormac, imploring him. "'ave a go at grabbing a couple of gems for yourself, and give me a chance to win that shiny ring on your 'and." Spike glanced down at the ring on his finger before withdrawing a cigarette and a lighter from his black vest, thoughtfully considering the invitation. "I'm sure the ovva Watchers at the outpost won't miss you for one night."

Spike took a long draw on his cigarette, flicked the ash and accepted Cormac's offer with a puff of smoke. The barracks door shut behind him.

Cormac's blue eyes sparkled as he turned, coming face to face with Ben, almost having forgotten that he was there. He glanced down at Ben's feet in the spreading pool of muck. "Per'aps I'll send for young Sarah to come clean your mess, 'ey? Sweet little lamb chop, she is." He shot a crude yellow grin at Ben, and then made haste for the door in the corner.

* * *

Ray woke up in the steam room, staring at the red grate, still wearing a foolish grin from his recollection. His tongue was dry, and his palms were clammy. His head throbbed. He was not sure whether that was due to the flashback or the sulfuric heat engulfing him in the hotbox.

He glanced around the cell. It seemed smaller. In the corner, the threads that had remained of his shirt had now wilted to a few burning embers within a heap of black ash. The other boys were silent, perhaps navigating their own memories for an escape from reality.

His gaze slowly drew back to the glowing mesh wire, almost as if some unseen force had control over his attention like a puppeteer pulling at ethereal strings. The fiery red brazier etched itself into his retinas, so that even when he scrunched his eyelids against the blaze, it did nothing but cast a spotlight upon the burning metal grill, like a hellish stage prop in front of a thin curtain of ruddy skin.

When he opened his eyes again, he was standing in his father's study. Jacob Rauder placed a hand on his shoulder, his bright green eyes delivering Ray some bad news.

"Dad!" Ray exclaimed.

His father moved closer, the golden glint of the medallion's necklace shining from underneath his shirt's collar. "Now son, I know that you're upset, but you need to understand –"

"No, I don't want to leave! You take Benji and you go, I can look after myself. You showed me that. When we were kids, you left me in charge and I looked after Ben while you went off filming your documentaries. Why should this be any different!?"

"Please, son," his father tried to persuade him in his world-weary voice. "Here, let me show you something," he walked around to the other side of his desk, rifling through a drawer brimming with stacks of paper and maps. "I'm part of an org–" he sighed as Ray stormed out of the room, slamming the door behind him.

Ray ran outside and through the streets of their neighbourhood. He could not run too far; it was just a small town, but at least the exercise would help to clear his mind. He hurtled past the other houses, past the school, the water tower, and the car yard. Eventually, he reached the diner at the main intersection of town. It was their favourite place to hang out after school. It was the only place to hang out after school.

He saw Dana inside, sitting with a group of her friends. He turned away, taking a moment to recompose himself before he pushed through the door. He asked her if they could talk in private. They walked over to a corner booth, their favourite booth, with the waitress clucking her tongue, knowing that he would not order anything.

For what seemed like an eternity, Ray stared at the table, studying the graffiti that he and his friends had whittled into the wood over the years, leaving their marks forever. *Ray was here* and *Ray and Dana for life* and *Berserker for president* were among the most deeply-carved grooves. It all seemed so childish now.

"What's up?" Dana smiled at him.

Ray could not bring himself to look up into her soft brown eyes.

"I'm leaving town."

* * *

Ben shook at his chains again, but to no avail. He did not want Sarah to see him standing in this stench, let alone have Cormac hounding after her.

The door creaked open before Cormac could reach it, and Sarah entered the cell house with a mop and bucket already prepared. She froze at the sight of the crude man advancing towards her.

"'ello sweet'eart," he grinned.

"CORMAC!!" Caleb bellowed, making him jump as the stern Watcher strode up the cafeteria staircase, returning from the tool shed. Caleb drew his shock stick. "Get back to work, now! The rebellion happened on your shift. Don't make me report *this* to the Warden, too."

The faces of inmates slowly filled the barred windows surrounding the cell house, their eyes staring at the two Watchers with keen interest.

Tension had been building between the pair of guards ever since Caleb had won the medallion from Cormac.

Cormac slowly wheeled around, gripping his own shock stick behind his back. "Touchy touchy, Caleb. Just making sure everything's shipshape up 'ere. Don't 'ave to go getting your knickers in a twist about it. I gave me sparker to Leon while 'e's down there in the pit."

"I'm warning you, Cormac, one more mistake and I'll send you back to the Desert Complex myself."

"Oh, a thousand apologies, Your Grace…" Cormac mocked him, bowing low and waving one hand dramatically in the air. He winked at Ben before descending the stairs into the cafeteria.

Caleb glanced at the mop and bucket in Sarah's hand, and then at the mess at Ben's feet, before marching up the barracks stairs to report his assessment of the damage.

Once they were alone, Sarah set her bucket down next to the chains rack. Strangely, Ben found that he was no longer utterly terrified at the thought of talking to her as he once was. "That girl, Mara," he said. "Why does she hate me?"

Sarah plunged her mop into the bucket of water, looking up at him with an apologetic smile. "I asked Mara to do this," she said, slapping the wet mop onto the floor and scrubbing away the muck, "So that we could talk."

"You knew our plan didn't work?" asked Ben.

"Ava saw Evander bringing your brother up through the cafeteria," she replied, mopping around Ben's sneakers. "I guess I kind of already knew though, once all the noise stopped."

"Yeah, we were all speechless when we saw the Lizardmen," said Ben, moving his shoes out of her way. He remembered something from the first time they had spoken, coincidentally the first time he was bound to the chains rack. "Before Caleb gave Joshua the black eye, you said that Joshua told him that there was more to discover inside the prison than there was outside in the pit. Were the Lizardmen what he was referring to?"

Sarah shrugged. "Ava reads to the Lizardmen from books stolen by the

Watchers. They have a study upstairs, through that passage," she pointed towards the door in the corner.

"Why would she read to them?" asked Ben.

"They want to learn our language, I guess. Ava started teaching them the alphabet. They want to read by themselves." Sarah seemed indifferent towards their existence.

"How long have you known about the, uh, what are they called again?" asked Ben.

"The *Kirzakai?* Oh, I knew early on. Ava told me on my first night here. I was afraid at first, but they keep to themselves." She smiled at the ground, "Actually, if you can look past his scales, Ophidirick is kind of like a funny old man."

"Don't be so naive, Sarah," said Mara, entering the cell house. Apparently, she had been listening in on their conversation. "Remember, they're the reason why we're trapped here."

Sarah blushed, returning to her work as Mara paced out of view to the empty row of cells.

"Hey, there was an alarm before," said Ben, remembering the abrupt end to the rebellion. "Did Joshua have something to do with that?"

Sarah looked up at him, brushing back a curtain of her silky chestnut brown hair. "While the inmates from the morning shift were fighting in the cafeteria, Ava snuck up to the study. The Lizardmen have a hidden passage to their quarters up there. Joshua asked her to help him open it."

"He must have used our riot as a distraction," Ben mused. "Do you know what he was doing?"

"No," she said, examining the head of her mop, then the bucket of water. "I think I need to rinse this out, I'll be back, okay?"

He nodded as she picked up her bucket, following Mara out of the cell house. The floor was considerably cleaner than before. The wet stone was still stained with smeared muck, yet at least all of the lumps had been washed away. He no longer felt the urge to dry heave.

Ben glanced to his right, looking over at the cells above the tool shed. Although only a handful of rooms had collapsed, the damage was extensive.

Even parts of the wall had fallen in with the floor of the cells affected. The displaced prisoners from the night shift had been relocated to empty cells until those above the tool shed could be repaired. As for who would carry out the repairs, he could not guess. His mind was preoccupied with thoughts of the bipedal lizards.

Ben recalled that his father was obsessed with all things reptilian. Many of his expeditions had been based on some myth about giant lizards. He wished that their father had spoken more about his work, rather than letting his absence speak of his devotion to it.

Maybe I can ask Uncle Joshua, he thought to himself, although he was not even sure if Joshua was still alive. It had been a strange thing to see the friendly man with the close-cropped hair and polo shirt whom Ben had known for so long to be thrown around like a ragdoll. He had not stirred before Ben had been ejected from the wrecked tool shed.

Joshua had mentioned that they had known about this place for some time. Surely it was no coincidence that there had been a rock carved with the same symbol as his father's medallion amongst the debris that had fallen from the cells above the room.

His thoughts turned towards the Warden's speech upon finding the symbol. The portly puffy-cheeked man had mentioned *these people*. Ben wondered who *these people* were. Perhaps there was some group opposing the Lizardmen. Or perhaps the Warden was just referring to Ben's father and his friends.

Soft thuds resounded from the cafeteria's flight of stairs. The heads of two Watchers appeared, dragging something behind them. Ben saw a pair of feet in the guards' hands. His chains clinked and pulled taut as he strained for a better view. They were dragging the body of a man. Joshua's head thumped up the last step.

One of the men dropped a foot to wipe away sweat beading across his brow. "Would've been easier dragging him up the ramp to the treasury," he said, stretching his back.

"You gonna argue with Caleb?" said the other.

"Reckon he'll say anythin' worth hearin'?" the first man picked up

Joshua's leg again.

"If Caleb can't make him talk, the Lizardmen at the Desert Complex will."

Ben watched as they resumed dragging Joshua towards the door in the corner, pondering what life he and his brother would have left to return to even if they *did* manage to escape. After all that had happened, they could not simply return to a normal life. But he knew that they could not remain in captivity forever either.

They needed a new plan.

* * *

Ray's eyelids snapped open. His throat was dry. Beads of sweat ran down his face. He licked at the salty moisture just to wet his tongue. It only served to increase his thirst.

His memory was returning. He wished that it was not. He wished that his memories of breaking up with Dana would have stayed forgotten with his all too short-term amnesia brought on by the venom snare. She had cried so many tears that day. He did too, although he did not show it. They had been forced apart by something neither of them could control. He would give anything to have her back in his arms once more.

He glanced down at the tan-line around his thumb again. He needed the ring back, to prove that he had remained faithful. To prove that his promise was unbroken.

Ray refocused his thoughts on Spike. He envisioned the glint of silver on the guard's hand when he first woke up in this dreadful place. That sunglasses-wearing leather-vested Watcher had stolen the ring.

Rasping voices rose up from below, breaking his imagination about what he would do to Spike's hand when he caught him. The inmate sluggishly got to his feet and swayed uneasily for a moment, steadying his balance before moving closer to the grate. The others seemed to be asleep, or at least not stirring. The heat emitting from the furnace was enough to burn his ear.

Through the dancing heat waves, he could only just glimpse a hazy figure stalking back and forth in a room beneath Ethan and Kenneth's hotboxes. The voices were just whispers, hisses that he could not understand. *Maybe that's where the Lizardmen live*, Ray thought to himself. *Or maybe I'm just imagining the hisses.* The walls of his cell shimmered in the sweltering heat, bending this way and that. Rashad had warned them about heatstroke.

Keeping his eyes trained on the hazy figure, he ventured too close to the grill and scalded his ear. He heard it sizzle for a moment, his body too slow to react. After the sharp pain seared his skin, he leapt back to the other side of the small room, fully awake now. He cupped his throbbing ear, biting back a groan and rocking back and forth as he tried to take his mind off the pain.

Two guards passed by the barred window, dragging something through the corridor. Ray could not bring himself to investigate further. Soon, a metallic clang reverberated throughout the passage, and the Watchers' voices receded around the corner.

Maybe Ben was right, maybe something of greater value does *lie in the pit.* Questions filled his feverish head. *Why else would the Lizardmen freely give away prized jewels to the corrupt Mayor Gaspar, and to the Watchers who aren't here out of their own free will? Are they after the gold? Why would a bunch of talking alligators need gold?*

It was far too hot for him to think. It felt like he was inside a volcano. He lay down on the hot stone floor and shut his eyes, forcing himself to sleep; the only escape from this sauna.

He recalled visiting a volcano with his father and Ben when they were children. He and Ben were taken along with the documentary crew to a tropical paradise. The island – connected to the mainland by a small bridge – was bordered by white sands and neon blue waves. The documentary crew needed to be escorted by town police and volcanologists up to the volcano, yet Ray, Ben and their father remained behind.

Their father had an argument with the brunette woman who had given them shelter in her hollow-brick and bamboo house by the beach. Ray and Ben had eavesdropped, but Ben would have been too young to remember.

The argument had been something about a message their father was trying to deliver, which he refused to convey through her.

The tropical paradise fell away again, and Ray returned to the swamp.

He remembered how they had been ambushed, and their father's sacrifice, buying them time to escape, yet all in vain. He remembered carrying Ben to safety and removing the venom snare covering his face before rushing back through the mud-sodden swamp to where he had last seen their father.

He found the camera crew on their knees, surrounded by people wearing red. His father and Joshua refused to submit. Ray charged into the melee with a flying double-kick to the nearest Watcher, some redneck local. He flailed valiantly at the attackers, throwing wild punches left and right, until he was hit with a venom snare from the Deputy Sheriff.

He looked towards his father, who yelled, *"Take care of your little brother!"* before being struck down. At this, Joshua fell to his knees in surrender, and Ray staggered back to Ben, collapsing nearby.

Ray woke up, breathing hard. His shirtless body was covered in a sheen of sweat. Rivers of what little moisture his body had left streamed from his forehead, dripping onto the floor. He knew that he had been dreaming, but as he stared into the furnace, the events, the objects and the faces of the people in his dreams lingered in his vision.

His memory had returned.

* * *

Sarah returned to the cell house with a fresh bucket of water, her mop cleaned as best as she could.

"How easy would it be to escape through the barracks?" Ben asked in a low tone.

Sarah looked at him with admiration in her gentle eyes. Here he was, cuffed to the chains rack as punishment for attempting an escape, and now he sought to plan another.

"You really don't waste any time, do you?" she said, shaking her head with a smile. Ben blushed slightly, catching her sweet fragrance as she came closer to whisper her answer. "If you could manage to sneak past the Watchers that are on patrol, there are still those who are off-duty. The stairs in here lead up to their lounge area, and there are always a few guards in there."

Ben recalled the first time he had been bound to the chains rack, when he had seen a glimpse of the off-duty guards through the barracks door, swigging from pale brown bottles of ale just after breakfast.

"Could we run past?" asked Ben, feeling himself start to sweat at her proximity.

"We'd need the code to open the door to the garage," she said with a forlorn expression. "I've tried to read it when they punch it in, but I can only ever catch one or two numbers. There's a vehicle inside the garage. Caleb has the keys. He and Evander sometimes leave for a few hours at a time to buy materials for the quarry's retaining walls."

"We can escape on foot though, right?" asked Ben. "Can we reach the roof of the cell house without a code?"

"We can," said Sarah, "But there's a barbed wire fence around the whole building." Finished with her work, she slid the mop back into the bucket. They had been talking for so long, the floor around the chains rack must have been the cleanest in the entire prison. "Anything else I can help with?" she asked sweetly.

His chest tightened, but he pushed himself to ask. "The other day in the pit, when you hung up fishnets for the retaining walls... Levi tried to talk to you. What did he say?"

Sarah cringed at the mention of his name. "I don't like him," she said flatly. Ben breathed an inaudible sigh of relief. "He keeps bragging about how one day, he'll be some great Watcher, and all of the inmates will bow down to him. He asked me if I wanted to become a Watcher, too." Ben waited expectantly. Sarah caught his gaze, "Well of course I said no! But, does this mean..." Her eyebrows furrowed at him ever so slightly, "Were you watching me?"

She had put him on the spot. Ben looked away, his eyes too guilty to deny it. Before he could muster a reply, the barracks door opened.

A southern drawl addressed them, "Don't 'at just warm your heart?"

Ben looked up to see a man in a black cowboy hat and a matching button-up shirt sauntering down the stairs, followed by a team of people, all wearing red uniforms and bearing tools. Sarah's eyes widened, and she hurried out of the cell house with her mop and bucket.

"Aww, I ain't mean to break up y'all's little moment here," the southern man called after Sarah, but she was already gone.

The man stopped in front of the chains rack as the others marched downstairs into the cafeteria. Ben snapped his attention back to the group of red-clothed workers – he thought for a moment that he had glimpsed Sergei amongst them.

"What's the matter, boy, I ain't pretty enough for ya?" the southerner said. His protruding cheek bones and sun-damaged skin made his face resemble a rusty iron block.

Realisation of his identity dawned on Ben as the Sheriff tipped his hat back with a wide cheery grin.

15 - FRONT & CENTRE

He dreamt that he was falling face first. He could not move his arms. He was going to fall flat on his face and there was nothing to stop him.

Ben's eyelids snapped open, finding himself suspended above the stone floor of the cell house. He struggled against his chains for a brief moment of futility before straightening up. His chest throbbed from stretching his arms backwards, and his wrists glowed embers of red beneath his bonds. He had fallen asleep, held on an angle by the restraints. He did not know how long he had slept.

The last thing he could remember was seeing the Sheriff standing at the base of the now unoccupied set of stairs in front of him. He could not seem to recall the Watcher firing a venom snare at him, nor would the man have had any need to.

Ben's chains rattled again as he strained against the cuffs, just barely managing to wipe sleep from his eyes before looking around the cell house. The cells of the day shift inmates had all been shut, and the row of cells for the night shift workers now stood open. Voices of weary prisoners floated up from the cafeteria below. *It must be some time in the evening now,* he thought to himself.

At the sound of Ben's chains clinking together, heavy footfalls echoed up the steps from the cafeteria. An ominous black hat emerged from the flight of stairs, and the Sheriff sauntered up into the cell house with a no-nonsense expression, the hat upon his head casting a shadow over his protruding cheekbones from the spotlights above.

As he reached the top of the stairs, Sheriff Sullivan turned his gaze upon Ben, his rigid face breaking into a wide smile. "Well, I know I'm a handsome devil 'n' all, but I ain't *never* had no fella swoon over me like you done!"

Ben silently fumed, realising that he must have fainted at the sight of the Sheriff standing before him. *That's the* second *time I've fainted in the prison.*

The Sheriff sat upon the barracks stairs, stretched back, and then clasped his hands behind his head, his wide-brimmed hat falling low over his eyes. "Boy, I tell ya, it's been a long day. I'm about ready to hit 'at old dusty trail 'n' kick off the boots."

"*Hey!*" Ben yelled, rattling his chains in protest, disturbing the Watcher's rest.

The Sheriff tipped his hat back, lazily looking up at Ben. "Some'n' you wanna say, boy?"

"What happened to my father in the swamp? *What did you do to him!?*"

Sheriff Sullivan let the hat fall over his eyes again as he answered, "'at was mighty unfortunate. But I want you to know, I ain't the one who done killed him."

"Then who did?" Ben demanded.

The Sheriff simply kicked up one of his boots onto his other foot, whistling to himself.

* * *

Ray panted in the heat of the steam room. His breath was shallow. His lungs burned with each inhalation of the sulfuric gases corroding his airways. It felt as though he had just run a marathon. His shirtless body glistened with sweat. The floor sizzled in wisps of vapour with each drop of his perspiration falling upon the hearth of the furnace.

He looked around and wondered if the cell had been shrinking, or if the grate had grown. The fiery furnace loomed large over him, towering above the inmate. The red grill glowed like the surface of the sun, engulfing the entire room in an inferno. Incomprehensible rasps rose up from somewhere below, through the burning heat waves of the metal mesh.

"I gotta get out," he croaked through cracked lips.

He clambered to his feet slowly, a spell of dizziness coming over him. He stumbled to one side of the hotbox and slapped the wall with the clammy palm of his hand.

"I gotta get out," he repeated in a scratchy whisper.

Ray dragged his feet to the other side of the room and hit the wall again. He trudged back and forth, hoping that some opening would miraculously reveal itself to him.

Something escaped from his trousers waistband and fell down through the opening of his pants leg. He looked down at the object clattering upon the floor with distorted focus. It was a rock with the word *TODAY* inscribed upon it.

"Who's there?" he demanded, whirling about before realising that it was he who had concealed the rock within his uniform a lifetime ago.

He stooped to retrieve it, almost keeling over. The rock's rigid surface was cold to the touch, offering cool relief to his sweaty palms. He rolled the stone across his face and neck as though it was an ice cube, ignorant of its rough edges scraping his skin.

Ray stared for an immeasurable amount of time at the cell window and the three iron bars that separated him from freedom into the narrow corridor beyond. He tossed the rock from one hand to the other in silent contemplation. Its coolness already expended, he thought of a new purpose for the stone to serve.

He gripped the rock tighter in his hand, his knuckles turning white before slamming it against the hardwood door, a dull thud echoing in the tiny room.

Not even a splinter.

A red haze misted down over his eyes. He struck again and again and again. His hand began to bleed from the tremors of impact.

He paused for a brief moment to assess the damage. At some point in his feverish fury, his strikes had strayed from the door, hammered across the stone wall and scuffed fresh white marks into the corner. His boots stood in the ashes of his charred green shirt. Inspecting the door, he staggered back in disbelief. All he had managed to do was whittle a few scratches into the wood.

He spun around the room with giddy laughter. The walls, the red grate, and the cell window all flashed together in a whirling spiral. Lunacy overpowered logic, the rasping whispers from below becoming clear. They beckoned to him.

"There is only one path out of here," Rashad's voice echoed in his head.

With a sudden burst of mad inspiration, Ray threw his hand with the rock against the red grate. A metallic clang bounced his arm back like a springboard. He bashed at it again, harder. The clash of stone on steel filled the cell. He grinned in his delusional state, fancying himself a blacksmith, hammering in his forge. The others stirred at the commotion.

Jack attempted to pierce his cloud of unhinged madness, "Ray, calm down, mate!"

CRASH!

"You'll overheat!" Ethan yelled, "Sit down and take some deep breaths!"

CRASH!

"Ahoy!" Kenneth now tried to break his frenzy, "How 'bout you go back to arguin' with yourself in your sleep, boyo? I'd like to hear how the conversation ends!"

Their efforts failed, and they turned to calling for the Watchers instead.

* * *

The barracks door swung open, and two people clothed in red emerged carrying building materials. One, a thickset man with stubble, bore planks of wood over his broad shoulder and a pair of hammers. The other, a girl around Ray's age, with long black hair and caramel skin, carried boxes of nails and wore power tools around her exposed waist.

Ben wondered aloud where they could have come from as they passed by the chains rack and descended into the cafeteria below.

"What, you thought this was the only place 'em lizards are runnin'?" the Sheriff asked, "Warden only sends for 'em when things get bad. Even pulled me outta 'at backwater shanty town earlier'n usual. From one to another, I s'pose."

Ben did not like the idea of talking to the Sheriff, but he was the only one with the answers. "What are they doing here?" he asked.

Just as the Sheriff leaned forward to answer, panicked inmates' yells resounded from the passage beyond the door in the corner. He ignored their screams. "Well," he said, "Since y'all *insist* on not lettin' me catch some shut-eye, they're here to fix up 'at little mess y'all made downstairs. What you were oglin' at just now are the *Watcher Recruits*. They'll be sure to fix up 'at tool shed good 'n' proper so's some'n' like 'at don't happen again when it's their turn to guard you little miscreants."

The Sheriff sprang to his feet as crashes of metal began echoing louder and louder through the door in the corner. "Excuse me while I go check this out," he said, drawing the shock stick from his belt. "Never a dull moment 'round here," he muttered between murmured profanities.

The inmates' shouts were briefly amplified as the Sheriff opened the door. Ben strained against his cuffs, craning his neck to see inside the small passage, yet he could see nothing but a wall. He wondered what was happening to Ray and the others in the steam rooms. Their yells were muffled again as the Sheriff slammed the door behind him.

Just as one door closed, another flew open, and Lygia descended the barracks stairs with a wicked smile. Ben's chains rattled as he shivered openly at the sight of her blackened teeth glistening under the spotlights' glare.

"Oh, what joy!" she cried in her shrill voice, "*WHAT! JOY!*" she rushed towards him and pinched his cheek between her pasty gnarled fingers, "Together again, my dear boy!"

Inmates from the morning shift woke up at the sound of the banshee's wailing screeches. They moved to their cell windows where they watched with horror as Ben struggled to escape from Lygia's loathsome reach.

"I'm not your boy!" Ben yelled in disgust. Desperate to ward off her touch, he snapped his teeth at one of her long fingers.

Lygia withdrew her hand with a mocking cackle, raking his cheek with her claw-like fingernails, leaving bright red marks. "Oh, but you *are*, my dear boy, *you are!*" she shrieked, "No one... NO ONE LEAVES THE RACK!!" She paused to smile with her black teeth, "Not until they face punishment for their *ssins!* Now, how shall I chasstise you...?"

His heart hammered as she disappeared behind the chains rack. It felt like a giant spider vanishing from view; out of sight, yet ever present. And Ben *hated* spiders.

"Lygia!" a sharp voice boomed from the cafeteria steps. Caleb marched up into the cell house, scrutinising the faces of the prisoners watching behind bars. "Our inmates have finished their meals, and your shift is still in their cells!"

Ben shuddered again as Lygia's skeletal face came back into view. "But the boy musst be *punished*, Caleb," she wailed, *"WOULD YOU DENY HIS PUNISHMENT!?"*

"I shall see to it myself," Caleb answered, moving in front of the chains rack. "And I shall report your misplaced priorities to the Warden. Where's Gremlin?"

"Rifling through your belongings FOR ALL I CARE!" Lygia shrieked in a fit of rage, maddened by Caleb revoking her opportunity to inflict pain.

The stern guard turned to Ben. "Do not think this a kindness, inmate. If she had not been tardy to her shift, I would have encouraged her to leave permanent scars, as a reminder of the cost of insubordination," he said, before striking Ben's temple with the back of his hand.

* * *

"I gotta get out..." Ray rasped as the others continued calling for the guards to come.

CRASH!

"I gotta get out..."

CRASH!

"I gotta get out! *NOW!!*"

Ray leaned back and thrust all of his weight into the next strike, punching a hole straight through the corner of the grate, rending the iron so that half of the furnace stood on an angle, bent backwards into the heat vent.

He scalded his forearm on the twisted metal and accidentally dropped the rock into the depths of the shaft. He pulled his arm back into the cell as a wave of unfiltered steam blew up into the hotbox as if in answer to his offering, drowning out the panicked yells of his fellow inmates.

Breathing in the overwhelming sulfur and staring at the broken grate, Ray allowed his rage to take full control of his remaining senses. He clenched and unclenched his fists, readying himself to wrench the scorching metal from its foundations with his bare hands in his heatstroke madness.

The hardwood door slammed open from behind. Ray turned and a shock stick caught him across the neck, the volts of electricity travelling in a blue flash over his sweat-covered body. He grasped the pulsing baton and threw himself against the Watcher, the pair of them landing in a tangled heap in the corridor outside.

In a flurry of movement too fast for his bloodshot eyes to follow, Ray lost hold of the shock stick. A few swift blows to his crown took the fight out of him, and he was kicked over onto his backside.

Ray stared up at the man towering over him. A shadow seemed to hover above the Watcher's head. The man reached up into the circle of darkness, tipping his wide-brimmed black hat back.

The red glow from the broken grate illuminated the guard's grinning face. "How many times I gotta see you on your backside, boy?" the Sheriff said, staring down at him with a mixture of pity and amusement. "Sure ain't look like no picnic in there. If you could see yourself now..." he chuckled to himself.

Ray gazed up, a wave of hatred flowing through him at the sight of the Sheriff, one of the men who had been responsible for his father's death. But in his current state of dehydration, he was powerless to take vengeance.

His head lolled to one side, and he stared back at the steam room through the open entrance. The broken red grill stood both dreadful and inviting, flickering in flame.

"Now how's about we put all 'at extra energy towards some'n' useful?" Sheriff Sullivan said, taking Ray by his feet and dragging him out of the corridor.

They entered the small passage that led to the cell house. Ray shivered as he was hauled farther away from the warmth of the corridor, the cold stone floor sliding beneath him like a river of ice.

A row of empty cells entered his vision and the Sheriff dropped his legs. Ray tossed his head around to look at the other side of the room. He caught a glimpse of an inmate cuffed to the chains rack, his body leaning forward in slumber, suspended by his bindings.

"Benji!" Ray croaked, his throat parched.

His younger brother's chains clinked, but he gave no answer.

Sheriff Sullivan hoisted Ray up by his armpits. "Here ya go, nice 'n' easy now. They'll sort ya out." The Watcher let go of him for a moment, and the inmate swayed at the top of the stairs leading down to the cafeteria. "Ain't my problem, now…" he muttered, then, with a kick to Ray's backside, the Sheriff sent him head over heels down the staircase.

Ray rolled and tumbled down the flight of stone steps, flailing his limbs out before him to protect his head and neck. He landed hard on his elbow at the bottom of the stairs.

Sitting up to massage his numbed bone, he was suddenly aware of all of the prisoners staring back at him in the cafeteria, some with their spoons half-raised to their mouths. Ray flexed his arm and struggled to his feet. He felt exhausted and cold, but he still managed to stagger into the queue for some gruel.

Caleb, standing at the front of the cafeteria, noticed the new addition to the line-up. "Inmate!" he yelled, "Front and centre!"

Ray leaned sideways out of the queue, all eyes in the room upon him. He trudged to the front, some of the teens in the queue gasping at him as he passed by. Evander's prior contempt for him softened into pity as the shirtless inmate approached.

Caleb bore his steely gaze into Ray. "What are you doing out of the steam room?" he demanded. Ray looked up at him blankly. "*Speak*, prisoner!"

"Sullivan… he pulled me out," Ray's choked voice was barely more than a whisper.

"Gremlin," Caleb said without breaking eye contact, "Change his manacle to the current shift." Evander glanced sidelong at Caleb, yet said nothing. Rough hands worked around Ray's ankle, and he looked down to see a new manacle on his leg flashing with a blue light. "Don't think you've finished your punishment yet," said Caleb. He turned to Lygia, the pasty white Watcher with bug-eyes bulging from underneath her stringy black hair. "Assign this inmate to the mattock gang."

Lygia looked Ray up and down before throwing her head back and laughing in a shrill cackle, revealing her forked tongue nestled between two rows of blackened teeth.

In a jolt of revulsion, Ray turned back to the line. The other inmates were surprised by his lack of complaint in being assigned to a shift – on the mattock gang, no less – after spending time in one of the hotboxes. He even welcomed it with a smile. Anything was better than the steam rooms.

Ray caught sight of the water tap above the bench of bowls and spoons. He lurched towards it, expecting to have to shoulder his way through the other prisoners, yet they stepped back to let him pass. He swept the bowls aside and propped himself up on the wooden table, drinking straight from the tap. He coughed and spluttered at the first mouthful, and the second and third, the water like a foreign poison after his ordeal. He forced himself to drink though, feeling the liquid revive his organs as it washed down his gullet.

The other inmates gave him his space. Even the Watchers allowed him a moment's reprieve, Evander placing a restraining hand upon Gremlin's shoulder who had thought to smite Ray for his arrogance.

After quenching his thirst, Ray picked up a bowl and bore it before the gruel pot. He looked up to see that in Ava's place, Mara stood behind the cauldron. She looked over him with concern.

"Ray, what happened to you?"

He looked down at himself. Burns and scratches amid the grime on his shirtless body marked his skin. He wiped his face, and his hand revealed blood mingled with sweat. He dimly remembered rolling the cool rigid surface of the *TODAY* rock across his face and neck. It had given him such relief earlier, yet now the other prisoners stared at him like he was a carrier of some highly-infectious plague.

Mara ladled him his gruel in the silence.

Ray coughed and then said loud enough for all to hear, "I cut myself shaving." He squared his jaw at the Watchers.

Caleb snorted, narrowing his flint grey eyes back at the prisoner. The other inmates whooped and cheered at Ray's defiance as he trudged towards an empty seat, yet they still avoided him, having already heard what had befallen the other instigators of the rebellion.

Ray lifted the gruel up to his mouth and savoured the taste of sustenance, foul as it was. He leaned towards the nearest inmate. "What shift?" he rasped.

"Morning," the boy mumbled, averting his gaze.

Morning. Ray could not believe it. They had been in the steam rooms since just after breakfast, and now it was midnight. He could only imagine how long the others would have to stay in the hotboxes.

As if on cue, Kenneth rolled and tumbled down the flight of stairs, landing on his bad leg with an eloquently constructed chain of curse words at the Sheriff, who chuckled up out of sight in the cell house above.

Kenneth scrambled to his feet and limped towards the gruel pot, the queue having already dissipated. He lay back on the wooden table and drank from the water tap in similar fashion to what Ray had done. Mara slopped a spoonful of gruel into his bowl as his manacle was changed over.

Inmates avoided eye contact and shuffled away from him as well, branded as another of the rebellion's ringleaders. Kenneth sat down a few seats away from Ray. He did not appear as dehydrated, although the Irish prisoner had not had the same bright idea of burning his shirt upon his arrival in the steam room.

"How's your leg?" Ray croaked.

Kenneth glared at him, "It was a lot better yesterday, boyo."

Ray raised an eyebrow. "Don't blame me for what happened."

"You're right, it was all *Ben's* idea, wasn't it?" Kenneth said angrily.

"You leave my brother outta this," said Ray, getting to his feet.

All eyes in the cafeteria turned towards Ray and Kenneth arguing back and forth, and the inmates began drumming the tables in anticipation for a fight.

* * *

Ben slumped forward, his entire body suspended in place by his restraints again. Caleb had knocked him unconscious, and he had been sleeping ever since. It was only a light sleep though, as he stirred at the sounds of inmates clamouring for a fight down in the cafeteria.

His chains rattled as he blinked groggily. The barracks stairs before him seemed to rock from side to side like the deck of a ship sailing through stormy seas. He fought the urge to vomit as he stood upright, especially after Sarah had spent so long cleaning the floor.

The Sheriff chuckled to himself nearby, standing at the top of the stairs to the cafeteria, watching the scene below. He turned towards Ben. "Well, it's about time you get back to your cell 'n' quit askin' me questions." The Watcher withdrew a set of keys and released the prisoner. Before Ben could rub at his raw wrists, Sheriff Sullivan seized him by the arm and dragged him to the centre of the cell house. "Now tell me, boy, which one's yours?"

Ben weakly pointed towards his cell in the corner of the room with his free hand, the only cell with a fresh pair of inmate uniforms and a clean chamber pot beside the door.

"Day shifter, huh? Y'know, you could'a lied and had a spot on the night shift if you wanted, get you out the sun for a while," the Sheriff grinned. "But you ain't no liar, are ya, boy?" The cheery man considered him for a moment before making up his mind. "Naw, you ain't got the guts for it. Speakin' o' lyin', I got me a poker game tonight," he said, hauling Ben in the direction of the cell, "And I do so sorely think it unbecomin' to leave a prisoner unattended."

Sheriff Sullivan unlocked the door and flung it open.

Ben's eyes widened at the sight of the village boy in his tattered brown shirt and flip flops crouching before them in the doorway, ready to attack, yet the Sheriff simply shoved Ben forward so that they both fell to the floor of the cell in a heap.

Chuckling, the Watcher threw the fresh uniforms at the pair of prisoners and kicked the clean chamber pot inside the cell. The village boy scrambled out from underneath Ben to attack again, but he was too late. The door slammed shut just before he could reach it.

The villager turned around with a disappointed expression as Ben dusted himself off. "I'm wait so long for a door to open," he said in a harmonious Americanised accent, and yet with broken English.

"I'm sorry," said Ben, then, placing his hand upon his chest, he said slowly, "My name is Ben Rauder, what is your name?"

The boy laid his hand across his own chest and said with pride, "Me, Juanico Ricardo Vicente."

"Wow," Ben smiled, forgetting the dull aches of his throbbing head and wrists. "That's a long name, do you have a nickname?"

"My teacher say to me, *Juan*, but yucks, I don't like. I like *Nico*," he beamed back.

"Nico, you have very good English, where did you learn it?"

"Thank you so much, I learn on my school," he bowed solemnly, before brightening up with another smile, "And then I learn much more in a movies!"

"Nico, can you tell me where we are?" asked Ben, returning his smile.

"We're in the mountain. The other side to the volcano," he answered as if it was common knowledge.

"No, I mean, *where* are we? What country is this?"

"Philippines!" Nico said excitedly. "You don't know where are you?

We're in the Philippines!"

Ben's knees quavered and he sat down on the lower bunk bed to stop himself from falling. He knew that they were far away from home, but he did not think that they would be *on the other side of the world.*

16 - ROYAL FLUSH

"Bang on. Bang on. Bang on!"

The cafeteria was alive with inmates chanting and thumping tabletops and clambering over their stone block seats for a better view of Ray and Kenneth. The two former allies faced off against each other, the Irish prisoner laying the blame on the Rauder Brothers for what had happened to his leg during the rebellion.

Ray and Kenneth paused, glancing around the room to see inmates and Watchers alike jostling for the best view before the pair of prisoners went head to head. Not to be gambled upon for everyone else's entertainment, the two shared a begrudging nod and slowly sat back down, still glaring at each other. The sound of drumming ceased, and was replaced by a collective groan of disappointment.

Lygia leapt up onto one of the tables and shrieked in a high-pitched wail, her forked tongue giving her a lisp. "Sstop sstuffing your faces, *it'ss time for work!*" she stepped on the arm of an inmate who had a spoon raised halfway to his mouth. "DID I SSAY YOU COULD FINISH YOUR MEAL!?" she screamed, kicking him off his seat. "Get up! *Get working!!*"

Inmates leapt off their stone blocks and followed Gremlin and the other guards out of the cafeteria. Lygia jumped over to Ray and Kenneth's table, standing in between the pair of prisoners. The sickly green-skinned woman was dressed in layers upon layers of black rags, with grey streaks through her stringy black hair and blackened teeth to match.

Ray wondered to himself what her favourite colour might be.

With resentment burning in his eyes, Kenneth picked up his bowl and hurled it against the wall, gruel splashing down to the floor. Both inmates rose out of their seats and trudged out into the corridor.

A group of people donned in red uniforms marched in and out of the tool shed, hauling loads of rubble and building materials. The corridor was filled with the sounds of sawing and hammering. Makeshift workbenches had been set up haphazardly throughout the corridor, where they were busy cutting planks of wood down to size.

Must be inmates from another prison, come to clean up the mess. Ray stopped in his tracks, remembering the red group of people who had ambushed them in the swamp alongside the Sheriff and the rednecks. Although he could not recall the faces of those responsible, he knew that one of them had killed his father. He watched the red group shuffling to and fro, hoping to recognise someone.

"Ignore the Watcher Recruitss, unless you want to join them!" Lygia shrieked from behind. "Go sstraight down to the pit, where your tools are waiting!"

Suddenly, Ray no longer feared being sent to the Desert Complex. He would only see it as an opportunity to find out who killed his father and bring about a swift end, or a slow one, to the person responsible.

As the morning shift marched through the corridor, Ray and Kenneth glimpsed a familiar face in the red group.

Kenneth, feeling reckless in his frustration and hunger, called out to him, "Ahoy, Chubby Chekhov! Did you put on some weight, you big tub of lard?"

Sergei turned with a twisted gleam in his pig-like eyes. He dropped the bundle of planks he was carrying and swung a hammer at Kenneth, catching him off-guard in the meat of his shoulder. Kenneth yelped in pain and fell to his knees, clutching at his upper arm.

Ray came to his defence, throwing a punch at Sergei, yet his prolonged dehydration in the steam rooms still dulled his agility, and Sergei dodged the blow. Ray's swing betrayed him, his momentum sending him to the floor at Sergei's feet.

"Sergei is here to fix problem!" the Russian skinhead declared, producing a galvanised steel nail from his pudgy hand. He placed the tip of the nail upon Ray's forehead, and then forced the kneeling inmate's head against the wall. Ray grabbed Sergei's hand in protest, yet the goon's arm was too heavy to cast aside. "Say mercy to Sergei!" he yelled, lifting the hammer above his head with a mad grin.

Ray's eyes widened, his legs kicking out frantically.

Just before Sergei could swing the hammer, he was spear-tackled by a man from the side. Ray looked up, and for a moment, he thought he caught a glimpse of Rashad. He rubbed at his eyes to see that his saviour was just some other beefed-up Watcher Recruit.

The pair of red-uniformed workers scrambled to their feet.

"You *dare* to challenge Sergei!?"

"You didn't give him a chance to say *mercy*," the thickset man with stubble replied.

The Russian skinhead lifted his hammer again, this time aiming at the new challenger. The burly man disabled Sergei with a flurry of movement, twisting his wrist behind his back and forcing him to drop the hammer before chopping him in between his blocky bull-neck and shoulder with an open palm, sending him crumbling to his knees like a broken stack of tiles.

Sergei reached for the hammer again, yet before he could clutch it, a long trident was thrust dangerously close to his throat. A previously unseen reptilian warrior – not Pythrisse – emerged from the tool shed, charged with the supervision of the Watcher Recruits. Sergei raised his hands and smiled in surrender, focusing his twisted gaze upon Ray, who had been at his mercy a mere moment ago.

Ray and Kenneth got to their feet, Kenneth refusing Ray's assistance even as he struggled to shift his weight onto his one good leg. They dusted themselves off and tramped outside into the hot night with the rest of the morning shift.

Only one section of the pit was illuminated by the floodlight, the area resembling a bright slice of pie within a circular tray of darkness. Lygia and Gremlin took their seats underneath the umbrella, in shadow even from the light of the moon and stars stretched out across the dark velvet curtain of night sky.

"No wonder they're so pale," Ray said aloud as they marched down the slope. His insult went unanswered. He had already spent enough time in the steam room, any more time in the hotboxes and they would kill him.

The inmates trudged over to where the mattocks and shovels awaited them in front of a shelf of rock. Ray picked up a mattock, and Kenneth grabbed a shovel set in the ground, as instructed by the Watchers.

Ray lifted the mattock overhead and brought it down upon the shelf of rock, cleaving through the dirt, rocks crumbling at the impact. He raised the mattock again for another strike, admitting that this felt more natural to him than what shovelling ever had. He turned back to look at Kenneth, who clumsily dug his shovel into the piles of earth steadily building up.

Kenneth misjudged the distance to one of the minecarts behind the shovel gang and threw his load of dirt just short of the barrow. He glared at Ray, "How 'bout we swap, boyo?"

"NO SSWITCHING TOOLS!" Lygia shrieked from the veil of darkness beyond the floodlight, "ESSPECIALLY NOT *YOU!!*"

Kenneth cursed under his breath and continued shovelling.

* * *

Ben sat upon the dingy lower bunk with his new cellmate, still grappling with the idea of being held in a prison halfway across the world. It was just past midnight, the moon sailing high in the star-studded sky, shining its pale light down through the shaft in the ceiling.

In his silent defeat, Ben glumly watched Nico, the boy from the village, venturing into the square patch of moonlight to inspect the chamber pot. He stooped to drink the water from the metal bucket.

"No, don't drink that!" Ben exclaimed. Nico looked up at him enquiringly, the water cupped halfway to his mouth. Ben pointed at the chamber pot, "That's the *toilet* bowl, don't drink from there, it's not good for you," he warned, which was more than what Little Danny had ever done for him.

From his squatted position, Nico examined the water underneath the skylight, the warm night sending a pleasant breeze down into the cell. It was then that he saw the oily remnants of detergent rippling in the water. The village boy dropped the water back into the rusty bucket and dried his hands off on his ripped jeans.

Ben picked up the pair of fresh uniforms that lay crumpled upon the floor. He handed Nico a set of clothes, and asked him not to look as he turned around to undress. He thought to ask his new cellmate if he could have the lower bunk bed to avoid hitting his head on the cell's low ceiling, but this would have to wait until after he had tested an idea that he had formulated while cuffed to the chains rack.

"Your skin so white," Nico mumbled, folding his old clothes upon the lower bunk bed.

"I told you not to look!" said Ben, crossing his arms over his pale skinny chest, yet the awestruck boy could not turn away.

"I only see so white in a movie," said Nico, "And if the men come down the mountain."

"Which men?" asked Ben, pulling his shirt on and sitting down beside Nico's old clothes.

"They come our village, and then go in a bar," said Nico, sitting against the wall upon the floor.

Ben had a mental image of Watchers like Cormac and Leon taking full advantage of Lungsod's hospitality. Even as he imagined it, he thought he could hear their callous laughter floating down from above.

"What do you know about this place?" asked Ben.

"In my village, it's not allowed for coming here," Nico replied.

"But you came here anyway," said Ben, furrowing his eyebrows. "Or did they capture you?"

"My Papa say the jungle is haunted," said Nico, speaking gravely as he leaned forward. "My Papa say the *Aswang* will going to eat me if I come in the jungle. Many people already try to come, and then, never come back. But me, I like to explore. Last day, Lungsod don't have a power, it's brownout."

"You mean *blackout?*" asked Ben.

"Yeah," said Nico, "But here, we say a brownout. Last night, I sneak out. Nobody see me in my village. I come to the jungle, and then!" Ben raised his eyebrows. "I'm waiting for the sun. I don't like the *Aswang* to eat me. And then, in the morning, I climb the mountain. I see the…" he stood up, mouthing with difficulty, "*Volcano... Monitoring... Station...* It still have a light. But when I look in my village, still brownout."

The volcano monitoring station must be a Watcher outpost of some kind, like the rednecks' house in the swamp, Ben thought to himself. He looked out through the cell door window where the spotlights illuminated the cell house. *There must be a backup generator somewhere within the prison. Maybe Rashad was right about that after all.*

"I try to explore the road only," said Nico. "I like to see the other side to the volcano. And then, there's a many yelling. The men in the station try to catch me, but me, I'm so fast. And then, they shoot me." He covered his face and re-enacted his struggle with the venom snare, choking to the floor. He looked up, "I thought I'm dead. The *Aswang* will going to eat me now. And *then!*" Nico shrugged and sat back against the wall, "No more, I'm here."

They stared at the floor in silence for a while, until Ben suddenly straightened up. Recalling the idea that had occurred to him while he was on the chains rack, he took the sweat-stained bed sheet from the upper bunk and, moving Nico's old clothes aside, he laid it over the sheet on the lower bunk. Nico stood up with a puzzled expression as Ben folded the double layer of sheets lengthways.

"I need your help," said Ben. "I think I know a way to escape."

Hearing that magic word, Nico obliged in a flash, taking one end of the linen. Soon, they had rolled the bed sheets into a makeshift rope. It was not thick, as the sheets were barely large enough to cover their small mattresses to begin with, yet Ben deemed that it would have to do.

Stepping up onto the lower bunk, he began to feed the bundled linen through the skylight's bottom set of bars.

Nico tugged at Ben's shirt with a disapproving look, "Give me," he said, holding out his hands.

Bemused, Ben gave him the cloth. The village boy pulled the makeshift rope out from the iron bars, the thin material unfurling at one end as it sailed down to the floor.

Squatting, Nico hurriedly twisted the sheets back together, ensuring that they were tightly wound. He held up one end of the rope to Ben so that it did not unfurl again. He then dipped the other end into the chamber pot water, wetting the sheets so that they would retain their shape.

Nico ran the entire course of the cotton cable through the water. The bundle of sheets, wet upon the floor, now looked as though a long snake had slithered into the cell. He beamed up at Ben, handing him back the rope.

Water dripped from the fabric as Ben tested its strength. He reached up again to feed the rope through the rusty iron bars, coiling it around the one in the middle and giving the other end to Nico. They pulled down on either side. Nothing. Nico jumped and forced his bodyweight down upon the rope, causing Ben to soar up and hit the ceiling with his head.

They tried again, jumping in synchronisation this time. The stone surrounding the bar cracked a little as it gave way, but it did not break off. Ben rubbed his head, part in thought, and part in massaging the throbbing pain atop his skull.

Just as Ben was considering using the bunk bed as a counterweight, Nico pointed to the floor, "Just try to pull, I will going to try something," he said with another burst of inspiration.

Ben pulled the rope down using his weight, and Nico's feet lifted off the floor. Ben wound the rope around his arms and stuck his legs beneath the bunk to keep Nico suspended. In midair, the village boy flipped upside down and planted his feet on the ceiling like a sleeping bat. Ben gritted his teeth as Nico pulled himself up into a crouching position. Ben thrust his knees up into the bed frame as Nico pushed out with his feet.

Cracks appeared in the ceiling, and dust motes floated down through the shaft of moonlight. Nico's veins popped out in his exertion, and the iron bar snapped from its foundations. The rope acted like a slingshot, launching the iron bar down. Ben threw himself to the side as the bar narrowly missed his head. It landed with a loud metallic clatter and rolled away. Nico twisted his body in midair so that he fell on his side.

They grinned at each other. *It worked!*

"You 'ear that?" a voice came down from above.

Ben held a finger to his mouth.

"Hear what?" a gruff baritone growl answered.

"Thought I 'eard something."

Nico stowed the rope out of sight of the skylight shaft. Ben got to his feet, picked up the iron bar and tried to refit it, but it would not take hold. He listened carefully. No footsteps.

"I ain't hear a thing. We still playin' or you just tired o' losin'?"

"Yeah, quit stallin', Mac, it's your turn to deal."

The pair of inmates heard the faint shuffle of cards, and they breathed a sigh of relief, but there was no turning back now. If they stopped, the Watchers would soon discover the damage in the morning. And if they waited until the guards were gone, the sheets would dry out and lose their pulling strength.

Ben examined the water in the chamber pot. Roughly a third remained.

Together, they laid the thin musty mattresses from the bunk beds out on the floor. They pulled the remaining two bars from the bottom of the skylight's shaft, both the bars and Nico landing with soft thuds.

Then it was time for the bars at the top of the skylight. They were lucky – only a thin ledge of stone skirted each end of the bars, so they could still pull the bars down, but the cotton cable was not long enough for Ben to serve as an anchor on the floor again.

With some deliberation, and taking care not to make too much noise, they dragged the bed frame underneath the skylight and placed a mattress on the floor on either side for both of them to land on. Standing upon the top bunk, Ben was able to reach up and coil the rope around the first bar.

The only problem was that the whole process of rearranging the tiny room was very time consuming, and the sheets had lost most of their moisture. Working quickly, they planted their feet on the ceiling on either side of the skylight, straining and wrenching at the rope.

The bar snapped off, and when the rope stretched taut across the top bunk, the inmates still holding both ends of the cable crashed into each other through the centre of the bed frame. They smiled ecstatically at each other as they lay upon the wooden slats of the lower bunk.

Wasting no time, Ben climbed up and coiled the rope around the second bar, and again, they wrenched it free, yet this time, when the cable pulled taut across the top bunk, they heard a *RRRIP!*

As if to mock their misfortune, Cormac's voice descended from above, "Royal flush! 'and it over!"

They inspected the length of rope – it was only slightly damp now. They had taken too long. Nico pulled the rope over to where the chamber pot lay. Ben watched with hope as the villager dipped one end into the water with a shallow splash, and running it gently through his hands, he wet roughly half of the cotton cable. He tipped the chamber pot upside down for its last few drops before looking up at Ben with a morose expression.

* * *

As the shift wore on in the quarry, Cormac's booze-fuelled laughter echoed from above with glee, reverberating down into the pit from the viewing deck.

Ray squinted up to see the faint outline of the sun, even in the night, waving from the strange flag fluttering in the soft breeze on the surface. Rashad's words echoed in his mind again, *"Like an eye watching us all in our toil."*

A silhouette appeared next to the flagpole, casting a shade of darkness across the stars glittering overhead. "I'm the king of the world!!" Cormac slurred his drunken declaration.

Flying objects rained down into the pit, erupting in explosions of glass shards. Ray and the other inmates covered their heads and crouched behind the rock shelf. Watchers laughed from the viewing deck, and Lygia's shrill cackling filled the pit, drowning out Gremlin's amused squeals.

Objects continued to fall upon the dirt floor, and Ray chanced a glance from between his fingers to see fragments of pale brown bottles lying all around them. Another shattered against one of the minecarts and he shut his eyes again. His eyesight was bad enough.

The hail of glass bottles eventually subsided, and Lygia screeched, "Did I *ssay* your shift is over? *No?* THEN WHY AREN'T YOU ALL WORKING!?"

Amidst the profanity amongst the prisoners, Ray caught one inmate calling her the *Wicked Witch of the Morning Shift*, her shrill banshee-like wails spurring them to resume digging.

Ray recalled having thought that the screams he had heard on previous nights had been shrieks of pain coming from the female cell house, yet now he realised that it had been Lygia's terrible wailing voice that had kept him awake at night. He found strange comfort and revulsion in the thought as he swung the mattock.

* * *

Ben stared up at the final bar. They would not be able to fit through. Even with his skinny frame, he had barely managed to climb up through the shaft to coil the rope around the bars.

Accepting defeat, he looked past the iron bar towards the stars in the clear night sky. *If only it was the rainy season.* Maybe this small window of stars each night was the closest he would ever get to freedom. That is, if he would even have the privilege of a skylight after the Watchers discovered the damage they had done the next morning.

ZZZIP!

Ben looked over at Nico. A thin stream glittered in the moonlight, landing with a padded patter on the coil of linen beneath him.

Nico turned with a smile. "We will not going to sleep here tonight, it's

235

not need for this one," he said, indicating the bundle of sheets. Ben shot up out of the bunk bed, lifted from his misery. Nico stopped, stooped and rolled the cable over. "Just try to put more to the other side."

"Okay," said Ben, wholeheartedly obliging. "But this time, really, *don't look.*"

He relieved himself, already overjoyed that they were going to escape. They could race down to Lungsod, find the hardware store owner, send for help and break out the other inmates from the prison. He would make all the headlines. He imagined himself posing for photos, renowned as a hero for freeing so many lost adolescents and kidnapped teens who had been forced into manual labour, exposing corruption in the local authorities, and maybe Sarah would even stand by his side as he accepted his awards.

His fantasy stopped at the end of his stream, and only one question remained: *how are we going to pick up the linen?*

He shook and turned back to Nico, who had already picked up his old clothes. He wrapped his tattered brown shirt and ripped jeans around the pungent end of the rope before climbing upon the top bunk. With catlike flexibility, he managed to avoid the rope's touch in the skylight as he coiled the soiled linen around the final bar before lowering himself down on the other side of the bunk bed.

They wrestled with the ends of the rope, dislodging the last bar that stood between them and freedom. They crashed into each other a third time and Nico quickly cast aside his end of the rope, Ben releasing his side so that the bundled sheets slipped down into a corner of the cell.

Ben climbed up the bed frame with shaky limbs.

Beneath him, Nico murmured, *"Bang on. Bang on. Bang on..."*

With his knees wobbling as he straightened up, Ben nervously poked his head above the upper limits of the skylight's shaft. He shot down again under cover with barely a glimpse of the roof, about-faced, and tried again. All he saw was a table and empty chairs. The entire roof was free of the Watchers.

He hoisted himself up and onto the roof.

No sirens. No shouts of alarm.

The night sky was so open and beautiful. Stars were infinitely studded across the black veil above from horizon to horizon. On one side of the open stretch of concrete on the cell house's roof stood what Ben assumed to be the barracks. He could see lights emanating from inside the glass window panes overlooking the roof, but nothing stirred from within.

Turning, he saw the remains of the Watchers' poker game: beer-stained cards, cigarette butts and upturned chairs. The wooden viewing deck lay beyond, the prison's strange flag looking out over the quarry pit where an artificial light radiated upwards into the night sky.

Ben laid his eyes upon the barbed wire fence that encircled the complex just beyond the edges of the roof, separating the dull grey building from the sea of shadowy green jungle bordering on all sides. He had planned for the barbed wire fence too.

Bending over the square hole he had emerged from, he could see Nico beaming up at him. He whispered to his fellow escapee to hand him a mattress. Nico disappeared for a moment, rolling one into a bundle and reappearing to push it up through the skylight shaft. For the first time, Ben was grateful that the mattresses were so thin. Setting it aside, he reached down and helped Nico up.

"Stay low, okay?" said Ben, indicating the barracks windows on the other side of the roof.

Nico nodded solemnly, yet neither of them could contain their excitement. Their hearts leapt within their chests as they crawled across the cell house roof, dragging the mattress along with them.

They passed by other skylights as they worked their way eastward. Ben decided that they should steer clear of the grates in the roof, just in case Levi was awake and listening to their faint scratches along the concrete surface.

He smiled to himself. He had planned everything out so perfectly during his time upon the chains rack. Another moment of gratitude passed in his mind for not realising the flaw in the prison's design until *after* his previous cellmate had been relocated. Cormac's son would have been halfway to the barracks by now, announcing the escape.

Passing over the damaged and unoccupied cells above the tool shed, they reached the edge of the roof. The grass below was long and untended, but it was only a short distance from the building to the barbed wire fence. They tossed the mattress down onto the turf below with a *WHOOSH* and a soft thud, flattening the long stalks of overgrown grass before lowering themselves down the side of the building, landing gently on top of the mattress.

Nico looked sidelong at Ben with admiration.

Ben moved to step off the mattress, yet the villager shot out his hand with a sudden change in his expression.

"Wha–"

Nico shushed him. "Just try to hear for a snake," he whispered.

The pair of inmates stood wreathed in darkness upon the mattress for a few mere moments, but to Ben, it seemed like an eternity. Tropical insects within the shadowy rainforest beyond the fence chirped noisily, clicking their mandibles as large bats swooped from tree to tree, the nocturnal hunters in search of prey. The ocean's waves clashed against cliffs in the middle distance, and the earth-scraping noises of some less fortunate inmates digging below in the quarry rose up to the surface.

Satisfied, Nico nodded at Ben.

They hoisted the mattress up onto the fence, smothering the barbs on the top rows of wire. Scaling over the thin mattress, Ben could still feel the spikes jabbing into his hands, but it was a small price to pay for the freedom that awaited them on the other side.

Ben landed upon his feet, and already, the sense of liberation washed over him. The air felt cleaner, fresher, and less muggy. His body felt lighter, as if he was riding upon a cloud.

Nico dropped down beside him.

They were standing at the edge of the jungle now. Vehicle tracks over flattened grass led farther eastward into the depths of the shadowy jungle.

"We'll going to take the road?" asked Nico. "Maybe the *Aswang* will wait in the trees."

"The *Aswang* isn't in the trees," said Ben, not even sure what the *Aswang* was. "They caught you on the *road*, remember?"

Nico looked at the jungle's undergrowth apprehensively. Ben was just as terrified of the eerie woods, maybe even more so, but he refused to let his fears be responsible for their recapture.

* * *

Down in the pit, Ray felt a clump of earth break on his backside. He ignored it. Inmates working around him laughed. Another hit him and sprayed over his shoulder. Ray turned back to see Kenneth with a shovel full of dirt, ready to lob another at him a third time.

"Throw it, see what happens," Ray dared him, practising a baseball bat swing with his mattock.

Kenneth reconsidered openly throwing the dirt at him, tossing the load into a nearby cart with a look that promised *this won't be the last time*. Ray turned back to the rock shelf and swung his mattock with renewed vigour, imagining Kenneth's uninjured leg splayed out before him with each strike.

He gritted his teeth, remembering watching Ben being beaten by bullies, small as his tormentors were, yet Ray would do nothing to keep them away from his brother. He had wanted to see Ben fight for himself, as he thought that even if Ben *lost* each fight, he would still become stronger from the experience.

He had wished for Ben to become independent. Having no mother, and a travelling father, Ray was the only person who Ben could depend upon. And if something were to happen to him, Ben would have had no one else to look to for help. He recalled judging that his inaction would eventually benefit his little brother, even if it hurt them both.

Another volley of dirt struck him in the back. The other inmates laughed as they, too, threw dirt at him, as though somehow the rebellion had failed because of Ray. Their earlier ovation at his defiance towards the Watchers in the cafeteria had quickly turned to disrespect, at Kenneth's encouragement.

He could feel the rage building up inside him. The heat caused his clammy hands to slip, the humid night worse than the arid day. He clenched the mattock's handle tighter. Buzzing gnats incessantly bit at his shirtless body, feeding on the inmate's straining muscles as he worked through the early hours of the morning. The ear-piercing screeches of Lygia, the banshee above them, sounded like a kettle reaching boiling point. All of this served to fuel the fire of his rage, and Kenneth had been the spark to ignite it, disappointed with the outcome of the rebellion.

It seemed that all of the inmates would direct the searing frustration of their crushed hopes of escape towards him. Ray thought that he would only appear more vulnerable to their flame each time he was engulfed. *The burn will have to stop here.* He could not afford to defy the Watchers and defend himself from the other inmates at the same time. He could not give the blaze the impression that he was flammable. Ray had to make sure that these inmates knew *they shouldn't be playing with fire.*

With only one more toss of dirt at his back being his breaking point, the inmates were distracted by the sound of the water carts trundling from the top of the quarry down into the pit. Ray chose to bide his time, making a mental note of each one of the inmates propping up their shovels in the dirt – four in total.

The prisoners gathered around the carts. No orderly line was established. No inspection of calluses took place.

Ray elbowed his way to the front, the physical activity required by the intensive labour had restored his strength quicker than any amount of water or rest ever could. He drank fast before he was flung out of the pack by the other inmates. They crowded around the carts like animals at a waterhole.

He got to his feet and, marking his targets, he seized advantage of their distraction. Balling his hands into fists of fury, he landed his first blow into the kidney of one unsuspecting inmate. Another turned his head to look down at his fallen friend, and Ray clocked him across his slack jaw.

He spotted his next victim, who cried in alarm, pushing farther into the pack of prisoners standing around the water carts.

Kenneth limped across Ray's path. "What d'you think you're doing, boyo?"

Ray front-kicked him just above his good leg's kneecap. Kenneth dropped to the floor with the blow in an effort to prevent his knee from completely snapping in the wrong direction. The others scattered as Ray pursued the last inmate, backing him into a water cart. Snatching him up by his legs, Ray dunked the inmate headfirst into the remaining water.

All of the prisoners squealed in pain as volts of electricity burned through their manacles. Ray's leg buckled, but he continued to hold the thrashing teen underwater. Letting his anger take full control, he drew up his own pulsing leg, his manacled foot almost over the edge of the cart.

A new wave of electricity surged through Ray's shirtless backside and he fell backwards. Still gripping his victim's feet, they both went down together, tipping the water cart over and splashing themselves with muddy sediment.

The electrical volts coursing through their manacles ceased before the water could come into contact with their ankles, and Gremlin's pallid pointed face looked down upon Ray, his vicious malice mingled with fear.

Ray jumped to his feet, shoved the short Watcher aside – even as he held the shock stick and the sparker remote – and he roared at the quavering inmates, "Come on, throw some more dirt! I DARE YOU!!"

He marched over to his mattock and resumed work, striking with enough ferocity to tear craters out of the rock shelf. Everyone in the pit held their silence. Even Lygia kept her mouth shut. Kenneth stared in bewilderment at Ray, seeing him in a new light.

All of the prisoners cautiously picked up their tools and moved to the other end of the rock shelf, the inmates and Watchers alike avoiding Ray as much as possible.

* * *

Ben and Nico stayed a short distance away from the winding path as it gradually turned from flattened grass to a dirt road. Covered by the line of trees, Nico led Ben steadily downhill in the direction of Lungsod. The village boy's flip flops slapped against the heels of his feet as they ran.

It felt good to run, crashing through the wet grass and vegetation underneath the sprawling canopies of dark palm trees. Ben wondered why he had not engaged in physical activity more often, before he and Ray had been captured.

Away on their left, on the other side of the dirt road, he could hear waves breaking on rocks somewhere far below, their crashes echoing up from the foot of a cliff facing the ocean. Salty sea air wafted inland, borne on a light breeze over the expanse of the ocean.

The moon behind them was descending towards the horizon, and the night sky was beginning to give way to the dawn approaching in the east. As the trees on their right lessened in density, revealing thick shrubs and vegetation beyond, the vast shape of a volcano began to materialise, catching the first rays of sunlight upon its eastern rim.

Nico stopped as they came to a break in the tree line. He turned to Ben and grinned, "We will going to the other side, see?" he pointed ahead.

Through the trees on the other side of the now gravel road, Ben could see a faint glimpse of Lungsod. Small dots of people were stocking fishing boats docked at the harbour and setting up market stalls in the early hours of the morning. Church bells pealed across the small town to announce the dawn service, and roosters crowed in response.

"Just one thing before we go," said Ben. "What does *bang on* mean?"

"In Filipino," Nico smiled, "*Bangon* means *Rise*."

** * **

As time wore on and daylight began to grow in the sky above, Ray's limbs weighed down heavily with the lactic acid swimming through his body. The chemical reactions releasing energy into his muscle fibres dispersed more inhibiting acid with each swing of the mattock. He persisted anyway. To show weakness now would only serve to make him appear vulnerable again.

He lifted his mattock above his head, when suddenly, a man's yell emitted from the viewing deck. A ragdoll of a body was cast down into the pit. Catching hold of the fishnet retaining wall, the falling man managed to slow his descent somewhat. The fishnet gave way under his weight, and wooden pegs ripped out of the quarry wall as he dropped the remaining distance to the pit floor, causing a small landslide to fall on top of him.

Joshua's bloodied face was engulfed by dirt, right where Ray would have swung his mattock only a mere moment ago. Ray dropped his tool and dug the dirt away from Joshua with his bare hands.

Half-buried, Joshua opened his mouth to speak. "Ray. Find a way to contact your uncle," he whispered weakly. "Tell him, *it's the Dragonstone... Tal– Tell him inh–*" Joshua meekly coughed up blood, his head lolling to the side.

Ray shook the colourless man, yet he did not stir. *Uncle* and *Dragonstone* were the only words he could decipher. He looked up at the viewing deck to see the unmistakably stern figure of Caleb standing in the gathering dawn, the first beams of sunlight falling upon his stony face before he disappeared from view.

In all the confusion, Lygia shrieked that the shift was over. Ray attempted to pull Joshua from the landslide, yet he was ordered by the guards to return his mattock back to the tool shed immediately.

He resigned with weariness, knowing that he would have nowhere else to go but the steam rooms if he defied the Watchers once more. He picked up his mattock and trudged back up the slope, the other inmates following at a measured distance behind. Ray stared down into the pit at Joshua's motionless body half-buried next to the rock shelf.

They entered the tool shed, which was now fully repaired. The Watcher Recruits were nowhere in sight. The roof was held in place with support beams running horizontally across the ceiling, and a wall now covered the portion of the room where the drainage pipe had been, making the tool shed appear no wider than the corridor outside. Ray hung his mattock on the rack, unable to deny their industrious efficiency.

The inmates were lined up along the back wall of the cafeteria – Ray and Kenneth almost collapsing where they stood – when Caleb strode down the stairs and across the room, directly towards them. Withdrawing his shock stick, he plunged the weapon into Ray's grimy bare chest.

Ray's legs buckled and he fell to his knees, gasping for air. Without a word, Caleb hauled him back up the stairs.

Kenneth and the other inmates did nothing to defend him.

17 - JAWRESH

It was a glorious morning for The Cull. Not a single cloud tainted the azure blue sky, the crystal clear ocean surrounding the tropical island reflecting its brilliance. Colourful exotic birds trilled from vast green canopies of coconut trees and densely packed mangrove trees alike. Gulls wheeled and called over the dirt clearing in the centre of the *Kirzakai* village.

The square was a bloodbath. Hundreds of savage Gravelhide Lizardmen descended upon one another in a frenzied carnage, sinking their jagged fangs into the muscle-packed scales of their brethren. Weaponless, they bit and clawed at each other, tearing chunks of gravelly flesh from their victims and spraying the onlooking crowd with clouds of blood mist, the victors slathered in frothing dark red juices as they gnawed at their slain tribesmen with mad gleams in their yellow eyes.

Tangled writhing bodies littered the blood-stained dirt, snarling and rasping and wrestling for dominance underneath the passive rays of sunlight, many unsure of who to trust in the slaughter – one *Kirzaka* could aid another in bringing down a fully grown warrior, only to launch a second attack while the other feasted on its carcass.

The melee was not restricted to the mature adults either – the young and old alike were forced to take part in the butchery. They hunted each other in packs, each member hoping to inflict the death blow. The one rule of the annual Cull was: none could leave until they had made at least one kill. Only the most ferocious fighters ever survived. That was how the Gravelhides ensured that only the worthiest warriors continued to live in the strongest of the *Kirzakai* tribes.

It was near impossible to track those who had made a kill in the macabre massacre, yet yellow and brown Bluetongues armed with halberds and poleaxes surrounded the square, commanded by the Chieftain of the Gravelhides himself to slay any who emerged without blood and flesh hanging from their teeth.

It was truly *kill or be killed.*

Orange Frillnecks watched the brutal show of barbaric bloodshed from a safe distance, lounging upon rocks and against trees, wherever they could fit their immense girths as they idly gnawed at the fruits and slimy crawling insects brought to them by the obedient Redcrowns. The ornate platters nestled upon the Frillnecks' laps were wrought of silver and gold and inlaid with bright sparkling gemstones, their rainbow of colours a dazzling contrast compared to the grisly display before them. Small birds perched upon their scaly orange hides, pecking at the morsels of food that fell between the folds of the Lizardmen's excess flesh.

Savarish, along with many of the more compassionate and peaceful Redcrowns had already volunteered themselves to watch over the *Kirzakai* youths in the farthest reaches of the Command Complex, as far away from the battle as possible, although some of their less docile tribesmen stood side by side with Teguresh and his ever-watchful colour-changing Blackbeads.

As ever – since Boaresh's exile – the coiled Horntail slaves lined the outskirts of the island, their rough thorny hides giving them the appearance of boulders embedded in the shore or rocky outcrops resting upon the elevated sand bars in the seawater that encircled the island. They guarded the perimeter from any humans foolish enough to venture too near to investigate the war cries and cheers brought on by the chaotic spectacle.

The red-eyed Gravelhide Chieftain, Jawresh, a staggering nine feet of pure muscle, let out a deafening roar in the centre of the flesh-filled square, blood dripping in meaty globs from his serrated teeth. He savoured the onslaught. The genocide would usher in a new generation of battle-hardened soldiers for the inevitable warfare with the humans to come.

He watched as Kuttrick and Gatorisse – two of his most promising fighters – went head to head, as they did every year. They clawed and gouged and snapped their jaws at each other, the cutthroat lovers ripping one another to shreds, working themselves up into a blood-fuelled frenzy. Then, establishing that neither's time had yet come, they formed an alliance, and savagely turned on the would-be predators sneaking up on injured prey.

As Jawresh smiled at the slaughter, another trio of challengers sur-rounded him – two fully grown males and one fierce young female – loyal to one another until they could bring the titan to his knees. They lashed at him with the tips of their tails, testing his range and his speed.

The Warrior Chieftain did not flinch. Instead, he laughed, *"RAHA-HAHA!!"* Blood slathered from his jaws down to his iron grey chest, now painted in dark red with the life force from the last group of his opponents.

The female was the first to strike, edging in close to wrap her powerful tail around his neck, pulling with her body weight to one side in an attempt to throw him off balance. The other two latched onto his thick arms, their long snouts snapping shut above his elbows. With mouthfuls of dense flesh, they shook their heads from side to side in an effort to saw into his hide.

"Is thix all you can do!? YOU ARE NOT WORTHY!!" Jawresh thundered, plunging his claws deep into the belly of the *Kirzaka* on his left and lifting him up high, ripping the young male's teeth from his jaws to remain as inch-long studs in the Gravelhide Chieftain's shoulder. Jawresh threw him to the ground and coiled his massive tail around the challenger's head, feeling the fallen warrior's skull crunch in his bone-crushing grip.

The Lizardwoman's grasp around his neck faltered as Jawresh set his blazing red eyes upon her. He grabbed her tail with his right hand, the other male still attached, and squeezed until she detached her tail in agony. Unbalanced, she fell to her webbed hands and feet and crawled away, a pack of Gravelhide youths soon descending upon her without mercy.

The last remaining challenger broke off his attack, pulling away to examine the bite mark, which was merely a flesh wound. He had not even managed to puncture the muscle beneath. Standing a full head below the Warrior Chieftain, he looked up at Jawresh with sheer terror in his eyes and stumbled backwards over the scattered bodies of fallen tribesmen.

Jawresh laughed in his wake, "*RAHAHAHAHA!!*" The retreating *Kirzaka* made for the Bluetongues at the square's perimeter, having already reached his killing quota to exit The Cull. The colossal predator gave chase. Just as the craven male reached the edge of the arena, Jawresh grabbed his tail, wrenching backwards so hard that the cowardly warrior smashed his snout flat upon the ground.

The Gravelhide Chieftain turned him over and, in both hands, held him up before the crowd. The craven male dropped his tail in futility, and Jawresh crushed the writhing appendage with one clawed foot. The *Kirzaka* titan opened his immense maw, salivating at his prey's struggle before locking his jaws around the flesh between the wretched worm's neck and shoulder, a fountain of blood spouting forth from his victim's throat and washing over Jawresh's face and chest in a fresh layer of gore.

A waste of fine warriors, he thought to himself, *but every challenger must be broken.*

A rustle of awkward applause from the crowd brought him back to earth, most of the spectators unsure of whether to cheer or turn away from the gruesome scene. The remaining Gravelhides in the square exited the arena, many of them joining the other victors already in the hot springs to cleanse themselves. Some of the more seasoned warriors preferred to wear the blood of their dead tribesmen like badges of honour. After all, many of the fallen had fought both valiantly and savagely to their last rasp.

For those young ones who had just taken part in their first Cull, they did not shiver. They did not shake and they did not sob and they did not moan with remorse for the acts they had done, for this was the way of their tribe. As it always had been, and always would be. Any *Kirzaka* who would show signs of trauma from the whole experience did not deserve a place amongst the strongest of the *Kirzakai* tribes.

* * *

With the square cleared of the fallen and the blood of his victims now dried upon his iron grey scales, Jawresh marched north through the village to answer Tyrax's summons. Thick foliage overhead screened his movements from the carrion birds that circled the island in the morning sun, wheeling and calling in celebration with a feast of their own.

He passed by the *Colossiboa* cage, the vast snake pit slithering and hissing in a tangle of gigantic writhing bodies. Under Tyrax's reign, the Great Snakes were no longer defanged before their use in the underground network of tunnels connecting the other *Kirzakai* Complexes. A subdued *Colossiboa* would never attack its rightful masters anyhow, so this only served as an extra precaution against any intruders who happened upon one of the subterranean labyrinth's entrances.

Next to the coiling snake pit were the aviaries that now housed those of the Elder Race. In the early days of Tyrax's leadership, the wise winged serpents had threatened to overthrow the brood son of Thorax and find a suitable replacement. Kalarish and her flesh tank Frillnecks had been uncharacteristically quick to quell their dissent, hurling cloths and rags covered in pungent crushed herbs over the Elders until they fell into deep slumbers. Now, they were fed a daily dose of concoctions to keep them placid and sluggish, routinely farmed for their eggshells and corrosive *Mirak'i* venom.

If ever they were lucid enough to become aware of their own movements and escape, Kalarish had doubted that any of them would ever be capable of taking flight again, their wings having grown deformed and crippled after years of captivity.

Jawresh ascended the wide earthen stairs that were bordered on both sides by dense jungle until he reached Tyrax's chambers. Dirt was spread over the floor of the octagonal room, held in place by a low palisade wall rising up on all sides, just like the rest of the village. The northern three faces of the chamber overlooked the ocean beyond the closely-packed line of mangrove trees rising out of the seawater lapping at the rocks below. Dominating the centre of the chamber was a large gleaming slab of gold mined from the Quarry Complex to cover Tyrax's burrow in the earth.

"Hail, Chieftain of Chieftains," Jawresh rumbled.

Dirt showered down from the entrance of the burrow as Tyrax ascended up into the chamber. He was a tall youth at seven feet, his hide coloured a walnut brown, splotched with small patterns of yellow to match his pale underbelly where his peppered brown scales became scarce in turn. His vertical blade-like tail coiled around him as he considered Jawresh with his dark brown eyes.

"Jawresh… Congratulations on another ssuccessful Cull," he hissed in a low raw tone. The Gravelhide Chieftain eyed him impatiently, awaiting his command. Tyrax slinked towards the palisade wall overlooking the ocean. "Furesh has ssent word that a Faction sspy has arrived at the Desert Complex. He has invited me perssonally to extract the information from the human mysself."

"I shall accompany you, Tyrax," Jawresh said at once, eager to meet Furesh once again, and challenge the Ridgeback to a show of true strength.

"No," Tyrax turned away from the ocean, "I ssensse a trap. If he truly wishes for me to interrogate the human, then he can ssend it to me. He plans to assail me, I *know* it," his forked blue tongue slithered out from between his lips, tasting the air as if Furesh's treachery was upon it.

Jawresh stomped over to join him by the wall. "Why have we not crushed that puny worm yet? Let me xerve as champion, *I* will prepare our xoldiers for war. *He* is no longer fit for the title. Look at the Frillneckx he xent back. *Veterans* he calls them, *worthy of rank*… They are ALL! FLESH TANKX!!"

Tyrax stared up at the colossal brute, matching his gaze, "He cannot teach those who will not learn. Those of the other tribes have always returned to uss as warriors. Bessides, if I left all of our ssoldiers' training to the Gravelhides, they would all be dead within the week."

The Warrior Chieftain slammed the bulk of his massive tail against the gleaming slab of gold, and for the briefest of moments, the soft malleable metal warped inwards as it absorbed the shockwave of impact, and the next moment it was gone, crashing through the palisade wall and barrelling end over end into the dense jungle.

Jawresh dripped red-tinged saliva from his jagged teeth with half a mind to tear the young leader's head from his neck with a single snap of his jaws, yet he decided against it. *The* Kirzaka *has a plan for all of us, I cannot harm him*. Fuming, he addressed the Lizardman youth, "You wound me, Tyrax."

The Chieftain of Chieftains turned away from the seething giant and his burrow – now laid bare – to stare out over the ocean again. "Like it or not, Jawresh, when the war comes, we will need all the sstrength we have… Including Furesh and his Ridgebackss." He laid his webbed hands over the top of the palisade, training one eye upon the scaly titan beside him. "As for thiss Faction sspy… you shall go in my sstead. Learn all you can from the human, and report back immediately. Once we know their location, our war can begin.

* * *

Tyrax had wished for Jawresh to take a heavily-armed escort of his twenty finest warriors with him. He only needed six. The two older, more cautious *Kirzakai* had gone to the trouble of affixing metal barbs to their tails – the signature weapons of their tribe. Jawresh and the four younger warriors had not bothered to arm themselves. To do so would have been an insult to their own strength against the Ridgebacks.

The half-dozen Gravelhides – still painted in the blood of the fallen – followed in their Chieftain's wake without formation across the beachhead towards the sandy mound in the centre of the oval-shaped beach. Revelling in each other's grisly stories from The Cull, they entered the camouflaged bunker into a wide underground tunnel, supported by beams of roughly hewn timber stretching far away into the darkness. Large empty rolling cages stood to one side of the cavernous tunnel, meant for prisoners and other loads that could not be transported any other way.

It had been a long time since Jawresh had felt the need to travel. Clawing along the side of the tunnel, he ripped an unlit torch from the wall, its brazen bracket falling to the ground. He kicked sand across the floor of the dark tunnel, searching for the bronze gong. The Gravelhides were not well-known for their ability to see in the dark.

A Redcrown warily approached the grunting warriors. "Here it is, Chieftain," he said, humbly leading Jawresh to the centre of the tunnel.

Jawresh shoved him out of the way, sending the Redcrown servant reeling on all fours. The giant brute swung the metal torch down upon the large gong set in the ground. The sound was muffled against the sand, but its vibrations shook dirt down from the walls and ceiling.

Soon after the earth's trembling subsided, another series of quakes came forth from farther down the tunnel. Jawresh tossed the broken firebrand aside as a pair of great luminous slits materialised, a gigantic snake slithering its twisting charge towards them in answer to their call.

In the enclosed space, the *Colossiboa* looked twice the size of its kin in the snake pit. Its sleek scales shimmered in the darkness like a shallow stream over river stones on a moonless night. Eyeing them with its narrow reptilian slits, the Great Snake's forked tongue flitted in and out of its bridled mouth, tasting the air for the slightest sign of fear. Satisfied, the *Colossiboa* turned its head around, revealing twin sets of bony ridges spanning the entire length of its back.

The giant serpent hissed as the Gravelhides climbed aboard, the Lizardmen lying flat on their bellies and gripping the ridges with their webbed hands. A fully grown *Colossiboa* such as this could have carried the score of warriors Tyrax had commanded, but their weight would have slowed it down considerably.

Jawresh climbed on at the very front, just behind the worn leather harness strapped around the rear of the Great Snake's skull. The Redcrown appeared next to the *Kirzaka* titan with a short stick in hand, gazing at him warily. "What is your desstination, Chieftain?"

"Desert Complex," Jawresh rumbled.

The Redcrown servant played a melodic tune upon a small xylophone mounted on the back of the serpent's bridle. The *Colossiboa* hissed in acknowledgement and the Redcrown danced out of the way as the Great Snake turned around in the tunnel, the surrounding rocks groaning as the serpent's scales chafed against the walls.

The Gravelhides lowered their snouts to the scaly back of the giant snake as the *Colossiboa* bunched up like a coiled spring. Impatient, Jawresh lashed his tail at the serpent's body and the reptilian monster lunged forward, twisting its way down the dark tunnel into the pitch black void.

Stale dank air rushed against Jawresh's scaly face as the *Colossiboa* weaved through the winding tunnel at breakneck speed, gaining momentum with each twist of its giant body. Back when he had been young and seemingly invincible, the Warrior Chieftain would pass the time by standing upon the back of the giant serpents and seeing how long he could maintain his balance before the tunnel took an unexpected dip or a sudden turn and he was forced to take hold of one of the snake's bony ridges again. Once, he had been thrown from a *Colossiboa's* back by a low-hanging rock jutting down from the ceiling. After spending countless days filled with hunger and wandering the black abyss with only his sense of touch as guidance, Jawresh had decided to tone down his recklessness, little as the change had been.

Dark rocky shapes blurred past in the tunnel, and another memory began to take form. *Furesh.* Jawresh had not seen the likes of him since Tyrax came to power. The Ridgeback Chieftain had long since been a distant shade of the past. The only dealings they had with him was sending young *Kirzakai* to be trained as warriors – with the exception of the Gravelhides, of course, they could see to their own training – and giving food as payment.

He is afraid of me, the cowardly worm, Jawresh thought to himself. *That is why he does not dare to face me. So now I go to face him.*

* * *

After weaving through hundreds of miles of subterranean darkness towards their destination, the *Colossiboa* crested an unseen rise in the tunnel, and a tiny spark – like a single star in the night sky – appeared at the end of the underground passage. As they drew near to the shiny speck surrounded by blackness, its light grew to the size of a candle's flame, then to a burning torch, then to a blazing bonfire, until they exited the tunnel and pierced the heart of the inferno.

The sudden explosion of light was blinding even to their thin reptilian pupils. The half-dozen Gravelhide warriors shielded their faces from the flash as the *Colossiboa* skidded to a halt, yet their Chieftain bore the stinging pain of harsh brightness to his retinas, watching for the Ridgeback ambush Tyrax had expected.

Jawresh waited for the brilliant white glare to dissipate, their surroundings slowly materialising in shimmering waves, before dismounting. He stared around at the plain room as his soldiers fell in behind him. Its walls were made of smooth mud-brick, and sand covered every surface from floor to ceiling. The antechamber was big enough for the *Colossiboa* to turn around in, yet judging by its emptiness – save for the slab of rock and bronze gong set in the ground in the centre of the room – there was little other purpose that it could be used for.

Dazzling sunlight streamed in through a large open arch set in the opposite wall, and a similar, yet smaller, darker entrance to another room stood to their left. They saw no signs of any welcoming party or the trap Tyrax had feared, yet they could hear the sounds of sparring and rasping through the radiant archway.

Jawresh motioned for Gatorisse to tie the *Colossiboa's* worn leather harness to the slab of stone to ensure that it remained close at hand. The two older warriors silently checked the room on the left, finding it only to be a store of tools and building materials, the floor littered with threadbare burlap sacks. Without waiting for his soldiers to reform, Jawresh stomped over to the sunlit entrance, still having to duck his head underneath the archway despite its height, and emerged unannounced on the eastern side of a sand-filled arena.

Kirzakai warriors trained for combat across the square. Proud Blue-tongues hacked and slashed at each other with dull-edged poleaxes and halberds; slender Redcrowns perched atop a raised platform in the centre of the arena, thrusting and jabbing with their round-tipped spears and pikes; thorny Horntails attempted to take the higher ground from them, ascending wide wooden ramps and swatting at the spear thrusts with blunt maces, morningstars and ball-and-chain flails, and on the other side of the arena, a group of Ridgeback warriors oversaw the stooped Blackbeads practising their archery with shortbows.

Other archways surrounded the square, branching off to the smaller chambers of the vast underground cavern. A pair of empty stone-carved spectator stands – one opposite Jawresh and one to his right – commanded views of the arena from the second level, and above those were wooden catwalks and rope bridges overlooking the entire complex for the Ridgeback guards on patrol.

Jawresh savoured the harsh rays of the sun blazing down through the giant hole in the underground cavern's ceiling, his iron grey scales soaking up the scorching warmth of the sky above the Desert Complex, the light and heat most welcome after enduring the dark and gloomy tunnel.

All this should have been mine, he thought to himself as his clutch of soldiers filed out beside him. His reptilian eyes traced over the square, imagining the sand-covered floor stained with blood for weeks after each Cull, and himself roaring in all his glory upon the raised platform beneath the burning sun, and no humans within leagues of the complex to tremble at his triumph.

From a freshly cut archway in the wall to their left, a red-ragged human slave emerged, pushing a dirt-filled minecart out into the arena. At the first sight of Jawresh and the half-dozen Gravelhides, its eyes went wide, and it left the minecart, retreating back through the archway. The room was obscured by clouds of billowing dust, yet dark figures of other slaves and Lizardmen alike appeared to move back and forth inside.

Jawresh's soldiers clustered around him, preparing for a fight, but soon, over the clanging and grunting sounds of the other *Kirzakai* tribesmen sparring, they heard shovels and mattocks breaking up chunks of rock from somewhere within the hazy room.

Furesh strode out from behind the cloud of dust and into the arena, the steely grey Lizardman bearing his two curved scimitars in a non-threatening manner, yet the Master of Combat was ready for battle all the same.

"Jawresh," he said, stopping a few metres short of the new arrivals. Holding his head up high, he studied them over the trio of horns atop his bony-plated snout, his mantis green eyes flicking over the Gravelhide warriors, surveying the dried bloodstains of their brethren slathered over their scales with a mixture of disapproval and disinterest. "I had sent word to *Tyrax*, not *you*."

"Tyrax is busy, worm. He xends me."

"*Worm…* Your recklessness has not changed through these long years," said Furesh, pacing in a slow semicircle around the Gravelhides. The giant warriors shuffled to maintain position, rasping as they stepped on each other's feet and tails. "You should do well to remember: you can always grow more teeth, but you only have one tongue. Guard it well."

Jawresh snorted at the Ridgeback Chieftain, who stood two feet below him. "You dig like a worm." Without breaking eye contact, he turned his head towards where Furesh's soldiers and the human slaves continued to hollow out a space on the south side of the arena. "You and your puny tribe of worms should take the Quarry Complex inxtead. You can drop your weapons and claw at dirt like the warm-blooded wretches."

Furesh halted suddenly and faced him dead-on. The younger Gravelhides bunched closer together, but the veteran soldiers spread out to either side of the clutch, the metal barbs affixed to the tips of their tails curling up and down in anticipation.

"Another insult, Jawresh, and I will have you clawing at the dirt beneath your feet."

Jawresh stomped forward with a menacing snarl, rage burning in his bright red eyes. Furesh raised his swords in answer, yet before they clashed, he tilted the tip of one scimitar towards the south wall in warning.

Jawresh turned to see forty Ridgeback warriors all in formation, poised to unleash a barrage of javelins cocked over their shoulders. Another forty tramped out of an archway with heavy footfalls on their right flank, armed with tridents. The rope bridges overlooking the arena sagged with the weight of the patrolling guards, ready to rain javelins down from above. The entire complex was silent. The other tribes had ceased their sparring some time ago.

Tyrax was right, Jawresh thought to himself.

"Resume!" a slender maple brown Ridgeback Lizardwoman commanded the Blackbeads on the other side of the arena. Their bowmanship immediately suffered in her absence as she marched across the sandy square, wood clacking and blunt metal clanging as the other *Kirzakai* slowly returned to their training in her wake. She halted a few feet behind Furesh, digging the haft of her trident into the sand. "We stand ready, Chieftain. What is your will?"

Furesh posed a similar question. "Tell me, Jawresh, have you come here to die, or have you come for the prisoner?" Seeing himself and his clutch outmatched, the fight in Jawresh's eyes simmered down. Furesh lowered his curved swords. "Take him to see the prisoner, Sharisse."

"Your will, Chieftain," Sharisse bowed and turned to lead Jawresh back across the square.

When the Gravelhides moved to follow the *Kirzaka* titan, Furesh held up a scimitar, barring their way. "Your soldiers will remain out here. *Sit.*" He waved his trident-bearing warriors over to surround the six Gravelhides. A shadow of a smile played at the edges of his snout as he looked down upon them with scorn. "Feel free to claw at the dirt while you wait."

* * *

The ashen-faced prisoner looked half a corpse, lying in the corner of one of the small mud-bricked rooms off to the side of the arena. When Sharisse had led the Gravelhide Chieftain through the open archway, the frail man could only feebly turn over to face the wall, uttering a pained gasp when it had attempted to cover its head with its soiled clothes. The Watchers who had brought it to the Desert Complex only knew that its name was

Joshua – anything else it had told them during its short time at the Quarry Complex could have been a lie.

Jawresh had taken the majority of his rage out upon the Faction spy, hurling the puny human around the room like a ragdoll. At one point, he even brought the dour-faced prisoner outside to throw it halfway across the arena. Some of its bones were already broken before the Warrior Chieftain had even started, yet now the mangled human was as floppy as a fish. Its cries, moans and whimpers had amused Jawresh, especially when he had raked his claws across the wretch's chest, blood spilling forth in rivulets. But as broken as the sombre Faction spy's body was, it simply would not *break*.

No amount of taunts, threats or trauma could coax out any information on the Faction's whereabouts, what their plans were or how big their army was. The Faction was the one group of humans who were aware of the *Kirzakai*, and thus, their biggest threat. For reasons even the Elder Race – before their imprisonment – could not explain, it seemed that the Faction had never told the world's wider population of humans about the reptilian race's existence, based on the reactions of shock and horror from all of the prisoners they had taken captive over the years. Yet their silence could change in an instant, and the *Kirzakai* were not ready to go to war with the rest of the world. *Not yet.*

Frustrated by the amount of time the interrogation had taken, Jawresh left the sunken-eyed prisoner broken and bleeding in the room. He stormed out into the arena and headed straight for his seated tribesmen surrounded by the Ridgebacks' tridents. Hisses of alarm went up from the Blackbeads as he seethed through the pack.

"OUT OF MY WAY!!" he thundered, shoving a pair of duelling Bluetongues to the ground. The Gravelhide titan ascended one of the wooden ramps leading up to the raised platform, throwing a Horntail over the side. The Redcrowns scattered before him.

Stomping down another ramp and across the sand on the other side towards the perimeter around his Gravelhide brethren, Jawresh slammed his mighty tail into the rear of four Ridgebacks, sending them sprawling.

He entered the circle through the newly-made hole and commanded his soldiers to rise.

"What news of the Faction, Jawresh?" Furesh marched out of the haze of construction along the south wall again. He gestured for his fallen warriors to resume their positions, trapping the Gravelhides inside the circle with their weapons raised once more.

"The prisoner will not talk," Jawresh rumbled with impatience, grabbing one of his veterans by the arm and wrenching him forward. "Now I do not want to hear it talk. Now I want to cut the wretch's legs off and hear it *xcream*."

"He will bleed to death," said Furesh, measuring his words. A murderous gleam had re-entered Jawresh's bright red eyes, and this time, an argument would mean death, on both sides. He did not wish to risk the lives of his own kin over a Faction spy.

"We will cover its wounds," Jawresh fumed. He only intended on rubbing sand over the stumps of the prisoner's legs so that it lived long enough for them to cut off its arms, too.

Eyeing the Ridgebacks' unwavering tridents pointed in his face, Jawresh shoved his own warrior forward, who caught two of the three forked prongs with his neck, the weapon's points impaling his throat. Heaving the weight of his fallen veteran – still gurgling in his death throes – with ease, the Warrior Chieftain dragged him through the confused ranks of the Ridgebacks. He only needed the older Gravelhide for the metal barb on his tail anyway.

Kuttrick hissed with laughter at the bemused Ridgebacks surrounding them. One death was nothing compared to the massacre they had revelled in that very morning. The other three young Gravelhides joined his laughter. The one remaining veteran held his silence, knowing that he could have been chosen just as easily.

All of the *Kirzakai* had ceased their training yet again, only this time, they cleared a wide path for Jawresh and his dying tribesman. Some of the Blackbeads morphed their scales to take on the appearance of the mud-brick walls behind them.

"Jawresh, there is another way!" Furesh boomed while fighting a fierce inner battle with his own rigid moral code. Jawresh halted, but he did not turn away from his path. Furesh breathed slowly, for he could not take back what he was about to say next. "We can make him join us. He will tell us everything… if we use the power of *constriction*."

Despite their years of discipline, the Ridgebacks gasped at their Chieftain's words. Even some of the other tribes looked upon Furesh in a new light.

"*RAHAHAHA!!*" Jawresh rasped, dropping the dead Gravelhide in the sand and whirling around to face Furesh. "You, *Champion of the Chieftains*, you would lay down your honour for thix *warm-blooded wretch!?*"

"If you kill him, the Faction will bring an end to us all."

"Then I grant him life, but only if *you* conduct his *conxtriction*."

18 - AGAINST THE WALL

Ben and Nico left the cover of the jungle and stooped low as they ran across the gravel road to the grass on the other side, coming to the edge of a small cliff. Nico pulled Ben down beside him and they both lay flat on their stomachs.

Below them lay a small semi-circular glen, surrounded on three sides by a curving wall of rock. It was almost as if the basin had been cut into the mountain. In the clearing, an open field of lush green grass swayed in the light ocean breeze, dew drops glistening underneath the rising sun.

A signal tower wrought of crisscrossed metal stood tall on one side of the glen, rising above the cliff wall and overlooking the ocean, and a double-storey house with antennae and a satellite dish upon its roof had been built near the gravel road curving down the slope on the other side. Beyond the glen, a beach with white sand bordered by a concrete road led into town. A handful of native hollow-brick and bamboo beach houses overlooked the neon blue waves lapping the shore.

Nico pointed at the house in the small valley before them and said with difficulty, "*Volcano... Monitoring... Station...*" he turned to Ben. "The men who will going to shoot me inside that one."

Ben looked around. The cliff face was steep, yet it was the only alternative to taking the road, which was in plain view of the Watcher outpost. Even now, they were already exposed with the road at their backs.

"Come on," said Ben, and they scrambled down the rock wall.

They flitted across the open field, staying on the north side of the glen along the ridge between them and the ocean, Nico's flip flops slapping hard against his heels.

Suddenly, a light from the outpost flickered on, shining in their direction. The small bulb barely added any extra illumination to the field in the morning light, yet it was still cause for alarm.

Ben froze, dreading the thought of Watchers emerging and bringing them back to the Quarry Complex. Nico tugged him by his shirt and they ran towards the signal tower.

They lay flat on the ground behind the tower's base as footsteps resounded upon a wooden floor within the house. Ben peered over the top of the concrete foundation at the volcano monitoring station. The ground level was comprised of an open carport that housed a white pickup truck, and an exposed flight of stairs leading up to the second level. Most of the building was made entirely of concrete, save for the wooden veranda on the upper floor.

He ducked his head back down as a screen door flew open and crashed against the wall of the second level. The escaping prisoners hugged the earth in dead silence, only the sound of the waves breaking against the shore in the distance could be heard. Ben was grateful that their inmate uniforms were coloured green, effectively serving as camouflage in the lush grass.

The Watcher paced across the deck until his footsteps came to an abrupt stop. Ben seized all his courage and poked his head up for another glance. The light was off now, yet Spike, clad in his black jeans and leather vest, stood against the northern railing of the veranda, peering out at the surroundings with a pair of binoculars in one hand, his black sunglasses in the other, and his venom snare pistol holstered at his waist.

"That's the man who will going to shoot me," Nico whispered, his head also raised above the tower's base.

"Don't worry," Ben replied in a low voice, "We'll send him and all of the other Watchers to jail once we get the authorities involved."

Spike scanned the landscape thoroughly, turning his attention in the direction of the gravel road and focusing on the point where it became concrete paving as it led into town. Gulls wheeled and called overhead, flying low through the glen borne on the ocean wind, scouring the field for rodents and small insects in the morning light. The motion-detecting bulbs lit up all around the station, and Spike replaced the binoculars with his sunglasses.

"Damn birds," the Watcher muttered, lighting up a cigarette before re-entering the outpost.

Nico tugged at Ben's shirt with a broad smile. The coast was clear.

Ben prevented him from getting up, "Take off your flip flops before we go any farther," he said. Nico returned a confused expression. He pointed at the village boy's feet.

"You don't like me to wear a slippers?" he asked in confusion, and then realised, "Oh yeah, they're so loud."

Nico kicked off his footwear into the grass and they both raced towards the town.

* * *

Caleb hauled Ray by his feet to the all too familiar hot corridor of the steam rooms. The air was thick with sulfur this time. Ray stifled a gag as they entered. Caleb showed no reaction to the reeking stench. His stony face had not cracked since he had thrown Joshua from the roof into the quarry pit.

Ray did not even know what he had done wrong. Perhaps he had not spent enough time in the steam room. He wondered whether Kenneth would be coming to join him. More importantly, he wondered whether Jack and Ethan had been released yet.

Evander, masked in a bandanna to shield his airways, stood inside Ray's former hotbox, staring at the damage the inmate had wrought upon the metal grate. Caleb paused momentarily in the corridor as the dark-skinned Watcher stepped out to address him.

"Caleb, this grate's mangled. I don't think we can fix it."

Caleb stood in thought, almost like a statue, before turning his head slightly. "Kick it into the shaft," he said. "Let the Lizardmen make a new one."

Evander nodded, "Will do. But before I get started, I'm gonna check on that inmate with the head injury," he glanced accusingly at Ray lying on the floor, and then exited the passage.

Ray briefly remembered Aiden's motionless body lying at the entrance of the tool shed after the rebellion, his green sweatband soaked red with his own blood owing to a rock that had fallen from above. It was good to know that he was still alive, at least.

Caleb resumed dragging him through the corridor. They passed by the second steam room and halted again as they reached the first corner of the passage. The stern guard thrust a key into an obscure lock set inside the dark stone wall in front of them. A *click* echoed in the narrow corridor, and the wall receded backwards into a shadowy room beyond. The Watcher yanked the shirtless inmate up to his feet and shoved him through the dim opening.

Before Ray could get his bearings as he stumbled through the darkness, Caleb pushed him down into a steel chair. Cuffs tightened around his wrists and ankles. He struggled in futility, his weariness taking its toll on his aching body. He had not even had the strength to try to stand on his own two feet while Caleb had dragged him across the floor, so he was not certain why he was bothering now – perhaps it had become more of a habit for him to want to fight to escape rather than actually attempting to escape.

He tried to take in his surroundings. The red glow of the hot corridor cast a dim light into the small dark room. A foul metallic smell filled the chamber.

Just as his eyes began to adjust to the darkness, a glaring light snapped on overhead and burned into his retinas. Ray shut his eyes and jerked his head to the side at the intensity as if turning away from a nearby explosion.

A loud *clang* reverberated inside the room followed by another *click*, magnified in the small space. Ray's eyelids blinked open again, averting his gaze from the harsh light. In front of him was a gunmetal grey door. He had not seen this door in the corridor before, it was almost as if the door had been camouflaged to blend in with the other walls outside.

He looked around the otherwise plain room, glancing over a stack of wooden crates in the corner, yet a feeling of dread set in when he looked down at the floor. Patches of dried blood were spattered here and there, giving off a reek of copper. He hoped that Jack and Ethan had not been worked over in here while he and Kenneth had been down in the pit.

Caleb paced out from behind Ray. "You did quite a job on that grate in there, inmate," the Watcher stooped and patted at the legs of the inmate's pants. "But I don't expect that you did it with your bare hands."

Ray laughed aloud. "You should see what I can do to your face," he said, looking up at the stern guard with a defiant smile.

Caleb cocked his head to one side with a half-amused expression, and then hooked a fist into the teen's temple, sending lights dancing through his vision. Ray's gaze fell upon the bloody floor again. Both immediately and belatedly, he realised that he should not be joking around with this Watcher.

Caleb took hold of the armrests on the chair and bore his steely glare into Ray. "I should just cut out your insolent tongue. You'd be a much better worker."

The gruel in the cafeteria would taste so much better, Ray thought to himself, but this time, he chose to keep his silence.

The Watcher straightened up, "But in here, *that* would be counterproductive." He paced over to one of the crates in the corner of the room and took a seat, staring at Ray in silence. Vile odours of the crusting blood upon the floor mingled with their breaths. The scathing light idly buzzed overhead.

Ray swallowed. "Why am I here?"

"I'll ask the questions," Caleb replied. "What do you know about the *Faction*?"

"The *Faction*?"

"What are you, a parrot?"

What are you, a parrot? Ray resisted the urge again. A smile played at the corners of his lips, and he bit the insides of his cheeks to keep from laughing. He simply shook his head at the question, as if it needed answering.

"Then answer the question, inmate. You were captured with Joshua. Joshua was found to be a Faction spy. *What do you know about the Faction?*"

Ray sighed, looking around the plain room, "Never heard of it."

"Surely you must know something. He was a friend of yours, yes?"

"My *dad's* friend. Not mine."

"Ahhh, yes. Your father. How is he? Is he well?"

That struck a nerve. Ray fumed in silence. He was not angry at Caleb, but rather at himself. He should not have said that. He should not have been saying anything. The less the Watchers knew, the better. They could not exploit his past if he spoke nothing of it. In the back of his mind, he made a mental note not to declare Ben as his brother.

* * *

Powdery white sand flew up in their wake as the escaping inmates hit the beach. Ben slowed his pace to a jog as they cleared the ridge and the vast expanse of water opened up on their left. He could not remember the last time he had seen a sea so pure and crystal clear.

They were now in sight of a few native houses on the opposite side of the road overlooking the coast, but Ben did not wish to stop at any of these, on the off-chance that the houses were more Watcher outposts.

A large wave crashed upon the shore, and Nico jumped with both feet into the sea foam. Ben scampered higher along the beach to avoid the rolling tide. He could not help but admire the village boy, laughing joyously as he ran barefoot across the white sand.

Fishing boats drifted out from the harbour in the farther reaches of the town, embarking and setting sail for the day's catch. He remembered Joshua telling him of the hardware store owner who might be able to help them escape with the motorboat left in his charge.

Not until we've shut down the Quarry Complex for good, Ben thought to himself.

He looked up to see that they were approaching the end of the beach, marked by a building that extended from the street above down to the water's edge. Nico cut across his path and led him up the shore and onto the road's concrete flagstones.

His chest was heaving, and he called for Nico to slow down as they came to a quiet intersection. Nico walked across the junction to examine a fresh poster on a concrete wall on the opposite side. Ben, with both hands on his knees to catch his breath, surveyed their surroundings.

The building on their left appeared to be some kind of bar, devoid of any patrons in the early hours of the morning, save one, snoring face down on the ground outside, his long black hair strewn around his tattooed arms with an empty bottle in his hand. The bar stood upon the corner of three roads: one leading back the way they had come; another bending left, leading directly towards the marketplace in the middle distance beyond blocks of shanty houses; and the third road turning to their right, passing through paddocks of farmland bordered by a hospital and a cemetery. Ben thought their proximity to each other would be less than encouraging for any of the townspeople seeking medical aid.

He sidled up next to Nico, and saw the village boy's face on the poster, underneath a title in bold writing: *MISSING.*

Nico looked sidelong at Ben. "I think my Papa will going to look for me."

"Let's go find some help first, and then we'll find your Papa, okay?" said Ben, pointing towards the bustling marketplace. *Our safest option is to be in a crowd of people.*

Nico nodded apprehensively, and they jogged along the stretch of road towards the market stalls, passing by rows of housing on either side. The majority of the residences lining the road had been constructed with hollow-bricks and concrete, roofed with wood, corrugated iron, and in some cases, densely-packed dried coconut leaves. Loud voices arose out of the marketplace ahead as vendors declared their wares and buyers haggled for lower prices.

Roosters lent their own voices to the chatter, heralding the dawn as the village's morning gears turned. Pigs snorted happily behind concrete walls while tethered goats grazed along thin stretches of grass along either side of the road. Lazing haphazardly on the cool concrete flagstones, stray dogs watched the pair of boys run towards the marketplace.

They were approaching another intersection when Nico stopped dead in his tracks as a pair of motorbikes rumbled around the corner. The village boy slowly held up his hands. Ben breathed a sigh of relief and stretched out his arms too, welcoming the sight of the riders' blue police uniforms.

The police officers brought their bikes to a stop in the middle of the road. One patrolman spoke into a radio, while the other warily approached Ben and Nico.

"We're so glad to see you," said Ben, "Please, help us."

The policeman did not answer. He simply shoved Nico, his hands still in the air, to the side of the road. The officer gestured for Ben to join the other boy, placing a hand on his holstered pistol.

Ben looked down at his green prison uniform and the flashing red manacle around his ankle, and then back up at the patrolmen. "I know our clothes make us look like criminals, but the *real* criminals are on the other side of the volcano!"

* * *

Ray looked up at Caleb, stone-faced like a gargoyle sitting on his perch, staring back at the inmate. Ray's eyes fell to his father's medallion hanging from around the Watcher's neck.

Following his gaze, Caleb looked down, and then back up at Ray. "Does this hold some meaning to you?"

"Yeah, it's mine," Ray snarled, nodding his head towards the golden necklace.

Caleb held up the medallion, the faint etches in the pendant reflecting under the harsh light. "So, you *do* know about the Faction then," he said. "Why else would you have worn its symbol around your neck?"

"Why do *you?*"

"To lure Faction spies out of hiding," he replied coolly. "Joshua was friendlier towards me than any of the other Watchers, but he never *fully* trusted me with his secret – at least, not willingly." His gaze flicked down to the bloodstains on the floor, then back up at the inmate.

Ray's eyes settled on the gunmetal grey door, intent on keeping his silence. Caleb rose from the wooden crate and slowly paced around the small room, disappearing from Ray's line of sight.

"Perhaps what you're saying is true, inmate. Perhaps your father held secrets from you. Perhaps he gave you this trinket as a keepsake for your birthday and you know nothing of the Faction. But then again…" Caleb returned to face him, *"Perhaps not."* With frightening speed, he ducked and plunged his fist into Ray's navel, sending the prisoner along with the steel chair skidding backwards across the floor, crashing against the wall.

Ray leaned over the side of his chair, dry heaving. If he had been better hydrated prior to the interrogation, he would have vomited upon the floor. His spirit unbroken, he sat upright and struggled to take control of his shallow breathing, yet he only managed to wheeze small gasps of air into his traumatised lungs.

Caleb sat back down on the crate across the room. "I suppose it doesn't *really* matter whether you know about the Faction or not," he began. "With the way that traitor fell from the roof, I'm sure that soon enough, we will learn from Joshua all that is necessary for the Lizardmen to put forth their plans."

Ray recalled seeing Joshua's lifeless body half-buried in the pit. *Unless the Lizardmen can speak to the dead, they won't be getting any information about whatever this* Faction *is.*

"What is of more interest to me," Caleb continued, "Is Joshua's last words after he took that tumble into the pit. I couldn't help but notice the two of you having a nice chat together on his way out."

Ray silently reflected upon what Joshua had told him, although he did not have the slightest idea of what the message meant, or whether he even had an uncle to deliver Joshua's dying message to. He knew that he did not have an uncle while he and Ben were growing up, but perhaps some memories had been slower to return to him than others. *I need to talk to Ben.*

* * *

"Against the wall!" the officer ordered.

Ben cooperated, placing his hands on a concrete wall beside Nico where they were subjected to a search. The escapees exchanged expressions of concern as they were patted down. The policeman turned both of the youths around, his partner joining him.

Ben attempted to give an account of all that had befallen him, his brother, and all of the others. He tried to explain that Lizardmen had kidnapped dozens of teenagers, forcing them to dig into the side of the volcano, yet the officers simply exchanged puzzled glances. *I must be talking too fast,* he thought. With Nico's near-perfect English, he had not considered that there might have been a language barrier with the two patrolmen.

Nico tried speaking in their native dialect. Even though he had not seen the Lizardmen, he could at least tell them of the Watchers who had kidnapped him, along with the prison.

Ben looked back towards the intersection behind them to see a brunette woman jogging in the direction of the farmlands. She did not appear to be a native Filipina woman. *She must be a foreigner who owns one of the houses overlooking the beach,* he thought to himself, *or, more likely, she's just another Watcher.*

The police officers began to chuckle at Nico's far-fetched story, and the village boy's speech changed in pace and tone.

Ben, growing annoyed, interrupted them, "Look, we're not just a couple of kids with wild imaginations, we're –" he stopped mid-sentence as a white pickup truck rounded the corner.

The policemen burst out with laughter. Nico sidestepped towards the

270

marketplace. Both men unbuckled their holsters and pulled out their pistols, aiming directly at Nico's head.

"Against the wall," the first officer ordered, jerking the gun's barrel back in Ben's direction.

Ben saw that these guns were not just pistols modified to accommodate venom snares, they were genuine firearms. Their lives were in jeopardy, more so now than they had ever been. Nico stood with his fists clenched, the marketplace only a few blocks away.

"Nico, they'll kill us if we try to run!" Ben cried aloud.

Nico threw up his hands again. He narrowed his eyes at the two men as he slowly trod back towards Ben. Together, the prisoners slouched against the concrete wall, watching the stray dogs lying on the concrete road scatter as the white pickup truck pulled up to a stop next to the motorbikes.

"Well, look what we got here!" the Sheriff said in a cheery voice as he climbed out of the vehicle.

Nico burned his gaze into Spike's face as he came around from the driver's side of the truck. Ben hung his head in defeat, realising who the police officer had radioed upon their unfortunate encounter. Spike tossed a glittering rock at one of the corrupt patrolmen, who juggled his pistol dangerously in an effort to catch the gem.

"Send our thanks to Mayor Gaspar for helpin' round up these escaped convicts," said Spike. "These boys'll say *anythin'* to get 'emselves outta trouble." The policemen nodded profusely, although not a word had reached their ears as they stared with wonder at the shiny jewel. "Lost your sandals?" Spike asked, waving Nico's flip flops in front of the sullen village boy. The Watcher threw the flip flops over the concrete wall. "Whoops."

The four men chuckled as the inmates watched the footwear sail out of sight. At the sound of a muffled grunt, Ben turned back to see that Nico had fallen to the ground, clawing at a piece of cloth on his face, and Ben once again found himself staring down the barrel of Sheriff Sullivan's venom snare.

Before he even had time to blink, the snare flew out and latched onto his face. He collapsed, wrenching at the mask. He tried to call for help, clinging to a desperate hope that some good Samaritan would hear and come to their rescue, but instead, he choked on the venom snare's overpowering aromas.

"Seems familiar, don't it boy?" said the Sheriff, tipping his hat back and squatting beside Ben, "All outta luck 'n' on y'all's way to prison."

Ben's eyes grew wide as the vibrant colours of the world around him seemed to shimmer and blend together.

Spike's voice echoed with deep and unnatural bass, "Let's load 'em up."

Tossing Ben and Nico into the tray of the white pickup truck, Spike turned the car around and sped off. The pair of prisoners sluggishly watched as the policemen tore off the *MISSING* poster from the wall of the intersection before they shrank away into the distance.

* * *

"Hey!" Caleb cut across Ray's thoughts, "Done reminiscing? *Joshua's last words*, inmate. What were they?"

"Maybe you should go ask Joshua instead of me," he said, looking up at Caleb. "You'd have a better chance of his corpse telling you the answer."

"You know, you're a lot stronger than your brother," said Caleb. "I asked what Joshua had said to him only a few days ago, and he gave over almost instantly." Ray jolted in his seat, jerking at his restraints. "What? Did you really think I wouldn't discover that the two of you are brothers?" Caleb rose from his seat again, withdrawing something from his pocket.

He held an old photograph in front of Ray. Standing together in the photo were him and Ben, back when they were children, along with their father, Joshua, and a woman – the same brunette woman from his dream – in front of the same hollow-brick and bamboo beach house with the lush green rainforest in the background.

"This woman is familiar," said Caleb, re-examining the photo. "You know, I think I've met her a few times down in Lungsod." Ray raised an eyebrow. "Yes, this looks *exactly* like one of the houses on the outskirts of the village. Maybe I'll pay her a visit after I'm done with you."

"Go ahead, see if I care," Ray said flatly. The only connection he shared with the woman was a distant memory of her arguing with his father. If she had been around for the rest of his childhood, maybe then he would have been more concerned. In any case, he was not in any position to help her.

"You still think somebody's going to come and rescue you, don't you?" Caleb said as he produced a lighter and sparked up a flame, setting the photograph ablaze, the faces in the film melting together.

The Watcher let the burning image fall, floating down upon wisps of its own smoke to land at Ray's feet. They watched as it shrivelled, folding in upon itself until the flame died down, leaving only a black scrap of ash.

"I found that in Joshua's belongings, after his life was forfeit. Reckless for a Faction spy. We divided up his things, in the same manner as what we do with that of the inmates."

Ray imagined Caleb and a group of other Watchers gathered around the minecarts in the treasury, although in place of squabbling over gemstones and jewels, they claimed the inmates' belongings for themselves instead.

Caleb cracked his stony face with an unnatural smile, already guessing at Ray's thoughts. "No one's coming here to save you. But *don't be afraid*, I'm here for you," he winked.

The realisation dawned on Ray.

Rashad was right, he thought to himself. The Watchers had taken their father's journal and torn a page from it. Caleb dropped it into Ben's cell just to play some sadistic joke by stirring up a false sense of hope in the new arrivals.

Caleb stood tall over Ray, the painful truth sinking in. The stern Watcher opened his mouth to continue, perhaps to deliver one last stinging blow into Ray to shatter all hope for the inmate, making him surrender whatever information he held, when the door clicked open. They both snapped their attention towards Evander entering the room.

Caleb's flint grey eyes flared as the goateed Watcher hurriedly whispered something into his ear. "When? How!?"

"Not here," said Evander, glancing at Ray.

The two guards swept out of the room, slamming the door behind them. Ray sat in silence, straining his ears for any other pieces of conversation the guards might drop, but only their footsteps echoed down the passage, another door slamming in the distance.

* * *

The would-be escapees found themselves lying upon a ceramic-tiled floor. The air around them was cool and refreshing. Ben blinked hard, his vision was groggy. He looked up to see Lygia smiling her blackened teeth at him – a stark contrast to the gleaming whitewashed concrete walls behind her – as she lounged on cushions set upon a chair made of bamboo, eager to hear what would become of the pair of inmates.

Sheriff Sullivan stretched out with his hands behind his head on another chair nearby, slightly amused at the sight of Ben and Nico waking up in the barracks. Other off-duty Watchers were gathered around them as well, drinking from pale brown bottles, throwing gems and jewellery to each other, apparently having gambled on who would wake up first.

Evander turned to Caleb, "What should we do with them?"

"Oh yess, what will you do with them, Caleb?" Lygia asked in her high-pitched voice, "Cuff them to the chains rack again?" she threw her head back in a mocking cackle.

Caleb narrowed his hawkish eyes at her as he addressed Evander. "Let Cormac deal with them, I don't have time for this."

With that, he marched out of the room and into the cell house, slamming the door behind him, Lygia shrilly calling in his wake, "Oooh! Don't know what to do, *sso you throw them to the dogs?* YOU'VE GONE SSOFT, CALEB!!"

* * *

The glaring light droned lazily overhead as Ray sat alone in the stillness of the small room. Every tiny sound was magnified tenfold, even his breathing. He heard scratches in the surrounding walls. It was as if claws were scuttling behind him, yet he was already sitting with his back against the wall.

Thoughts of the Lizardmen watching him through invisible cracks in the walls invaded his thoughts, sending his hackles on edge. His eyes darted around the room, searching for some hidden serpentine eye gazing back at him.

Nothing.

He turned his wrists over within his restraints. The rattle of his cuffs sounded like a hailstorm showering a tin roof in the small space. With the lack of Watcher supervision, he strained harder against his bonds, yet still, they did not yield.

Ray unclenched his fists, relaxing before the next bout of exertion. Noticing the tan line on his thumb, he attempted to put thoughts of his old life out of his mind, yet he could not help but wonder what secrets his father might have been withholding from him and Ben.

It was certainly possible that their father had been leading a double life, especially with all of the time that he had spent away for work. Although, if their father knew about this *Faction*, he would have most certainly written about it in the pages of his journal, which was now in Caleb's hands. He shrugged, remembering that none of this would help him out of his current situation.

His eyes flicked over to the door. It had not clicked when the Watchers had left him alone. It was possible that they had forgotten to lock up in their haste. If only he could manage to break free of his bonds. He strained again at the cuffs, grunting with exertion, veins bulging within his skin.

The chains cut into his wrists and he was forced to slacken, falling back into the steel chair again. He needed to see past his pain, and blind himself with anger. He forced himself to think of the Watcher Recruits, the people who had ambushed them in the swamp.

A red veil fell over his eyes as he pictured their uniforms. He imagined his father kneeling in that mud-sodden mire, awaiting his execution; the Sheriff, the rednecks, and all the others standing around him, laughing in victory.

Ray's blood boiled in his veins. He felt the heat emanating from his pores. His cuffs rattled against the steel frame of his chair. Rage was building within him. If he could channel his energy, he might be able to wrench himself free of the restraints.

This time, he left his fists unclenched, pointing his fingers so that his hands might squeeze out through the cuffs instead. He slid the cuffs just below the halfway point of his palms. If only he had enough saliva to spit and grease his hands for the last fraction.

"Just a… little… more!" he said through gritted teeth.

The gunmetal grey door flew open with a crash against the stack of crates. Caleb stepped through the doorway and into the light of the glaring bulb above, casting a wide black shadow into the room. His stern gaze examined Ray's chafed hands.

"Thought you might try," said Caleb. "Pair of escape artists, you and your brother."

The Watcher strode across the small room in two steps, his shock stick drawn, and he tapped the steel chair with the baton. A blue arc leapt from the tip of the shock stick to the chair frame, climbed the chain-links of the restraints and fired volts of electricity into Ray's hands, still wedged halfway through the metal cuffs. In his throes of pain, the back of his skull smashed against the wall behind him, leaving the taste of copper in his mouth.

Caleb shut the door and sat back down upon one of the wooden crates in the corner of the room. "Well, inmate, I have good news and bad news. Good news first?"

Ray managed to subdue his involuntary muscle spasms just long enough to muster a response. "You're letting me go?" he asked, still twitching. His cocky confidence had returned to him during his brief respite.

"I forgot to mention," Caleb said, ignoring Ray's chuckle, "Your friend, or should I say, your *father's* friend, survived that little fall, and he is still clinging to life. He's been sent back to the Desert Complex for further questioning. The Lizardmen have other, more *persuasive* methods of extracting information. Even as we speak, they are learning what other secrets the traitor holds before he dies, *properly* this time."

"Well, that's great news, Caleb, I'll be sure to spread the good word!" said Ray, feigning enthusiasm.

The Watcher sat unmoved by the inmate's sarcasm. "Bad news," he said, "It looks like it won't be long before your brother sees this side of the prison." Ray jerked his hands against the restraints again in protest. Caleb leaned forward, levelling his hawkish eyes with Ray's. "I'm also assigning you additional duties henceforth, until you divulge to me, and me alone, what Joshua told you in the pit."

* * *

Ben and Nico groaned as Evander hauled them both to their feet in the barracks. The other off-duty guards watched idly as the goateed Watcher struggled to open the cell house door with his arms full.

"Say now, what kinda hurt can we dish out to 'at boy there?" Sheriff Sullivan pointed at Ben. "I don't take kindly to bein' woken up early after a long night o' drinkin.'"

Evander kicked the door handle, letting a wave of the cell house's hot air breach the cool atmosphere of the barracks as the door swung open. "Pretty soon, all of the inmates are gonna get punished as a group after what they did in the tool shed, from what I heard," he replied.

Ben twisted his head around in Evander's solid arm as they stood in the open doorway, and he saw Cormac climbing up the cafeteria's stairs into the cell house.

"Ah! Them's the two what I thought we was missing today!" Cormac said cheerfully. A glint of silver shone from one of his grubby fingers under the spotlights' glare as he approached.

"Maybe we could give 'em a good whippin,'" the Sheriff suggested, "Learn 'em some discipline for tryin' to escape, *again*."

Lygia squawked her approval at the idea, laughing with delight. "Well, it'ss up to Cormac now, *isn't it?*" she shrieked hysterically. "Come on Cormac, let'ss hear what YOU have in mind!"

As he hung limp in Evander's arm, Ben silently hoped for the chains rack, although his luck might have well and truly run out by now if Cormac was to decide their fate.

Evander attempted to quell the other guards' excitement, but he was interrupted by Cormac, who drew up next to him. All who were gathered in the barracks leaned forward, eagerly listening to what the crude Watcher had to say.

The yellow-toothed man blinked his eyelids humbly in the stillness, soaking up the suspense of his bated audience. Only the whirr of the air conditioner battling the heat rising up from the cell house could be heard.

Before his theatrical pause wore on for too long – to everyone's surprise – Cormac spoke up on the inmates' behalf. "Be a shame if these two was to miss yet another shift," he began, "Just so's they can laze about while the others are breaking their backs in the pit. 'ow's about Evander looks after them while they work the night shift, 'ey?" he lingered for a moment, searching the faces of each guard sitting in stunned silence, before his imploring face wrinkled into a mischievous grin at the inmates, "And then it's off to the steam rooms until your next shift starts!"

19 - JUST LIKE US

Watchers were gathered inside Ben's cell in the corner of the cell house, Gremlin amongst them, peering up at the damage Ben and Nico had caused in their escape attempt.

Nico, just now coming to his senses, found himself suspended above the stairs platform outside the guard barracks in one of Evander's solid arms alongside Ben. Both inmates had just recently been recaptured on the outskirts of Lungsod.

Ben's new cellmate shook himself free of the guard's grasp, falling to the floor. Instantly, Cormac caught hold of him from behind with a firm grip.

"You've 'ad your fun for today, sunshine, now it's time for work!" The crude man grinned as he hauled the struggling village boy down both flights of stairs and into the cafeteria.

Ben, on the other hand, merely looked up at Evander with large pleading eyes. The kind guard looked over his shoulder at the judging Watchers in the barracks behind them before shutting the door on their scorn. Lygia's mocking high-pitched cackle pierced the heavy wooden timbers.

Evander set the inmate down on the staircase platform. "Come on," he gestured for Ben to follow him down the stairs and into the cafeteria. Seeing nowhere else to go, Ben climbed down the steps after him. "Other prisoners have tried your escape plan before you came along," said Evander. "Sometimes, I'd find bed sheets torn in half and crumpled on the floor. But it never worked, not until now..." he said in a slightly impressed tone as they descended the cafeteria's staircase.

The sounds of inmates settling in for the evening meal filled Ben's ears. Stone seats scuffed the floor, spoons scraped wooden bowls and rowdy banter could be heard both at the tables and in the queue for the gruel pot.

"I guess we just got lucky," Ben replied, silently acknowledging that his escape plan would have had the same result as all the others if it had not been for Nico's ingenuity.

Evander stopped abruptly at the bottom of the staircase. He lowered his voice so as not to be heard by the other inmates nearby. "Luck's one thing," he said, "Taking chances is another. Word to the wise: *lay low*. I've never seen the higher-ups get so riled up before. Even Caleb is starting to lose his temper. Things are about to change. And in here, *change is never a good thing.*

Ben nodded, heeding the kind Watcher's advice before he moved off towards the front of the cafeteria to join the other guards while Ben lingered upon the stairs. He would still be in last place for the queue, in any case.

* * *

In a small room on the other side of the prison, Caleb yanked Ray up from his steel chair by his upper arm. Battered and shirtless, Ray massaged his wrists, the skin rubbed raw by his attempts to break free of his restraints. The stern Watcher pulled the gunmetal grey door open and shoved the inmate out into the steam room corridor.

Ray held his breath as he stumbled through the hot passage. It still reeked with thick fumes of sulfur. Caleb's stony facial expression did not change as he breathed – it was as if his lungs were immune to the air's toxicity.

As they passed by two of the hotboxes on the left, Ray stole a glance through the first barred cell window; Jack had been released, and most likely Ethan, too. His own cell – the damaged steam room – had now been sealed off, its small window covered by billowing bed sheets draped across the door. The fiery furnace from within shone through the window, the three iron bars casting a trio of silhouettes within a glowing red square upon the cloth. The foul odour of rancid meat continued to fill the corridor despite the covering, seeping through the linen's fabric and lingering in the dense air like steam in a sauna.

Caleb pushed Ray through the door to the small adjoining passage, and then into the cell house beyond. Ray dropped to his knees and coughed at the first wave of fresh – albeit humid – air filling his lungs. The flint-eyed guard left him heaving upon the floor and strode halfway across the cell house.

Reeling on his knees, Ray rocked back on his ankles and looked up in a spell of dizziness to see the day and night shifts' cell doors all flung open. *I must have been in that room since this morning,* he thought to himself. The cafeteria below was filled with noises of weary prisoners settling in to eat their detestable dinners.

A few Watchers were gathered inside Ben's cell in the corner, staring up at the low ceiling with keen interest. Even straining his eyes from his position on the floor, Ray could not see what had captivated the guards' attention.

Caleb boomed at the group of Watchers, "Gremlin!" The ivory-skinned guard with greasy black hair trudged out of Ben's cell, his malicious green eyes flitting between Ray and the stern Watcher. Caleb waited patiently for the unpredictable man to venture closer before giving him orders, "Ensure this inmate assists with other duties around the complex."

"Ray?" Mara called out from behind, emerging from the adjoining passage, her dark brown eyes tracing over the fresh welts and bruises forming over his shirtless body.

Caleb turned at the sound of her voice while still addressing the other guard, "Start him off with the chamber pots," he said before marching towards Gremlin and jabbing a finger in the short man's chest, "And if anything goes wrong, I will hold *you* personally accountable."

Gremlin scowled up at Caleb, yet his disdain soon wilted under the hawkish Watcher's gaze. After staring back down at the disgruntled guard for far longer than necessary, Caleb descended the flight of stairs into the cafeteria, leaving Gremlin and the two inmates to their duties.

* * *

Ben surveyed the inmates shovelling food into their mouths, and the guards gazing out over the crowd for any signs of trouble. It was only then that he realised how much the prison's normal routines had been shaken up since their arrival: the inmates spurred to rebellion, destroying the tool shed; Joshua's betrayal of the Watchers; the unveiling of the Lizardmen; and now, a second escape attempt. All within the space of a few shifts.

A hard kick in his backside sent him careening down the remaining stairs. Sprawled upon the ground, he looked up to see Caleb striding towards the other Watchers at the front of the cafeteria. Apparently Ben had been in his way.

He got up and dusted himself off, joining the queue of inmates just behind Nico. The village boy stood hunched over his folded arms, shifting his weight from one bare foot to the other as he anxiously peered out towards the front of the line, nervously awaiting whatever ill fortune would befall them next.

Ill fortune indeed – woe to anyone who ate that sickening porridge.

"Relax," said Ben. "We're just going to get some food and water."

Nico looked around at him in alarm. "But I'm not bring a money to pay!" He sheepishly shuffled forward beside the table of bowls and spoons as the queue ahead of them dwindled.

Ben could not help but laugh. "Don't worry," he reassured his cellmate, "It doesn't matter whether you have money or not, everyone is treated the same here." Then, a chill shot up his spine as unbidden words flew from his mouth, *"Welcome to Paradise."*

Ben filled up dishes of water from the tap on the wall for Nico and himself and they greedily drained the bowls a few times each – the one perk of being at the back of the line.

Ava looked up at Ben as she served him a spoonful of gruel. "I'll tell

Sarah you're back."

"Tell her…" his pulse quickened. *I came back for her... No, no, no. I was recaptured, that's a lie... I didn't want to leave without her…* Ava cleared her throat, staring at him expectantly. He lost his nerve, "Tell her I said *hi*," he decided, before mentally kicking himself.

Ava raised an eyebrow with a look that said *really?*

Cormac, standing by the gruel pot, smiled mischievously at the pair of inmates. "Tell 'er I said 'i, too. Or shall I tell 'er meself?"

Leon chuckled nearby.

Ben's fist tightened around his spoon, remembering how they had manhandled Sarah across the cell house during the assembly. His heart hammered even harder, but he caught a disapproving glance from Evander.

"Keep moving!" Leon barked. Ben turned to find a seat, remembering Evander's advice, although a spoon against a shock stick hardly seemed wise anyway. "Hold it!" Leon growled, "You forgetting something?"

The prisoner stopped in his tracks and drew in a long breath. *What does he want now?* Turning slowly, he found that the grizzled guard was staring up at Caleb questioningly, who met his gaze. Neither man wavered. Ben and Nico exchanged puzzled expressions.

Leon broke the tension. "You forgot to change their manacles."

Ben glanced down at the red light of the day shift flashing upon his ankle. For a while, he had not noticed that the metal bracelet was even there.

"Your man, Cormac, assigned them to the night shift," Caleb answered sternly. "It was *he* who forgot something."

"It's *your* shift, sunshine," said Cormac, taking offence, "'ave some responsibility, 'ey?"

"You watch who you're calling *sunshine*, Cormac," Caleb shifted his dark eyes towards the grinning Watcher.

Evander stepped between them, holding up a pair of manacles flashing with the yellow light of the night shift. He thrust one into Cormac's chest, the force of his push sending the callous Watcher off balance. Before Cormac could voice his indignation, Evander spoke up, "We're all guards here. We all share the same responsibility for this prison."

Both Watchers silently agreed to change the manacles of the two inmates, Cormac muttering curses under his breath as he worked roughly around Ben's ankle.

Leon drew closer to Caleb, lowering his voice to a gruff whisper. "You're losing your edge, Caleb. Won't be long before those keys to the truck end up in someone else's pocket."

Caleb bore his hawkish gaze into Leon's challenging eyes, the grizzled guard turning his head upwards to spit over the taller man's shoulder.

Evander patted Nico's leg and came to Caleb's side again before the situation escalated. Cormac finished locking Ben's manacle and shoved the prisoner towards the tables, joining the hushed argument between the Watchers. The quarrel soon ended on an unresolved note, with promise of revisiting the subject once more, as soon as they were out of sight of the inmates.

Humbly thanking Ava for the ladle of foul-smelling porridge, Nico followed Ben to a table. Ben spotted a pair of familiar faces, Jack and Ethan, deep in conversation with a few other inmates on one side. He and Nico settled in unnoticed a few seats away on the other side, listening in on their conversation.

They were talking about the sudden appearance of the Lizardmen. The prison was rife with speculative rumours and theories to explain the new race's origins.

"Maybe it was a lab experiment gone wrong, some kind of mutation?" Ethan suggested.

"What d'you reckon of this," said Jack, "What if they've always been around, and *we're* the lab experiment that's gone wrong?"

Ben was famished, he had not eaten anything since the morning of the previous day – although, before they had been taken prisoner, he would usually skip his meals when he was alone in his room, reading his books from early morning until late into the night – yet all the same, he chose to eat his fill before weighing in on the subject of the Lizardmen.

Sitting across from Ben, Nico bowed his head and murmured Grace before setting spoon to porridge. *I wonder if he'll be so thankful when he tastes the food*, Ben thought to himself. He watched as the village boy raised the first spoonful of gruel to his mouth, expecting him to spit it out immediately. Nico grimaced at the taste, but he continued to eat without complaint.

"How in the world can you stomach this stuff!?" Ben asked, bewildered. Nico returned a similar expression. Ben had been so surprised that he had forgotten their slight language barrier. He pointed at Nico's bowl and rephrased, "Doesn't it taste bad?"

"I'm just thankful for a food," his cellmate answered, finishing his mouthful. "Many children in my village from a poor family, sometimes they will not going to eat." Nico smiled sadly and continued eating in silence.

Ben felt a pang of compassion for his cellmate. He appreciated the small things in life, however simple they were. Even the green uniform was better than the tattered and ripped clothes he had been wearing upon his arrival to the Quarry Complex. Yet still, this prison should not have been the place to have afforded him such basic necessities.

He chewed thoughtfully, thinking of the patrolmen who had accepted the sparkling gemstone as a bribe for their assistance to the Watchers in recapturing the escapees earlier that day. It upset him to think of riches passing so carelessly through the hands of greedy men while the hungry pleas of the impoverished young and needy fell upon deaf ears.

* * *

Mara helped Ray to his feet as Gremlin drew his shock stick and sparked up a blue arc of light. The vicious Watcher approached them, electricity crackling from the glowing baton. Ray steadied himself for yet another test of his endurance when Mara suddenly pulled him in the direction of the night shift's row of open cells.

"Come on," she said, "You look like you've had enough for one day." He looked back, and Gremlin lowered the shock stick as the inmates went about their duties. Once they were out of earshot, she added, "Besides, there's too many of them for just the two of us."

The other guards emerged from Ben's cell in the opposite corner of the room and, entering each unoccupied cell along the two rows of open doors, they bore out bundles of bed sheets and made their way up the stairs and into the barracks.

Mara started at one end of the night shift's row of open cells and emerged carrying a chamber pot. Testing Ray, she thrust the reeking metal bucket into his arms, and she was surprised by his lack of revulsion.

"I've done worse," Ray smirked, although he still averted his gaze from its contents.

Mara raised a thin eyebrow at him, faint traces of a smile playing over her dark lips. She entered the next cell, emerging with another chamber pot held at a distance.

She led him past the chains rack and through the door in the corner that she had come from, Gremlin warily following in their wake. Ray saw the other three doors in the small adjoining passage again. The first one on the right led to the steam rooms; that much he knew. What lay beyond the second door on the right and the last one on the left, he believed he was about to find out.

Mara kicked the door on the left open and trudged inside. The room was just another cell house, almost identical in comparison to the other side of the complex. To their right stood a flight of stairs leading up to what Ray assumed to be another entrance into the barracks. Only a handful of cell doors were open in the entire cell house.

"There aren't that many girls here," she explained. "Girls aren't really on high demand when the Watchers are out kidnapping people for hard labour."

The only other difference in this cell house was that next to the staircase to the girls' own cafeteria, in place of a chains rack, there was an additional flight of stairs in the middle of the room. Steam rose up from the second room below.

Gremlin shoved Ray forward from behind, and he nearly spilled the contents of the chamber pot upon the floor. Catching his balance, he felt a sudden impulse to make the pale guard wear the foul bucket as a hat, yet by some miracle, he managed to suppress the urge.

They climbed down the second set of steps, Ray narrowly avoiding a low-hanging pipe as they broke through a thin veil of mist.

The room was alive with activity. A dozen female inmates were all busily scrubbing and cleaning in the cluttered laundry. Water splashed from a wash trough in the corner, and droplets rained across the floor as uniforms were wrung dry. Thick vapours rose from clothes presses, enshrouding the ceiling's network of ruddy pipes in a cloud of steam.

The prisoners folding uniforms stopped at the trio's entrance – Sarah and Amelia standing among them – all work ceasing momentarily as they stared at Ray and Gremlin with startled expressions. Ray suddenly remembered that he was standing before them without a shirt, his last uniform having been reduced to a smouldering pile of ash in the steam room. At a snarl from Gremlin, the girls quickly turned back to their work without question.

"We don't usually get many visitors on this side of the prison," said Mara. "Come on, let's dump these buckets."

She led Ray and Gremlin past stacks of clothes and cupboards to the other side of the laundry. A square stone slab with a circular metal lid was housed in an isolated corner of the room with another rusty wash trough nearby.

She set her chamber pot down on a nearby wooden bench and uncovered the hatch set in the square slab, revealing a hole measuring roughly one foot across in diameter. The rim around the stone hatch was stained black. Holding the metal lid in one hand and covering her nose with the other, she motioned for Ray to dump his waste into the shaft.

He approached, yet the stench was almost overpowering. Even Gremlin shrank away in revulsion, slinking back to the staircase. The shaft downwards into the deepening shadows was void of all light, although judging by the foul reek wafting up, Ray thought that it was probably for the best that the pit at the bottom remained shrouded in darkness and out of sight. He mustered his will and poured the slopping contents of the chamber pot down into the hole.

"The other one, the other one," said Mara, her voice muffled by her hand as she nodded towards her chamber pot on the wooden bench.

He dropped the empty bucket and picked up the second, throwing the sludge down the shaft, finding himself wondering whether one of the big gruel pots was waiting somewhere down below.

Mara dropped the lid on the hatch, collected the two empty buckets and dry heaved into the nearby wash trough. She grabbed a reel of hose from the trough and squirted water into her mouth, swishing it about and gargling before spitting into the sink.

"I can never get used to the smell," said Mara, noticing him thirstily eyeing the hose in her hand. "Here, want some water?" Ray wholeheartedly obliged. Taking the hose from her, he thumbed the nozzle and sprayed the pressurised water over his face and body before drinking his fill. "Just don't let the hose touch your mouth, it's what we use to wash the chamber pots," she added timely.

He spluttered, spitting the water out, "Could've said something before!"

"It's a *laundry hose*, just be glad the water's safe to drink," Mara replied as she scooped washing powder into the empty pails. He handed her back the hose with a look of indignation, and she rinsed out the chamber pots, a smirk creasing the corners of her mouth.

Someone tapped Ray on the shoulder from behind. He whirled around with a fist half-raised, expecting to see Gremlin trying to hurry them up.

The girl named Sarah stood before him, startled by his reaction. She timidly held out a folded green shirt. His hand dropped instantly with an apologetic look, his fist opening to accept her offering. He thanked her, and she smiled politely as he donned the fresh uniform. Gremlin grumbled impatiently from the foot of the staircase, and Sarah quietly returned to folding clothes alongside Amelia.

Ray and Mara picked up the chamber pots and climbed back up the stairs, soapy bubbles frothing over the sides.

"So, how long do your shifts usually run for?" he asked as they re-entered the male cell house. "I've seen you in the pit when you were hanging up fishnets, and that was during the day shift, and then when I came out of the steam room last night, I saw you serving up gruel at midnight." His stomach grumbled at his own mention of gruel. He remembered he had not eaten anything since last night, and that was two shifts ago now.

"We might not work as hard as you guys," she shot him a sideways glance, "But we definitely work longer hours. *Someone's* gotta cook, and clean, and wash all the dirty clothes… Three times a day. I'd rather work out there in the pit. You guys have it easy."

They split up and placed the clean chamber pots in their original cells, and then grabbed the next pair of sloshing buckets.

"How'd you get stuck with this job anyway?" Ray asked as they walked back to the other side of the prison.

"I got caught eating food while I was working in the kitchen," Mara sighed. "See, the Watchers eat *real* food, and we're forced to cook it for them while we're all stuck eating that porridge." She glared back at Gremlin as he shadowed their footsteps.

They set about emptying the chamber pots again. Ray was glad that the sulfuric gases in the steam room corridor had somewhat desensitised his sense of smell, it was perhaps the only thing that made the removal of the waste hatch remotely bearable. The stifling odours, if nothing else, thankfully served to ward off his growing appetite.

They trudged to and fro, cleaning out the chamber pots and returning them filled with soapy water. Ray could feel his eyes growing baggier and bloodshot, his sleep-deprivation beginning to take its toll. His last good night of sleep was on the eve of the tool shed rebellion. He hardly counted his feverish dreams in the steam room as rest.

* * *

"There's no way to know how long they've been around though," said one of the inmates at the other end of the table, still discussing the origins of the *Kirzakai*, interrupting Ben's thoughts.

Having finished his meal, Ben broke his silence and chimed in. "I think you're both half-right," he said. "I think it was some kind of genetic mutation." Jack and Ethan both turned and exclaimed at the sight of him. "Evolution," he continued, remembering a science book he once read. "That's genetic mutation. The reptiles of early life on Earth might have taken a different route, similar to monkeys and humans. It's possible that they've always been here, just like us."

"Mate," said Jack, dropping the subject, "We thought you made it outta here last night."

"Yeah," said Ethan, "We saw the Watchers running in and out of your cell, yelling something about an escape. Wanna tell us what happened?"

"Night shift, *on your feet!*" Caleb commanded, marching the length of the mess hall with Evander and the other evening guards.

"Well, to be continued," said Jack as they rose from their seats, Nico following suit.

Cormac swaggered over to Little Danny and Levi, who sat together at the foremost table in the cafeteria. Cameron and Bryson were sitting a few tables away. Being lackeys to Sergei and Levi had been bad enough, but at least they had the good sense of knowing where to draw the line when it came to associating themselves with the son of a Watcher.

"Come now, Danny, you can talk to your new friend tomorrow," said Cormac, hauling his reedy son up by the scruff of his shirt and throwing him into the pack of assembling inmates. Little Danny straightened up, glumly distancing himself away from the others.

"It's about time you got back to work, Ben," Levi sneered from across the room. "Try not to faint again!"

Ben turned his back on the gloating teen, ignoring the insult.

Jack retorted on his behalf, "Don't worry about him, buddy, you just try not to have yourself another nosebleed! Wouldn't wanna go ruining that awful shirt you've got on, would ya?"

Levi looked down at his identical green uniform with the rest of the boys from the day shift chuckling at him as they were shepherded towards the stairs.

Jack turned to Ben as they shuffled towards the exit. "Smug kid had a blood nose when the smoke cleared in the tool shed yesterday morning. Think your brother might've had something to do with it."

"That reminds me," said Ben, "Where's Ray? I didn't see him in the cafeteria."

"Beats me," Ethan shrugged, "Haven't seen him since he got dragged out of his steam room. I'm sure he'll be alright though," he added quickly, catching a glance from Jack. "He held himself together better than any of us in there."

Maybe I can ask Sarah for some news about Ray, Ben thought to himself. It would give him an excuse to talk to her again, too.

Caleb and Evander led the inmates into the tool shed. Ben stopped at the doorway, examining the repaired room. It was different. It seemed as though the rebellion had merely been the first phase of a renovation to strengthen the tool shed.

Support beams now ran horizontally across the ceiling, holding the slabs of the concrete roof in place. The room was smaller in width than before, owing to the new wall now standing in front of where the drainage pipe had been.

The Watcher Recruits had completed the repairs over the course of a single day, and the room was now impervious to its previous weaknesses. Although impressive, it was still cause for alarm, as any escape attempt that the inmates tried, they would only ever have one chance at making it work.

* * *

After all of the chamber pots had been emptied and rinsed, Ray and Mara re-entered the male cell house to find that the cell doors along the far wall were now closed, all except for one: *Ben's*.

Ray's eyes strayed towards his brother's empty cell in the corner. Mara caught his stare. In the absence of the other Watchers, the consequence of disobeying Gremlin did not seem like much of a threat. Ray let his curiosity take hold. He and Mara approached the cell in the corner, despite the short man's disgruntled snarls behind them.

What little furniture there had been inside the cell now lay in disarray. The bed frame leaned against the far wall, the one mattress beneath it barely visible amidst dust and slim fragments of stone. The iron bars in the cell's skylight had been wrenched from their foundations in the concrete at the bottom and top of the square shaft in the low ceiling.

"I didn't think he had it in him to go out on his own," Ray smiled, shaking his head in disbelief.

"It doesn't look like he was alone," said Mara, pointing at a pair of ripped jeans and a tattered brown shirt cast upon the rubble-strewn floor.

"I 'eard you was skulking about in 'ere," foul breath filled the cell from behind.

20 - VIPEROD

Rays of early morning sunlight pierced through the overcast sky to shine down upon the wide murky river as it ribboned its way through the rich green rainforest. The water was calm, gently flowing downstream in a slight curve between sheer walls of jungle. Gnarled tree roots on either side reached down into the riverbed, disappearing underneath packed deposits of muddy sediment lining the riverbanks, with clumps of silt occasionally breaking off against the current's flow and adding to the brown tinge of the water.

From the uninhabited rainforest on either side of the river, it would have taken a keen eye to distinguish the dark figures moving just beneath the surface of the clay-coloured water. From a bird's-eye view though, the host of silhouettes teeming in the river would have seemed like a mass exodus of giant fish, yet no bird of this world could ever even hope to prey upon one of these man-sized beasts.

Viperod – an adolescent *Kirzakai* warrior fresh from the Desert Complex – swam downstream alongside his Redcrown brethren. The Redcrowns were so aptly named for the red-streaked flat crest that ran from the top of their wedge-shaped heads to the tips of their tails. They were also intrinsically agreeable to any given command, as long as it was for the good of the *Kirzakai*.

The water was colder than Viperod would have liked, and his lower back complained each time the hafts of his spear and javelins slung over his shoulder slammed into the blood red streak down his vermilion orange hide with every stroke forward; yet Tyrax had wished to strike fast and undetected, and so they had been given no other choice.

He surfaced for the briefest of moments, just long enough to take a new breath and lick silt from his lidless eyes. The morning sun was away on their left. *A curious thing*, he thought to himself, plunging his head back down into the water. It had been just past midday when they had departed from the Desert Complex not long ago. He had not yet grown accustomed to the time differences between the complexes.

A swell in the riverbed marked a turn in the flow of the river, yet Viperod was too slow to react, and he crashed into one of his kin. Basirick, one of the Redcrown veterans, elbowed him back on course before swimming on ahead.

Viperod was in the centre of the Redcrown host. He was not a soldier of note, nor was his skill in combat well-recognised. He should not have been removed from training as far as the Ridgebacks were concerned. He had been given leave to join the army despite his youth, yet only as a cruel jest between the new Frillneck officers.

He had always dreamed of becoming a great warrior, respected by all, yet since the day he had been hatched as a Redcrown, he was already at a disadvantage. The more conventional members of his tribe never ceased to remind him that their purpose was to be kind, compassionate and accommodating for all of the *Kirzakai*, and that the stronger tribes would provide for them in turn – yet he would rather be a soldier than a servant.

Another bend in the river's course, and another elbow to his side. Even his brethren who had already been drafted into the military looked down upon him with scorn. *Young and stupid*, they said. The others of his tribe had been conscripted for the inevitable war against mankind, yet Viperod had pledged his life to Tyrax's army out of his own free will.

And now the war was upon them. After the *constriction* of the Faction spy had confirmed the location and weaknesses of one of the humans' strongholds, Tyrax had been quick to command all of his forces to rendezvous at the Jungle Complex – the former home of the Blackbeads.

Tyrax brought forth the majority of his warriors from the Command Complex, while Jawresh took charge of all of the soldiers still in training. Furesh and the Ridgebacks however, had neglected to join them in battle for some odd reason – and they would not share the reason with those outside of their own tribe.

Viperod recalled that the Faction stronghold, Quartz Hall, was once the location of a great battle between the Lizardmen and the humans. They had long since thought that the murky river had swept over it and destroyed the city completely, but it was not so. The wretched humans had simply hidden their city underneath it.

The river ahead flattened out into a shallow delta, the muddy sediment dispersing across the breadth of a wide underwater plateau, and the rocks scattered across the riverbed were suddenly replaced by a solid smooth surface. The Redcrowns pushed themselves up out of the water as they ran aground.

This portion of the river was somewhat cleaner, and the water was clear enough for Viperod to see through. The thin vertical slits of his red-tinged reptilian pupils widened at the sight of the dull shade of his own reflection staring back up at him out of the riverbed. His long pink tongue slithered out of his snout to lick his eyes clean, and he dropped to his scaly hands and knees to prod at his faint mirror image embedded in the riverbed, only to streak his webbed hand across a thick glass panel.

He leaned closer, peering down through the glass to see the vast subterranean city stretching out beneath them.

The square-cut buildings beneath varied in differing heights, some occupying only one level, others rearing up in multiple tiers. A market square existed in the northeast corner of the highest level, merchants and vendors setting up their shop fronts for the day's trade. Away to the northwest corner on a lower level, livestock – that appeared no bigger than insects from this height – idly grazed upon an elevated field of grass, securely fenced in to prevent them from plummeting to their deaths.

Smaller still were the tiny dots of people scurrying about the cobblestone streets at the ground level. Two colossal iron statues standing on either side of the underground gate along the northern edge of the city stared up in awe of the blue-grey granite stone keep dominating the centre of the stronghold. In fact, the entire city seemed to have a steel blue aura cast over it, the water passing over the glass ceiling painting the stronghold in its hue.

Scum, Viperod thought, snapping his canine-like teeth as he climbed to his feet. He did not understand why the warm-blooded wretches needed a city of this size, nor did he care. The people of the Faction were the direct descendants of those humans who had hunted and killed his ancestors for sport. Not just the Redcrowns, but the proud warrior races as well; Horntails, Bluetongues, and even the Ridgebacks. But never the Gravelhides.

Although centuries had passed since then, and all those responsible were long dead, the memory of Thorax's assassination during his mission for peace was still fresh in the minds of the *Kirzakai*, and so they would see the human stronghold's blue aura turn red with fire and blood before the day was through.

A distant roaring filled his senses, and he looked up to see the backs of his Redcrown brethren already silently wading into position, following the river that spread out into a horseshoe before cascading down on three sides into a deep gorge, a cloud of mist rising up from the rushing waters far below.

The shimmering outlines of camouflaged Blackbeads watched as the Redcrowns moved to the edges of the waterfall. Tyrax had sent Teguresh and his tribesmen out first to stealthily scout the way ahead while waiting for Jawresh to arrive from the Desert Complex. Now they stood near-invisible atop rocky outcrops and wooden bridges and observation decks with their shortbows. The disguised Faction sentries and oblivious tourists alike on the surrounding walkways were either masked unconscious beneath a venom snare or lying face down with an arrow in their back.

Viperod attempted to take up a position in the middle of the waterfall's central edge, yet he was shoved away to the left-centre by his older and slightly-larger counterparts. He snarled, yet he crouched at the new position all the same. None of them actually knew where the hidden entrance to the south side of the city really was.

The Redcrowns were to be the probing assault. Their orders were to find the entrance and mark its boundaries with a pair of javelins for the main force. They were perfect for the job; their bodies were designed to be natural climbers. Tiny hair-like needles grew from the scales of their fingers and toes, giving them extra traction against most surfaces.

A clutch of Horntail slaves emerged from the river behind them, maces and morningstars hanging from their belts. Soon, the rest of the *Kirzakai* army would arrive.

Viperod readjusted the weapon strap over his shoulder as he scanned the cascading torrents for a protruding rock or ledge or *something* jutting out of the waterfall. Nothing. The veil of fog hanging over the mouth of the roaring gorge only served to further obscure the hidden entrance's location.

"What are you waiting for!?" Tyrax hissed as he and the Bluetongues appeared behind the Horntails, "Find it! *Find the entransse!!*"

A handful of other Redcrowns lining the eastern and western rims of the waterfall began to haphazardly cast themselves over the edges. Viperod saw this as his chance, his opportunity to become recognised as a warrior worthy of respect amongst Tyrax's army. He cast himself down too, thrusting both of his hands into the rushing waters, scrabbling for purchase upon a wet rock as his tribesmen fell all around him, disappearing into the mist, their splashes lost in the roaring torrents far below. Perhaps their hands had not been made to climb waterfalls after all.

The muffled sound of a trumpet's *HARROOOOOOOOOOOO* echoed all around the concave waterfall, followed by muffled *pop, pop, pop* blasts.

They had been spotted.

Too fast for the eye, a hail of tiny blunt spears flew from unseen sentry holes, rocketing through the veils of cascading water and finding their marks in the Lizardmen crowded around the gorge's rim. It was almost as if they had kicked a beehive as more angry metal hornets zipped through the curtains of water, whizzing by overhead at tremendous speeds, ricocheting with tinny *pings* off the surrounding rocks or ripping through scales and burrowing deep into flesh.

Their battle line around the waterfall's edge thinned rapidly, as with each Redcrown warrior that fell to a projectile, another dove into the mist after them, determined to retrieve the body so that the world's wider population of humans would not discover their existence.

One tiny missile grazed over Viperod's arm in a metallic blur, bouncing off the cliff wall and leaving a jagged gash of blood in its wake. He flinched in pain and one of his hands slipped from the wet rock. He reached up to curl the elbow of his good arm around the handhold before looking back down at the waterfall's yawning gorge, its gargantuan jaws seeming to widen as if to tear a chunk of flesh from the belly of the sky and swallow it whole along with the tiny reptilian morsels clutching to its teeth.

Time slowed down. Two by two, his brethren fell from the cliff's rocks all around him. A long swirling tongue of fog caught them all, enshrouding them in mist. Borne on the roiling vapours, the buzzing swarm of hornets whistled past each other, each with a single-minded determination to reach their destination. More metal drones shot through the air as the sound of clapping continued to reverberate from within the walls of the waterfall, the Faction sentries giving a crackling applause at the spectacle.

As he stared with dread at the swirling tongue of fog surging up to greet him, another Redcrown cast herself off the edge, slamming into Viperod on her way down, knocking him from the ledge so hard that he somersaulted backwards. He would have closed his eyes if he had the lids. Just as he resigned himself to an unknown fate at the bottom of the waterfall, one of his flailing hands caught onto something just beyond the veil of water.

His webbed fingers closed around the metal rod faster than a frog could catch a fly, the weapon strap sliding off his shoulder at the sudden jerk of inertia. Viperod caught the strap with his free hand. Before he could even begin to pull himself up, the other *Kirzaka* wrapped her tail around one of his legs.

He let out a pained rasp, and then put his head through the screen of cascading water to find that he was holding onto a balcony's railing. He could not hope to pull himself and the other Redcrown up with just one hand. He hurled his weapon strap over the railing, the javelins landing with a clatter upon stone. Viperod attempted to pull himself up again, with two hands this time, but it was no use, he was not strong enough. He blamed the bloody gash on his arm, streaming down in red rivulets at his strain.

Sensing his struggle, the female Redcrown used her tail to swing herself up and onto his backside. Scrambling up his shoulders to the balcony, she reached down with one hand to pull him up. "I do not take your glory, Viperod," she assured him as he swung his leg over the railing, "You are the firsst to breach Quartz Hall."

"Anarosa?" he said incredulously. She was the brood daughter of Savarish, the Redcrown Chieftain. Savarish had allowed her to train in combat at the Desert Complex, but she had not been given leave to join the army. "What are you doing here? You are no warrior!"

"Nor you," she smiled, her pale lips curling up from her short snout. Her slight red eyes seemed to kindle fire beneath the spiky eyelash-like fringes lining the flat wedge atop her honey-coloured head. "I wished to ssee the war everyone has talked of for sso long, and you *know* my brood mother would never have approved if I had requessted to join the army. In all the confusion while Jawresh was leaving, I sslipped into the throngs of warriors."

Young and stupid. Viperod smiled back at her, a true Redcrown's smile, despite the fact that she had almost knocked them both down into the abyss just mere moments ago. "I will keep you ssafe here. Your brood mother would surely kill you *and me* in her rage if you returned now. Take a weapon for yoursself, but leave me my sspear."

Anarosa flashed the rose red streak down her backside as she turned and stooped to hand him a pair of his javelins from the floor, and Viperod stabbed them into the cliff faces on either side of the balustrade, their wooden hafts jutting out through the rushing torrents.

Poking his head through the curtain of water one last time, he called up to the remaining Redcrowns still surrounding the rim of the waterfall to follow in his wake. Their cheers were drowned out by the dissonant *pop, pop, pop* and the roaring of the churning gorge below.

As she handed him his spear and the javelins remaining in his weapons strap, Viperod had a chance to assess their surroundings. The *constricted* spy had claimed that the unseen flaw in the city's design was actually an entrance into Quartz Hall through the living quarters of the Faction's Overseer. The Faction had only ever anticipated attacks incoming from the gorge's mouth – and, to a lesser extent, the underground northern gate, which was also heavily defended – but not from atop the waterfall itself.

They stood upon evenly-set tiles of black granite, and diagonal wooden planks lined the walls on either side of the balcony. On their left was a large tub of bubbling water, similar to the hot springs in the Command Complex, and on their right was a row of long flat wicker chairs, shaped like the slabs of rock the *Kirzakai* preferred to bask upon. Through the tinted glass wall at the opposite end of the deck, they could see faint outlines of rich leather furniture scattered around the spacious living quarters inside. Two long-haired creatures seated within the chamber let out high-pitched screams, dropping their glassware and hurtling across the room, escaping through a dark wooden door.

Just as the rest of the Redcrowns began to gather around the thick glass ceiling directly above the balcony to make their descent, a series of drumming footsteps echoed up from a staircase behind the hot spring tub on the other side of the glass wall, and a thin man with a head of golden hair appeared, investigating the screams. The warm-blooded wretch shrieked at the sight of the two *Kirzakai* warriors staring dumbfounded at it, and then bolted for the exit, hurtling outside without even pausing to slam the door in its wake.

Viperod licked his eyes, giving his reptilian pupils clarity over the glass wall before them. He spotted a neatly cut crack running from ceiling to floor down the centre of the window pane, and with a running leap, he thrust both his feet into the tinted glass.

The disguised double doors swung wide open with a simultaneous *CRASH* against the windows on either side, raining frosty shards across the deck and carpet alike. *A strange entrance*, he thought to himself.

Anarosa pulled him upright, glass fragments coursing from his scales, and together they headed for the open door, their clawed feet crunching upon the broken glass with each step.

They emerged on the south side of the blue-grey granite keep, a narrow stone walkway bridging the distance between the Overseer's quarters and a gap in the keep's battlements. The human's mop of blonde hair disappeared down a stairwell in the keep's roof just beyond the walkway. Not a single soldier was in sight, yet shouts of alarm rang throughout the city. Scurrying merchants and vendors in the market square away to the northeast corner of the city crashed into each other, dropping their wares and scrambling for the nearest shelter. Far below the bridge on the cobble-stone streets below, insect-sized humans scampered about, calling for help.

None is coming.

Viperod clutched his spear tight, glanced at Anarosa beside him with wide eyes, and then charged across the walkway and down the stairs into the heart of the keep, determined to reach the Faction Overseer before any other *Kirzaka* could take his glory. With Anarosa shadowing his long strides, taking two and three stairs at a time, they vaulted down into a vast chamber.

It appeared to be some place of worship, lined with rows and rows of wooden benches all facing towards a white-clothed altar set upon a dais at the far end of the hall. A rich blue carpet extended from the stairwell to the raised platform's steps. Light streamed down from ornate chandeliers set in the high ceiling, reflecting off the white marble walls and columns. Aside from the two Lizardmen, nothing else stirred within the room.

The *Kirzakai* spun around, yet before they could set foot upon the stairwell again, the sounds of men yelling and footsteps shuffling and weapons rattling free from their holsters carried up into the echoing hall from somewhere down below. Viperod pulled Anarosa behind him as the noises grew louder, and they slowly backpedalled up the blue carpet, Viperod holding his spear out before him with Anarosa's javelin poised upwards over his shoulder.

Heavy footfalls and rustling war gear announced the Faction soldiers' arrival, and a half-dozen brave men ventured out from the stairwell. Each man wore a black vest of padded armour covering them from shoulders to waist, with packed pockets and pouches clinging to their midriffs like overfed parasites. Some wore blue-enamelled helmets, yet most of them still gathered in the stairwell did not; they had not been given enough time to prepare. Each human carried a small metal device in its hands.

At the sight of only two Lizardmen, another six soldiers filed out from the staircase. The Faction soldiers spread out across the hall, four flanking from the left, four from the right, and another four pressing up the middle, their paltry weapons raised. Kalarish and Ophidirick had discovered the names for the human weapons in their research; *pistols, handguns, firearms* – they had also warned how deceptively deadly the dwarfish devices could be.

"There are too many, Viperod," Anarosa hissed behind him, both of them still retreating slowly down the aisle.

"We take the higher ground," he said, remembering his brief training upon the raised platform in the Desert Complex. "The others will be here ssoon."

"Not if they move as sslow as we do," she replied.

Anarosa stumbled backwards over the platform's steps with a startled snarl, and Viperod whipped his head around at her. Taking advantage of their moment's distraction, one quick-triggered soldier from the four men in the middle barked his gun with a deafening *CRACK*. Viperod ducked and weaved, grabbing Anarosa around the waist and pulling her to the ground between two wooden pews.

Gunshots rang off the walls as the other Faction guards opened fire, the sharp blasts reverberating around the hall. Outside, the sounds had been mere crackles underneath the curtains of cascading torrents, but in here, the barrage of bullets burst with bass-filled roars, escalating into a rapid crescendo of war drums.

Hungry hornets crunched through the wooden benches, showering the pair of Redcrowns with timber and sawdust while stray slugs sang their death song overhead, embedding themselves into the marble walls and columns behind them with plumes of powdery dust.

Then, as sudden as it came, the chaos was replaced by a near-silent *click, clicking* over the undertone of stifling white noise that was peppered with the occasional *BLAM!!*

Icy tendrils of fear gripping his insides, Viperod steeled his nerves and sprang up to his feet, hurling two javelins one after the other at the men creeping up along the side as they worked to reload their guns. His throws veered off-course. One javelin hit a soldier square in the chest – he had aimed for the throat – yet it was too weak to pierce the armour of the padded vest. It clattered harmlessly to the floor. The other javelin plunged clean through the knee of another soldier, drawing out a girlish scream, although Viperod had intended to impale the head of the man in front.

The retaliation did have the desired effect though. The Faction guards scattered around the hall, diving for cover behind the wooden benches. Anarosa leapt over the shattered remains of the pews, racing up the stairs to the dais and crouching behind the white-clothed altar. Viperod picked up his spear and followed in her wake.

"Surrender and die!" a haughty youth shouted over the rattles of fresh clips of ammunition.

"Surrender *or* die," one of the older men chided, yet all of the warm-blooded wretches shared the same knowing grin as they cocked back the slides on their pistols.

Viperod's heart running circles within his chest, he chanced a glance over the altar and looked to the stairwell at the other end of the room, the steps crawling with even more Faction soldiers, and he wondered where their Redcrown kin were. He looked to Anarosa by his side, her javelin shaking in her trembling hands, yet the brood daughter of the Redcrown Chieftain stared back at him, resolute and ready to fight.

"By tooth and claw, we go to war…" he murmured as the blazing gunfire started up again.

"March sspear and ssword, into the maw," she recited, her scaly hands tightening into a python's grip around the haft of her weapon. The Faction soldiers were in a semi-circle halfway up the platform's stairs now, edging closer and closer.

"*For blood and gore, we roar, we roar!*" they yelled in unison, launching to their feet.

"BY BLADE AND JAW, WE GO TO WAR!!" Tyrax himself led the charge down the stairs, lunging with the spiked end of his halberd and Bluetongues swinging their poleaxes and Horntails whirling their ball-and-chain flails and more Redcrowns hurling javelins and thrusting spears at the panicked humans frozen in fear.

In all the confusion, Viperod kicked the white-clothed altar so that it toppled over into the encroaching Faction soldiers, clearing an exit from the dais. He and Anarosa leapt down the steps, stabbing wildly at the downed men. Javelins flew over their heads at the remaining wretches still fumbling for a target, and the pair of Redcrowns rushed to rejoin the *Kirzakai* warriors storming down the stairs into the room below.

The library was filled with distant echoes of gunshots and slain guardsmen and teeming reptilian scales by the time Viperod and Anarosa reached the bottom of the staircase. Blood-spattered books and scrolls littered the shelves, and plainly dressed men – unarmed upon their knees – screamed for mercy. One clutched at Viperod's tail, and he drove the point of his spear straight through the lowly creature's chest.

Sensing that the fighting was done, Frillneck officers gingerly filed down the stairs, each carrying a dagger and a pungent pouch of venom snares to sedate the prisoners.

Tyrax was already rasping orders to half of the Horntail slaves to clear the keep's lower levels of any Faction scum that remained. "Bluetongues, Redcrowns…" they gathered around him, hammering the ends of their weapons into wood and stone in a drumming chorus. "Long ago, we were hunted, rounded up like animals and executed for ssport… now, we take our vengeansse upon the warm-blooded wretches. Now, it is their turn to run and hide! *Let the hunt begin!!"*

The warriors roared their approval, thirsty for blood, hungry for revenge. They broke off the thrumming tremor of weapons and followed him towards the library's exit, shoving through the aisles and sending racks of books and parchment crashing to the floor in angry clouds of dust.

Tyrax motioned for a nearby *Kirzaka* to throw open the exit's wooden double doors, granting them all a glimpse of the keep's lower parapet wall before – *BOOM* – the warrior and a few standing behind him folded over gaping holes in their flesh left by a row of smoking shotguns. The Faction soldiers were lined up directly in front of the keep's entrance, standing halfway up a stone ramp that led down to the cobblestone streets.

The salvo was immediately answered by a hail of javelins, many thrown out of instinct rather than precision, clattering off the inner stone battlements, yet some found their marks in the row of half-hidden shooters.

The ranks of Lizardmen hurled themselves to the sides, sending packed shelves toppling over as each man cocked another shell into their gun's chamber.

Tyrax hissed over the next blast of bass-booming buckshot, "Horntails, *advansse!!"*

The brown chevron-patterned warriors formed up in the centre of the library, linking arms and marching backwards in a shield-wall formation, the next round of pellets bouncing off their naturally all-encompassing carapaces and showering the floor in shrapnel.

Their eyes wide, the Faction soldiers turned to flee for safety, yet before they could step more than two feet down the ramp, a trio of Bluetongues were upon them, decapitating the row of heads with long sweeps of their poleaxes.

Directly opposite the thronging mass of Lizardmen pouring out of the library's double doors, the two colossal iron statues reared up on either side of the underground gate lining the northern wall of the city, towering high above the inner keep's lower parapets. Despite how tall the iron giants were, their motionless heads were geared upwards at the keep, as if staring up in awe at its magnificence. The archer on the left of the gate had his bow shouldered, one hand shading the sun from his vision. On the right, the swordsman's helmet was in one hand with his shield held by his side in the other. Bathed in the steel blue aura of the Faction metropolis, the *Kirzakai* momentarily halted their attack to admire the statues' grandeur.

GUVV!! GUVV!!

Sharp metal fingers woofed down from the heights of the northern wall's battlements to tear through scales and flesh as snipers bearing bolt-action rifles leaned over the parapet wall to take aim at the Lizardmen venturing out of the library. Not even the Horntails' armoured scales could deflect these projectiles, many of them falling prey to the riflemen's long piercing reach.

The *Kirzakai* warriors rushed out of the library in a teeming mass, crouching behind the inner keep's parapet walls and peering up at the top of the gatehouse. All that could be seen of each sniper was half a helmet and a long barrel.

In futility, the Lizardmen hurled their javelins upwards, yet the angle was wrong, and their throws either sailed overhead or clattered harmlessly against the stone wall, falling back down to litter the cobblestone streets with broken hafts. Despite taking refuge behind the keep's battlements, the riflemen had no problem picking off the burly reptilian beasts one by one.

Just as Tyrax was halfway through railing off another order to the Redcrowns to storm the gatehouse, they were drowned in shadow by an immense dark figure sailing across from the top of the keep to land upon the giant archer's head.

"*RAHAHAHAHA!! TEAR IT DOWN! TEAR IT ALL DOWN!!*" Jawresh roared from above.

The Gravelhide titan leapt down from the statue's head, throwing all of his weight against the massive iron bow. The statue groaned. Hanging off the bow amidst gunfire in midair, the reckless Warrior Chieftain wrenched at the statue with a series of jolts and jerks.

A foot lifted from the statue's platform, and the colossal giant leaned back far enough to snap from its foundation's supports, sending the statue crashing through the curtain wall behind it and into an unseen tunnel outside the gate, taking a chunk of rubble from a neighbouring building on its way down.

The townspeople away on the other side of the city screamed in fear at the rumbling thunderclap. Livestock brayed from the elevated paddock above as dust and debris rained down. The snipers from the top of the gatehouse gazed up at the shaking glass ceiling in silent dread, yet the thick panes held steady.

The *Kirzakai* gave up grating cheers for Jawresh, and more Gravelhides soared out from the top of the keep to land upon the other statue and the gatehouse's battlements alike.

Viperod pushed Anarosa back inside the keep. "Sstay here with the Frillneckss," he cautioned.

"I wish to fight!" she shouted above the roaring Lizardmen, gazing over his shoulder at the carnage.

"The Faction's army is broken," he rasped before looking around at the ruined library cluttered with fallen maps and charts and stacks of parchment. He added, "No doubt Tyrax will want to learn our enemy's ssecretss, and no doubt the Gravelhides will desstroy them before he can. Keep them ssafe."

She nodded dutifully, filled with new purpose.

Viperod turned and circled around to the west side of the keep, staying to the battlements while his brethren rampaged in the streets below. Horrified screams and blood-drunk roars resonated throughout the city. A fire blazed through the second-storey windows of a long stone building nestled against the western wall.

Blue-helmeted Faction soldiers charged around the southwest corner of the keep, their black armoured vests wet from guarding the waterfall. They could barely halt and take aim before a clutch of Redcrowns descended upon them, slashing and stabbing with their spears, slaughtering them all.

Viperod jumped down to the cobblestone street to join his tribesmen, their weapons coated in blood to match the dark red streaks down their orange hides. Amongst them, Basirick hissed with approval at the crimson tip of Viperod's spear.

A group of Gravelhides tore past, heading eastwards, stampeding towards small blocks of housing in the distance. The Redcrowns moved to follow the sounds of screams and rending destruction until they spotted a pack of humans trying to escape towards the northern gate on the other side of the keep.

Five stragglers lagged behind in the crowd: a shoulder-length brown-haired man carrying another long-haired creature, too frozen with fear to move on its own accord, followed by three young males bearing long kitchen knives.

Two of the warm-blooded worms whirled upon the Redcrowns, brandishing their weapons and hurling threats as they backpedalled, buying the others time to escape.

Viperod cast a fleeting sidelong glance at Basirick and his brethren, prowling forth like a pack of wolves toying with their pitiful prey. Now was his chance to prove his combat prowess to the veteran warriors.

He burst through the ranks of his kin and lashed out with his spear. One of the wretches parried his thrust and countered with a high slash. The *Kirzaka* ducked and swept his tail under the human's leg, knocking it down to one knee.

Just as he raised his spear for the death blow, a grinding metal groan reverberated throughout the entire city as the second statue lurched from its foundations, blasting rubble as it came crashing down, exploding through the keep's northeast wall section. Viperod instinctively threw up his elbows, covering his face and lidless eyes from the showering debris.

A sharp length of steel bit into the flesh just above Viperod's hip as the pair of worms used the billowing dust cloud to escape. He dropped his spear, the weapon clattering to the ground.

Young and stupid! Viperod chided himself.

Clutching at his side and staggering into the haze, he spotted a lone silhouette trying to climb the keep's wall. With one webbed hand holding his wound, he reached up over his shoulder and fumbled for a javelin from the weapon strap slung across his back.

He grasped one of his wooden missiles. It was not with his preferred hand, but he did not care. Coiling low in the fog of destruction, Viperod sprang up and let the javelin fly. A high-pitched shriek called out to him in the darkness.

The Redcrown waited for the dust to clear before licking his eyes clean. The long-haired human was crumpled in a heap upon the ground, his javelin sticking up out of its back. Viperod ambled over to the creature's carcass and planted his heel upon its neck before ripping the weapon from its flesh, blood pooling out from the wound and staining its shirt like a red flower opening its petals.

He spotted another of the young worms – the third one who had hoped to flee with the others – crouched next to the fallen swordsman's statue that now blocked the path to the gate. The whelp's knife dropped from its trembling hand, tears streaking the cowardly youth's face beneath an overgrown shrub of hair as yellow as dead grass.

Viperod raised his bloodied javelin, eager to put the quaking critter out of its misery, when he heard a forked tongue cluck disapprovingly. He scanned the faces of Basirick and the other Redcrowns behind him, but they were all looking up towards the keep's parapet wall with bitter expressions.

Blood streaming from the side of his torso down his leg, Viperod turned around to see the clutch of Frillneck officers watching from above, Anarosa amongst them, lured out by the iron statue's rending crash.

One of the Frillnecks had managed to squeeze his massive girth between two battlements like a fat turtle in its shell. It was Kobrick, a flesh tank who had done nothing to deserve his rank, much like the rest of his tribe.

"And to think – Tyrax had zuch high hopez for the Redcrown volunteer," the officer rasped to his peers in a derisive tone before looking down at Viperod indifferently. "Now, I wonder: will he reward you for being the firzt to breach the Faction's Quartz Hall? Or will he *punish* you for wantonly killing our prisoners?"

21 - THE INCOMPETENT FOOLS

"Keep it moving!" Caleb ordered, his stern voice reverberating around the newly-repaired tool shed.

Ben snapped back to attention, approaching the rack of shovels. He examined the palms of his hands, finding that his blisters had now crusted over and formed into slight calluses, even though he had only worked a total of three shifts in the pit.

Jack, Ethan, and an uncertain Nico grasped shovels beside him, and all of the inmates trudged out into the quarry, Little Danny wheeling a minecart at a short distance behind them.

They shaded their eyes as the sun descended in the afternoon light, casting one final glare at the prisoners before disappearing over the western edge of the dustbowl's rim. Nico wandered out through the weathered support pillars, stopping beside the downward slope to behold the quarry. Ben joined him, cautiously peering over the brink.

A new level had been cut into the ground at the far end of the pit, and wooden pegs had already been hammered into the bare cliff walls of the previous level, naked without the dirt-retaining fishnets. Broken brown bottles and shards of glass strewn upon the ground glinted underneath the orange-tinted clouds as dusk approached, evidence of the Watchers' poker game from the previous night.

"They will going to dig?" Nico asked in his harmonious Americanised accent, watching the other inmates pass by down the ramp. Ben nodded at his curious cellmate. "Why?"

"For the gems and gold in the ground," said Ben, although remembering the broken sword, shield and arrowheads that they had uncovered, he suspected that there was more than just riches lying in the dirt.

They followed Jack, Ethan and the rest of the shovel gang down the dirt ramp and into the pit, Nico curiously running his hand over the fishnets as they passed by. The inmates with mattocks picked out their sections of the rock shelf and began working. Little Danny pulled his minecart to a stop and lurked in the gathering shadow of a cliff, away even from the other minecart pushers.

Ben plunged his shovel into the first pile of dirt and threw it into one of the barrows. The work was easier for him now. His muscles did not shriek in agony as they had during his previous shifts. Nico shovelled beside him, kicking his spade into a heap of earth with his bare foot.

Jack and Ethan chuckled on Ben's left. He turned to see the rest of the shovel gang flinging clumps of dirt at Little Danny rather than the carts. The peevish runt reared backwards, retreating from the volleys and sitting halfway up the slope instead.

"He thought he'd be safe working with us after ratting out on everyone yesterday in the tool shed," said Jack. "He thought *wrong*."

"Now he doesn't have his daddy watching his back either," Ethan added, stooping to pick up a rock and lobbing it at the scrawny boy.

* * *

In Ben's ruined cell, Ray and Mara turned around to see Cormac standing in the doorway with Gremlin peering anxiously over his shoulder. Ray caught sight of a familiar-looking silver ring gleaming from one of Cormac's grubby fingers resting upon the hilt of his shock stick.

Is that the ring Dana gave me? Ray thought to himself. *I thought Spike had it.* He could not tell if it was the same ring without a closer inspection.

"I've got a job for ya," said Cormac. "Mainly 'cause I don't wanna do it meself." He turned and shoved Gremlin aside, walking back across the cell house. Gremlin seethed in silence, his green eyes filled with spite at the other Watcher. "Come on then, I don't 'ave all day," Cormac called over his shoulder.

The pair of inmates exchanged a glance before trailing after him, with Gremlin bringing up the rear.

Cormac turned at the top of the barracks stairs. "No, no. Not you, Sheba. Be off and go paint your nails… before I changes me mind on what else you can do for me," he winked at Mara. With a mixture of contempt and relief, she glared up at the crude Watcher before exiting the cell house. "Touchy touchy, she's a feisty one, 'ey?" he chuckled, turning his attention to Ray. "Come on, sunshine, I've got work for ya."

Gremlin pushed him up the stairs as Cormac opened the door to the barracks. The smell of rancid meat filled his nostrils as they entered.

"Nothing like a bit of fresh air, 'ey?" Cormac grinned at Ray, who coughed between shallow breaths.

The room was lit naturally from the outside, the westering sun shining light through floor-to-ceiling windows on either side of the door behind them. To their right was an open elevator shaft, leading down into the treasury below. The elevator platform was sitting on one of the lower levels, leaving a hazardous open square in the white ceramic-tiled floor.

The whitewashed concrete wall across from them housed a single closed door on the right. To the left was a corridor with more doors to the guards' quarters set on either side, the most prominent of which being the one at the end of the passage, with what appeared to be a keypad next to the door handle.

Heaped on top of a wooden table next to yet another closed door on the left side of the room was a musty pile of soiled and sweat-stained bed sheets. Three Watchers loitered amid cushioned bamboo furniture, with bandannas masking their faces. They paid no attention to Ray, Cormac and Gremlin. The trio of guards instead stared with dread at the handle set within a red-glowing grate on the wall – a smaller version of the grills in the steam rooms.

"Again!" the unmistakably shrill voice of Lygia shrieked out from behind a bandanna, and one of the Watchers pulled the grate down like an oven door. Lygia and the other guard threw bundles of bed sheets into the open hatch as the room filled with sulfur.

Cormac inhaled deeply, the toxic air filling his lungs, and he uttered a deep sigh of elation. For Ray though, the fumes were too much. Coughing heavily now, he turned back towards the staircase. Gremlin blocked him off.

His eyes beginning to burn, Ray caught sight of the handle of a glass door set within one of the adjacent tall window panes. Hacking and wheezing, he lunged towards it, shoving it open and advancing out a few paces onto the vast expanse of concrete roofing the cell house.

A fresh salty ocean breeze kissed his skin and nourished his lungs with clean air. He took in deep breaths. Though tinged with the foul stench of acrid gas spilling out from the barracks behind him, the atmosphere up here was far cooler and cleaner than the heat and humidity that he had grown accustomed to within the lower levels of the prison.

Gulls wheeled and called overhead, soaring on the sea wind, searching for prey within the openings of skylight shafts ringing the outer edges of the plateau. Scattered clouds floated across the sky, infused with orange hues of the sunset.

Ray staggered forward, his sight falling upon a tropical rainforest beyond the edges of the cell house roof. Big coconut leaves swayed back and forth in the ocean breeze like giant fans. The thick band of treetops stretched east, eventually giving way to a volcano looming in the distance.

He saw his opportunity to escape. He bounced on the balls of his feet, preparing to run, when a baton thwacked him across the back of his knees. The tropical jungle's picturesque image soared up out of his vision as he crashed down on all fours to face the concrete roof.

"Thought I'd make it that easy, 'ey sunshine?" asked Cormac, hauling him up by the scruff of his shirt.

Ray threw an elbow back at the patchy-scalped guard, yet he only managed to throw the Watcher's stubby fingers off his uniform. He stood up, wincing at the pain in the back of his legs. Cormac flashed his yellow teeth in a crude grin, and invited the inmate to follow with a jerk of his head.

With Gremlin silently shadowing them, they walked along the side of the barracks, crossing over to the roof of the adjoining cell house and walking in between the skylight shafts. The row of glass panels on their right was interrupted by a hollow-brick wall that housed the adjoining passage to the other side of the barracks, the windows continuing again after a short distance.

Cormac dragged his dirty hand across the glass looking into the second half of the barracks, leaving a streak of grime in his wake before opening up another glass door. Ray lurched through, leaving the warmth of the sunset's orange glow to be hit by a wave of cool air as he entered, almost an alien atmosphere in the prison.

This side of the barracks was crowded with off-duty guards – it seemed not all of the Watchers were as insensitive to foul smells as Cormac. On the left side of the room was a dining area decorated with more cane and cushion furniture, the table sitting underneath a large air conditioner set high up on the wall. It was not exactly luxury, but it was still far better than what the inmates were treated to.

The rest of the room seemed almost identical to the other side of the barracks, with only minor differences. The elevator platform on the right was on their level, covering the square hole in the tiled floor. A door in the corner next to the platform stood closed, sealing off the connecting passage to the barracks' living area. Guards' rooms branched off another corridor along the far wall, but this corridor stopped abruptly in a dead end – no door with a keypad on this side of the barracks.

Cormac shouldered past the other Watchers, causing them to spill their beers as he led Ray and Gremlin towards the door on the other side of the elevator platform. He turned back as one guard cursed, looking down at his freshly-stained shirt. Cormac approached the guard with his eyebrows raised, a mischievous twinkle in his eye.

The guard shut his mouth and turned away, glancing at Leon who was eyeing them both from across the room, toying with his shock stick on the dining table.

Cormac laughed as the bitter Watcher retreated to the fridge for another beer. Satisfied, he turned and opened the door next to the elevator platform, flicking on a light switch. Dust motes swirled as the air-conditioned breeze swept into the cluttered storage room. The three of them navigated their way across, past boxes and crates, to a door on the other side.

The next room appeared to be quite plain. Absent of any chairs, a wooden workbench stood on the left. A rusty metal minecart was propped up on railings on the other side of the room, the tracks running between two closed doors. The light from a caged tungsten bulb overhead intermittently flickered on and off.

"Seem familiar?" asked Cormac, turning to Ray. "You woke up while they was searching ya, if I 'eard no lie."

Ray looked around the room. It seemed smaller than when he had first arrived. He thought of recreating the scene of his admittance into the prison. He turned to see Gremlin sidling over by the table, warily gazing at the inmate with his shock stick drawn and ready. He would only need to push the small guard over the table and take out Cormac before Gremlin got back up.

But then he would need to contend with all of the other Watchers outside, while all of the prisoners currently out of their cells were working far away down in the pit. He guessed that this was the reason why the female inmates never raised a hand to the guards, despite not being shackled by manacles. He was outnumbered, and in the barracks of all places to start a rebellion.

"Yeah," he turned back to Cormac, "I remember."

* * *

"So, how far out did you boys get?" asked Jack, "See anything interesting?" The ears of the other inmates working nearby prickled, listening intently.

"We made it as far as Lungsod," said Ben, "The fishing village just past the volcano, that's where Nico here is from." He introduced his smiling cellmate as he continued, "We almost reached the marketplace to find some help, and that's when we were apprehended by two patrolmen."

"More Watchers?" asked Ethan.

"Not quite –"

"Gaspar's guards," Nico interrupted in a bitter tone.

"*Gaspar...?*" Jack's shovel blade hung in midair.

"Mayor Gaspar," said Nico. "He's the only big belly in my village. Many people is hungry, and he'll going to do nothing," he fell silent, clenching his jaw as he kicked his shovel into the dirt.

"They radioed the Watchers stationed in an outpost near the volcano," said Ben, "And then held us at gunpoint until they arrived. Now we're back here."

"Where exactly is *here* anyway?" asked Ethan.

"Here? We're here in the Philippines!" Nico answered, his dark eyes brightening up again.

Mattocks glanced off the rock shelf and clumps of dirt fell short of the minecarts as many of the inmates faltered, dazed by the news. They worked in silence for a while, only the sounds of mattocks striking the ledge and shovels scratching the ground and chunks of earth being lobbed into the rusty wagons could be heard.

"I gotta ask," said Jack. "How'd you get out?"

Ben briefed them on how they were able to break the iron bars from the skylight using wet bed sheets, but after seeing the tool shed's rapid repair and structural reinforcement, he did not think that the Watchers would allow anyone else to make a second attempt.

"Well," said Jack, turning to Ethan, "I can think of another reason why I want this shift to be over already." They scraped their shovels against the mounds of earth steadily building up. Jack broke the monotonous silence again, "Let's make the shift go a bit faster, boys."

Ethan struck up conversation, calling across to Nico. "So, what's life like living in the Philippines? What's your school like?"

"If someone will going to attend to a school, they're so lucky," said Nico.

"Many my friends never finish in a schooling."

"Is that because their parents can't afford the fees?" Ben asked, more bluntly than he had intended. He had read somewhere that impoverished families in first-world countries could still enjoy some level of welfare, yet for those in other areas of the world, every day was a struggle.

"No," said Nico, shaking his head. "When the children is get bigger, they will going to work for support their family too, and then, there will going to more foods to eat."

"So… are you going to school?" asked Ethan, trying not to cause offence.

"When I'm a small, but not in now. Sometimes, if I saw them, my classmate or my teacher will talk me about school, and then I always said, someday, maybe, me and my Papa will have a money for the foods and a schooling again."

"What does your old man do for work?" asked Jack.

"My Papa? Well, when I'm a small, my Papa will going to cut the trees, and then we have a many foods and I will going to school. And then, the rainy season will going to come, and then, there's a landslide," Nico planted his shovel upright in the ground to animate with his hands. "Many houses is no more, wash out in the ocean. Even our house is no more. And then, my baby sister will going to drowned."

The inmates working the rock ledge nearby faltered a second time, their tools twisting in their hands.

"And then," Nico continued, "Mayor Gaspar say it's the fault of a logging, and the trees will going to stop on the landslide. So, my Papa's work is no more, and then our house is no more, and then my Mama is so mad on my Papa and my family will going to move to the city, in the mainland. But I don't like city, so I will going to remained with my Papa and I give a helped in our store. Still I didn't see my family, but it's okay, someday." He finished, picking up his shovel.

Ben blinked hard.

Ethan sniffed.

"And we thought we had it bad here," said Jack, digging through the piles of dirt.

Nico seemed completely normal after sharing the tale of his childhood, as if such sad stories were normal to hear while growing up. He smiled up at the others, "It's okay, it's just trial, testing to prove if you're a strong. And then here, in the Philippines, we always said *bangon*."

"So," said Ben, taking a deep breath to stifle the sob building in his throat, "What kind of store does your father own?"

"We sell some hardwares near at the marketplace," said Nico. "There's many fishermen will going to be our customer."

Jack paused, staring up at the fishnets hanging from the surrounding dirt walls. "Well, at least this place is helping your old man pay the bills."

"Wait," said Ethan, "Does that mean you recognise Caleb and Evander up there?" he pointed at the two men standing upon the rock shelf among the other guards in the fading light. "They're the ones who bring in all the supplies."

"No," Nico answered. "I will going to work in our stocks room only. I'm not see our customer."

Ben paused for a moment, and an image of the wooden chains rack in the cell house flew into his mind. The first time he had been shackled to the rack, Joshua had said that there were people in the fishing village who would be willing to help them when called upon, and that the local who ran the hardware store was one of them.

He gave voice to his thoughts, "Nico, did you or your father ever meet a man named Jacob Rauder?" His cellmate considered the name, and then slowly shook his head. "How about Joshua?" Nico shook his head again.

Ben resumed his silence, thinking that perhaps Nico's father was the same storekeeper who Joshua had spoken of. *And if he hasn't met Caleb and Evander before, then of course he wouldn't have met anyone else from however long ago Joshua said we came here. But without Nico's confirmation, there's no way to be sure.*

He could not guess at how many other hardware stores there might have been in Lungsod, and they could not hope to enlist the help of just any storekeeper with Gaspar's guards roving the streets. They could not risk exposing themselves to another person on the Watchers' payroll, if they ever had another chance to escape. Nico's father would be a great start in finding help though.

Maybe we should have headed straight for Nico's house, instead of running to the marketplace, Ben thought with the bitter taste of regret.

* * *

Cormac sauntered across the small room towards the minecart sitting on the twin set of rail tracks bolted to the floor. "Take these to the library," he said. "Gremlin'll show you the way." Ray approached the cart, bemused by the sight of jumbled scrolls and books piled high inside. Cormac caught his eye. "Don't ask me why they want it, they just want it. And when you're done wiv this lot," he pushed open a door to reveal a whole row of other carts waiting in a dark tunnel outside, "Come back for the ovvas."

Gremlin opened the door on the right to reveal a flight of stairs leading downward, the twin set of rails extending out of the room and down the steps. A wave of hot air clashed with the air-conditioned breeze from the barracks. Gremlin was halfway down the stairs when Ray decided to kick the cart down after him.

The ivory-skinned Watcher gave a cry of alarm, scampering down the steps and around the corner before the minecart sailed off its tracks and crashed into a wooden door below with an eruption of loose papers.

Cormac laughed crudely behind Ray at the other guard's misfortune before pushing the inmate down after him. Ray stumbled down the first few steps as the door slammed shut behind him. Regaining his balance, he casually walked down the rest of the stairs, with Gremlin glaring up at him from the bottom.

The grumbling Watcher led the way through the small passage. Grabbing hold of the barrow, Ray lifted his shirt up to cover his face as the foul sulfuric gas filled his nostrils again.

The rusty wagon scraped the walls as they took the sharp corners, trundling past the steam rooms and the gunmetal grey door. The reeking stench continued to seep through the fabric of the billowing bed sheet hanging over the entrance of the hotbox with the broken grate. Gremlin opened the corridor's exit and Ray pushed the minecart after him in a hurry, slamming the door behind him.

They were in the small adjoining passage between the two cell houses again, and Gremlin opened up the door on their right, revealing another flight of steps leading upwards. This was the same door that Ray had seen Ava exit from when he had first seen her. No rail tracks had been laid upon these steps to help him haul the cart up, and the ill-tempered guard did not seem to be the collaborative type. Ray heaved the minecart up backwards by himself, the metal wheels clashing upon stone and echoing in the stairway with each step.

Dragging the laden wagon through the doorway, Ray paused to look around. They were standing in a small sombre room with two large mounds of dirt heaped upon the floor, one sporting a densely-packed crater, and the other with barely an indent. Between them sat a simple wooden chair, set in front of an all too familiar red-glowing grate.

Dimly seen through the furnace, Watchers continued to throw bundles of bed sheets into the heat vent on the other side of the shaft.

A pleasant voice broke the silence. "I'm glad they sent *you*." Ray turned to his left to see Ava standing at the entrance to another room. "Bring it through," she said, standing to one side of the doorway, inviting him to wheel the minecart into the next room.

Bookcases lined each wall of the wide well-lit room, with two rows of shelves in the centre, although the library was far from being fully-stocked. Mounds of dust were broken by one or two books here and there.

"I've never seen *so many* before," Ava exclaimed as she peered at the cart's contents. "I wonder where they've all come from."

"I didn't think the guards knew how to read," said Ray, purposefully glancing back at Gremlin, who snarled from the other room. "What do the Watchers want with all this?"

Ava looked up at him, her eyes strained and mildly baggy. She shook her head. "Not the Watchers. The Lizardmen." She caught his puzzled expression. His question did not need to be voiced. "They ask me to read all of the seized literature to them."

"And that's what you do all day?" he asked.

"Yes," she nodded.

Her tangled blonde hair full of split ends made sense to him now, her proximity to the dry heat blowing from the furnace in the room behind them cooking all of the moisture out of her body on a daily basis.

"The Lizardmen want to learn our language," she continued. "They want to uncover information regarding the whereabouts of a group called the *Faction*."

"The *Faction*?" he repeated. "I've heard of them before, who are they?"

"I'm not entirely sure," she said, her gaze returning to the books and scrolls in the cart. "Maybe this will give us some answers."

Gremlin grunted from the doorway, his impatience flaring at their babble.

Ray upended the minecart, the books spilling out onto the floor. "Why are you helping the Lizardmen?"

"They treat me nice enough," Ava shrugged as she knelt to begin sorting through the pile. "Besides, it's better than what the other prisoners have to go through."

Ray agreed as he lowered himself onto the floor beside her, thinking of all the inmates straining down in the pit day and night, and Mara braving the stench of that horrible shaft in the laundry.

* * *

Little Danny took one of the minecarts and pushed it up the dirt ramp by himself, the skinny runt having trouble with the heavy load. After the inmates had been betrayed following the tool shed rebellion, the prisoner who was normally responsible for wheeling that particular barrow – and normally, would have welcomed the help – had taken up a mattock instead, preferring arduous labour over assisting someone who would give up his own friends so easily.

The sky darkened as night fell. Scudding clouds obscured the light of the stars, and thin wisps blew across the moon, intermittently veiling it like a curtain in the breeze.

Just as the inmates' eyes had adjusted to the gradually deepening shadows, Caleb strode over to the floodlight set above the shelf of rock and flipped the switch. A loud buzz reverberated around the walls of the pit, and all of the inmates were temporarily blinded by its blazing brightness.

Ben dared to open his eyes again, looking down upon the ground. It seemed as though the sun had returned, yet only a small portion of the quarry was now visible. Anything that fell beyond the borders of the floodlight's aura was wreathed in shadow.

The sound of a trundling minecart travelled down the slope, and all of the inmates breathed a sigh of relief. Finally, the water carts had come, marking the halfway point in the shift. Inmates tossed their tools aside and began to form a line for the water, comparing blisters and calluses under the light of the lamp.

Ben and Nico planted their shovels upright in the earth, casting long shadows upon the quarry wall behind them. They stood roughly halfway in the queue, with Jack and Ethan a few paces ahead. Ben examined his palms, thankful that his blisters had not burst again.

He also noticed that no one was calling him a *dreg* anymore – probably owing to his part in planning the tool shed rebellion – but he knew that the inmates who worked the day shift might not be so friendly after what had happened to Rashad, Kenneth and Aiden.

Nico turned over his hands too, as other inmates came to check the newcomer. Not even a blemish had appeared across his palms. His skin was as tough as leather.

"You belong up front with these hands, kid," one of the burly teens remarked before moving farther down the line.

"What happen now?" asked Nico, his eyes full of curiosity.

"We're halfway through the shift now," Ben explained. "Now we can drink some water."

Nico made a sound of approval. Ben had noticed that for the entire afternoon, his cellmate had laboured without making any complaints about the work, his thirst, or hunger. He stifled a smirk as he likened Nico to who he would have imagined to be a younger version of Rashad.

The cart came into view at the bottom of the dirt ramp, yet water did not spill over the sides. At a collective groan from the inmates, the cart proved to be full of fishnets. The figure behind the cart moved into the light, revealing himself to be a Watcher. Other silhouettes moved down the slope behind him.

"Leave it here," Caleb ordered. "We'll take care of it."

The Watcher nodded and pushed his way past the other moving shadows, who the prisoners soon recognised to be the female inmates coming down to hang up the fishnets. Many of the boys straightened up, momentarily forgetting their thirst.

Ben leaned out of the queue, searching for Sarah amongst the crowd. *There she is!* He smiled widely as he caught sight of her trailing behind Mara and Amelia. Together, the three girls climbed up the rock ledge to the higher level.

The water carts arrived soon after, and all of the inmates fell back into line. Little Danny and the other minecart pushers set about hauling fishnets from the first cart, but almost immediately, the scrawny imp caught himself in a tangle while trying to throw the nets up to the girls waiting on the upper level. Seizing the opportunity, Ben exited the line and came to his former cellmate's aid, the other prisoners jeering behind him.

"Thanks, Benny. I knew you was gonna forgive me sooner or later," said Little Danny, his sky blue eyes twinkling in the floodlight's glare.

Ben ignored him, and to his delight, he looked up to see Sarah crouched at the rock shelf's edge.

"Ben!" Sarah cried, "Ava told me you were back. I'm sorry they caught you, but I sure am glad to see you again."

His heart leapt within his chest. Her soft gentle eyes lingered upon him, waiting for him to answer, yet his mind struggled to muster a reply.

"Here," he said, handing her a bundle of frayed fishnet cords.

"*Smooth,*" Mara commented, sidling up next to Sarah and snatching the mesh up from Little Danny, hoping to catch his reedy fingers between the tangled knots.

"Sarah," Ben began, trying to pace his jittery voice, "Have you seen my brother anywhere?"

"Yes," she smiled, "I saw him earlier today, in the laundry. But he seemed exhausted."

"What was he doing in *there?*" asked Ben, puzzled.

"Helping me clean the chamber pots out," Mara answered out of the side of her mouth. "Don't know what for. As a punishment, I suppose."

"What's it like out there?" Sarah asked, her silky chestnut brown hair catching the light as she gazed up in wonder at the rim of the surface.

"It's beautiful," Ben replied, refraining from commenting on her own beauty, "There's a tropical rainforest, and a beach full of powdery white sand, and waves in the ocean as blue as the sky."

"That sounds a lot like where we were when I was captured," Sarah mused as she bent down to reach for another bundle of net.

Ben turned back to the queue for the water carts to see the other inmates pushing their way past a confused Nico. His smile faded somewhat as he pointed towards his new cellmate. "See him? That's Nico. He's a local from the fishing village nearby; he said we're in the Philippines."

Sarah's eyes widened, yet Mara cut across her before she could reply. "That's enough for now. We've got plenty up here." She looked down at Little Danny, who was still offering a bundle of fishnet up to her. "Actually…" she reconsidered, "One more couldn't hurt."

She bent down and took the entire net from him. Little Danny stood beaming up at her, waiting for an expression of gratitude. With a sly smirk, Mara opened up the net to its full span and cast it down upon the peevish runt.

"*Mara!*" Sarah cried indignantly as the sniggering girl disappeared into the shadows.

"'elp! 'elp!" Little Danny squealed in his reedy voice, collapsing and thrashing wildly beneath the bundle of mesh like an animal caught in a snare.

Other inmates crowded around, laughing at the struggling traitor, with Ethan moving to pull another net from the minecart nearby. Sarah felt pity for the scrawny child, and she looked towards Caleb and Evander for help. They stood watching like silent sentinels, allowing the prisoners to fight amongst themselves. As long as the guards were not under threat, they let the inmates have their short-lived amusement, even if it was at the expense of Cormac's son – and for some of the Watchers, especially if it was at the expense of Cormac's son.

"'elp!" the pathetic boy cried out again.

"Ben, don't just stand there!" Sarah pleaded.

A wave of disappointment washed over him. *He deserves this*, Ben thought to himself. But then again, he could remember when he himself had been in that same position. Not too long ago, *he* had been the scrawny child on the ground, with a group of bullies laughing in a circle around him.

Ben moved towards Ethan and laid a hand on his arm before he could pull the net out of the cart. Ethan cocked his head to one side in confusion before shrugging, letting the fishnet fall back into the barrow.

Weaving his way through the other inmates gathered around Little Danny, Ben stooped to lift the net pinning his former cellmate to the ground. He ignored the other inmates' ridicule. Nothing else mattered as he looked up to see Sarah smiling down at him.

"Alright boys, it's been fun," said Jack, raising his arms, "But let's not mess with the kid *too* much. We don't want him dirtying up the water tomorrow night, do we?"

Little Danny scrambled to his feet and brushed himself off, scowling at all of the inmates gathered around him. Worming his way through the begrudging crowd, he resumed his perch halfway up the slope in the darkness.

As the other inmates returned to their tools, Ben rejoined Nico at the water carts. They did not need light to see that only the dregs of the water remained in the dark depths of the carts. Small pieces of dirt floated upon the surface. Ben sighed, yet he had no other choice. His throat was dry, even in the absence of any sunlight. He cupped his hands together and plunged them into the water, feeling the muddy sediment spill into his sore palms.

"Just wait," said Nico, the barefoot villager taking off his own shirt.

Ben shook his hands free of the goop he had scooped up and gave his cellmate some room. Nico plunged his shirt into the cart, waving the cloth back and forth in the murky water before holding up the soiled uniform. Tilting his head back and holding the wet shirt above his face, Nico wrung the water into his mouth. The droplets rained down, catching the light of the lamp and twinkling with far better clarity than Ben had expected.

All of the other inmates watched in amazement, never having thought of this themselves. Ben removed his own shirt, revealing his pale skinny chest, and followed suit. The taste was terrible, but at least he was not drinking pure mud. He swished the water around the dry corners of his mouth, although it was not long before the refreshing liquid sank down his gullet to the parched arid caverns below.

He stared sidelong with silent admiration for Nico, who tossed his damp shirt aside. He wondered what the astute Filipino boy could have achieved if he had been given the chance to continue attending school.

Ben had his shirt halfway back on, afraid that Sarah would see how pale and skinny he was, when Nico protested. "No. You will going to sick. Just try to wait for a while."

Ben nodded and laid out his shirt to dry. He was not going to question Nico's advice.

"Nice trick," said Jack as the pair of inmates resumed their work, "I'll keep it in mind for whenever I get stuck at the back of the line."

Nico gave a humble smile.

"What I don't get," Ethan began as they tossed dirt into the minecarts behind them, "Is how a satellite photo of this place hasn't come out in public yet."

"Well," said Jack, "If they've got this Mayor Gaspar on their side, who knows how high up the corruption goes?"

"Maybe someone like to see in here, but I think they're not come," said Nico.

"Why not?" asked Ben.

"Well, there's a many NPA rebels, the *New People's Army*, in the mainland," said Nico. "They will going to be the one who fight the corruption, but still, no change," he grinned at that, as if it was a well-known fact that the militant group had failed to accomplish anything except add to the country's list of problems. At their bemused expressions, he continued, "And then, I think if someone like to see in here, they will going to scared because the NPA."

"So, does that mean even if we do escape," said Jack, "We might not get past the NPA?"

"Maybe," said Nico. "The NPA will going to ask for the payment. There's a bridge they will going to guard, and then it's our only way for the mainland if you didn't got a boat."

"Wait," said Ben. "If there's a toll bridge, why didn't you tell me that *before* we escaped this morning?"

Nico shrugged sheepishly, "Well, when we go on my village, I'm already escaped to my home."

* * *

They sorted through the pile of literature, separating the scrolls from the books.

Ben would've loved this job, Ray thought to himself. He glanced at maps and landmarks scrawled upon some of the parchments – blueprints of strongholds hidden in remote locations.

He examined the covers of the novels, *The Construction of Quartz Hall, The Adventures of Lance & Shaft, Rocksport: A History*. He stopped sorting momentarily. "I haven't read a whole lot of books, but these ones have some pretty weird titles."

Ava's eyes widened with each cover she scanned. She looked up at him with excitement. "All of this could be *original* Faction texts!"

"Wait until you see all the other carts."

"There's more?" she asked in disbelief, "That must mean... The Lizardmen must have found them already."

With an exasperated sigh, Gremlin marched across the room and thwacked Ray across his shoulders with the shock stick.

Ava leapt up with an indignant cry, "Why would you hit him!?"

Not in the mood to be punished again, Ray shrugged it off and resumed sorting through the pile. "He probably just wants us to hurry up," he assumed, looking back at the Watcher.

Gremlin grunted, his pointed face nodding with impatience.

"If you want us to work faster," said Ava, her voice heightening an octave, "Why don't you go and fetch the other carts yourself!? We aren't going anywhere!!"

Gremlin's face twitched, pained by her words. He raised his baton to strike at her instead, but Ray was on his feet in a flash. The short man wavered, his eyes darting between the pair of inmates. Fuming in silence, Gremlin flitted out of the room with the empty cart.

Ava went after him, shutting both doors as the minecart crashed down the flight of steps. Ray cast his eyes upon the heap of literature, speculating the significance of what the Faction might be to the Lizardmen.

"Come on, we don't have much time," Ava whispered behind him. She led Ray to the side of one of the bookcases in the centre of the room, pointing towards a particularly thick novel standing in the middle shelf by itself, clear of any dust. "Pull this book when I say," she said in a hushed voice, walking around to the other side. *"Now!"*

He was confused by her urgency, but he tugged at the book's spine all the same. At first, it did not budge. He gripped it with both hands and yanked backwards.

A *click* resounded from somewhere within the rack, followed by chains clanking and well-oiled gears turning.

In his peripheral vision, he saw one side of the shelf rising up to the ceiling. The two inmates reunited at the end of the rack, where an entrance to a dark passage beneath the bookcase was now revealed. Hot air blew up the hidden stairway to greet them.

"I think there might be an escape route through here," she whispered. "Be careful though, this is where they caught Joshua."

So that's what Kalarish meant when she said they found Joshua in their quarters, he thought, remembering the alarm blaring only *after* the rebellion in the tool shed had been quelled, and Pythrisse dragging Joshua's limp body into the ruins of the room shortly after.

"Gremlin could be back any minute," she urged, glancing at the closed door, and then back at him, "Who knows if he'll get another cart for us?"

Ray stared at her blankly and weighed up his options. He could sit there in the library and learn more about the Faction, or, he could explore the dark tunnel and try to find a way out. He shrugged. "Guess it doesn't matter if they catch me down there. We're already in prison."

He took a few cautious steps down into the passage, losing the light of the library at the bottom of the staircase. He ventured into the shadows, blindly navigating with his hands, feeling his way along the stone walls.

His hand slipped off the wall on his right, and he turned to see tiny shafts of light piercing the darkness enshrouding the corridor beyond. Rounding the corner, he heard a pair of voices coming through the wall.

He peered through one of the miniscule holes emitting the light to see ruddy copper stains upon the floor, and a glaring light lazily droning above a gunmetal grey door. It was the same room he had been interrogated in.

Cormac leaned back in the steel chair, both hands clasped together behind his spotted scalp. Leon sat on one of the wooden crates in the corner.

"Caleb's getting soft, 'e is," said Cormac. Leon growled in agreement, although Ray did not seem to think so after his interrogation. Cormac continued, "Lashing inmates to the *chains rack*, when's the last time we done that? Today, 'e couldn't decide what to do wiv those two what got caught in Lungsod. 'e left it up to me to dish out the punishments."

"Aye, Evander's rubbed off on him," Leon replied gruffly, "He's even got one of the newcomers hauling chamber pots back and forth instead of dirt and rocks."

"I took 'im off that job quick enough. 'e's got an attitude, that inmate." Cormac broke into a laugh, adding, "If I didn't 'ave work to be done, I'd 'ave made that inmate's cell the new drop-off for the chamber pots!"

Leon chuckled. "We'd make better second-in-commands in this place than Caleb."

A minecart trundled by outside the room, Gremlin scraping the walls of the steam room corridor on his way back to the library with another batch of seized Faction literature.

"I reckon you'd 'ave a shot at it, if Caleb wasn't 'ere," said Cormac. "Then we'd 'ave the pickup truck to make trips into town just like 'im and Evander."

Ray's ears prickled at this. If he could somehow get Caleb's keys to the pickup truck, they could make a fast escape.

"That's right," Leon growled. "Evander's too soft on the prisoners. Lygia and Gremlin and all the rest of them are useless. They were made for taking orders, not giving them. And we need Spike and Sully to look after the other mongrels on the outposts."

A hand shot out of the darkness to clutch at Ray's shoulder. He almost threw an elbow back until he caught a glimmer of Ava's blonde hair in the light cast by another hole in the wall. She squeezed his arm softly, taking his hand and leading him back around the corner and up the stairs, leaving Cormac and Leon to plot their regime change.

The pair of inmates exited the passage to hear the cart slamming backwards against the stairs outside. They raced around the sides of the bookcase.

"*Push!*" she urged in a strained whisper as the crashes of metal upon stone ceased.

He knocked the thick book back into place and the end of the shelf began to lower. They settled back onto the floor next to the pile of books and scrolls just as Gremlin threw the door open.

Ray and Ava worked in silence as the small Watcher wheeled the cart into the library. He looked the room over. Satisfied, Gremlin settled beside the minecart, flinging scrolls and books into their organised piles with devilish giggles.

* * *

The moonlight pierced through the black shrouds in the night sky, illuminating the shadows of the pit. Small insects buzzed around the inmates, attracted to the floodlight's glow. With his semi-dried shirt back on to protect himself from bites, Ben waved a hand over his shoulder, warding off a mosquito hovering too close to his ear with its tell-tale high-pitched drone. Nico swatted at the gnats landing on his skin with startling speed.

The female inmates, having finished their work hanging up the fishnets around the quarry walls, dropped down from the upper level. All digging slowed to a halt as they walked through the pizza-slice field of light.

Mara kicked Little Danny's legs on their way past, who had apparently fallen asleep against the quarry wall. Sarah smiled at Ben as they climbed up the ramp with Amelia rolling her eyes by her side. Ben waved back with a foolish grin.

"When's the wedding, mate?" Jack asked with a cheeky smile.

"So, uh – uh, Nico," Ben stammered, "What made you leave Lungsod in the first place?"

"I like to explore," said Nico, happily shifting the attention away from Ben. "In my village, it's not allowed for come here. And then, for the mainland, it's so expensive if the NPA will going to ask for the payment. And then, it's allowed for a swimming, but it's not allowed for a swimming so far. There's another island near on my village, but my Papa say it have an *Aswang* at there also."

"Sounds like Lungsod is just another prison if you can't go anywhere," said Ethan.

"Yeah," Nico agreed. "And then, I decide, I will going to explore in the other side to the volcano. And then, I will going to swim so far in the island. And then, maybe someday, I will going in the mainland to visit my Mama on the city."

"Right, I'm up for a ghost story," said Jack, "Tell me about this island with the *Aswang*."

Nico's brown eyes shone. "Well, it's like in here, many people already try to come, and then, never come back. If a fishermen will going to come too close in the island, maybe they will going to be eat by the *Aswang*. But still, I like to explore," he said with a faraway look, throwing another load of dirt over his shoulder.

Ben thought of the crystal-like ocean bordering the fishing village as Nico told them of the days he would spend with his friends swimming by the shore. Nico asked them what their beaches were like where they had come from.

"I wouldn't know," said Ben. "I don't know how to swim," he admitted, almost shamefully.

"But I thought many people know how to do the swimming," Nico said in surprise.

"Where I'm from, the water's too cold to swim," Ben replied. "I was always afraid that I was going to get sick, so I never learned. And besides, isn't it scary to swim out to another island? Aren't there sharks and crocodiles here?"

"I'd say there's a fair chance of alligators around these parts," Ethan said with a broad smile, referring to the Lizardmen.

"Yeah, that island might be full of crocs for all you know," said Jack.

Nico shrugged. "If you're not conquer fear, you're scared forever your life."

The others fell silent. Ben was inclined to agree with his cellmate. He had always thought that the normal life everyone else chose to lead – being active, adventurous and daring, like his brother – was just too tedious for him. Or that was what he would tell himself. Secretly, he yearned for it. He longed for an adventure in his own life, yet he was too afraid of making such a radical change.

He had never experienced the life that everyone else his age had been living; being renowned for athletic abilities, going on dates and trying new things. No, he merely eked out his own mundane existence, taking the backseat throughout life, being too afraid to summon the drive and initiative to take his own road. And now that he had been thrust into the driver's seat, he still could not seem to get his life into gear and get out of this place.

Perhaps this imprisonment was his punishment for not doing anything worthwhile with his time. Or, perhaps all of this was exactly what he had needed to spur him into action and take back control of his life.

* * *

Eventually, having run out of objects to throw, Gremlin hauled Ray up to his feet by the scruff of his shirt and shoved him in the direction of the rusty metal wagon, gesturing for him to fetch another. The Watcher paced the room, coming to a stop just behind Ava, fixating his malicious green eyes on Ray.

Ava gazed up at Ray with trepidation, leaning away from the unpredictable guard. The crisp sheets of paper in her hands began to rattle in the still air as she trembled at the thought of being left alone with the short-tempered Watcher.

Ray pushed the empty minecart towards the door, and Gremlin peered over Ava's shoulder as she uneasily rifled through the scrolls and parchments. Ray turned back to see that the Watcher was off-guard.

Years of experience decimating padded opponents on the football field gave Ray the advantage.

He charged at Gremlin, tiger-leaping over Ava and spear-tackling him to the ground. The short man fell to the floor winded, his baton rolling away with a metallic melody. Gremlin breathlessly squirmed and writhed underneath the weight of the inmate. Hissing, he dug his fingers into Ray's sides, squeezing with unprecedented strength.

With black stars of pain swimming in his vision, Ray thrashed around for a weapon. The bookcases were bare, and the shock stick had rolled out of reach. He flailed an arm out and swept a handful of dust from a nearby shelf onto Gremlin's face.

The Watcher gagged, and Ray unleashed a bare-knuckled barrage. Each punch was reduced in force somewhat, as the agony in Ray's sides began to spread over his entire body.

Shaking off the dust and clenching his teeth through the bludgeoning blows, Gremlin began to wriggle his way out from underneath the inmate, sitting up so that Ray's vision was filled with the Watcher's snarling pointed face. Gremlin dug his pale unrelenting fingers into the inmate's midsection even farther, like overgrown maggots burrowing into flesh, and Ray's fists froze mid-flight as he grimaced in anguish.

Ray was slavering at the mouth, silently fighting a losing battle to give voice to his pain, when Ava drew up from behind with the shock stick and thwacked the Watcher across the back of his head. Gremlin stiffened, his green eyes widening with surprise before losing focus.

Ray ripped the guard's hands from his hips, and Gremlin's arms fell limp upon the ground. Ray pushed himself up onto his feet, reeling from the trauma in his torso. He felt as though his innards had been twisted and torn. He took the shock stick from Ava, her hands shaking from the adrenaline coursing through her.

Staggering over to the empty minecart by the doorway, Ray wheeled it back and turned it over upon the unconscious Watcher, trapping the small man inside. "Let's open up that passage again," he wheezed. "You sit on this cart while I'm gone, okay?"

Ava continued to tremble as the two inmates unlocked the hidden doorway again. Ray entered the stairway, descending into darkness and rounding the unseen corner. No thin shafts of light pierced the shadows now. Cormac and Leon were gone.

Ray sparked up the shock stick, following the crackling light of the blue arc of electricity down the narrow passage. He had no plan, and he had no idea where the tunnel would take him, but he ventured deeper into the shadows all the same.

As he turned another corner, he heard voices whispering, the same rasping voices that he thought he had heard while he was in the steam room. A red glow from a room below cast a faint light on another set of stairs in his path.

The voices grew louder as he crept down the stone steps. A chamber opened up before him, and another red grate set in the side of the heat vent along the opposite wall greeted him at the bottom of the stairs. Two arched entrances to adjoining rooms along the left wall revealed large slabs of rock and stone counters brimming with bushy herbs, obscure jars, and bowls filled with thick and pungent pastes.

"We offer our congratulations on your victory, Tyrax," a rasping voice resounded from just around the corner to the right, "But, all is not well in the Quarry Complex. We are no clozer to locating the *Dragonztone.*"

"*Dragonstone,*" Ray whispered to himself, remembering Joshua's last words.

Another voice – like static in the distance – answered in a series of hisses, although Ray could not make out the words. He peered around the corner to see a room bathed in the heat vent's red glow, washing its fiery gloom over more indented mounds of dirt, the floor littered with fish bones, broken crab shells and coconut husks.

Craning his neck farther, he saw two Lizardmen with their backs towards him standing within a small niche next to the hidden passage's staircase. He recognised the plump orange head of Kalarish, donned in her purple robe, and Ophidirick, the spindly old moss green creature standing beside her.

"We have no uze for the Watchers now. Zend no more of the incompetent fools," Kalarish continued. A wave of relief washed over Ray, as he would not need to deal with Sergei again. A new fear gripped him now though, at the thought of something far worse replacing the Watchers. Kalarish confirmed his dread. "Tyrax, it is with great shame that we humbly requezt a garrizon of *Kirzakai* warriors to guard the Quarry Complex."

A wave of outrage blasted the pair of Lizardmen, and a metallic green orb soared above their heads. Ray's jaw dropped as he was caught in the gaze of two fierce black serpentine eyes just above the green orb, the swirling image in the sphere revealing another Lizardman caught mid-sentence at the sight of the eavesdropping intruder.

The orb floated backwards and disappeared into obsidian darkness, a large hooded snake's mouth closing around it with a hiss before the sleek silver-scaled serpent receded into a crevice in the wall.

The Lizardmen turned around, and Ophidirick immediately changed his scales to mirror the dungeon wall behind him. Perhaps once, back when the overgrown reptile was much younger, he would have appeared as a three-dimensional silhouette, dismissed as a mere trick of the light, but now, in his old age, large splotches of his underbelly were clearly distinguishable in the fiery red glow of the furnace.

Mostly camouflaged, Ophidirick leapt upon Ray, agile for his elderly appearance, wrestling the intruder to the scrap-strewn floor. Kalarish hissed something incomprehensible as his arms were pinned to the ground by the bony reptile.

Lumbering clawed footsteps filled Ray's heart with a wave of dread and soon, Pythrisse loomed out of one of the adjoining rooms. She poised for an attack on the trapped inmate.

Ray managed to break his arm free of Ophidirick's stealth grip and thrashed out at Pythrisse with the shock stick. He caught her leg with the tip of the baton, electricity crackling harmlessly upon her smoky grey scales.

She laughed in a series of rasping hisses, and with a single sweep of the iron barb attached to her powerful tail, she cleaved his shock stick in half, the baton erupting in an explosion of sparks.

Ophidirick's weight lifted, and the defeated inmate watched the array of dead brown scales float away as the Lizardman disappeared around a corner, an alarm blaring soon after.

Kalarish stood above Ray as Pythrisse held him at bay, the iron barb on her tail hovering menacingly above his throat.

22 - IT'S JUST US NOW

An alarm pealed from somewhere within the prison, the high-pitched pulsating siren reverberating around the quarry walls and descending into the shadowy depths of the pit. Something was happening inside the complex. The lamp of the floodlight upon the rock shelf cast its glare across the inmates' faces as they fell into disarray, glancing from side to side, exchanging puzzled expressions and trying to discern whether they should start a riot, or if one had already been started.

"A heads-up would've been good, Ben," Jack murmured, tightening the grip on his shovel.

"I don't have anything to do with this!" Ben exclaimed, just as confused as the others.

As the Watchers standing on the higher level of the pit all looked up towards the entrance of the prison for any indication of what was happening inside, the line of inmates broke away from the rock ledge to form their own small groups. Ben, Nico, Ethan and Jack huddled together.

"What do you think is happening up there?" asked Ethan.

Nico strained his eyes up into the darkness beyond the floodlight's glare. "I'm not see something," he shrugged.

Small blue arcs of electricity flared up on either side of the floodlight like fireflies droning around a blazing beacon, the silhouettes of the Watchers returning to the edge of the rock shelf and looking out over the lower level of the pit.

"What do we do now?" was the question on everyone's lips – guards and prisoners alike.

***

The shock stick cloven in two upon the scrap-strewn floor flickered its last blue embers before dying out, and the fiery red blaze of the heat vent's grate once again enveloped the Lizardmen's quarters.

The warbling alarm was deafening, but Ray did not dare move to cover his ears. Pythrisse's tail barb licked at the intruder's throat as he stared up at her looming figure, his eyes wide, taking in every tiny detail; the flakes of her smoky grey scales glistening even in the gloomy red darkness of the chamber, the sheen of her razor-like claws, even the frayed threads of the open blue vest draped over her dark yellow underbelly swaying in the hot breath of the furnace.

Hunched over a wooden staff beside her guardian, the plump Lizard-woman, Kalarish, sneered down at the trespassing inmate with his back upon the floor. The purple robe donned around her shoulders could only do so much to hide the excess flesh sagging from her neck, yet the cold cruel look from her amber orange eyes was more than enough to instil fear into the heart of any man. "Enough, Ophidirick!" she rasped, the smell of fish escaping from her long snout.

The siren promptly came to a halt, and the spry old Ophidirick scuttled back into the room, his camouflaged scales slowly returning to a perceivable spectrum as he reverted back to his moss green hide. He clasped his webbed hands humbly, blinking down at the subdued prisoner upon the ground.

It took a while before Ray's eardrums registered that the noise had ceased, echoes of the alarm still lingering in his head. He stared blankly at the dimly-lit stone roof above, Pythrisse's long tail coiling and swaying back and forth across his vision, the guardian toying with the intruder.

Just as he began to wonder whether he would be quick enough to wrestle with the Lizardwoman's tail before she could slice his throat, Pythrisse pressed the metal barb against his skin. The pressure was not enough to draw blood, yet it provided ample reason for him to remain still.

Extremely still.

* * *

Following the wailing siren's abrupt end, ripples of sound bounced off the cliff walls of the dusty basin before being lost in the night. The inmates breathed heavily in the still air of the pit. Adrenaline had seized hold of them, yet they had no course of action.

"Back to work, everyone," said Evander.

The youths exchanged furtive glances. They were all scared, yet it was not every day that the alarm rang. Perhaps someone had instigated another rebellion somewhere within the prison. Perhaps salvation was at hand.

"Last chance!" Caleb warned, withdrawing a sparker remote and holding it into the light for all to see.

One boy – wielding a mattock at the front of the throng of inmates – saw his opportunity to strike, and he swung his tool over the top of the rock ledge. Evander jumped up just in time to avoid the mattock's cleaving blade, yet the force of the swing followed through, knocking the floodlight to the ground. Caleb leapt clear of the lamp's explosion of glass and flame as shards and sparks hailed down upon the prisoners scattered below.

The inmates gave up a cheer and prepared to mount the rock shelf, striking at the Watchers' feet with their tools in order to drive them back and gain a foothold on the ledge.

The dying lamp of the floodlight had a strobe-like effect upon the charging inmates, their attack resembling a stop-motion animation in the night. Some were already halfway up the rock shelf when a sudden burning sensation pulsed through their legs. Caleb had recovered quickly, his thumb crushing the sparker remote. He and the other guards stood their ground, beating back at any prisoners still capable of attempting to scale the wall.

Ben fell to the dirt floor, Nico collapsing beside him, the villager confused by the onset of volts surging through his ankle. Nico sat up and began hacking at the manacle with his shovel. Ben bit his lip and forced himself into a sitting position. He attempted to break off his own manacle as well, yet his leg was twitching too violently for him to get a clear shot.

It was not long before both Ben and Nico threw themselves back against the ground, convulsing and writhing in agony along with the rest of the inmates scattered across the pit. Even as the poorly-executed rebellion was quelled, the electricity burning through each of their legs did not cease. The inmates were defeated, and in the absence of the siren, whatever had arisen within the complex was no longer in their favour either.

* * *

Kalarish stooped over the incapacitated inmate, filling Ray's vision with jagged teeth protruding from either side of her snout. The Matron of the *Kirzakai* addressed him in a soft wicked rasp, "Gratitude for your aid, wretched human." He raised an eyebrow in surprise. "Your timely appearanze put forth an argument to our leader far more compelling than I could have ever presented. Know that if you had entered our domain at any other time, we would have delighted in your zuffering."

She signalled to Pythrisse to withdraw the iron barb pressing into his neck. Ray slowly reached up to massage his tender throat, examining his fingers for traces of blood.

"As a reward for your azziztanze," Kalarish continued. "We will zpare you that pain. The girl will not be zo lucky…"

Ophidirick nodded, "The Faction sthpy may have found his way to usth by chancthe." His rattling voice almost sounded as though he was speaking into a small electric fan, and his tongue had been caught by one of the fan's blades, "But a sthecond time is beyond coincthidencthe."

Pythrisse hauled Ray to his feet with minimal effort and shoved the inmate towards the stairs. He whirled around to face them, wary of the possibility of being struck from behind. The three reptilian monsters stared back at him with their serpentine eyes.

He was apparently free to leave unpunished, yet his curiosity still took hold. "Who are you?" he croaked, his throat stinging. "Where did you come from?"

"The nerve of the worm!" Pythrisse hissed with laughter.

Kalarish tilted her scaly orange head upwards, looking down her long snout at Ray. "Only the Watchers are granted privilege to learn of the *Kirzakai*. Join uz, and you will know…" She stood with her plump arms stretched out wide, ready to receive the inmate's servitude, *"Kneel before your mazters!"*

"Don't we already work for you?" he said, still defiant even as Pythrisse's hulking figure towered over him. "What more do you want from us?"

Kalarish rasped in exasperation, letting her arms fall to her fleshy flanks, the butt of her wooden staff thwacking the stone floor.

Ophidirick solemnly bowed his hunched head even lower over his clasped hands, curling the edges of his short snout into what appeared to be a smile. "You and your wretched kind shall know before long," his beady black eyes darted towards Pythrisse, "For now, flee!"

The guardian lunged forward, forcing Ray to retreat up the stairs. The reptilians' hissing laughter followed him as he blindly searched his way through the dark passage and up the next flight of stairs into the light of the library.

Ava greeted him from her perch upon the overturned minecart, Gremlin still trapped underneath in unconscious silence. "What did you see?" she asked.

He whirled around at the top of the steps, peering down into the darkness of the passage. Nothing was trailing in his wake. To be sure, he strode around to the side of the bookcase, found the thick book lever and shoved it back into place.

Ava cautiously shifted her weight off the cart and worked the hidden switch on the other side of the shelf. They met each other at the end of the rack just as the entrance closed with a small thud. "What did you see?" she repeated.

"They caught me as soon as I turned the corner. There's no escaping that way."

"Maybe there is, and you just didn't see it," she said, trying to remain optimistic.

"You wanna check it out yourself? Be my guest," Ray replied. Then in a softer tone, he added, "They know you helped me. They know you helped Joshua."

Her gaze dropped to the floor, eyebrows furrowed. She had not even thought to consider that by exposing the hidden passage, she had also exposed herself. "It'll be okay, I'll be okay. They couldn't – they *wouldn't* – do anything to hurt me," she spoke more to herself than to Ray.

"I hope so too, for your sake," he said, opening the door to the room beyond.

Crestfallen, Ava moved to follow him out, but she turned at the doorway. "What, what about him?" she asked.

Ray looked past her towards the overturned cart with the unconscious Watcher still inside. "He didn't see you hit him. I'll deal with the consequences later." After all, there was not much else they could do to punish him.

They closed the door to the library, Ray descending the stairs two at a time, Ava struggling to keep up as he entered the adjoining passage between the two cell houses.

She caught hold of his shoulder so that he turned to face her. "The night shift will be over soon," she said. "I should be getting back to my cell…" Her hazel eyes stared up into his as they stood alone in the small corridor.

"See you at breakfast then," Ray said bluntly, turning from her lingering gaze and exiting into the empty male cell house.

He massaged his throat again, still processing the near-death experience. That burst of adrenaline brought on by the Lizardmen had spiked his energy levels, but now, he felt exhausted, unable to remember the last time he had slept.

A clash from the barracks door jolted him upright again.

"Where has that Gremlin sslunk off to now…?" the pasty bug-eyed Lygia muttered in a low yet shrill tone, "You, inmate!" she jabbed a long gnarled finger at Ray, "Downstairs, into the cafeteria! You didn't THINK you were going to resst *now*, did you?" she threw her head back in a mocking cackle as other Watchers filed out from the barracks behind her.

The guards busied themselves with opening up the morning shift's row of cells. Ray's stomach rumbled, and he willed his weary limbs to trudge down the staircase into the cafeteria.

The room was empty, save for Mara wheeling the gruel pot into position. Ray doggedly staggered towards the side table, banging his thigh into the wood, rattling the bowls and spoons.

"Hey, you okay?" asked Mara.

He pressed the heels of his hands up against his eyelids, offering the strained blood vessels within some cool reprieve. "Never better," he answered, picking up a bowl and filling it to the brim with water, first splashing himself in the face, and then drinking his fill.

"They sending you back out?" she asked, ladling him a generous serving of porridge.

Ray shrugged with a detached smile as inmates and Watchers from the morning shift filed down the stairs.

"Ahoy, get a load of this, lads! What's made him so special to have all that?" said Kenneth as Ray turned to find a seat. The queue of prisoners stared at his brimming bowl with envy, glowering at him as he passed by.

He sat at the corner of a long table at the back of the cafeteria, as far away from the others as possible. He was far too exhausted to entertain any confrontation now.

* * *

Caleb jumped down into the pit to walk amongst the groaning night shift inmates as they lay upon their backs in the dirt. "Are we done yet?" he asked, aiming a kick at one of the downed prisoners to punctuate his words, "Ready to continue working now?"

Evander was right, Ben thought to himself, *Caleb really is starting to lose his temper.*

"Shift's over, Caleb," Evander called from atop the rock shelf, his dark face hidden by shadow. "It's midnight. Look." He pointed upwards to the moon sailing high above in the centre of the patch of open sky visible from the bottom of the pit. It was the only illumination offered to them, the embers of the fallen floodlight's lamp flickering out.

"Fine," said Caleb, finally taking his thumb off the sparker remote, "Back to the cafeteria, inmates! *On your feet!*" he ordered. The other guards soon joined him, and they began roughly hauling the prisoners up by the scruffs of their green uniforms.

Despite the near-miss of the mattock to his legs only moments ago, Evander jumped down into the pit and civilly helped the inmates onto their feet. Ben attempted to massage some feeling back into his numbed ankle when he was yanked up sharply by Caleb. He soon lost his balance and collapsed to his knees.

"Come on, inmates, pick up your tools and get moving," said Caleb, glaring at Ben with his flint grey eyes. "Last one back works a double shift!"

With the added incentive, inmates leaned on their tools and on each other for support, stumbling after the Watchers up the dirt ramp. Little Danny tottered down from his position halfway up the slope, dodging the other ambling prisoners and catching hold of his minecart at the bottom. Ben and Nico passed by, their arms slung over each other's shoulders amid the stragglers.

"Won't you 'elp me, Benny?" his former cellmate pleaded in his reedy voice.

Ben paused, turning to face him. Seeing Little Danny's child-like face bent over the minecart filled almost to capacity, he felt compelled to help the small malnourished boy.

Jack limped between the two, putting a hand on Ben's shoulder. "Come on mate, you know that's a favour he'd never pay you back for. I reckon he'd ditch you at the top and let you work the double shift."

Little Danny's sky blue eyes blazed with sudden anger and, reaching into the cart, he threw a clump of dirt at the back of Jack's head.

Jack faced him, chuckling, "Yeah, emptying that cart is about the only way you're gonna get it up the ramp by yourself. You won't be seeing any help from us." He turned on his heel while Ethan pushed the skinny runt into the dirt on his way past.

Ben and Nico idly stood by, looking on at Little Danny's misfortune. Ben felt as though he had become a bully simply by his inaction, although he could not say that the boy did not deserve the mistreatment.

Ethan paused halfway up the dirt slope to look down at Ben and Nico. They were the last inmates in the pit besides Little Danny. "Come on guys, let's get something to eat."

They looked back at the scrawny child scrabbling in the dirt to get back on his feet. It was a piteous sight, yet neither of them wanted to work an extra shift. Tearing their gaze away from him, they continued their slow climb up the slope, Ben explaining to Nico what Little Danny – Cormac's son – had done to betray his friends after their rebellion in the tool shed.

Nico glanced over his shoulder at the boy haggardly bent over the minecart, struggling to push it up the ramp with one numbed leg. "Maybe he didn't know that will going to happen on you and then on your friends," he said. "Maybe he will going to tell his Papa after his Papa is asking."

As they passed out of the moonlight and through the weathered support pillars underneath the overhanging cells, Ben considered the possibility that Little Danny was just being a loyal son to his father. Recollections of his ex-cellmate flashed through his mind; the impulsive behaviour, his uncontrollable fits of laughter, and the mad gleam in his eye whenever someone tested his short temper. He was definitely Cormac's son.

"Maybe..." he said finally, still unconvinced.

Ben and Nico entered the tool shed and hung their shovels back on the racks before filing out into the cafeteria, other inmates of the night and morning shifts already lined up for the gruel pot.

Jack and Ethan were ahead of them in the queue. Kenneth limped towards a table. His leg had not yet recovered from being wedged between the drainage pipe and the overturned cart in the tool shed.

"Hey, Kenneth," Ethan called out to him, "You good?"

"Well, that depends," the freckled Irish teen turned to look them over, "Are you still sidin' with *them?*" he shot a glare in Ben's direction, who stood bemused with Nico at the back of the line.

"We're all on the same side, mate," Jack answered.

"I wonder if you would feel the same way if it had been *your* leg under that pipe," Kenneth replied. "And I don't suppose you've already forgotten what's become of our good friends, Aiden and Rashad? Aiden still hasn't even woken up yet! All he does is talk in his sleep and choke on his food, at least that's how Evander tells it." Jack and Ethan exchanged glances. "To answer your question, lads, it appears I'm good, but you're certainly not." With that, he limped away to one of the centre tables.

It was clear that Kenneth no longer wished to be affiliated with the Rauder brothers after the injury he had sustained during the rebellion. *After all, it* was *our idea to start the riot*, Ben admitted to himself. Before he and Ray had come along, Kenneth was held in the highest regard on the day shift, and now, he would have to work his way back up through the ranks of the morning shift before he could hope to gain the same level of authority.

The queue shuffled forward so that he and Nico stood beside the table of bowls and spoons, Jack and Ethan passing by them without a word.

Ben picked up a bowl and together, he and his cellmate took turns drinking from the tap, cleansing and purifying their insides with the clear water. After quenching his thirst, he turned to see Mara standing impatiently behind the cauldron of goopy gravy.

"Where's Ava?" asked Ben.

"What?" Mara snapped at him, "Just because I lug chamber pots around all day, I'm not good enough to dish up food for *Your Highness?*"

"No, no, it's not that," he hastily offered his bowl to her with shaky hands. "I'm j-just wondering where she is, that's all."

"We all have to sleep *some time*, don't we?" she said bluntly.

"Won't be ssleeping sso PRETTY after the changes we've made!" Lygia mocked from nearby, twisting her mouth into a sour smile to reveal her blackened teeth.

Mara fell silent as she splashed gruel into Ben's bowl.

"*Changes?*" he echoed.

"You'll find out soon enough," said Caleb, standing a few feet away alongside Evander.

"Not sso fasst, Caleb!" Lygia erupted in a shrill cackle. "These boys are bound for the ssteam rooms after they've finished off their newspaper!"

"The steam rooms?" Caleb repeated, shifting his gaze to Evander, who nodded to confirm.

"Yess…" the pasty white Watcher narrowed her bulging bug eyes, "It was YOU who told Cormac to decide *how* they were to be PUNISHED, *don't you remember?*"

"I thought he would've come up with something better than that," Caleb answered.

Ben and Nico backed away from the Watchers before Caleb could impose an additional punishment upon them.

* * *

Ray cast his head down to look at the bowl in front of him. Despite its murky consistency, he could not detect the usual foul scent wafting up into his nostrils. It was no surprise though, after handling the reeking chamber pots and corroding his airways in the sulfur-filled chambers of the complex.

He raised a spoonful of goop up to his mouth, immune to its cardboard taste, yet still, his body rejected it. His previously rumbling stomach hardened instantly, bile rising in his throat. Within the space of just a few moments, his hunger had completely diminished. Sleep deprivation had altered his physiology to the point of refusing sustenance, vile as the sustenance was. He forced the sickly meal down his throat with even more gruel.

Looking up from his bowl, Raw saw Kenneth settling upon a stone block a few tables away. The fiery-haired inmate narrowed his eyes at Ray, who returned the stare. Neither one of them wavered. They both refused to back down from the challenge. Only one crucial difference broke their contest. Kenneth had slept since the hardships of the previous day, and Ray had not.

He blinked, and his eyelids snapped open to see Kenneth smirking at his momentary lapse in concentration. Victorious, the red-haired inmate bowed his head to eat his meal.

Ray turned his attention back to his own food. In a dull daze, he lifted his spoon and completely missed the wooden bowl, scraping the table with the utensil. He was almost ready to keel over and slip into unconsciousness.

"*Bang on*," a familiar voice floated down to him from nearby.

Groggy-eyed, he looked up to see Jack settling in beside him, and Ethan dropping down to sit opposite, blocking Kenneth from view. "What're you talking about?" Ray mumbled.

Jack and Ethan exchanged a glance.

"*Bang on*," Ethan repeated, "It's a word the locals use. *Bangon*. It means *Rise*."

"Same thing, different language if you ask me," Jack said around a mouthful of gruel. "We haven't seen you since the steam rooms, mate. Thought you got shipped off to the Desert Complex to be honest. Wouldn't have put it past Caleb, he was riled up enough."

Ray raised his tired brows at them, revealing his bloodshot eyes.

"It looks like he doesn't even *remember* the steam rooms," said Ethan.

"Heat got to you pretty bad," said Jack. "You were saying some crazy stuff in there, talking about your brother, your dad, some sheila named Dana."

"It was like you were in a trance, or a bad dream," said Ethan. "You didn't even snap out of it when Joshua was begging for mercy just a few feet away from us."

"What do you mean?" Ray straightened up, willing his senses to return.

"Ahoy, now he's back with us," said Jack. "While you were out of it, Caleb and some of the other guards were grilling Joshua in a room nearby."

Ray thought of the room with the gunmetal grey door and the ruddy bloodstains on the floor. He could almost taste the reek of copper in the air, or maybe that was just the sensation of his bloodshot eyes burning.

"He just kept saying, *the Faction, the Faction*, over and over," said Ethan.

"Like a broken record," Jack agreed, scraping up the remnants of his gruel. "I reckon Joshua poked his nose where it didn't belong while we were all busy having a good time in the tool shed. Pretty sure that's why that alarm went off when it did, too."

"What about the alarm?" another voice broke into their conversation.

"Benji? I saw your cell, what happened to you?" Ray asked as his younger brother and another boy took a pair of stone block seats beside Ethan.

Ray looked the other boy over as he quietly muttered Grace over his bowl. He appeared to be no older than Ben, yet his compact muscles bulged out beneath the pale brown skin of his lean frame. "How did you end up back here?"

Ben examined his brother under the dim light of the cafeteria. Dark circles lined his sagging cheeks, contrasted with the bright red rims of his bloodshot eyes. "Well, what about you? Was it you who set off that alarm earlier?" he answered with his own series of questions.

"Guess I'll start off first then," said Ray. "The four of us got dragged to the steam rooms; me, Jack, Ethan and Kenneth." He looked past the shoulders of Ben and Ethan to where Kenneth sat a few tables away. "Kenneth lost his head in there. He blames us for what happened to his leg. I lost it a bit myself too, apparently. Then around midnight, that clown wearing the Sheriff's hat dragged me and Kenneth down to the cafeteria."

"So that's where you guys went," Ethan mused.

"I reckon we had it easy compared to you boys," Jack added. "He just chucked us back in our cell and that was the end of it. We weren't swearing up a storm like Kenneth was though, maybe that's why the Sheriff cracked the whip on him."

"That's just a metaphor, there wasn't actually a whip," Ethan explained, the others still not yet accustomed to the Aussie's slang. "Sometimes, even I struggle to keep up with this guy's lingo."

Jack grunted with an amused smile on the other side of the table.

"We worked the morning shift," Ray continued. "It seemed just like any other day here, only difference was digging in the dark. Things were pretty normal up until Joshua took a tumble into the pit. Caleb threw him off the roof."

"Joshua's *dead!?*" Ben exclaimed.

"Might as well be," Ray shrugged, "They sent him back to the Desert Complex for further interrogation. Right after Joshua blacked out, Caleb dragged me into a room and grilled me with questions about some group called the Faction. Do they sound familiar to you?" Ben shook his head with a bewildered expression. "Well, after that, Caleb tasked me with additional duties until I would agree to tell him Joshua's last words."

"What were they?" asked Ethan, curious.

Ray looked him over for a moment before purposely misinterpreting his question. "First, they had me hauling chamber pots in and out of the cells with Mara."

"Phwaw mate, I leave some nasty ones in that bucket," Jack grinned, a piece of oatmeal stuck between his teeth.

Ray smirked back. "It wasn't until Cormac had me bringing in some seized literature to the library –"

"We have a library here?" asked Ben, excitedly intrigued. The others leaned in closer.

"That library's not for us," he replied, piquing their interest even further. "The books and scrolls that were coming in were all about the Faction. Ava, who reads books to the Lizardmen, said that one of the Faction's bases might've been raided. She'd never seen so much information on the group. Gremlin was with us, but he left us alone for a few minutes."

Ethan made a suggestive hum.

"She showed me a hidden entrance." Ray continued, ignoring Jack's burst of laughter and having to speak over the top of Ethan as he pounded the table. "It led down into the Lizardmen's quarters. I heard them talking about changing the guards from Watchers to… something worse. That's when they caught me."

"And that's when the alarm went off," Ben concluded. Ray nodded. "Well, they had me cuffed to the chains rack until midnight before they threw me back in my cell. I think I would've been cuffed there for longer if it wasn't for Cormac hosting a poker game with some of the other Watchers."

Ray remembered Cormac and the other guards upon the viewing deck the previous night, drunkenly hurling their bottles down into the quarry prior to Joshua's demise.

"That's when I met Nico, my new cellmate," Ben gestured towards the quiet Filipino boy sitting next to him. "He's one of the locals from Lungsod. Spike brought him in just after the rebellion."

Ben recounted the events of their escape; breaking out of their cell, running through the jungle, sneaking past the Watcher outpost with the motion-detecting lights, and eventually being recaptured by Gaspar's guards as soon as they entered Lungsod. Ray thought back to the avaricious Mayor Gaspar dirtying up his long-sleeved white shirt with armfuls of freshly-unearthed jewels in the treasury.

"The patrolmen radioed the Watchers from the outpost," Ben continued. "Soon after that, we were venom snared and thrown into the back of a white pickup truck… And now we're here."

Ray closed his eyes and massaged his temples, taking it all in and refocusing his thoughts. Just when the others thought that he was about to fall asleep, he groggily muttered, "I overheard Cormac and Leon mention that Caleb has keys to a truck too… And I'm thinking it's nearby."

"That's right," said Ben. "Sarah told me that he's got the access code to the garage and the keys to the vehicle inside."

An image of the keypad next to the door in the barracks flashed in Ray's mind. "Well, we're gonna need those keys to outrun that other truck, and Gaspar's patrolmen too."

Jack and Ethan held their silence, wondering what the brothers were planning now.

"But we can't escape to the mainland," said Ben, "There's a toll bridge nearby, manned by the NPA, soldiers of the New People's Army."

"If we didn't have a money to pay," Nico chimed in with his Americanised accent, "They will not going to let us to pass. And then, maybe they will going to shoot on us."

"But there must be some other way to get across to the mainland, right?" asked Ethan.

Nico shook his head.

"That's easy," said Ray. "We can grab a couple gems from the treasury and bribe whoever gets in our way."

"*Or*," said Ben, "Maybe we can find that motorboat Joshua told me about."

"Yeah, maybe if Joshua was still with us, Benji," Ray replied in a bitter tone.

"Would've been nice to have Rashad, Aiden and Kenneth on board too," said Ethan.

"Look, it's just us now, so we're gonna have to deal with it," said Ray. "First, we've gotta get to that truck."

"Do any of us know how to drive though?" asked Ben.

The inmates looked from one to another with expectant faces.

Jack shook his head in admiration at the two brothers, leaning back with a smile. Finally, he broke his silence. "Mate, I dunno how you blokes do it. Some of the boys in here have been trying to get out for *years* from what I've heard. Then you two rock up and try to get out in just a couple *days*. Ben actually got past the fence!"

"I couldn't have done it without Nico," said Ben, patting the newcomer on the back. Nico smiled with a sheepish shrug, maintaining modesty despite his achievements.

"No worries, boys," Jack said with a grinning wink, "I'll cover the driving."

23 - TRY NOT TO DIE

Leon and Cormac climbed halfway down the cafeteria's stairs, peering out at all of the inmates gathered at the tables for the midnight meal. Cormac descended the rest of the staircase and walked to the front of the room, engaging in a swift conversation with the other Watchers gathered behind the stone bench.

At the back of the cafeteria, the Rauder brothers and their friends scraped up the gruel remaining in their bowls, all except for Ray, whose exhaustion overpowered his hunger.

Ray looked over to Leon, who still lingered upon the stairs. He rubbed his bloodshot eyes, wondering what the two men were up to, since the pair of guards usually monitored the day shift, at least as far as he had seen.

Ben was too preoccupied to notice the guards' arrival, having a full-length conversation in his own mind as he shovelled cold chunks of porridge into his mouth. *All we need is access to the garage and Caleb's keys to the truck,* he thought to himself. *But how? Maybe I could ask Sarah to help us find out the security code for the garage door's keypad next time she's ordered to clean the barracks.*

The door leading out to the corridor swung open, and Little Danny entered the cafeteria after finally having wheeled the laden minecart from the pit up into the treasury, his laboured breathing painting his usually hollow cheeks into a puffy red. His wide sky blue eyes surveyed the room, growing larger with each bowl of gruel that they beheld. His searching gaze fell upon the bearded man standing halfway up the staircase.

Ben followed the boy's stare to lock eyes with Leon, who spat at a nearby table and clapped his hands together for the inmates' attention before barking his announcement, "Everyone up into the cell house! Morning and night shifts, start moving, *now!!*" Having said his piece, the shaggy-maned guard loped back up the stairs.

Ray looked down at his half-eaten meal, his shrunken stomach far too full to eat another bite. He prodded at the hardening gruel with his spoon, the cardboard-like porridge seeming to have lost the little warmth that had made the meal at least bearable. He and the others rose from their stone block seats, along with the rest of the inmates, eager to delay the commencement of the morning shift.

While the Watchers were distracted with coordinating the prisoners up the stairs, Little Danny haggardly moved towards the unmanned gruel pot, yet too many other inmates now stood in his way. Just as he was searching for a clear path to the front of the cafeteria, a new idea entered his simple mind. Scouring the tables for scraps, he fixed his eyes upon Ray's leftovers. He climbed up and scampered across the long table on all fours like a wild raccoon, knocking over empty bowls in his wake. Ray looked back at his cold meal and shrugged it off, letting the scrawny imp have at it. He was far too weary now to antagonise the little runt for his betrayal.

Ray, Jack and Ethan shouldered through the thronging inmates gathered around the foot of the staircase and shoved their way up the packed steps, Ben and Nico shadowing their footsteps before they could be cut off by the crowd.

The prisoners fanned out across the cell house, the boys from the day shift already gathering, rubbing at their eyes and grumbling about having been disturbed from their sleep. Only Kenneth's old cell remained closed. Aiden was in no state to stand at the assembly.

A few Watchers led the female inmates into the cell house through the adjoining passage in the corner. Ben stood on his tiptoes like a meerkat searching for Sarah amongst them. As their heads turned and whispers rippled throughout the crowd, the girls scurried along the left wall in a fit of panic, giving the barracks staircase a wide berth.

Kalarish and Ophidirick stood together upon the stairs platform outside the barracks, preparing to make an announcement. Below, flanked by Watchers, Pythrisse and the portly Warden stood between the staircase and the crowd of murmuring inmates.

Other prisoners of the morning and night shifts stared wide-eyed at the reptilian humanoids looking out over them, some gasping in horror at the Lizardmen. Despite having heard the rumours, many of the inmates were seeing them now for the first time.

"*Aswang*," Nico muttered under his breath at the sight of the scaly monstrosities.

"Hey, Benji," Ray said in a low voice. He looked around to make sure that only his brother was listening as the rest of the inmates filed into the cell house. "Do you know whether we have an uncle? I can't remember."

Ben blinked back, taking a moment to process the odd question. "Not that I know of, unless Joshua counts as one... why?"

"It wouldn't be Joshua. In his last words before he got taken away, he told me to deliver a message to our uncle."

"What was the message?" asked Ben, also lowering his voice.

Ray stared back at him, holding his younger brother's curious gaze, considering whether he should share the secret. He looked around again at the prisoners packing closer together. He turned back to Ben. "Something about the menu here, he had a complaint about the lack of variety."

Intrigued, Ben stood eager to hear more, thinking that this must be some kind of code, yet Ray simply turned away with a chuckle. *The less he knows, the better*, he thought to himself, shifting his attention elsewhere.

Ray squinted over the tops of the other inmates' heads at the Watchers gathered at the bottom of the barracks stairs. Caleb and Evander stood on either side of the Warden. From the distance, he could just barely make out Caleb's narrowed eyes staring straight back at him, still intent on learning what Joshua had told the inmate.

Ben turned to look at his cell in the corner of the room. The bed frame was still out of place, and the one remaining mattress was lying amongst the unswept dust and rubble scattered across the floor.

"Where we will going to sleep?" Nico asked, catching his gaze.

Ben turned his eyes downcast before looking back at his cellmate, "It's the steam rooms for us, after this."

Ray began pushing his way through the packed crowd of inmates to get closer to the front. Jack and Ethan followed after him, wondering what he was up to now. Nico took a few steps forward with uncertainty, but Ben had a different idea in mind.

He signalled for Nico to follow the others before navigating his way through the mob until he reached the left wall. A group of close-knit female inmates blocked his path, Mara in their midst.

"What do *you* want?" she asked, raising a thin eyebrow at him, her metal nose stud glinting in the overhanging spotlights' beams.

"I need to ask Sarah something…" said Ben, his voice breaking. "… It's important."

Mara tested him under her unwavering glare. "Better be," she warned, nodding at the girls standing on either side of her.

* * *

"Oi, watch who you're shoving, dreg!" a snide weasel of an inmate protested. The owner of the voice, Levi, turned around, his pupils dilating at the sight of Ray.

Ray laughed and elbowed the smug prisoner in the ribs, sending him gasping to the floor. Having gained a better vantage point, he surveyed the Watchers again. He breathed a sigh of relief – there was still no sign of Gremlin.

I wonder how hard Ava hit him, he thought to himself, impressed.

A silver gleam caught his attention as Cormac waved his hand in front of Spike with a yellow-toothed grin, marvelling at the splendour of some prize. Over the din of the inmates, the crude guard's gloating was just barely audible. "Looks better on me, 'ey Spike?" he said. "I'd invite ya to come 'ave a play to win it back, but it looks like there's nothing to take off ya now, innit?"

The leather-clad Spike smiled as he made his reply, although Ray could not hear what was said. His focus was solely on Dana's promise ring around Cormac's grubby finger.

* * *

The female inmates cleared a small path for Ben, and Mara led him through the crowd. He could feel their eyes tracing his every step with suspicion. He broke out into a sweat, never having been in such close proximity to so many girls all at once.

Just as he considered turning around to seek out Ray instead, he caught sight of Sarah's silky chestnut brown hair flowing down past her shoulders, her doe eyes gazing up at the Lizardmen at the top of the stairs.

Mara shoved Ben forward, yet he managed to catch his balance just behind the gentle brunette girl. He tapped her on the shoulder, her slender figure quavering at his lingering touch.

"Ben?" Sarah said in surprise, turning to face him.

"Hi, I –"

"*QUIET!!*" Lygia shrieked from the front of the room, hushing the crowd of murmuring inmates almost instantly, many of the prisoners and Watchers alike standing within her blast radius nearly doubling over to hold their throbbing eardrums.

Ben uncovered his ears only to hear a whistling white noise. The entire cell house had fallen into a harsh stillness.

* * *

Jack, Ethan and Nico sidled up next to Ray. Before he could ask them where his brother was, Kalarish held up her scaly arms to address the crowd.

"Look upon your leaders, and dezpair!" she rasped. "Too long have you opposed our dominion, without knowing your true mazters!"

Pythrisse raised her tail high at the inmates' disbelief, the Lizardwoman whipping her iron barb down upon the floor with terrifying speed, a great *CRACK* of stone reverberating around the cell house. Prisoners sprang back as chunks of debris flew up from the impact. She withdrew her tail barb with a snarl and slowly paced around the room, a metallic scraping noise following dreadfully in her wake, terrorising the inmates and forcing them to huddle closer together.

"In anzwer to your defianze," Kalarish continued, "We have devised a collar to quell those who would rise up to challenge the might of the *Kirzakai!*"

* * *

"You told me this was important," Mara grunted with impatience.

"What is it?" Sarah smiled.

Ben tore his gaze away from Pythrisse as she stalked around the edge of the crowd, finding comfort in Sarah's sweet brown eyes. "Can you figure out the code sequence for the keypad to the garage?"

"But, Caleb has the code," she replied uncertainly. "I can only ever see one or two numbers whenever he enters it."

"I need you to try, Sarah, please," said Ben.

"Okay, I'll try again," she said, expecting him to say something else, yet he quickly averted his gaze, turning to face the Lizardmen.

Ophidirick unfurled his coiled tail, laying it gingerly upon Lygia's shoulder as she stood by the barracks staircase.

The black-toothed Watcher smiled at the touch of his scaly appendage before throwing her head back to screech, *"BRING IN THE CART!!"*

As the other inmates who were gathered towards the front of the cell house reeled from her second ear-piercing screech, Ben stood up like a meerkat again, craning his neck to see a minecart trundling out from the doorway in the corner, Gremlin wheeling the wagon between the drawn lines of the guards and prisoners, coming to a halt before the staircase.

Caleb, Evander and the Warden examined its contents, the Warden's plump lips curling sour at the sight of the Lizardmen's distasteful devices. From what Ben could see, the minecart was filled with many metallic tools, although he could not discern their exact shapes, as they all seemed to be tangled together.

Inmates shoved Ben from behind as panic rippled through the crowd. He turned around to see Pythrisse skulking along the left wall, Mara and the other female prisoners bunching even closer together. He and Sarah struggled to retain balance as they were pushed against each other. His heart somersaulted within his chest.

"Hey! Don't get any ideas," Ava warned him, appearing from behind. Undaunted by Pythrisse's looming figure, she pulled Ben and Sarah apart and wedged herself firmly in between the two teens.

Sarah smiled at Ben from behind her overprotective cellmate, and the surrounding female prisoners breathed an audible sigh of relief as Pythrisse emerged from the crowd to stand by the minecart, having completed a full circle of the inmates.

* * *

Ray parted a pair of prisoners blocking his view to see Gremlin shrinking away from the Lizardwoman, massaging the back of his neck pointedly. His pallid face turned and caught sight of Ray. Their stares locked, the Watcher's green eyes lighting up with wicked malice and a promise of later retribution.

"What it is?" asked Nico, peering at the contents of the cart over Ray's shoulder.

"I wouldn't be so keen to find out," Jack said dubiously as he looked at the minecart full of what appeared to be scrap metal.

Kalarish and Ophidirick ambled down the stairs to approach the metal wagon. Caleb, Evander and the Warden respectfully parted before the Lizardmen. Gremlin bowed his head and fell in beside the other Watchers, but not before smiling at Ray with vicious vengeance burning in his eyes.

Ray tilted his head back, squaring his jaw at the small guard, ready for the challenge.

Kalarish reached into the minecart and withdrew a broad circular piece of rusty metal, waving it aloft for all to see. She turned the object over in her scaly grip. It appeared to be a medieval version of a footballer's shoulder pads, or the top quarter of an old suit of plated armour; that which protects the neck, shoulders and chest, forming a grisly metal collar.

"Behold, the *torc!*" she declared. Inmates whispered among themselves, exchanging puzzled expressions. "Long ago, it was a great honour amongzt the *Kirzakai* to wear metallic bands named torcz as jewellery."

"Charmin' necklace for a charmin' lady," Kenneth shouted from somewhere in the pack of prisoners, "Let's see you put it on!"

Pythrisse reared up, stretching to her full height of seven feet to search for the heckler in the room. Ophidirick blinked at the unruly crowd with his wide eyes and shrank closer to Kalarish, who shook the macabre piece of metal at the inmates, rasping, "Your anzeztors shackled our proud kin with these girdles, naming them torcz in mockery of our culture. To wear our jewellery now brings uz great shame as we remember our pazt… But now, you wretched humans shall be zubject to their bind!"

"Good luck getting that thing on me," Ray murmured to himself, squaring his broad shoulders and flexing the muscles in his neck.

* * *

Ben shuddered at the idea of wearing one of the rusty metal collars. He hoped that there were no sharp edges, fearing a tetanus infection.

The portly Warden shuffled forward to address the edgy crowd, holding up his sweaty palms and launching into a speech of his own. "These are all purely as precautionary measures intended to protect the management of this facility. If I may, I would cite the recent uprisings as threats to our safety, and justification of the need for additional security. Fear not however, the torcs will only be mandated for those working an active shift. Further improvements to security are to follow in the coming days."

Evander, standing behind the puffy-cheeked man, shifted his eyes towards Ben as voices of dissent filled the cell house, drowning out the Warden's calls for calm.

"I've got some more threats to your safety, right here," one inmate called out.

"You can shove your improvements up your fat arse," another shouted.

"It's the Rauder brothers that brought this on us!" Kenneth yelled. "They're the reason why we're gettin' leashed up like dogs!"

Ben looked around to see the other boys staring back at him with hate and hostility. He was safe for now in the close-knit pack of female prisoners, as they never had to wear the same shackles as the boys anyway, yet the moment that he was back amongst the pit workers, he would not last long. Breathing hard, he scanned the crowd for Ray and their friends.

* * *

Jack and Ethan stood to one side, whispering together and shooting glances in Ray's direction. Nico, failing to comprehend the Warden's speech, looked around in confusion.

"Morning shift, front and centre!" Caleb ordered.

Without waiting for the morning shift's inmates to present themselves, the line of Watchers pressed into the crowd, scattering the prisoners into disarray, each guard more than eager to find those who were scheduled to work the next shift all on their own.

Ray suddenly lost all desire for his clearer vantage point at the front, and he backpedalled through the teeming mass of inmates, leaving Jack, Ethan and Nico. He looked to the row of cells belonging to the night shift, fixating his eyes upon the open doors. He shoved his way through the pack towards them, thinking that he might be able to slip inside one of the cells unnoticed while the rest of the cell house erupted in chaos.

Just as he broke free of the crowd of prisoners, a pair of hands looped underneath his armpits and over his shoulders, clasping the back of his skull with interlocked fingers.

"Kenneth, *what are you doing?* They'll take us both like this!" Ray said through gritted teeth.

"I'm not Kenneth," a snide voice murmured into his ear.

Ray turned and caught a glimpse of Levi in the corner of his eye. He threw an elbow back at his attacker, yet Levi simply jumped back, dodging the blow and forcing more downward pressure on the back of Ray's head.

"You're not gonna rib me again that easily," Levi said smugly.

With his chin almost touching his chest, Ray thrust his head upwards despite the jarring strain on his neck, drawing Levi closer as he shuffled forward to maintain the hold. Ray stomped down on his feet.

Hopping in pain, Levi called out to the guards, "I've got one! I've got one from the morning shift!!"

Reaching up, Ray pulled one of Levi's fingers away from the rest, bending it backwards over his hand until the bone snapped. Levi's grip faltered as he let out a girlish scream. Ray kicked back again, digging the heel of his boot into Levi's shin and scraping down to his ankle. He released Ray, falling to the ground to nurse his injuries.

Ray whirled around, keen to give him one more injury as the cherry on top. He threw his entire bodyweight behind a punch aimed dead-centre at Levi's face. His nose splattered in an eruption of blood, the red fluid spraying out across his cheeks and gushing down his chin. Levi's hands flew to his face to staunch the flow of blood, tears and mucus, his broken finger hanging at an odd angle.

Ray backed away from the grisly sight and ran towards the open cell doors. He took two steps in his sprint when he was stopped dead in his tracks, the wind knocked out of him. Struggling to wheeze air into his lungs, he looked down in confusion to see a baton laid across his sternum, Leon wielding his shock stick like a baseball bat.

"Would've scored me a home run with that one," Leon growled, pleased with himself. "Bring a torc over here! I've got another one ready for work!"

Ray collapsed to his hands and knees, eyes wide and seeing stars at the lack of oxygen travelling to his brain. Over the sounds of his own laboured breathing, he could hear Leon clucking his tongue at Levi, who still moaned in agony on the floor.

"Thanks for your help, inmate, but word from the top says we aren't hiring any more Watchers. Looks like you're gonna have to start making friends again!"

Panting on all fours, Ray felt the cold bite of a metal torc closing around his neck, the weight sliding over his shoulders pulling him closer to the ground. A bolt locked into place behind his neck. To add insult to injury, Leon kicked his hands out from underneath him, making Ray fall flat on his face against the hard stone floor.

* * *

Ben and the female prisoners watched as most of the inmates offered themselves up freely, fearing the consequences of not cooperating. Others were not so quick to oblige. Amongst those who openly resisted was Kenneth, who fought heartily against the Watchers trying to subdue him while balancing the majority of his weight upon his good leg.

Prisoners of the day and night shifts backed away to watch the fight, yet the open space only invited more guards. Gremlin scurried in behind Kenneth, kicking his good leg out from underneath him before beating him with a flurry of punches and savage kicks, mostly aimed at his bad leg.

Cormac stood back, laughing crudely as the Watchers beat their way through the crowd. "Don't use the sparkers, it'll take all the fun out ovvit!" he shouted above the chaos, then, turning his attention to the female prisoners, he looked over each of them ravenously while the others in the cell house were distracted. "Oi!" he yelled suddenly, catching sight of Ben, "Look at this ladies' man, 'ey? No 'iding from the steam rooms for you, sunshine!"

Caleb stepped forward, and the Warden huddled closer to Evander in fear of being left alone in all the confusion. "I'll handle this prisoner," he said. "Make yourself useful and help the others, Cormac."

Cormac flashed his yellow grin as he advanced wholeheartedly into the pack of inmates, yelling callous curses with each blow of his shock stick against the youths, regardless of their shift.

Caleb strode towards the rows of girls in front of Ben. They stood resolute, linking arms and staring up at the stern Watcher, determined to hold their lines. Sarah reached past Ava to clutch at Ben's arm in fear of what might happen to him. Caleb raised his shock stick at the defiant prisoners standing before him. Some of the girls wavered, but not one of them was willing to break their chain of linked arms.

"Wait!" Ben called, placing his hand upon Sarah's and gently lifting it from his arm, "I'll come willingly."

"Ben, no…" said Sarah, her eyes downcast.

Ava pulled her away as Mara, Amelia and the other girls hurried him along with all haste. The sooner Ben was out of their ranks, the sooner the Watchers would leave them alone.

Caleb grabbed Ben by the collar of his shirt and pulled him over to the front of the cell house beside the minecart. "Find the other one, Evander."

The goateed Watcher nodded and went off in search of Nico.

One by one, the morning shift's inmates were rounded up and forced to their knees. Torcs were slid over their shoulders, and a bolt locked behind the neck of each collar. Many of the disgruntled prisoners assembled in the cell house stared at Ben with resentment. After all, the new security protocols had been in direct response to the recent escape attempts engineered by him and his brother.

Nico soon joined him, and Ben could not have been gladder to be led to the steam rooms, away from Lygia's screeching calls for order and the glowering glares of the inmates.

Caleb twisted Ben's arm so that he was almost bent over double as he was shoved through the door in the corner of the cell house. They entered the small adjoining passageway with three other doors, two on the right and one farther down on the left. Ben recalled that there had been plenty of foot traffic through here each time he had been cuffed to the chains rack. The Watchers paused in the passage for a moment.

Out of the corner of his eye, he could see Evander tying a bandanna around his face, and Caleb covering his nose and mouth with the neck of his shirt.

They pushed the inmates through the nearest door on the right, and Ben almost gagged at the acrid smell befouling his nostrils. Nico, behind him, coughed and spluttered in the sulfur-filled hallway.

The corridor was sweltering with heat. It was even hotter than the midday sun in the pit. On the right side of the corridor, a large sheet of cloth had been draped over a small square glowing red. It fluttered and billowed with the torrid reeking fumes issuing forth.

"Evander, seal this door up properly," Caleb said as they passed by. "We want them to *suffer*, not *suffocate*."

"I'll take care of it," came Evander's muffled reply.

Another door stood open beside the rippling sheet of cloth. Caleb threw Ben to the floor inside, nearly dislocating the boy's arm from his shoulder. The steam room's door slammed shut behind him, a similar sound echoing from around the corner as Nico was secured. Ben sat up, massaging his upper arm while taking in his surroundings.

The room was tiny, even smaller than those in the cell house. The only distinct features in the hotbox were the door behind him, and directly opposite, a huge metal grill that spanned the entire wall, emanating heat from its fiery red furnace.

Caleb's masked face appeared in the square window of the door, behind the three vertical iron bars. "Try not to die, inmate. There's dirt that needs digging."

* * *

"Morning shift, report for duty!!" Lygia shrieked.

Kenneth and the rest of the inmates scheduled to work were already at the front of the cell house. Ray pushed himself up and got to his feet, still reeling from the blow to his chest. Nearby, Bryson knelt over a shuddering Levi, compelled to help his cellmate or suffer through endless nagging for his lack of support. Cameron watched Ray with a measure of pity as he staggered to fall in line.

Even as all eyes in the room were upon him, and with the wind knocked out of his chest, Ray let out a shallow laugh at the thought of Levi's broken nose healing to become just as bent as Cameron's, but maybe his nose would curve to the right instead.

Suddenly, he was set upon from the side, and his legs swept out from underneath him. Landing on his back with a metal clang of the torc upon the ground, he looked up to see his attackers: *Jack and Ethan.*

"This is your fault, Ray! You brought this on us!" they yelled, pummelling him mercilessly.

Inmates around the cell house cheered them on, Kenneth being the loudest. Ray threw his hands up to protect his face from the savage attack stemming from the dwindling remainder of friends that he had left in this horrible prison.

Where are Ben and Nico? Ray thought to himself, his mind detaching from his body as he was pounded again and again. *Are they just gonna leave me to be beaten on the ground?*

A flash of Ben in a similar position in a school hallway entered his mind, with Ray idly standing by, watching it all unfold. He remembered thinking back then, *there's only one way you're getting outta this. You've gotta fight your way out. Fight until you've got nothing left.*

With an enraged roar, Ray lashed out with newfound energy, surging to his feet and throwing wild punches left and right, although his brutish blows could not connect. He looked up to see Pythrisse towering over him, holding both Jack and Ethan in the air.

The Lizardwoman threw them half the distance of the cell house, the crowd scattering to avoid their impacts. Kenneth and a few of the other prisoners jeered, but they quickly fell silent as Pythrisse hissed, "Dead prisoners do not work!"

"Get in line," Leon growled, yanking Ray up by his shirt, almost tearing it beneath the torc.

Ray dragged his feet to join the others standing at the front of the cell house, passing by Gremlin, who threw a pair of torcs at Jack and Ethan's feet with a devilish grin.

Cormac caught the malicious guard's intent and he murmured aside to Leon, "Maybe they can finish 'im off down in the pit."

24 - A DEAR FRIEND OF MINE

The door to the entrance of the sweltering corridor slammed shut behind Caleb and Evander, leaving Ben and Nico locked in their separate steam rooms as punishment for their escape to Lungsod the previous night. Caleb had seemed to think that they had been let off easy.

In the stillness, Ben stood staring through the iron-barred window set in the hardwood door of the tiny room. The only sound that he could hear was the hissing heat issuing forth from the giant red grate set in the wall behind him. He felt as though the climate outside in the quarry was a cool autumn's day in comparison to this oversized oven.

His lips cracked in the shimmering air of the steam room, the arid heat cooking the moisture from his hair and skin. Acrid fumes seemed to waft into the cell from the hallway, rather than emanating directly from the fiery furnace within.

The burning smell of sulfur pervaded his senses. Despite his best efforts not to inhale the toxic gas, he began to hyperventilate. Panic set in as he wildly searched for an escape from the miniscule hotbox. He gripped the iron bars of the cell window, releasing them within an instant and uttering a garbled cry as the metal scorched his skin. The palms of his blistered hands throbbed with a violent shade of red.

"Just try to relax. Take your seat," Nico's calm voice sounded from a cell nearby. The other inmate had been locked in a steam room just around a bend in the torrid corridor.

Ben wavered for a moment, bringing his nerves back under control, and then, seeing that there was no escape, he sat cross-legged in a corner, opposite the glowing furnace.

His heart still pounding, he found that the surface of the stone floor was cooler and the air was cleaner, the fumes spilling in from the hallway less thick at this height. He cooled his burnt hands upon the lukewarm floor and attempted to regulate his breathing.

He had been in the steam room for barely over a minute.

* * *

Watchers emerged from the crowd of inmates gathered in the cell house, resuming their positions on either side of the trio of Lizardmen. Jack and Ethan joined the line-up for the morning shift, Kenneth high-fiving them on their way past for their unprecedented attack on Ray.

The assembly of prisoners looked upon the row of shackled inmates standing before them with a mixture of pity and dread, as they would each have their own turn to wear the rusty neck restraints before the day was through.

The weight of the torc upon Ray's shoulders was stifling. He tried to shake the metal collar around his neck into a more comfortable position.

"Don't tamper with the torcs!" Leon barked at him. Ray eyed the grizzled guard, begrudgingly letting his arms fall to his sides. Leon gruffly addressed Cormac who stood only a few feet away, yet he spoke loud enough for all to hear, "I think a demonstration is in order."

A crude grin flashed across Cormac's face as he fished around in his pocket. "You might feel a little sting, sweet'earts."

The mob of inmates watched with cringing anticipation as Cormac withdrew a new sparker remote from his pocket, his bright blue eyes twinkling with mischief. Ray focused his attention upon the silver gleam of Dana's promise ring upon Cormac's grubby finger, the one that the callous Watcher had won from Spike.

Ray's thoughts were interrupted by a yelp of strangled pain escaping from his own lips, along with all the other inmates in the line-up. He fell to the ground, his teeth chattering uncontrollably with the vibrations rattling up his neck. Blazing ice scorched across his body, the torc's volts of electricity stabbing his spinal column and coursing throughout his entire nervous system.

He reeled upon his hands and knees in shambles, his vision exploding with black fireworks, fighting the urge to gag. He screwed his eyelids shut, feeling as though his eyes might pop out, feeling as though his head was about to explode. Then, as suddenly as the freezing burn had assailed the inmates, the torture stopped.

The prisoners panted and dry heaved in the after-effects of the electrocution. Ray struggled to his feet, his muscles still shaking and twitching. The crowd of inmates before them were wide-eyed and mortified at the display, many of them standing with their hands clapped over their mouths, others quivering in shock, humbled by this new threat. The row of convulsing teens looked up to see Caleb facing Cormac, the taller of the two Watchers now holding Cormac's sparker remote.

"We was just 'aving a bit of fun wiv the new toys, Caleb," said Cormac.

"These are *tools*, not toys, and it's high time you learned the difference," Caleb said sternly. "By your blatant lack of responsibility, Cormac, I hereby revoke your clearance to carry a sparker remote."

"And leave the day shift without a sparker?" Leon stepped in between the pair of guards. "That's a risk to the security of this complex, Caleb. You should know better than that!"

Evander came to Caleb's side, and the entire room held their breath in anticipation as the Watchers squared off against each other, the four men being at odds for some time now. Kalarish and the other reptilians sneered at the breakdown of authority amongst the guards.

The Warden broke out into a nervous sweat, furtively glancing at the Lizardmen who, at any moment, could throw his leadership of the prison into question. "It is clear that Cormac no longer possesses the necessary attributes of a model guard," he said, attempting to regain control of the situation. Caleb nodded his head in agreement, his hawkish gaze relenting slightly as the Warden continued, "It has been noted however, that Leon has displayed many traits of an ideal Watcher, and so, I declare that he is to be entrusted with the day shift's sparker remote."

Caleb reluctantly dropped the remote into Leon's outstretched hand. Cormac grinned his yellow teeth from behind his bearded counterpart at the other pair of Watchers.

Caleb met his gaze, "Don't forget to bolt a torc on your son, too. He has a double shift to look forward to."

Cormac's smile faltered as he turned to Little Danny, the reedy-limbed boy quavering amongst the pack of onlooking inmates.

Leon, holding the sparker remote high in the air, barked in triumph at the crowd, "A warning to all: if anyone tries to tamper with their torc, you will be sparked; if an inmate acts out of line on – or off – their shift, you will be sparked; and lastly, if I even hear the *whisper* of another attempt to escape, *you will be sparked!*"

At a sign from the Warden, Caleb reached into the minecart and handed Spike a pair of torcs, for use on any more trespassers who he might apprehend at the Watcher outpost overlooking the road into town, should the effects of the venom snares be short-lived.

The Warden addressed the assembled prisoners once more, "At present, we only have an adequate amount of torcs for the residents who will be working an active shift. However, more can be manufactured for those who are not on duty, should you choose to continue to act in such an unruly manner. For now, the manacles upon your legs shall remain as an additional precaution."

Many inmates who had hoped that they would be free of the bracelets around their ankles shifted their gazes to the floor.

Pleased with the overall effect of the announcement, Kalarish hobbled forward with her wooden staff to further dishearten the crowd. "In rezponze to your defianze of late, Tyrax, leader of the *Kirzakai*, has decreed that a garrizon of our warriors is to be established. Zoon, the Quarry Complex shall revert to itz prior zecurity arrangement, and the idea of your freedoms shall be little more than a memory."

Crests fell even further as the echoes of her rasping hisses dissipated in the cell house. Inmates and Watchers alike exchanged expressions of concern, wondering what new rules would accompany a garrison of Lizardmen guarding the complex. The trio of upright alligators hissed with laughter as they ambled out of the room.

The silence that followed was broken by Lygia's horrible ear-piercing screech, "The moonlight'ss fading, prisoners! Did I *ssay* you could sstand around? I DIDN'T, DID I!?" she marched over to the nearest inmate and slapped him hard across the face, turning his ear into a red cauliflower. "Now get back to work, BEFORE WE SSPARK YOU AGAIN!!"

The stunned crowd parted to allow the morning shift through. While the Watchers spurred them on with shock sticks from behind, Ray and the others hurtled down the stairs into the cafeteria and through to the tool shed.

Ray trudged towards the rack of mattocks and laid a hand on one of the tools, hoping that only a short shift awaited him before he could rest at last. Jack grabbed the mattock next to his, cheerily winking at the weary inmate.

A flat metal blade slammed Ray's backside, just beneath his shoulder blades and the protection of the torc. He fell to his knees, the wind knocked out of his chest and the taste of copper in his mouth. He looked around in a daze, half-expecting to see Kenneth, but instead, he laid eyes upon Gremlin wielding a shovel with a devilish smile, eager to take his revenge for what had befallen him in the library.

The greasy black-haired Watcher tossed the shovel to Ethan, who stood nearby amongst the prisoners forming a semicircle around Ray, many of them grinning with their arms crossed. They all bore a grudge against him for his part in bringing about their new neck-brace shackles. No help was coming for him this time.

Ray leaned on his tool's wooden handle to support himself in the struggle to get to his feet. Then, with a surge of strength, he thrust the flat-headed business end of the mattock up into Gremlin's pointed chin. The Watcher went down with a squeal of surprise and pain.

Eager to finish off the guard once and for all, he attempted to lift the mattock over his head, yet the torc stifled his arms from reaching above shoulder height. He took on a sideways stance instead and tried to hack down at the terrified Watcher, yet to his dismay, his swing was blocked by Kenneth.

The fiery-haired inmate held the weight of the mattock steady with his shovel. "You tryin' to make it worse, lad? You gone mad?"

Still short of breath from the blow to his back, Ray thought it best not to argue. He shoved his way through the throng of inmates, using the metal torc to shoulder past those who did not yield.

Arguments broke out among the prisoners as their collars tangled together. Little Danny ducked his way through the pack of bickering inmates over to the minecarts, grateful for the distraction as he avoided their attention; their anger at his betrayal still outweighed their grudge for the Rauder brothers.

* * *

The crackling rasps from the brooding red furnace grew louder in the silence. In an attempt to cope with the stifling heat, Ben imagined that he was somewhere cold, and he instantly thought of home. He pictured himself in school, sitting in the library. No. In the science labs. It was always cold in those classrooms.

He remembered his teacher giving a lecture on hot air balloons. A bead of sweat tracked down from his forehead at the mere thought of hot air. He focused on what his teacher had said. *"... Hot air from the gas burner is lesser in density than the cold atmosphere, thus, the hot air rises, inflating the balloon and lifting the basket from the ground..."*

"Hot air rises," Ben repeated, looking around. The room was small, yet it was just wide enough for him to lie down flat. A blanket of cold seemed to draw over him. He breathed the refreshing coolness into his lungs. "Lie down on the floor, Nico," he said, wishing to share his science teacher's lesson. "It's not as hot down here."

"Yeah, I know it already, it's just the same like my house in a hot night," Nico answered from the other cell. "It's okay, I'll just sleep. Maybe just try to keep your shirt too, it's will going to help."

Ben pondered this, glancing down at his shirt that was already halfway off. He recalled that whenever he had worked in the quarry, only his exposed skin would feel the humidity. Something in the crispy smooth fabric of his green uniform somehow protected him from the heat. He pulled his shirt back over his stomach, trusting in the village boy's ever-helpful advice, especially on dealing with the heat in his own country.

Closing his eyes, he thought of their failed escape to Lungsod. If only they had turned right at the fork in the road instead of left towards the marketplace, perhaps they could have avoided the patrol of Gaspar's guards. They would have only had to contend with the brunette woman who had emerged from one of the houses along the beach, jogging in that direction after they had been apprehended.

I wonder whether she was another Watcher like those men in the volcano monitoring station, or if she was coming to help us escape. In any case, she was either too afraid to oppose Gaspar's guards, or she was just another person on the prison's payroll.

At least one glimmer of hope remained. The person who had scrawled 'DON'T BE AFRAID' on the back of the note dropped into his cell could still be somewhere within the complex. The presence of his father's journal from which the note had been torn was unknown to Joshua, and Ben had a strong feeling that it may have been Evander in a stealthy attempt to give them some encouragement. Although, with Evander being paired alongside Caleb, it might prove to be more than difficult for the kind Watcher to sneak any other offer of assistance past the stern guard.

Or, maybe Rashad had been correct all along, and maybe it was all just a mind game being played by one of the Watchers to give them false hope. Maybe it was Cormac's idea of a joke to drop the note into his cell's skylight during one of the guards' late-night poker games, and then dragging his own son, Little Danny, to the steam rooms as punishment for eating the note the next day to conceal any evidence of the message.

Who knows what depths he *would sink to for his own amusement?* Ben thought to himself.

***

Ray passed through the weathered support pillars and out onto the overlooking ledge. He was the first inmate to set foot in the quarry.

The moon sailed by overhead in the blotchy night sky. The stars were obscured from view behind blankets of dark cloud. A shadowy figure, materialising into a Watcher, tracked up the dirt slope bearing the floodlight, its globes shattered. Ray wondered what they would use to illuminate the pit as he descended the ramp before more prisoners plodded out behind him.

He could not tell whether the pit had become deeper. Perhaps it was the darkness of the night that made the quarry seem even more ominous while wreathed in shadow, or perhaps the previous shifts had already dug into a new level. Shards of brown glass scattered across the basin's floor twinkled under the dim moonlight, remnants of Cormac and the other guards' drunken revelry when they had hurled the volley of empty bottles from the viewing deck.

As other inmates descended into the gloomy pit, Ray's adjusting eyes fell upon another shadowy figure standing on top of the rock shelf holding a staff or a pole of some kind.

Ray shielded his face, his instincts proving correct as a glaring white light washed over the dirt floor and walls, prisoners around him gasping in pain at the sudden bright flash.

Lygia's shrill cackle reverberated around the quarry. "You can thank those FILTHY MAGGOTSS on the night shift for that. *Another* floodlight broken! Now, who ssaid you could lie about? GET TO WORK!!"

Ray peered out from behind his free hand, allowing his eyes to adapt slowly. Inmates were crumpled upon the ground rubbing at their eyes, others staggering around blindly and bumping into each other, their torcs catching together and sending them even further off balance.

He dropped his hand just in time to stare down an advancing Gremlin, his pale face shocked by the inmate's clarity of vision. The Watcher grumbled to himself and climbed up the rock shelf to stand next to Lygia and the other guards, taking refuge in the shadows.

Ray trudged over to the far end of the earth wall, away from the dirt ramp and the other prisoners still recovering from the dazzling flash as they were harried on by Lygia's shrieks. He raised the mattock, yet his arms caught again on the torc's shoulder guards. The resulting strike was pitifully weak, barely breaking pebbles free of the ledge.

He stood side-on instead, swinging the mattock like a baseball bat into the rock. From this position, he could simultaneously work and monitor the rest of the pit, keeping an eye on the Watchers and the other inmates, those wielding mattocks soon copying his technique.

A vein of tiny blue gemstones appeared in the rock wall as he worked, and he pondered what *Dragonstone* might look like. Joshua had told him to pass the name of the strange mineral on as a message to his uncle, whoever that might have referred to.

He then remembered Kalarish reporting to her leader, Tyrax, that they were no closer to finding the *Dragonstone*, confirming that he had heard Joshua correctly, but to what end, he had no idea. He turned the thought aside as the glittering jewels embedded in the rock fell to the ground with each of his swings, lost amid the dirt steadily piling up.

A trio of inmates wandered over to his worksite – Jack, Ethan and Kenneth.

Jack took up position with his mattock on the other side of the gemstone vein, Kenneth drawing up behind him with a shovel, and Ethan digging at the pile of dirt at Ray's feet. Ray's grip tightened around the wooden handle of his mattock, his knuckles whitening. He knew that he could only swing once before he would be overwhelmed by his former friends, so he would have to make it count.

"Sorry about before," Ethan said behind him. "We had to make it look real."

"What!?" Ray and Kenneth exclaimed in unison.

"Jack and I thought it would be a good idea to watch your back after everyone started pinning the blame on you for the torcs," Ethan explained. "We needed to get ourselves put on your shift somehow."

"And beating me down was the only way for you to get a double shift?" Ray asked over the top of Kenneth's profanity-laced outrage.

Jack shrugged. "It worked, didn't it?"

"We thought Kenneth might try something," Ethan turned to face the Irish prisoner, whose freckled cheeks were red with anger, realising that he was the one who was outnumbered now. "As soon as he laid the blame on you and Ben, we started planning."

"And here I was thinkin' you lads had come to your senses!" Kenneth said amid another impressively diverse string of curse words.

"It's you that needs to get your sense back, mate," said Jack.

"We need to come together," said Ethan. "It's no good fighting amongst ourselves while the *real* enemy stands up on that ledge laughing at us argue." The four inmates looked up at Lygia, Gremlin, and all of the other guards standing by the floodlight, watching over the prisoners working below.

"Look," Ray said to Kenneth. "We can get outta here a different way, but you need to –"

"Need to *what?* Need to wreck me other leg? *No!* I was perfectly fine before you and your brother came along."

Jack and Ethan exchanged a glance, sensing the tension mounting between the pair of inmates again. "Didn't reckon they'd have a spare floodlight lying around," said Jack, changing the topic. "I was looking forward to working without the bugs biting for once."

The others continued digging in silence. As if in answer to Jack, a mosquito droned past Ray's ear, landing on the back of his neck. He tried to smack it, but his arm got caught on the torc and the gnat escaped unscathed.

"Hey, Kenneth," Ray ventured as he ripped his mattock from the rock wall, "I think I might take you up on that offer to switch tools now." Kenneth grunted his disapproval. "Guess that's a *no,* then," said Ray, plunging the mattock back into the rock.

A broken bottle rolled over the ledge and shattered upon Ray's pile of dirt, setting the others on edge.

"I've got an idea," said Jack, bending down to pick up some of the pieces. "Let's chuck these shards in with the gems. Maybe some of the Watchers'll cut up their hands later."

Ray smiled, remembering the guards sorting through the minecarts in the treasury with their bare hands. Ethan chuckled as he scooped up the broken glass with his shovel.

"Maybe they'll think twice about what they're throwin' into the pit," Kenneth grinned.

* * *

Rhythmic knocks from outside jolted Ben from his slumber. He rose to his feet and stretched. With the heat flushing his face, he found himself choking halfway through a sulfurous yawn, immediately reminding him of where he was.

The top half of Caleb's stony face appeared at the hotbox's iron-barred window, his nose and mouth covered by his grey shirt. "Warden wants to see you."

Ben narrowly avoided the heavy wooden door as it swung inwards. He masked his face with his uniform before venturing out into the passage behind Caleb.

Evander, wearing a bandanna, knelt in the corridor as he hammered nails into a plywood board over the top of the sheet of cloth billowing with acrid fumes from the adjacent steam room. The kind Watcher's measured knocks paused for a brief moment as he nodded at Ben.

"Now, inmate!" Caleb said impatiently, turning the corner and expecting him to follow.

With his shirt drawn up over his nose and mouth, Ben hurried to keep pace with the striding guard, not wishing to remain any longer in the toxic passageway. "Is Nico coming?" he asked, glancing through the window of his friend's cell. They soon turned another corner, the stern Watcher ignoring his question.

Caleb directed Ben to walk before him so that he could keep an eye on the inmate. They approached the end of the corridor. On their right was a closed door, and on their left was a flight of stairs leading upwards to another closed door. A twin set of railings ran diagonally up the staircase, most likely for the transport of goods or fresh inmates in minecarts between the two levels.

Assuming that they were heading up to the barracks, Ben placed a foot on the first step, but he was yanked backwards, his shirt falling from his face and exposing his airways to the corrosive fumes of the corridor again. Before he could clap a hand over his spluttering mouth, Caleb shoved him through the freshly-opened door on their right into another room.

It seemed that he had been thrust into the treasury. Watchers were bent over minecarts, throwing handfuls of dirt to other empty barrows and shoving glittering gems into their pockets. Cormac and Leon were among them, perusing the unearthed riches. None of the guards noticed the new arrivals.

Nuggets of gold lay amid cloths and brushes on a wooden workbench nearby, but Ben's thirsty eyes fell upon the water tap on the other side of the room, set in the wall next to an open service elevator.

Caleb shoved Ben towards the elevator platform and thumbed a switch on a nearby panel. The elevator's motor whirred to life beneath them and the platform rose up with a jerk towards the room above, which was only visible through a square hole in the ceiling.

Ben's attention snapped back to the treasury as a fight broke out among the Watchers. Leon elbowed one of the jostling guards in the face and stood back to admire a brilliant green emerald clutched within his gnarled fingers.

Others advanced on the grizzled guard, but Cormac came to his defence, sparking up his shock stick and issuing a challenge to the other Watchers. "'ey? 'ey!?"

"Animals," Caleb muttered as the rising elevator platform obscured the scene.

The clamour below fell away from Ben's mind as the cool breeze of an air conditioner swirled around him. He closed his eyes for a moment, savouring the serene tranquillity before the elevator ground to a halt on the upper level.

They were in the barracks now.

Ben opened his eyes to see the brightly-lit lounge filled with bamboo furniture, off-duty guards lazing upon the cushioned cane wood chairs while drinking from pale brown bottles. Before he could look around any further, Caleb stepped off the platform, opened up a door on their right and threw him onto the white ceramic-tiled floor of the room within.

* * *

The sound of the water carts trundling down into the pit was greeted by a ritualistic collective sigh of relief. Ray passed by the other inmates, all of them angrily glaring at him for the restrictive torcs around their necks, yet they would not make a move with Jack and Ethan flanking him. Even Kenneth seemed to have lightened up on his grievance, if going from irate to resentful was any improvement.

The labourers crowding around the water carts begrudgingly made space for Ray and the others. Ray scooped water up to his mouth, although his arms collided with the torc yet again and he spilled the water before he even had the chance to take a sip.

Little Danny's reedy laugh was quickly silenced by glares from the other prisoners, and he retreated halfway up the dirt slope to safety.

Ray bent over the edge of the water cart farther, when a sudden wave of electricity shot down his neck, bringing all of the inmates to their knees. He grabbed the side of the cart to steady himself, but in his convulsions, he tipped the barrow over, the water splashing out across the dirt.

Kenneth and the other inmates shouted their abuse at his clumsiness. Gremlin's pointed face grinned from ear to ear as he stowed away his sparker remote. Ray, Jack and Ethan recovered before Kenneth could rile

381

up the other inmates against the three of them. They cautiously moved back towards their tools in the far corner of the pit, having zero chance of getting near the other water cart.

"Nico's water filtering trick would've been handy, if it wasn't for these rusty collars," said Jack, tugging at his torc.

Deprived of sleep and now water too, Ray sluggishly swung his mattock at the rock ledge, barely scratching a groove into the wall. He was spent, depleted. He tried to work with one eye shut, but this only served to throw his already staggered stance further off-balance. His vision clouded over, everything seeming to swim and blur before his eyes, even objects near at hand. He thought to himself that perhaps his bad eyesight had finally deteriorated altogether.

At some point in his hazy trance, the sun had risen.

Lygia's screeches and Jack's guiding shoves propelled him up the dirt slope, dragging his tool behind him in the dim light of the early morning. Ray returned the mattock to its rack with Ethan's help. He did not even notice the torc being unfastened from his neck to be fitted to the day shift's inmates filing into the cafeteria.

A splash of water and a bowl of gruel allowed him just enough energy to follow the others up the stairs into the cell house. He even let Gremlin unceremoniously kick and push him into a new cell along the left wall that housed the other boys from the morning shift. Ray staggered towards the bed frame and flopped onto the bottom bunk, snoring before his head even hit the mattress.

* * *

"Will that be all, sir?" asked Caleb.

Across the office, behind a mahogany desk, sat the Warden, his forefinger caught between two pages of a hardcover novel, *The Construction of Quartz Hall*. He glanced up from the book, mopped his sweaty forehead with his handkerchief and peered over his desk to see the inmate sprawled upon the floor. He settled back into his armchair with a nod, dismissing Caleb with a wave of his hand.

Caleb took his leave at once, but not before stating that he would be waiting outside in the lounge if he was required any further.

The Warden resumed his reading, making notes as he leafed through the pages, allowing Ben to draw himself up into a cross-legged position upon the floor.

The office was neatly arranged. Two bookcases stood on either side of a closed door behind the Warden. Leafy green pot plants occupied the four corners of the room. A bench made of bamboo served as a couch on one side of the office, and along the other wall were a small refrigerator and a water cooler.

Ben's eyes lingered on the water cooler, but his gaze soon strayed above the unit with curiosity towards an oddly-shaped parcel hanging upon the wall. It had the figure of a rifle, with a long barrel and a thick handle, yet what was underneath its brown paper packaging was a mystery.

He turned back to the Warden, noticing for the first time the ornament placed upon the corner of his desk. It was the same carved rock that had fallen from the ceiling during the tool shed rebellion. The symbol on the rock was identical to the one on his father's journal, and his father's medallion that now hung around Caleb's neck, the very same symbol that adorned the front cover of *The Construction of Quartz Hall* clutched in the Warden's clammy hands.

The puffy-cheeked man set the book down, finally turning his attention towards the inmate sitting upon the floor.

"Please," he gestured towards the bamboo bench. Ben got to his feet and sat on the cushioned cane wood chair. It creaked beneath him, despite his small frame. "Would you like some water?" the Warden offered.

Ben licked his parched lips with a dry tongue, glancing back at the water cooler again before nodding profusely. The portly Warden lifted himself from his armchair and ambled around his desk to the cooler. His Hawaiian shirt revealed sweat stains running down his back and under his armpits as he bent down to fill two plastic cups, one for himself and one for the inmate. Ben drained his cup before the Warden could sit back down again.

He toyed with the empty cup nervously as he wondered what the man would ask of him.

The Warden took a small sip of the water, relishing its coolness before clearing his throat. "Sheriff Lee Sullivan informed me of the regrettably violent encounter in the swamp. Your father, Jacob, was an important man here."

Ben crushed his plastic cup in surprise.

"Sorry," he said, setting the broken cup aside, "Did you say *here?*"

"Yes, and my sincerest condolences for your loss," said the Warden. "He was a dear friend of mine during the foundation of the Quarry Complex, and perhaps the only person I could trust at the time. In our humble beginnings, Jacob *embraced* the idea of serving our masters, the *Kirzakai.*"

"Liar," Ben said hotly, "My father wouldn't have had anything to do with a place like this."

"On the contrary," the Warden replied, "Jacob revolutionised our operations with his ingenious suggestions. He introduced the idea of using our labourers as guards instead of the *Kirzakai* warriors. This opened up a world of possibilities. It enabled us to establish relations with the nearby village, and help a certain Eduardo Gaspar to climb the rungs of the political ladder."

"Are you saying that *you're* responsible for the local government's corruption?"

"Not necessarily. We merely financed the budding candidate's campaign, adding our donations to the income stream of his pre-existing extortion endeavours. Years later, after your father's departure, the village's logging activities threatened to uncover our operations, and the honourable Mayor Gaspar returned our favour by blaming a devastating landslide on the lack of trees on the town's side of the volcano."

Ben felt nauseous, knowing that Nico's family had split up after his father was put out of work as a lumberjack following the landslide. He stared down at his dirty brown sneakers as the Warden prattled on.

"The blame may have been well-placed. It was a violent storm, after all, yet the loggers had to be quelled somehow. Then, to ensure our privacy, our good Mayor went on to secretly spread claims that the jungle was haunted, and the beings who dwelt there were angry at the villagers for destroying their homes, and that the landslide was merely retaliation. The locals are a superstitious folk, so the rumours were not hard for them to believe."

Ben recalled his cellmate's sad childhood story. *Nico's baby sister drowned in that storm.* He blinked at the floor.

The sweaty Warden finished his cup of water before clucking his tongue at Ben's silence. "Do not let this tarnish the memory of your late father, dear boy. Jacob won many arguments for the humane treatment of our residents: chain gangs were replaced by manacles and sparkers; whips and other crippling devices were replaced by shock sticks; and of course, he gave people hope with the opportunity of one day becoming a Watcher. Jacob was sure to become Warden, and I second-in-command, which is why it was such a surprise when he chose to depart unannounced."

Deep in thought, the Warden rose from his armchair and approached the water cooler again. "I had expected Jacob to return at some point, as he had left something behind, something very dear to him." The Warden traced his fingers along the gun-shaped object hanging on the wall. "But of course, I understood his reluctance to return."

"Where did the Lizardmen come from?" Ben blurted out, snapping the Warden from his far-off gaze.

He shrugged, turning to resume his seat with another cup of water. "They have always been here on Earth, hiding in the shadows, waiting, waiting…"

"Waiting for what?" Ben croaked, his throat dry and scratchy again as his thirst returned.

"For the work in the quarry to be completed," the Warden answered. "It will guarantee our victory over the Faction, and then, the world. Despite what you may think, it is possible for us humans and the *Kirzakai* to live together in harmony, if both parties are willing."

"Is this your idea of living?" asked Ben, his voice coming out in a hoarse whisper now.

The Warden finished his cup in silence before clapping his hands twice. Caleb entered almost immediately, dragging the prisoner off the bamboo bench and back down below.

They returned to the steam room corridor to see that the plywood board covering the sheet of cloth had been sealed on all sides with duct tape, although the reeking fumes still lingered in the hallway.

Caleb threw Ben to the floor, securing him inside the hotbox once again. "Do not think yourself favoured, inmate. If the air, and company, were not so foul down here, the Warden would have spoken to you through the bars of this window. The day shift has already been assembled, but it would be unfair to the other prisoner if you were punished less severely by being allowed to spend time upstairs. Now, you can wait until the night shift before you are released." With that, the stern Watcher turned on his heel and strode out of the corridor.

Ben slumped down against the door, thoughts racing through his mind. He wondered if the little he had known about his father was even true at all. Only the notes left in the marked leather-bound journal hidden somewhere within the prison could answer all of his questions concerning the Lizardmen, the Faction, and of course, his father.

As he settled down for another sweltering sleep, the rock on the corner of the Warden's desk entered his mind, and a thought struck him: *maybe the Warden has my father's journal.*

25 - WE WERE SAFE

Eventually, Ben was released from the steam rooms and dragged down into the cafeteria for the night shift. With his face flushed red, his green shirt soaked with sweat and his tongue as dry as a cactus, Evander reasoned with Caleb on the inmate's behalf that he would not last more than a few minutes in the pit.

Caleb glanced sideways at the prisoner, panting on the floor of the cafeteria, and he reluctantly agreed with the kind Watcher. He even allowed Ben to drink his fill of water, although he strictly prohibited the inmate from receiving any food.

Ben was brought to one of the centre cells along the back wall of the cell house, where Nico slumbered. His cellmate seemed no worse for wear after working the day shift, despite his time in the steam room.

With Nico already stretched out upon the lower bunk – as much as one could stretch on the tiny bed – Ben exhaustedly climbed onto the upper mattress where he slipped into a feverish dream. Images of the Warden's office, the Lizardmen, and the Faction symbol on his father's journal and medallion swirled in a dizzying vision before him; each room, face and object bathed in the gloomy red glow of the steam room's furnace.

Shivering with cold sweat clinging to his face and neck, Ben shook out of his troubled sleep, startled by a low growl from nearby. He jerked upright only to hit his head on the low ceiling. Stifling a groan, he glanced around at the new cell, the bed frame creaking under his weight as he turned over on the thin mattress.

No morning sunshine streamed down through the skylight just yet. *Has it been seconds or days?* He could not tell.

Looking over the pale stone walls illuminated by the spotlights shining in from the cell house, his eyes widened in horror at the sight of three jagged lines scratched into the wall, just above where his head had been only moments ago.

Was that there before? Were they from a Lizardman's claws? Is it... is it still in here!? Slowly, carefully, he leaned over the side of his mattress to check on Nico. He was still sleeping peacefully upon the lower bunk.

Still hanging his head over the side of the bed, Ben heard another sound tracking across the underside of his thin mattress – a tiny *pitter patter* like drizzling rain on soft grass.

Overcome by curiosity yet frozen with dread, he watched as a small green lizard popped its thumb-sized head out from underneath the bed, staring back up at the shaking boy with its wide yellow eyes. Their gazes locked for a brief moment before the little gecko skittered across the bed frame and padded up the wall onto the ceiling, giving an almost inaudible hiss back at him from its tiny gaping mouth before disappearing up into the skylight.

Ben lay in confusion on the edge of his bed until he heard the growl again. Rolling back upon the mattress, he breathed a sigh of relief – it was only his stomach rumbling.

He felt around for a pillow, yet none was in reach, nor was there a bed sheet. Every piece of linen had been removed from all of the cells after he and Nico had managed to escape using the bed sheets to break open the skylight.

When one of the prisoners had complained about the uncomfortable new sleeping arrangements, a Watcher had gleefully declared, "Inmates can no longer be trusted with what little they have!"

* * *

Ray woke up alone in his new cell along the left wall of the cell house where all the other morning shift inmates were. He glanced down at his soiled uniform, realising that he had fallen asleep before he had even changed out of his last shift's clothes. He got up to wash himself with the soapy water from the chamber pot, yet all that remained in the metal bucket was oily water, the cleansing suds having dissipated while he had slept.

He looked over at the wall next to his bunk where his pillow would have been, if he had one. The stone slab was a blank slate waiting for him to scratch in his recording of the amount of days that he had been imprisoned. He shook out a small rock from one of his boots and reached over the bed, but he stopped halfway. He realised that he could not remember how many days it had been. After being assigned his additional duties designed to deprive him of sleep, he had lost track of time.

Doors began to open along his side of the cell house, heralding the beginning of a new shift, and all of the prisoners fell in line. As they filed down into the cafeteria, the torcs were taken from the returning night shift inmates and were secured around Ray and the others.

It did not take long before Caleb bore his steely gaze into Ray, asking whether he had changed his mind about keeping tight-lipped on Joshua's last words in the pit.

"Can't remember," Ray shrugged.

Caleb raised an eyebrow at the inmate's smug smile. Ray braced himself for a beating, yet to his surprise, Caleb released him from his additional duties, the prisoner having proven too much trouble for the extra responsibility anyway.

Ray worked through the drudging early morning hours while shooting glances over his shoulder, half-expecting Caleb to appear and badger him at any moment. Nothing happened. Kenneth threw a pile of dirt at his backside, but with a warning glare from Ray, the Irish inmate stopped.

When the shift ended, he and the others returned to the cafeteria, their torcs removed and given over to the next batch of inmates. Ray saw Caleb again momentarily, who scarcely acknowledged him. None of the other Watchers gave him any trouble either, not even Gremlin. He ate alone and then returned back to his cell.

* * *

Each day dragged on with the same repetitive routine, the only noticeable change being brought on by the passing weeks ushering in a new tropical season. The lengths of each shift in the quarry seemed to fluctuate at the whim of the weather. Dark storm clouds stretched across the sky more often than not, shrouding the light of the moon and the rise of the sun, obscuring when the shifts should begin and when they should end.

Ben was thankful for the cooler weather as it gave his skin a chance to recover from the various peeling layers of angry sunburn, although the sudden barrages of torrential rainfall accompanying the wet season did not earn his gratitude, nor did it earn that of the other inmates – their movements already stifled and off-balance underneath the weight of the torcs locked around their necks – they slipped and stumbled and swore as they struggled to slog through the squelching mud in the pelting rains.

The complications brought on by the wet weather did not stop there either. There was also the bug problem. Seemingly thousands of larvae swam in the stagnant water that pooled at the bottom of the pit after each downpour, the mosquitoes feeding like a plague of locusts on the never-ending buffet on display.

Equally affected by the vexing vermin, the Watchers made a habit of pouring gasoline into the puddles and burning the water's surface to cook the insects in their infancy, but they always came back, and with the lack of bed sheets in the cells, the prisoners could do nothing but cover themselves with their soiled uniforms to keep the mosquitoes in the night at bay.

All of the inmates cheered when Aiden finally broke through his feverish cycle of eat, sleep and repeat. He still wore his green sweatband stained red with his own dried blood around his forehead, although aside from his occasional complaints of different muscles aching while he adjusted to the new movement patterns forced upon them by the neck-bracing torcs, he was otherwise silent. Not even his former cellmate, Kenneth, could stir a conversation out of him.

As the days in the pit grew darker, Ray began to think that his additional duties were more privilege rather than punishment. He actually did not mind the extra time he had spent working alongside Mara and Ava – although Ava had since lost her light duties after having twice unveiled the hidden passage to the Lizardmen's quarters.

Amelia had taken her place as the reptiles' reader, as well as serving breakfast and dinner, while Ava was now cleaning the prison alongside Sarah, emptying chamber pots with Mara, and sometimes appearing in the cafeteria for the midnight meal.

Ray thought of ways to disrupt the order of things just to break the monotonous cycle of the prison, and with hopes of being reassigned more work, yet his plans always seemed to fall upon deaf ears, Kenneth having convinced the other inmates on the morning shift that things could still get worse for them if they continued to resist.

Following the punishments imposed upon the inmates, their disdain for the Watchers was as strong as ever, yet instead, the prisoners turned back to taking out their frustration in the safest way possible: fighting against each other.

Torcs, being able to defend the chest and neck from injury, provided the gambling guards with differing odds when they placed bets upon brawls in the cafeteria between shifts. Spear-tackling became the new ideal takedown technique amongst the squabbling prisoners. Kenneth's leg had already improved enough for the grudging inmate to charge at Ray whenever he could catch him unaware.

Ray did not see Ben, Ethan, Jack or Nico other than in passing. He was always being forced to linger and tidy up the tool shed before the day shift began, or his shift would be let out of their cells to eat early, swapping torcs with the returning night shift inmates and heading straight out to work.

Although he was separated from his brother, Ray knew that he could rely on the others to protect him. He was glad that Ben had made friends with those three. They had far more integrity about them than his brother's previous cellmate, Little Danny, and beyond that, any of his classmates in their school. In fact, they might have been the only friends that Ben had ever had.

However, with the other boys being on different shifts and Rashad far away in the Desert Complex, Levi took every available opportunity to bully Ben and Nico. Word had spread quickly of how Ray had broken the snide inmate's nose to evade being shackled with a metal collar the day the torcs had arrived, and in retaliation, Levi would slam his minecart into Ben's backside and roll the metal wheels over Nico's bare feet, or he would knock bowls of gruel out of their hands after a long day, just to get back at Ray.

It seemed as though nothing would unify the inmates anymore, who were in constant fear of the threat that the spine-rattling torcs would be distributed for everyone – not just those working an active shift – if they continued to step out of line.

***

Ben had seen Sarah cleaning in the cell house from time to time, which would always brighten up his nights even though not much more than a few words passed between them each time, yet now when she came to the bars of his cell, she was brimming with excitement. Like a child on Christmas morning, he leapt from his bed and stood before her.

"I know the code to the garage's keypad," she whispered happily. "Well, it was all thanks to Ava. It was her idea to clean the barracks while the Watchers were playing poker. Spike got upset about losing, and he left in a hurry to go back to the outpost. He didn't see me behind him while he was keying in the code."

Ben returned her smile. "Now all we need is a plan to get into the barracks."

At that moment, the door to the adjoining passage in the corner of the cell house flew open with a crash, making them both jump. Sheriff Sullivan sauntered in with a group of teens at his back. Though they did not yet wear the green uniforms of the Quarry Complex, the prisoners had been fitted with torcs.

As the Sheriff shepherded them down the stairs into the cafeteria, he looked up at Sarah, calling out to her in his southern drawl, "Ain't it past y'all's bedtime about now?"

"Just finishing up the day's work, sir," she replied shakily, backing away from Ben's cell.

"Well, it sure ain't look like it," said the Sheriff, his gaze following her out of the room before he descended the flight of stairs after the new prisoners.

A familiar trundling noise resounded from just beyond the open door in the corner, and moments later, a minecart appeared, wheeled in by Leon. Then another, by Cormac. And another. And another. The guards set about opening doors to any unoccupied cells they could find.

Awakened by all the commotion, Nico joined Ben at the barred window, looking out into the cell house as the Watchers wheeled dozens more metal wagons into the room. The smoky grey-scaled Lizardwoman, Pythrisse, loomed into the cell house behind them, donned in her open blue vest, followed by a band of other reptilian humanoids, all of them in varying shapes and sizes; their differently coloured scales of yellow and orange and fiery red dancing underneath the auras of the spotlights hanging from the four corners of the ceiling. Others, whose hides were dark grey and leathery brown, seemed to blend in with the dank stone walls of the gloomy prison. Each of the *Kirzakai* warriors dragged a pair of limp captives along the floor on either side of their slithering tails. These teenagers were not yet wearing the green uniforms of the prison either.

Other inmates startled by all the noise began to line the windows of the cell house.

Cormac yelled in alarm as one inmate jumped out at him from an unlocked cell. The Watcher beat the prisoner back with his shock stick. "'ere sunshine, 'ave some company!" he shouted, reaching for a nearby minecart and upending the barrow's contents, spilling an unconscious youth into the cell like a load of dirt before slamming the door shut.

"What happen?" Nico whispered, his eyes watching the Lizardmen uncertainly. Each of them bore crudely-made yet sharply-hewn weapons. Spears and javelins hung from straps over the brightly-coloured reptilians' shoulders. The darker ones wore maces and ball-and-chain flails from their belts. A few of the larger *Kirzakai* warriors in the likeness of Pythrisse also had iron barbs affixed to their snaking tails.

"They must be new inmates," Ben muttered, staring almost trance-like at the amount of prisoners being hauled into the cell house one after another.

Little Danny stood at the entrance of his open cell with indignation in his sky blue eyes as he pleaded with his father, "But Pop! You promised I would 'ave a room all to meself!"

"You 'ad one, and now you 'ave to share it," Cormac said through gritted teeth while hauling a body through the door. "Man of me word, innit?"

"What'd you do this time, kidnap a whole school bus?" Jack called across the cell house.

"Quiet down, inmate," Leon growled, thwacking Jack's window bars with his shock stick, narrowly missing the Aussie prisoner's fingers.

"Take your own advice," said Ethan, appearing at the window next to his cellmate. "We're trying to sleep here."

More inmates began shouting across the cell house, the new prisoners groggily waking up on the floor at the sounds of their yells. The Watchers became hard-pressed to place the new arrivals in their cells before they could fully return to their senses. At this, the caged inmates' yells grew even louder, chaos and confusion spreading throughout the cell house. Amused, Pythrisse and the other Lizardmen hung back and watched the guards rushing to and fro.

The amount of bodies scattered upon the floor soon dwindled. The Watchers were just shoving the last of the dazed captives into their cells when the barracks door swung open. The Warden, flanked by Caleb and Evander, entered the room. The puffy-cheeked man ambled down into the centre of the cell house, his arms held up high in a call for silence.

The yells and jeers continued around the room until Pythrisse raised her iron-barbed tail and whipped it down upon the concrete floor with a resounding *CRACK*. Almost instantly, a hush fell among the inmates. Only the *pitter patter* of rainwater beginning to trickle down through each cell's skylight could be heard above the silence.

"Yes, thank you," the Warden bowed his balding round head in Pythrisse's direction, a small cloud of dust billowing out from behind the Lizard-woman. He turned to address the crowd of inmates behind bars, "As I'm sure you're all well aware by now, our facility's security personnel will soon be replaced by the capable Pythrisse and her clutch of *Kirzakai* warriors."

The Lizardmen snarled in response, swelling with pride.

The inmates, on the other hand, were all wearing forlorn expressions. Even the Watchers scowled at the reminder.

"However," the Warden continued, "Something that you are perhaps puzzled by is the sheer number of new arrivals tonight. Following the fall of Quartz Hall at the hands of the mighty Tyrax, Matron Kalarish and I have together handpicked some new worthy candidates from our subdued enemy to join us in our great endeavour!"

"We never joined you!" a rebellious voice rang out. "Faction 'til we die!"

"Well, y-you did not die when the Faction fought back in f-f-futility," said the Warden, wringing his clammy hands together. "And, evidently, you are with us, so – so yes, you have joined us."

Ben had never seen the Warden so nervous, but it was most likely due to the towering figure of Pythrisse looming behind him, in addition to all of the other *Kirzakai* warriors listening intently to his speech.

The Warden withdrew his handkerchief and mopped his sweaty fore-head. "I expect all of our current inhabitants to be welcoming, courteous, and kind to our new guests. Please remember, they have just lost their home, but with your help, they can become a part of ours."

Cormac rolled his eyes and Leon spat in disgust at the Warden's words. Some of the inmates snorted. Even the Lizardmen hissed with derision. The Warden shrank closer to Caleb, and Ben almost felt a pang of sorrow for the portly man.

Caleb spoke up on his behalf, "Well said, Warden." He cast his stern gaze upon the inmates standing with bated breath at every cell. "In a few hours, you will be working together. As we are now reaching capacity in the cells, anyone who does not pull their weight in the next shift will be sleeping in the steam rooms. *Permanently.*"

Murmurs broke out among the inmates, especially the new arrivals. Evander glanced sidelong at Caleb, his face full of concern, yet Cormac, Leon and the other Watchers chuckled with crude grins.

After the Watchers and Lizardmen left the cell house, the inmates returned to their thin mattresses. It had been difficult enough to fall asleep without a pillow and a bed sheet, yet now with the rainwater streaming down through the skylight and smacking the stone floor and low gusts of wind whipping by overhead sounding like long wails of agony, Ben tossed and turned, trying to remember what freedom felt like.

* * *

Rain droplets splashed in the mud-sodden earth, the shadows of the drizzling rain dancing across the quarry walls as they traced over the floodlight's glaring bulb in the early hours of the morning. Ray's hands slipped on his mattock's wet handle. As he paused to readjust his grip, he glanced down at the fading tan line around his thumb.

He feared that somehow, if Dana's promise ring was not returned to his thumb before the diminishing outline faded from his hand completely, he would lose any chance of seeing the world above ever again, along with being able to reconcile his ill-ended relationship with her.

"GET BACK TO WORK, INMATE!!" Lygia's shrill voice filled the pit.

Ray tightened his grip on the mattock and swung at the rock shelf with a muddy *squelch*, contemptuously eyeing the silhouettes of the Watchers sitting dry beneath the large umbrella beyond the floodlight's reach.

Wrenching his tool from the mud, he paused, gazing over the top of the dark umbrella. Shadows were moving along the quarry wall and down into the pit.

It can't be the water carts already, he thought to himself. Not even one of the weaker boys had begun to complain about the working conditions yet – usually a sign that they were close to being halfway through the shift.

The other inmates noticed the movement, and the Watchers ventured out from underneath the umbrella. All heads turned towards the shadowy figures slipping into the floodlight's aura. The crowd shuffled out into the pit, tightly bunched together and attempting to readjust the torcs around their necks, staring in confusion at the prisoners already gathered.

Ray, Kenneth and the others stared back at the new arrivals, seeing their different clothes as almost foreign objects. Ragged though they appeared, the multitude of colours from the crowd's garments seemed to strike out as the newcomers huddled against the rain and shielded their eyes from the floodlight.

Lygia and Gremlin reached the edge of the rock shelf just as a man in a black hat sauntered to the front of the pack of new captives. He tipped his wide-brimmed hat back.

"Howdy ma'am," said Sheriff Sullivan in his dry southern accent, "Got a gift here for y'all, straight from the tippy top! New *volunteers* from the *Fact-she-awn.*"

Lygia stood with her arms akimbo in front of the floodlight, the lamp's brilliance reflecting an eerie luminescent glow from her sickly green skin. "And *why* are you dumping the *whole lot* down HERE in the middle of *MY SHIFT!?*" she shrieked.

"You kiddin'? The amount o' skinny little varmints 'em lizards bagged up, I'm surprised we even got enough rooms for 'em all up there," Sullivan jerked a thumb up at the black outline of the cell house beyond the dark curtains of rain.

A loud rumble travelling down the rain-washed slope caused the Sheriff to sidestep out of the way, a minecart careening out of the darkness and tipping sideways a third of the way across the pit, spilling tools out where the Watcher had been standing only a moment ago.

A long-faced blonde teen got up from behind the overturned barrow, its rusty metal wheels still spinning in the air. "I – I lost control of it in the rain," he said with rosy cheeks before sheepishly joining the crowd of other miserable dregs.

Sheriff Sullivan shook his head with narrowed eyes, and then turned back to Lygia. "Well, I'd love to stay 'n' splash around in the mud, but I got someplace drier to be." Chortling, the cheery Watcher climbed back out of sight and up the drenched dirt ramp.

All work in the pit having ceased, Lygia seized the sparker remote from Gremlin and tapped the button for a moment. Some of the long-standing inmates dropped to one knee at the shock, but the newcomers gasped and wrenched at their torcs.

"*Firsst! Warning!*" Lygia shrieked above their squealing. "Sstart working, because YOU WON'T GET A SSECOND!!"

Ray, Kenneth and the others turned back to their menial tasks, and the new captives begrudgingly followed suit.

A second mattock fang struck into the rock shelf where Ray was working. He looked to his side to see the blonde-haired youth struggling to free the tool from the muddy bank, a white shade of nervousness illuminating his face.

"Good way to make an entrance," said Ray. "A little to the left and you would've had him."

The boy ran a hand through his matted blonde hair, brushing the wet strands out of his eyes before straightening up proudly. "Yes, that's exactly what I meant to do, but as I said, I lost control of the cart." He offered a hand to Ray, "I'm Connor, pleased to meet you."

"Ray," he replied. Then, glancing at the other boy's mattock still embedded in the ledge, he added, "Pull it out from the top." Connor wavered awkwardly with his outstretched hand for a moment before he gripped the mattock just below the spike, yanking it from the rock shelf. "Where'd you guys all come from anyway?" Ray asked, watching the other prisoners clumsily learn how to dig in the rain.

"We're from the Faction," Connor answered, plunging his mattock back into the muddy wall with a loud *squelch*. "We dedicate ourselves to ridding the world of the inferior Lizardmen."

"If they're so *inferior*, how'd you end up here?"

"Well, we had a minor flaw in our stronghold, overlooked by many. Not by me, of course," the Faction teen added quickly. "Somehow, the Lizardmen found out about this one weakness, and within *minutes* of their attack, we were overrun."

Ray thought back to when Jack and Ethan had told him of Joshua's interrogation in the room with the gunmetal grey door; his pleas for mercy and repeating *the Faction* over and over. Perhaps Joshua had revealed a vital clue about the Faction's defences during his torture.

"So all those books and scrolls, they came from your people..." said Ray. "But those came in a few weeks ago, what took *you* so long to get here?"

"They seized our literature? *Ha!* Probably to light a fire to keep themselves warm, savages..." Connor said with mild amusement. "We put up a great fight, battled them for *weeks* in the upper levels of the city. Some of us were taken prisoner early on, but we kept going until our supplies ran out."

Ray glanced at him sceptically. "So, what did the Lizardmen feed you while everyone else was fighting?"

"*Everyone else?*" Connor exclaimed dramatically, running a hand through his hair again, "*I* was one of the *last* to be captured!" The newcomer swung his mattock again, gasping in pain as the skin of his soft palms blistered from the tool's handle.

Over the course of the shift, Connor complained about the working conditions of the quarry, his sense of importance faltering as his clothes became dirtier in the mud. The rain began to pour as the storm raging above heightened in intensity. On the surface, gales of wind blew large ferns and palm tree leaves over the barbed wire fence and into the pit.

One of the newcomers roared in pain when a big coconut crashed down upon his foot, causing all of the other prisoners to glance upwards every few seconds for any more windswept detritus and debris.

The inmates breathed a sigh of relief when Lygia shrieked that the shift was over. As the youths battled to slip and slide up the muddy slope, the building overlooking the pit swayed dangerously with the strong winds. With each violent gust, dust issued forth from the joints of the weathered support pillars underneath the overhanging cells. Ray wondered how long the columns had been in place for, and whether they could support the cells above for much longer.

With all the dregs clumsily tangling their torcs together, Ray managed to avoid being instructed to tidy up the tool shed. He had not seen his brother for a while, but now more than ever, he felt the need to see Ben, so that they could discuss the arrival of the Faction inmates.

He opened the door to the cafeteria and came face to face with Leon. The grizzled guard spat at the wall before gesturing for the inmate to come closer. As Ray moved through the doorway, the Watcher reached up and pulled Ray's head forward. With the prisoner's head bowed, Leon roughly unlocked the torc and threw the metal collar into a minecart at the foot of the stairs.

* * *

Ben woke up with a start, hitting his head on the low ceiling. He had dreamt that he was drowning. The walls and floor of their cell creaked, and the whole building seemed to sway all around them. The storm's ferocity had grown during their slumber.

"I think there's typhoon will going to come," said Nico, already awake, watching the rain pour down through the skylight. At Ben's confused expression, the Filipino boy explained solemnly, "Big, *big* storm. Like the one when I'm a small. So strong, and then our house is no more."

The building swayed again and Ben threw himself against the wall, fearing that the floor would collapse beneath their feet. He had never imagined that he would be so glad to see Cormac's yellow grin as the Watcher approached their cell window to announce the start of the day shift.

Ben and Nico exited their swaying cell in a hurry, the floor already waterlogged, the drainage grate in the centre unable to cope with the downpour. Inmates on their left and right tracked out of their cells with wet footprints too.

The boys from the Faction were confused at first, but eventually, an orderly line was formed, and the prisoners began marching downstairs to the cafeteria.

The morning shift's pit workers were already lining up for the gruel pot. Leon and a few other guards stood at the foot of the stairs with a minecart, fixing torcs to the inmates as they reached the bottom of the staircase. Once Ben's metal collar was locked in place, he wheeled around to join the queue.

* * *

Ray searched for his brother amongst the crowd descending the stairs until Connor lined up behind him and obscured his vision. Before the new arrival could strike up a conversation, Kenneth marched up and shoved Connor backwards, the inmates behind him stumbling backwards in turn with muttered curses.

"It'll be a cold day in the pit when the dregs eat before the old hands," said Kenneth, glaring at Connor and waiting for him to make a move. Without breaking eye contact, the fiery-haired inmate addressed the rest of the crowd shuffling and clamouring behind them, "Y'hear that, lads? Unless you're wearin' the colour, get to the back of the line!"

Connor pushed back at Kenneth, although with his leg now fully healed, the stout Irish inmate stood rooted to the ground like an oak tree.

Kenneth grabbed Connor's hands, twisted his wrists and clucked his tongue at the broken skin on the newcomer's palms, fresh blisters glowing bright pink. "Look at all these blisters," he said with sarcastic concern. "You'll be at the very back, boyo. Ray should've told you that, at least." Still holding Connor by his wrists, Kenneth whirled around to face Ray, who was inclined to agree.

"Gotta earn your place, Connor," said Ray.

Kenneth shoved the wide-eyed inmate out of the line. "Still lettin' your friends down, I see. Rashad never let you get pushed around, or have you forgotten about him already?"

Ray clenched his jaw.

* * *

Up and down the line of inmates, the boys who were not yet clothed in the green uniform of the prison were ejected from the line-up. The sounds of muffled grunts and clanging torcs filled the midsection of the queue as the jostling pack of prisoners lurched and shuffled, tripping over each other's shoes as they struggled with the bulky neck braces.

Ben and Nico, having learnt not to allow others to tread upon their feet without complaint, pushed back at the inmates in front. One of the fresh arrivals from the Faction turned around, glowering at the pair of prisoners and raising his meaty fists. Ben took a step back, as the Faction inmate was at least a head taller, yet Nico stood his ground.

Ben ducked under a swing from the big teen, and Nico ribbed him with a flurry of punches before grappling with him against the wall. Other uniformed inmates quickly came to their rescue, overwhelming the newcomer and shoving him towards the back of the line.

"Thanks, Nico," Ben breathed, his heart bouncing off the walls in his chest.

Just as the last of the new arrivals trudged towards the back of the line, a chant began to ripple through the front of the crowd.

"Bangon... Bangon... Bangon!"

Ahead, Ray was squaring up against Kenneth, yet to Ben's surprise, Ray took a deep breath and stepped aside, allowing Kenneth to take his place in the queue. Guards who had been discussing odds on the fight dropped the topic in disappointment.

Ignoring the jeers of the other inmates, Ray spotted Ben in the group of prisoners towards the back. He stood against the wall as the queue shuffled forward, letting the others pass by, and the two brothers came face to face again.

"We don't have much time," said Ray. "I think the guards are trying to keep us separated." Amelia ladled gruel into the brothers' bowls and they speed-walked over to one of the centre tables. "We've got the numbers for another riot," Ray kept his voice low as they settled in. "We could do it here, during a shift change, before they put torcs on the new shift."

Ben shook his head. "It won't work, not without Kenneth and the others on our side."

"Why wouldn't it work?" Ray cocked an eyebrow. "It's a lot better than trying to land a double shift and waiting for the manacles to get changed over in between, remember that idea?" he was referencing the major detail they had forgotten the day they had almost destroyed the tool shed. "It's the same plan, Benji, but now, we don't have to pull overtime for it to work. We'll have a full shift of fresh inmates without collars."

"You're forgetting," said Ben, glancing pointedly down at the red light flashing on his ankle, "We still have the manacles."

"Manacles are *nothing* compared to torcs. And we don't need Kenneth either. We can do this on your shift, or Jack and Ethan can start the riot. All we need to do is spread –" Ray stopped mid-sentence, warily eyeing Levi as he walked past with his bowl of gruel.

Ben resisted the urge to trip up the smug weasel of an inmate, especially now that his older brother was there to ward off any thoughts of retaliation. *That would make me no better than him and Sergei*, he told himself. He watched Levi join Bryson and Cameron at the far end of the cafeteria.

Ben's stomach rumbled. He could not neglect his hunger for any longer. Momentarily forgetting all thoughts of escape, he spooned the food into his mouth and wolfed it down, barely bothering to chew. Looking around, he noticed Nico sitting on his own a few seats away. His Filipino cellmate knew how much Ben had wanted to speak with his brother.

Ray watched the Faction inmates milling about without a clue as to what they were supposed to be doing. Squinting, he saw Connor settle down upon a stone block alongside Levi and his lackeys at the other end of the room. The long-faced blonde teen spat out the porridge and moaned in disgust.

"*Welcome to Paradise*," Ray muttered the words exactly as Levi mouthed them.

"I think the Warden might have our father's journal," said Ben, snapping Ray back to attention.

"Caleb's got it," Ray said around a mouthful of gruel, flecks of porridge falling to the table. "He burnt a photo of us when we were kids while he was trying to get Joshua's last words outta me. Rashad was right. Caleb tore a page from the journal and wrote 'DON'T BE AFRAID' on the back just to play some sadistic joke on us to give us false hope," he swallowed with a grimace. "What made you think the Warden had it though?"

Ben frowned, shifting in his seat. He had thought at the very least that Evander would have had the journal. "The Warden called me up to his office and told me that our father was involved in the quarry's formation. Apparently, he was the one who came up with the ideas of using Watchers as guards, and replacing whips with shock sticks and the chain gangs with manacles and sparkers." He left out their father's involvement in bribing the local politicians though, glancing at Nico nearby.

Unfazed by the news, Ray scraped up the rest of the gruel from his bowl before pushing it aside. Then, with a knowing expression, he leaned across the table. "And you believe *everything* you hear from a stranger?"

"Why else would the Warden have told me all that in the first place?"

"Because, Benji, the Warden is trying to get close to you, so that he can get close to me. Caleb *knows* he can't force Joshua's last words outta me, so they're trying a new tactic."

* * *

Soon enough, the morning shift's inmates were ordered back upstairs by Lygia's screeching wails. Water was gathered in small pools at the foot of every door in the cell house.

Ray trudged back to his cell, eager to change out of his mud-covered rain-soaked uniform and into a fresh set of clothes. He paused at the doorway, watching the rain spilling into the waterlogged cell through the skylight in the ceiling. Evidently, the downpipes in the floor could not drain the water gathering in each cell as fast as it was pouring in.

He closed the door behind him and walked across the sodden stone floor with tiny splashes. Tipping the clean chamber pot's soapy water over himself, he rinsed off the lathering suds underneath the downpour from the skylight. Closing his eyes, he savoured the familiar sensation of having a shower at home.

This is not my home, he reminded himself. Almost ashamed of having enjoyed the brief moment of peace, he snapped his eyelids open and donned the fresh prison uniform.

Thinking that the storm raging on outside might not pass for some time, he climbed up to the top bunk. Just as he was settling onto the thin mattress, the cell door swung open again, and Connor was thrown to the floor with a splash.

The new arrival scrambled to his feet and whirled around just in time to see the door slamming in his rosy-cheeked face. Grumbling aloud to himself, Connor attempted to wipe off the water soaking the front of his soiled clothes.

"Don't bother trying to dry yourself off," Ray said from the top bunk, "There's a uniform ready for you on your mattress."

"What if I don't want to wear the uniform?" he asked bitterly.

"Doesn't make a difference to me, just quit muttering to yourself while I'm trying to sleep," Ray answered, hiding a grin.

He lay back on the mattress as Connor resigned his defiance with a sigh and changed into the fresh green clothes piled on the lower bunk. Ray was glad for the company. He had been feeling quite alone in the cell by himself, although Connor would not have been his first choice for a cellmate.

* * *

Cormac and Leon began hauling inmates up from their seats. Ben and Nico stood out of their own accord and made their way to the tool shed before it became too crowded with the other inmates.

As they exited with their shovels, they saw that the newcomers had managed to jam themselves in the cafeteria's doorway, tangled together by their torcs. Chuckling derisively, Leon cleared the blockage with a quick shock of the sparker remote, sending them all to the floor. With wobbly knees, Ben and Nico staggered outside before they could be trampled.

Water spouted from the drainage pipes on either side of the entrance, gushing out into the pit, joined by the streams pouring down from the small circular grates in the row of cells above. Ben and Nico gingerly stepped out from beneath the overhanging building, the weathered support pillars tilting dangerously with the gusting wind.

It might have been morning, but the sunrise was nowhere in sight. The sky was bleak and grey, dreary storm clouds casting a dark blanket over the morning light. The quarry was strewn with rock-sized coconuts and enormous palm tree leaves, more debris flying down from above with the gale raging on overhead.

Brandishing their shock sticks, the Watchers forced the youths to trek out into the torrential rain. Slipping and sliding down the muddy slope into the pit below, the prisoners begrudgingly marched out to take up positions along the rock shelf, squelching with each step across the slushy earth floor.

As they dug through the sludge, Ben looked up to see the part of the building that jutted out over the pit still swaying with the wind. He feared that the support pillars would collapse under the strain and that the row of cells would come crashing down on them all. He swallowed with the sudden realisation that they were just as vulnerable inside as well, since that entire section of the building housed the cells of the day shift's inmates.

The quarry pit was soon filled halfway to Ben's knees with rainwater. Many of the disgruntled inmates lost their shoes in the sucking mud. Nico, on the other hand, was in high spirits, as he had constantly been ridiculed by Levi and some of the other teens for working barefoot. Now, everyone else would have to get by without a pair of shoes.

"See? I say you typhoon will going to come," said Nico, happily shovelling beside Ben.

"Yes, you did. At this rate, we'll be bailing out water instead of digging through mud by the time our shift ends."

"Look!" Nico pointed with a wide grin on his face.

Ben failed to stifle a laugh at the sight of Levi and Bryson struggling to push the minecart up the muddy slope. The rest of the inmates had been working with an unspoken agreement to load the barrows to the brim to get back at the minecart pushers for gloating and loafing around in the sun during the dry season.

Cameron tottered up the slope to help his friends, only to slip and fall in a pirouette before sliding back down the ramp on his rear-end, painting his pants in a lovely shade of brown. All work stopped momentarily so that the prisoners could cheer them on – even the reserved Aiden managed to crack a smile – and the laughing Watchers threatened to throw coconuts at them if they did not hurry.

While the guards were distracted with finding objects to throw, Ben seized his opportunity to find out more about the Faction. He approached a pair of prisoners who were not yet wearing the green uniforms and asked them where they had come from.

Gavin – a pale goose-necked boy – said that the Faction was a secretive organised group fighting against the Lizardmen. Samir – a pockmarked teen with jet black hair – swelled his chest proudly and proclaimed that they should be rescued soon enough, once the other Faction strongholds mobilised a retaliation force against the enemies now occupying Quartz Hall.

"What happened during the attack?" asked Ben.

"We were overrun within a few minutes," said Gavin. "Our soldiers didn't have a chance. There was no time to prepare. Most of them were killed unarmed. But I think that the Lizardmen had orders to capture kids and teenagers. Now, I can see why." Gavin craned his long neck as he peered around at the walls of the quarry.

"They wouldn't hurt us," said Samir, "Even when we killed dozens of their own. We were safe as long as we kept moving. We held out in the upper levels of the city for a few weeks, but eventually, our supplies ran out."

Ben opened his mouth to say more, but Leon's bark cut him off, his gruff baritone voice resounding throughout the pit above the sound of the roaring rain, "Get back to work you lazy curs, or we'll see what happens when you get sparked standing knee-deep in water!"

Having learnt what he could from Gavin and Samir about the Faction, Ben realised that he had stumbled upon an even greater revelation: no matter what they did, the inmates could not be killed. They could be hurt, yes, but not severely.

He looked over at Aiden, who Evander had closely monitored throughout his recovery, proof that they had to be kept alive in order to keep working. And as long as there was work to be done, *they were invincible.*

* * *

Ray felt the weight on his thin mattress shifting. He snapped his eyes open to see Connor climbing up to his bunk alongside him, his fresh green uniform already drenched. Ray cocked an eyebrow, resisting the urge to throw his new cellmate from the top bunk just long enough to hear his explanation.

"The cell's flooded," Connor said with a strained voice before scrambling to the foot of the bed.

Ray leaned over the side, and sure enough, half the cell had been submerged in water while he was asleep. "Good thing that's empty," he said, watching the chamber pot bobbing up and down, occasionally going under as more water gushed down through the skylight.

The downpour began to spill out through the iron-barred window, splattering onto the cell house floor where the water joined with streams pouring from all of the other cells.

An onset of frenzied screams sounding from across the cell house caused Connor to jolt with fright.

At first, Ray decided to stay high and dry on his mattress, but when he heard Jack calling out Ethan's name, he jumped down into the water. Chest-deep, he waded over to the cell window and strained his eyes at the opposite row of cells.

Many inmates around the cell house were huddled up together on the top bunks of each room, but Jack and Ethan were at their cell door. Ethan yelled wildly, trying to force his head through the tightly-spaced iron bars of the window while Jack desperately tried to restrain him.

Ray called out for help. From a cell nearby, Kenneth shouted for the Watchers to come. Soon, the entire cell house was in an uproar, and the guards burst out from the barracks to investigate.

"OH, *SHUT IT!!*" Lygia screamed as she unlocked Ethan's cell door.

Wide-eyed, Ethan shoved past the Watchers in the tide of water flooding out behind him.

At first, Ray thought that it was some kind of trick Ethan and Jack had hatched to take the Watchers by surprise, but the thought immediately vanished when he saw the panic, distress and desperation on Ethan's face.

"Looks like he has a phobia of water," said Connor, jumping down and wading beside Ray.

Ethan stripped off his drenched shirt, madly thrashing out at the guards trying to approach him. Jack leaned over the Watchers' restraining arms, shoving and elbowing and cursing in a frantic bid to reach his friend and calm him down, until Sheriff Sullivan pointed a charged baton in his direction. Jack backed off with his arms raised, not wishing to be shocked while soaking wet. Ethan, on the other hand, would not surrender. He attacked the advancing Watchers like a crazed animal.

Gremlin slowly drew up behind Ethan with his shock stick at the ready. He sparked it up and brought it down hard on the back of the prisoner's neck. Ethan stood stiff as a board before he went limp and collapsed upon the floor, eyes staring.

Silence fell in the cell house.

The Watchers backed away from the stilled Ethan lying face down on the ground with his neck bent at an odd angle.

Jack bellowed hysterically.

"YOU KILLED HIM! YOU KILLED ETHAN, YOU MURDERING DOG!!"

26 - HE'S DEAD

The mournful hush in the cell house was broken only by the sound of rainwater overflowing from every flooded cell's window, spilling out onto the floor and draining down the flight of stairs into the cafeteria below.

Jack shook with silent grief next to the chains rack in the centre of the cell house, overwhelmed with sorrow for his fallen friend. The wordless Watchers stood in a circle around the two inmates, water swirling past their feet.

Prisoners from all around the cell house stood chest-deep in the rainwater, staring out from their iron-barred windows gaping in silent horror at the slain prisoner. With the majority of the youths being in their mid-teens, they could not bear to look at the scene, yet they could not turn away either. For many of the inmates, this was the first violent death that they had ever witnessed.

Gremlin guiltily backed away from Ethan's crumpled body, retreating behind the other Watchers.

Caleb was the first to summon his speech among the surrounding guards, taking charge of the situation. "Open the cells," he ordered. "Bring all of the inmates down to the cafeteria. Lygia, inform the Warden."

"You wanna turn 'em all loose over one kid?" Sheriff Sullivan objected before leaning closer to Caleb, "You sure 'at's a good idea right now?"

"I'm ensuring we don't suffer any more losses in productivity," Caleb's flint grey eyes flicked towards Gremlin as he spoke. "Dead inmates don't work. We'll hold them all in the cafeteria until the storm dies down."

Evander placed a hand on Jack's shoulder, the prisoner still shaking with anguish, and the kind Watcher walked him down the flight of stairs.

Torrents of water gushed out from the cells as each door was opened, inmates and chamber pots alike streaming out across the wet stone floor with every wave. Under the threat of being sparked by the shock sticks while soaking wet, they mournfully trudged down into the cafeteria, staring wide-eyed at Ethan's lifeless body as they passed by.

Ray caught Little Danny's reedy voice as he muttered to himself, "Serves 'im right, that's what 'e gets for messing wiv me on all me shifts."

While the guards were distracted with unlocking the cells, Ray strode towards the stairs and tripped up Little Danny on the top step, sending the scrawny runt tumbling down the wet staircase with a startled yelp.

"You'll be next for that!" Little Danny yelled mid-roll, landing with a shallow splash at the bottom. Ray descended the stairs two steps at a time after him, causing the panicked imp to dart away to the other side of the room.

The cafeteria was just as flooded as the cell house. Water cascaded down from the level above, pouring over each step, flowing towards the back of the room and coursing out into the corridor. Shuffling through the ankle-deep water, all of the prisoners managed to find a seat in the crowded room, the inmates still reeling in shock.

Connor sat down on a stone block seat beside Ray in the uncomfortable silence, the newcomer not knowing who Ethan was, and not daring to ask about him. For a while, they watched Kenneth's attempts to console Jack. It was all they could do, as neither one of them was sure of what they could say to him themselves.

* * *

Thunder boomed across the dark sky, briefly illuminated by flashes of lightning as they licked the underbellies of the rolling storm clouds. Rain bucketed down into the pit as the typhoon raged on overhead. The quarry's walls seemed to be melting, mud oozing out from the holes in the fishnets surrounding the pit.

The rain-whipped inmates were standing waist-deep in the flooded quarry, digging in futility. Every murky load of goop they scooped up in their shovels fell short of the immobile minecarts stuck in the mud nearby. Levi, Bryson and Cameron had already given up on trying to heave the overflowing barrows back up to the treasury, so they had brought more empty metal wagons down from the tool shed instead.

Ben could barely see farther than two metres through the veil of water cascading down all around him. He hoped that the pit would not flood, his inability to swim adding further weight to his worries. He envisioned the quarry filling with water, the ramp becoming too slippery to climb, and himself being stuck in the murky depths of the pit, drowning in mud.

Nico interrupted his grim daydream with an elbow, pointing towards the dark figure of a man precariously ambling down the ramp through the pelting rain, slipping and sliding along the muddy slope.

The Watcher made his way through the pools of water on the level above the inmates to where Cormac, Leon and the other guards huddled beneath the big battered umbrella. Ben and Nico strained their ears to listen in on the conversation, yet Leon's growls and Cormac's crude voice were muffled by the tempest roaring overhead. The messenger soon departed, scrambling back up the muddy path.

The guards lazily strolled to the edge of the rock shelf to make an announcement.

"Shift's cancelled," Leon barked above the storm. "Everyone get back up to the cafeteria. Warden's orders."

Amid the sighs of relief from the inmates, Cormac's mischievous tone could be heard as he made a suggestion to Leon. "Come on, just spark 'em a little bit. Let's see what 'appens while they're in the water."

Leon's gruff laughter spurred the exhausted prisoners out of the murky waist-deep pool and up the slippery slope with renewed vigour. They held onto each other for support, gingerly testing footholds as they navigated their way up the slosh. Some inmates flailed out and clawed at the fishnet retaining wall to keep their balance, but in some sections it was as if the quarry's cliff faces had swallowed the mesh completely, with muck seeping out from the muddy walls.

"I hope my Papa will going to be okay," said Nico, shielding his face from the rain and staring upwards at the storm clouds. "I'm worry on Lungsod."

"I'm sure your Papa will be fine," said Ben, clinging to his barefooted cellmate as they made their way up the ramp. "I'm more worried about *us* right now."

Jets of water streamed from the downpipes of the overhanging cells above as the prisoners reached the building's opening, coupled with the strong torrents pouring out of the large drainage pipes on either side of the entrance.

Wading through the water, Ben and Nico splashed past the weathered support pillars and into the flooded corridor. More water flowed out from the cafeteria, which was already crowded with other inmates. They quickly hung up their shovels in the tool shed and padded across the passage into the packed mess hall. None of the Watchers came forward to unbolt their torcs.

They stood ankle-deep in the shallow current streaming down from the staircase, drenched from head to toe, searching for their friends. Nico caught sight of Kenneth sitting opposite an ashen-faced Jack, with Ray and a blonde boy seated nearby.

He must be one of the new prisoners from the Faction, Ben assumed, as he had not seen the inmate before.

Ray and the blonde boy looked up as Ben and Nico splashed through the shallow water, their green shirts sopping wet and their pants covered in mud after their work in the pit.

Ben sat down with a weary sigh. "Our shift got cancelled. Finally, some good luck," he said with a tired smile. "What's happening in here?"

Ray stared back at him, sizing up his brother, wondering if he was ready to hear the news. Ben shifted in his seat under his brother's gaze.

"Gremlin killed Ethan," Ray said bluntly.

Ben's jaw dropped, and Nico began fruitlessly searching for Ethan around the room.

A throat-clearing sound came from the long-faced blonde teen, and he explained what had happened in the cell house. After relaying the grisly details, he finished up by introducing himself as Connor Heidrun from the Faction.

Ray cocked an eyebrow at him. "Something tells me you're not great at making first impressions, are you?"

Connor shrugged and withdrew his outstretched hand, apparently unnoticed by the speechless pair of prisoners.

Ben thought of his own phobia of being submerged in water, and he wondered whether he, too, would have been driven mad by it. He had never thought that Ethan could have shared the same fear as him though. *Ethan always had a big smile, how could he have been afraid of anything?* Just yesterday, he had been trading insults with Jack, and now, he was gone.

Ben turned around in his seat. "Jack, I – I don't know what to say…"

"Don't say anything then," said Ray, catching Kenneth's warning glare at Ben for cutting across his comforting words. Ray decided to change the subject, "Looks like we'll be stuck in here for a while. Caleb wants all of us in the cafeteria until the storm eases up. I'll bet it's even worse out there in the pit…"

* * *

The brothers and their cellmates sat in silence, listening to the water pour down the cafeteria's stairway, swirling in shallow pools before flowing out to the corridor and into the quarry.

Gavin and Samir, along with the rest of the Faction captives, mingled freely with the seasoned inmates, putting aside their differences in light of Ethan's death, coupled with the general panic stemming from the typhoon bearing down outside. This was perhaps the longest amount of time that Ray had sat in the cafeteria without seeing a fight erupt among the prisoners.

Some of the younger boys were still in shock from what they had seen in the cell house, and Ben was struck by the realisation that perhaps the inmates were not as untouchable as he had thought, although now he wondered what would become of Gremlin.

The guards stood behind the stone bench at the front of the mess hall. Gremlin isolated himself away from the others, standing alone in the corner, ashamed of what he had done, yet still unpredictably dangerous, gripping his shock stick tightly in his hands and furtively glancing at both the inmates and the other Watchers alike.

Kenneth left Jack to his own thoughts and stood at the end of the brothers' table, all of the seats already taken by other teens. He spread his hands out on the wooden bench, leaning down to eye level and looking at each one of them in turn.

"If you lads are cookin' up another plan, now would be the perfect time," Kenneth said in a low tone. Ben and Nico were both taken aback at his sudden change of heart, but Ray was not surprised. "Look around, we've got the numbers. And I'd wager there are a lot of people wantin' revenge for what we just saw upstairs."

"We still need transport," said Ray, turning to Ben. "Did you find out that code for the garage's keypad yet?"

Ben nodded, recalling Sarah brimming with excitement outside his cell the previous night as she delivered her happy news, but something about Ethan's death made it seem like a vague memory to him now.

Ray eyed Caleb amongst the other guards standing at the front of the cafeteria, wondering how they would be able to get the truck's keys away from him.

"We should wait," said Connor, catching them all by surprise.

Ray and Kenneth exchanged bemused glances. The Irish inmate exhaled in exasperation. "And here I was thinkin' I had to make an apology to the dreg. I was right to shove you outta the line this mornin', you soft-handed coward."

"Look around, Connor," said Ray, gesturing to all of the prisoners gathered together in the cafeteria. "We might not get another chance like this again."

"Actually," Nico chimed in, "Many typhoon will going to happen in a rainy season. Maybe there will going to be another work cancelled in some days time."

Ray shot Ben with a look of bewilderment. He folded his arms across his chest, expecting his younger brother to support him and restore some sense to their fellow inmates, yet Ben saw the logic in the others' opinions.

"They're right," said Ben. Ray uncrossed his arms with a heavy sigh, looking over at Kenneth. "We need time to spread the word. And even though it might look like we have the numbers *now*, all of the Watchers are here now, too. We acted too quickly during the tool shed rebellion, and look where that got us. We need to plan properly this time."

"So, what's the plan then, boyo?" Kenneth said impatiently through gritted teeth.

Ben and the others turned to Ray. He stared back at them all before conceding, "Fine. Let's do it during tonight's shift change. We'll strike here in the cafeteria, at midnight." He glanced at Jack. "I know the boys on the night shift will be worn out, but so will Caleb and Evander. They'll be our biggest threats when it all goes down."

"The lads might be worn out, but they'll have a good reason to fight," said Kenneth, referring to Ethan.

"I'm gonna need your help, too," said Ray, staring pointedly at Kenneth. "Our shift won't follow me without your support."

"You've got it," Kenneth assured him. "Just don't go squashin' me leg again this time."

"And then how about me?" asked Nico, pointing a thumb at his own chest, wondering what the day shift could do to help.

"I have an idea," said Ben. "I need to talk to Sarah again, but maybe we can –"

"Attention, inmates!" Caleb's stern voice filled the cafeteria. Ben jumped, thinking that they had been caught plotting another escape attempt. Everyone fell silent, and they all turned to listen. "The storm has passed. In a few minutes, you will be returning to your cells."

In all their conspiring, they had not noticed that the rainwater pouring down from the cell house had slowed to the pace of a leaking tap. The water swirling about their feet had already begun to recede.

"I need four volunteers to help restore the cell house to a reasonable standard," said Evander. He stroked his goatee, waiting for someone to step forward. At the inmates' lack of charity, he said with a wry grin, "I guess the girls will just have to do it themselves then."

The cafeteria erupted in chaos, seats and tables toppling over, inmates shoving each other and slipping on the wet floor as they rushed for the stairs.

"Sarah might be up there," said Ben, more to himself than anyone else, jumping to his feet and launching into a run without a second of hesitation.

Ray and the others leapt up from their seats and charged headlong into the pack of thronging prisoners, following Ben as he desperately squirmed his way through the crowd. The guards laughed crudely at the sudden mayhem.

With three other inmates already halfway up to the cell house, Ben set his foot on the first step, but before he could climb any farther, he was seized from behind. Out of the corner of his eye, he could see Levi's sneering grin. Determined to keep moving, Ben threw all of his weight at the stairs.

Ray caught sight of his brother at the foot of the staircase, with Levi clasping his torc from behind. Pushing his way through the crowd, he jabbed the weasel of an inmate in the ribs, breaking his hold on Ben, who sprawled out onto the stairs, almost face-planting on the stone steps. Scrambling on all fours, Ben climbed up to the cell house before anyone else could follow.

Furious, Levi whirled around, yet his pupils dilated at the sight of Ray.

"Hey, Levi, you need a tissue?" he smirked.

"N-no," Levi stammered. "Why?"

"Because you're about to!" Ray yelled, winding up a fake punch.

"No, please, not again!" Levi exclaimed, covering his nose with both hands and disappearing into the pack of inmates.

With Evander promptly blocking off the top of the flight of stairs from any more would-be volunteers with an amused smile, the youths resentfully trudged back to their tables, cursing beneath their breaths. Most of the dregs fresh from the Faction had not even known that there *were* any girls in the prison, yet they sat panting from the melee all the same. Jack was still sitting at his table, unmoved by the commotion, just staring at the floor in silence.

"Did anyone see him make it up there?" Connor asked as they settled back into their seats.

"Well I don't see him down here, boyo," said Kenneth in his sing-song Irish voice, taking Ben's stone block.

"He's up there," said Ray, stretching his hands behind his head. "The real question is: will Sarah be up there?"

Nico peered all around the cafeteria, and then nodded back at them sagely. "I think yes, because I'm not saw her here, too."

* * *

It was as if the typhoon had hit the inside of the prison. Ethan's body was gone, but the rest of the cell house was in disarray. Drenched mattresses hung halfway out of each doorway. Leaves and other detritus that had swept down through the surrounding cells' skylights were strewn across the waterlogged floor, mixing in with the scattered contents of the overturned chamber pots spread out haphazardly like a minefield. Leftover droplets of rainwater dripped from the skylights, their tiny splashes like a symphony of leaking taps.

The three inmates from the cafeteria were already hard at work alongside Ava and the other female prisoners who were also soaking wet, having weathered the storm on their side of the prison. Mara was all too happy to stand back and instruct the boys on how to mop the floor.

Despite the mess, Ben could not help but smile at the sight of Sarah, her silky strands of chestnut brown hair falling gracefully about her shoulders as she cleaned the debris from the floor.

He moved quickly. They did not have much time.

Sarah looked up at the sound of his squelching footsteps approaching across the flooded floor. Her eyes filled with surprise, relief, and then pity. Suddenly becoming aware of himself, Ben realised that he was still wearing the torc from his shift. He had grown so accustomed to the weight of the metal collar around his neck that he often forgot when he was even wearing it. It also reminded him of why he had needed to see her so urgently.

"You don't wear torcs or manacles while you're working," said Ben, smooth as ever.

"Of course not," said Sarah, confused. "We're not that much of a threat to the guards."

"Good," he said, "We're going to make them pay for underestimating you." In a low voice, Ben told Sarah what they had planned for the shift change at midnight. "I need you and the other girls to create a distraction. That way, the Watchers downstairs won't get reinforced like they did last time in the tool shed."

Sarah bit her lip in thought, looking around at the other girls cleaning the cell house. "Apart from Ava and, maybe Amelia, I don't think they would help me," she turned back to him. "Ben, imagine what would happen to us if this doesn't work."

"That's okay, I think I know who they might listen to," he said, narrowing his eyes at Mara.

He had never understood why Mara only harboured scorn and contempt for him with her standoffish attitude. Perhaps he had not earned her respect yet, or perhaps, on a deeper level, she could sense his status in the social hierarchy of his former life, which had somehow followed him into this new life of captivity. *But all of that is about to change.*

* * *

Most of the inmates resigned themselves to drumming their fingers upon the tabletops, waiting for the cell house to be cleaned. Kenneth however, spread word of the plan, keeping a low profile as he covertly moved from

419

one group of prisoners to the next. Aiden's mute gaze followed his former cellmate around the room, but he made no move to hear the message, and Kenneth wasted no time on trying to tempt his interest.

Ray was glad to have Kenneth back on their side, but without making it known to the others, he began to have his own doubts in the plan. *What if the rest of the inmates are all afraid of dying like Ethan?* There would be no funeral. No heartfelt goodbyes. His friends and family, whoever and wherever they were, would never even know what happened to him.

He looked over at Jack, still staring down at the floor. The once charismatic Aussie adolescent was no longer in any shape to lead the night shift inmates to rebellion. Ray knew that he would need to set Jack straight in order for the plan to work.

He knelt beside the crestfallen prisoner. "You seemed like good friends, I know it must be tough…" his words of sympathy appeared to fall on deaf ears as Jack turned away. Ray looked around the room for guidance, searching for the right words when he decided to abandon the pity train altogether. He tried a different tact instead, "I know a way you can get revenge."

Jack snapped his gaze up, staring straight into Ray's eyes.

"He's dead."

"I know he is," said Ray, slightly startled by his sudden reaction, "But –"

"He's dead," Jack repeated, "He's dead."

Shaking with rage, Jack rose to his feet, lunging towards Gremlin, who was still slinking in the front corner of the room behind the other Watchers.

* * *

Summoning his confidence, Ben approached Mara, yet before he could open his mouth, he heard a yell from the cafeteria below.

"He's dead! HE'S DEAD!!" Jack's gruff roar resounded up into the cell house.

"Mara, I need to ask you something," Ben called, yet she simply ignored him, moving to investigate what was happening down below.

Ben and the others followed her to the top of the staircase, peering down at the scene in the cafeteria. Ray, Nico, Kenneth and Connor were gathered behind Jack, all four of them struggling to restrain the stocky inmate as he pointed at Gremlin's guilty face. Despite their best efforts, Jack slowly managed to inch his way forward.

"HE'S DEAD!!"

"Control yourself, inmate!" Caleb boomed. He and the other Watchers sparked up their shock sticks and formed ranks at the front of the room, with Gremlin trembling behind them.

The rest of the inmates were on the verge of rioting prematurely, banging on the tables with their fists, punctuating Jack's bloodthirsty roars, the entire cafeteria shouting over and over in frenzied unison.

"HE'S DEAD!! HE'S DEAD!!"

"I told y'all we shouldn't've let 'em out!" Sheriff Sullivan hollered over the uproar.

"Come and 'ave a go, then!" Cormac yelled, inviting them closer, his baton blazing blue. "Let's see 'ow strong the rest of your necks are, 'ey!?"

"Would you like to *join* your friend?" Lygia screeched, "WOULD YOU!?"

Seeing the cause for the mounting tension, Caleb grabbed Gremlin and shoved him out of the cafeteria through the door behind the stone bench, slamming it shut behind him before bellowing a command to the other Watchers, "GET THEM BACK TO THEIR CELLS, *NOW!!*"

As the inmates were forced up the stairs and Evander ushered the girls back to their own cell house, Ben stared after Sarah, hoping that she alone could convince the other girls to help them.

With Gremlin out of sight, Jack shook off his friends' grips and whirled around to look Ray full in the face, and with a mad grin, he whispered a vengeful promise.

"He's dead."

27 - BANGON

It was almost midnight.

Gusts of wind whipped by overhead, the forerunners of another storm approaching. None of the inmates cared. The weather conditions in the pit no longer concerned them.

The plan was to riot in the mess hall after the torcs were unbolted from the night shift, but before the morning shift were sent out to work, so that none of the prisoners would fall victim to the metal collars' spine-rattling shocks, and the guards would be split on either side of the cafeteria with the mass of inmates between them.

They had chosen for the riot to occur during the midnight meal, as most of the boys from the night and morning shifts were considered to be among the strongest and hardiest in the prison.

Ray, Kenneth, Connor and the others from the morning shift were led down the stairs into the cafeteria. The minecart at the bottom of the staircase that served to hold the torcs between shifts stood empty. They were early again. Caleb's strategy to separate Ray from his friends was now working against the Watchers.

Ray smiled to himself at the sight of Ava serving up gruel in the cafeteria – it meant that Mara would be elsewhere.

Ben had somehow managed to convince Mara and the other girls to take part in the riot. Their task was to create a distraction large enough to divert any reinforcements who might descend from the barracks – a key factor to the inmates' defeat during their uprising in the tool shed.

Lygia and Gremlin stood by the door next to the gruel pot at the front of the room. All of the guards behind the stone bench were oblivious as to what was about to happen.

Ray and Connor sat together, the entire morning shift eating the cold chunks of porridge in silent anticipation, forcing the vile gruel down for the last time. Kenneth moved between the tables, unnoticed by the Watchers, ensuring that everyone was ready.

* * *

Ben gazed up through the skylight as their cell began to sway and the walls creaked around them. Leaves rustled across the roof, borne on storm winds. Noises of the boys from the morning shift scraping at their bowls of porridge in the cafeteria resounded up into the cell house.

Nico joined him, also looking up at the square patch of the dark night sky visible through the skylight's shaft. "No star tonight," he said. "I think there will going to be some storm again."

"That's good," said Ben. "We can use the storm to cover our escape."

Throughout the waning hours of the afternoon's dim light following the morning's deluge, Ben had watched through the small grate of their cell floor's downpipe as the night shift tediously drained the flooded pit. Forming a bucket brigade, they had passed chamber pots full of water to each other from the depths of the quarry right up to the treasury, dumping the murky water into the heat vent so that the pit would be ready for the morning shift to resume work. The inmates however, had a different agenda.

The adrenaline of anticipation pulsed through all of the inmates in the entire prison, except for the unscrupulous few such as Levi and Little Danny. Sarah and Ava had spent the better part of the evening dodging out of the Watchers' earshot as they passed on the message to all of the prisoners.

Ben's heart leapt within his chest at the sight of Jack and the rest of the night shift doggedly marching underneath their cell's downpipe, the loss of Ethan still a heavy weight on their shoulders, although the promise of vengeance helped them bear the burden.

Nico fell to the floor on his hands and knees, pumping out push-ups to expel some of his extra energy.

In the cell house, Mara entered through the door in the far corner of the room. Sarah, Amelia, and a troupe of female prisoners followed in behind her. Ben was glad that Sarah had been able to convince the other girls to join in on their plan.

"Morning shift, on your feet!" Caleb's stern voice boomed up from the cafeteria.

"Any second now…" Ben said quietly.

* * *

Struggling to keep their zeal from surfacing, Ray, Kenneth, Connor and the others lined up along the back wall of the cafeteria, passing by Jack, who bristled with caged fury amid the night shift's inmates as they pretended to queue up for the gruel pot. Gremlin stood at the foot of the stairs, his back turned as he fished into the minecart filled with the discarded torcs.

The boys stood with bated breaths, waiting to see who would make the first move.

Just as the tension in the room had reached its peak, Lygia flung open the door at the front of the mess hall. Inmates gasped at the sight of Pythrisse and a clutch of armed Lizardmen warriors entering, their long tails snaking in behind them as they dispersed throughout the room, each of them bearing bundles of javelins slung across their scaly backs.

If the prisoners had not been so horror-struck at the arrival of the cold-blooded *Kirzakai*, they would have noticed the distinct differences between the three breeds of reptilians.

Brightly-coloured scales of yellow and orange adorned the more slender Lizardmen, each with a blood red streak that ran down their back from the top of their wedge-shaped head to the tip of their tail. The slim warriors gripped either wooden hafts of spears or tall iron pikes between their clawed fingers, licking at their eyes with long slithering tongues to adjust to the dim light of the room.

The rounder-bodied blunt-snouted Lizardmen were covered in chevron-patterned armour-like scales ranging from light tan to coffee brown, their all-encompassing carapace overlapping from head to toe. Rows of spiny thorns erupted from every perceivable surface of their hides, even across their yellow and black underbellies, their bodies matching the spiked maces, morningstars and ball-and-chain flails hanging from their belted loincloths.

The largest – and perhaps the most dangerous of the three breeds – were the gigantic bipedal serpentine beasts, whose muscular hides ranged from light pewter to dark lead grey, similar to Pythrisse. They had to stoop in order to enter through the doorway, and they snapped at each other with foaming red-tinged saliva almost as much as they snarled at the Watchers and inmates alike. Their mouths filled with rows of serrated teeth, they did not even need the iron barbs attached to the ends of their tails raking across the floor of the cafeteria like fingernails on a chalkboard.

The very sight of the villainous reptiles instantly dispelled the enthusiasm of the crestfallen inmates, their adrenaline dissipating with involuntary shakes and jitters. Little Danny, one of the few prisoners unaware of the plan, leapt up from his seat with a terrified squeal as one brushed past him, and he scurried halfway up the stairs in wide-eyed fear.

Ignoring the scrawny child trembling on the staircase, Caleb climbed up a few steps to make an announcement, "We planned to transition the prison's security over to the new garrison of guards in phases, but after the events of this morning, resulting in an inmate's death, the Warden has declared that the guardianship of the Quarry Complex will rest in the hands of the *Kirzakai* warriors, effective immediately."

The colour in Connor's face drained. Ray felt an icy shiver run down his spine, the warmth of his pumping heart turning cold. Kenneth shot a nervous glance at the pair of them, their confidence in the plan dwindling.

Gremlin began bolting torcs around the necks of the paralysed prisoners lined up against the back wall as Caleb continued, "Pythrisse and her warriors will be joining you for this shift to identify the key areas of the prison that will require close monitoring. This is for your safety, and ours," he looked pointedly at the guards, reminding them that they had nothing to fear.

Even so, Evander grimaced as Pythrisse drew near, her serpentine eyes curiously peering at the inmates and Watchers alike through her reptilian slits.

Jack stared at Ray, Kenneth and Connor, still ready to fight at a moment's notice, yet almost telepathically, they had agreed that it was too dangerous to go forward with the plan. Jack shifted his attention, burning his hateful gaze into the back of Gremlin's head as the pale guard reached Ray.

Ray clenched his fists, but hesitated at the sound of the Lizardmen's hissing laughter. His chest tightened around his shrinking heart as the torc was fitted around his neck and shoulders, the metal collar's bolt locking into place.

"Bet you didn't ssee *thiss* coming! DID YOU!?" Lygia's shrill cackle pierced the silence as she swept towards the moping inmates.

"Shut up, witch," Kenneth muttered under his breath.

Catching his insult, Lygia slapped him with an open palm, waggling a gnarled finger into his face. "YOU WATCH YOUR MOUTH!!" she screamed. Then, as if greeting a long-lost relative, she stroked his reddened cheek and her rotten lips curled into a fond smile, peeling back from her blackened teeth, "Or would you prefer it if *Pythrisse* PUNISHED you instead? *Hmmmm?*"

Ray knew the answer he would have picked, yet Kenneth merely pulled away from the vile woman's skeletal white hand.

With her bug-eyes bulging, Lygia shrieked at the morning shift's inmates to march into the tool shed. Pythrisse and the other Lizardmen filed out into the corridor behind them, exchanging strange hisses in their differing reptilian dialects as they pointed out key guard positions. The *Kirzakai* warriors roamed up the stone ramp into the treasury, taking a brief tour of the main areas of operation.

Lygia, Gremlin and the other Watchers of the morning shift supervised the inmates as they absentmindedly tinkered around in the tool shed. Each of them silently contemplated working another day in the quarry pit, and for the rest of their lives, as it seemed, under the new Lizardmen guards.

Kenneth gripped his shovel with both hands and locked eyes with Ray, jerking his head slightly towards Gremlin, but Ray shook his head. His mind had retreated, grappling with his own guilt, knowing that he had been responsible for the change of guards, having given Tyrax enough paranoia to establish a reptilian garrison after his intrusion into the Lizardmen quarters below the library.

The inmates trudged out of the tool shed and through the corridor to the quarry's entrance. The cells above them teetered on the weathered support pillars with each violent surge of the approaching storm.

Ray felt the wind gusting past him, cold on his face in the midnight air. He closed his eyes. Connor stopped beside him as the crew of inmates filed past. Gremlin grunted his impatience behind the pair of prisoners, sparking up his shock stick.

Lygia paused next to the green-eyed guard. "WHAT'SS THE HOLD UP!?" she screeched in her high-pitched lisp.

Ray ignored her, not wishing to face reality.

* * *

Ben shifted nervously from one foot to the other in his cell, wondering what was taking so long. No sounds of rebellion could be heard from below, only Lygia's shrieks spurring the inmates on, coupled with the windswept debris skittering across the cell house roof above. The light tinkling from the chamber pot behind him sounded like a waterfall; it was Nico's third time in the past hour.

The girls in the cell house began to grow anxious, glancing at each other uncertainly as they stalled for time, pausing at the open doorways of half the cells on the left side of the room. Sarah looked over at Ben, who could only shrug in response as he peered at the cafeteria's staircase.

As if on cue, Little Danny's ragdoll frame scampered up the stairs and bolted across the room into his cell, slamming the door behind him.

That's a good sign, Ben thought to himself. *Maybe Ray and the others have started taking out the guards in silence.*

The barracks door flew open, and Sheriff Sullivan stepped out onto the landing to investigate the noise from Little Danny's slammed door. The idling female inmates retreated into the cells, emerging with dirty laundry and chamber pots held at a distance.

Mara stared up at the Sheriff in defiance as the others gathered around her.

Standing with his hands on his hips, the Watcher returned her icy glare. "Say now, ain't you normally do all 'at by yourself?" he asked, gesturing at the other girls bearing chamber pots.

Sarah looked towards Ben.

Something is wrong, he wished he could call his doubt out across the room. *Ray and the others should have come up the stairs into the cell house by now.* He shook his head at Sarah.

Sheriff Sullivan sauntered down the steps with a no-nonsense expression, standing inches from Mara. "Answer me."

"It's part of the new changes to security," Sarah spoke up on her behalf. "It's meant to keep us all in the same area. You can check with the Warden if you don't believe us."

He caught the strain in her voice, raising his eyebrows, yet Mara spoke before he could question them any further. "It looks like you haven't been doing your job as a guard if an inmate knows more than you about the prison's new arrangements."

The Sheriff raised his arm, showing the back of his hand for her insolence, causing all of the girls to gasp. Just as Mara braced for impact, he dropped his arm by his side. "Now, 'at would be downright unbecomin' o' me, strikin' such a fine young lady as yourself." Mara withdrew in revulsion as he tipped his wide-brimmed black hat at her. "How's about I stay 'n' make sure y'all clean this place out proper-like, bein' the *dutiful guard* I am 'n' all," he winked.

All eyes in the cell house watched the girls exit the room.

The Watcher sat down on the barracks stairs. "You boys are gon' scare 'em all off if y'all keep on starin' at 'em like 'at."

A collective groan sounded from the back wall of the cell house as Ben and Nico watched Jack and the rest of the night shift emerge from the cafeteria staircase, trudging back to their cells with drooping shoulders. One of the new inmates from the Faction knocked on Little Danny's door, nervously glancing back at the crowded mess hall stairway.

"They must have called it off," Ben said in a tone of disappointment.

Nico slumped onto the lower bunk of the bed frame.

Confused, Ben thought of calling out to Jack, but with the guards following them up the stairs into the cell house, he silently resigned himself to hoping that the rebellion had merely been postponed.

Caleb, Evander, and the other Watchers ambled past the Sheriff on their way up to the barracks just as the girls re-entered the cell house to collect the second half of the chamber pots.

Sweat erupted across Ben's forehead. *I hope they can figure out that the plan has been put on hold.* They would not get a second chance if they exposed the plot now.

The incoming gale picked up speed, buffeting the prison and causing Ben's cell to sway.

Unlocking Little Danny's door and shoving the Faction inmate inside, Sheriff Sullivan turned around to see every confined inmate staring out through their barred windows.

The lone Watcher in the cell house clicked his boot heels together and tipped his black hat back, squaring his jaw. He crossed the room, approaching the girls emerging from the cells and grabbed Sarah by the wrist, causing her to drop the chamber pot with a metallic clang, its foul contents sloshing over the sides.

"Y'know, I think ya done told me a lie. I'm gon' take you up to see the Warden myself."

As he started towards the barracks stairs, Mara broke out from the pack and struck him from behind. He let go of Sarah with a startled yelp as he fell to the floor next to the chains rack. Amelia ran forward to shower the dazed guard with the contents of her chamber pot. The rest of the girls threw up a cheer.

The distraction without a rebellion.

Hyperventilating, Ben threw himself to the floor as the cell swayed violently in the wind. Looking through the downpipe's metal grate, he could see Ray and Connor standing side by side between the groaning support pillars. "Ray, this is our only chance!" he yelled. "You have to do something!!"

* * *

Dust fell from the support pillars as they creaked beneath the weight of the lurching cells. The sound of the storm's whistling gale was broken only by Ben's voice calling down to Ray through one of the downpipes above.

Gremlin's footsteps shuffled forward, the malicious Watcher drawing in a sharp breath, poising to strike.

Ray snapped his eyelids open. Holding his tool's handle in a vice-grip, he spun around, side-swinging the mattock in a blur, but Gremlin jumped back, and the tool's spike plunged into the support pillar instead, knocking out a chunk of concrete from the column.

A Watcher nearby gave up a shout, and Connor front-kicked him in the chest so that he fell backwards into the quarry pit below. All of the inmates turned to Ray, still fearful of the presence of the Lizardmen drawing up guard positions in the treasury, but they would take whatever he had planned over a lifetime of slavery.

Ray pulled his mattock from the support pillar. "LET'S BRING THIS PLACE TO THE GROUND!!" he struck again. The column shook with the impact, and more chunks of concrete sprayed out from the weathered foundation, exposing the steel rebar within.

Connor and the other mattock-wielding inmates joined him, chopping madly like a mob of frenzied lumberjacks.

Gremlin's glowering glare now a skittish scowl, the pale guard gave up a strangled cry of alarm, which soon became a low warble in comparison to Lygia's banshee-like wail. The Watchers rushed forward, but Kenneth and the rest of the shovel gang held them off.

In delayed response, Gremlin drew the sparker remote from his pocket, and Kenneth snatched it from his fingers, flinging it to the ground.

"Better watch yourself, boyo, Jack wants you dead!" Kenneth shouted, crushing the remote beneath his boot with a triumphant grin at the guard, *"He's dead! He's dead!"*

Gremlin's eyes widened in fear as all of the inmates echoed his words in a bloodthirsty chorus.

* * *

The back row of cells shook with a series of heavy thuds as Ray and the others hacked at the support pillars below, sending up vibrations that rattled the floor and walls even harder than the typhoon's buffeting winds in the midst of Lygia's unmistakable shrieking wails.

"Ben, they will going to fight, did you saw it?" Nico stood at the barred window, staring out into the cell house where inmates all around the room cheered the girls on.

Crouched beside the downpipe's grate, Ben tore his gaze from the scene below to join Nico at the window. The Sheriff had taken his black hat off, revealing his greying hair. The southern man did not seem so intimidating now, lying upon the stairs holding the hat over his face as a floppy shield against the foul contents of the chamber pots being hurled at him.

Sullivan's cries of alarm drew more Watchers from the barracks. Sarah and the others threw the metal buckets and dirty laundry at the approaching guards coming to his aid, causing them to trip and stumble down the staircase.

Mara backpedalled to the chains rack and, pulling a long length of metal from the stand, she swung it over her head and whipped it at the Watchers, lashing several guards across the face.

A bunch of female prisoners swarmed Leon, wrenching his torc sparker away from him. Amelia wrestled a set of keys from the downed Watcher, throwing it across the melee to Sarah. Nico whooped and hollered wildly with the other inmates as Sarah rushed across the cell house to their door, frantically trying to work the lock.

Behind her, Cormac caught Mara's chain, wrapping it around his shock stick and sending volts of electricity up its length with his blazing blue baton. Dropping the chain in snarling anguish, she ran back to the wooden rack for another, but without her harrying the guards, the Watchers began to overwhelm the girls.

****

Down below, the inmates glimpsed Pythrisse and her Lizardmen hurtling down the treasury ramp behind the rows of Watchers. Just as the reptilian beasts came within reach of the rioting prisoners, Ray struck the central support pillar one last time, and the strained steel rebar inside snapped, the column crumbling from the ceiling down to the mattock's bite-marks like sand in an hourglass.

The sudden burden of additional weight caused the other pillars to give way on either side. The floor of Ben's cell groaned, and stones fell away from the corners of the room as the walls began to shift and rupture.

Just in time, Sarah unbolted the door and flung it open, beaming at the pair of prisoners.

Ben and Nico were about to rush out into the cell house when the floor fell from beneath their feet.

Below, Ray and the other inmates dodged out from underneath the collapsing ceiling as it rained down in a cloud of billowing dust and rubble, sealing the entrance to the complex and serving as a wall between the prisoners and the guards.

Finding himself half-buried in the fallen rubble, Ben's vision was groggy and clouded. Something heavy must have fallen on his head. For a split second, the copper taste in his mouth reminded him of Aiden lying unconscious next to him in the tool shed, his green sweatband turning red with his own blood. He fought the urge to vomit.

Ray spotted Ben amongst the wreckage and the other dazed inmates. Shoving the debris off of his brother, he pulled Ben up to his feet.

"*BANGON!!*" Kenneth roared, climbing up over the rubble with his shovel into what remained of Ben's cell, leading the charge through the open doorway into the cell house.

"Ben?" Sarah called down to him as she plucked the set of keys from the lock, flattening herself against the door as the mob of inmates swarmed past. "Are you okay down there?"

Doubled over in a state of shock, Ben stared around at his surroundings, trying to get his bearings. Some prisoners were trying to scale the fishnets hanging from the quarry's walls up to the barbed-wire fence on the surface. Others were searching in the rubble for guards they held personal grudges against, making sure that the Watchers stayed buried. Nearby, Connor was busy helping Nico out of the fallen debris.

Ray dusted his brother off and yelled to Nico and Connor, "Stay close!" He grabbed Ben by his shoulders, shaking him out of his dizzy daze and back into consciousness before hauling him up by the hand over the pile of rubble, the others following in their wake.

* * *

The guards had a full-blown riot on their hands. With Sarah busily releasing the other confined inmates from their cells, pairs of prisoners gleefully joined the skirmish against the handful of guards in overwhelming numbers. The female inmates backed away from the Watchers, letting the boys take over the fight.

Levi, Bryson and Cameron huddled outside their open cells, but at the sight of Ray entering the room with his mattock, ready for battle, Cameron declared his allegiance to the inmates. "*BANGON!!*" he yelled, dashing into the melee. Levi and Bryson followed hesitantly, but their strides became surer with every step.

The Warden, Caleb and Evander stood together at the top of the barracks stairs, surveying the chaos in the cell house. The portly man trembled as the unruly inmates lashed out at the backpedalling guards. With a sweeping gaze of the room, Caleb quickly ushered the Warden back inside the barracks, beckoning Evander to follow.

Ray caught sight of the Sheriff in the crowd, one of the men responsible for killing his father, now thrashing out at the advancing inmates like a cornered animal. Vengeance consumed him. Leaving Ben at the doorway of his cell, Ray charged into the fray, gripping his mattock like a samurai sword with Connor and more from the pit bringing up the rear.

In a tactical retreat, the Watchers backed slowly up the stairs, taking the higher ground of the platform. Bypassing Kenneth and the thronging crowd of inmates, Ray ran around to the right side of the staircase. Kicking himself up off the wall, he swung the mattock like a baseball bat, sweeping the Sheriff's legs out from underneath him.

Sullivan landed flat on his back, his eyes wide with surprise, the muck-covered Watcher lying dumbfounded and momentarily helpless. Ray could practically taste revenge. He tried to raise the mattock above his head for a cleaving blow, but with the restrictive torc still locked around his neck and shoulders, his grip faltered, and the strike fell short.

Ray let out a pained snarl as Sheriff Sullivan struggled to his feet, retreating through the door to the barracks.

Jack appeared alongside Ray, reaching up and wrenching a Watcher down by his ankle. He shoved the squealing guard into the swarm of inmates clamouring around the stairs, and they latched onto him like a pack of piranhas.

Jack turned to Ray with a fierce hatred burning in his eyes. "WHERE IS HE!?"

"Gremlin? He's downstairs, next to the tool shed," Ray barely got the words out of his mouth before Jack sprinted towards the cafeteria stairs.

Kenneth and the mob of inmates gained the platform, and they swung their tools into the locked hardwood door of the barracks, showering the raving crowd below with splinters.

* * *

Nico threw his arm around Ben outside the doorway of their cell, just as shaken by the floor's collapse as Ben had been.

"Aiden?" said Ben, seeing the lone prisoner totter out of his room, "Aiden!"

The ropy fair-skinned teen stared at the scene in the cell house with his mouth ajar. His green eyes seemed to absorb the chaos; focusing, sharpening, evoking some primal part of him, reaching past the residual brain damage the fallen rock had left behind and triggering his fight-or-flight response, snapped synapses fusing back together.

Aiden snapped his attention towards Ben. "What's our move?"

At that same moment, Sarah hurtled towards the three of them, all of the cell doors now opened. "Help me find Ava," she said between breaths. "I think she left to block our cell house's entrance to the barracks on the other side of the prison."

Without waiting for an answer, she took hold of Ben's hand and led them towards the door in the corner of the room, passing by Gavin and Samir among the crowd of inmates hurling wild punches at the unfortunate guards who had been left behind in the cell house.

Levi, Cameron and Bryson were among the prisoners massing around the Watchers, taking cheap shots at the guards as they attempted to retreat into one of the open cells.

Little Danny was trying to stop the rebellion, lingering near the pack and holding the arms of inmates behind their backs so that they were free targets for the Watchers' shock sticks.

"Who are all these dregs?" Aiden muttered, peering at Nico curiously and catching brief glances of the Faction inmates' faces as they made their way across the room.

The four of them had almost reached the door to the adjoining passage when Ava burst forth and tore past. "Not that way!" she screamed. "EVERYBODY, *RUN!!*"

Sarah immediately pivoted and yanked Ben after Ava. Ben caught Nico around the torso with a flailing arm, winding him in the sudden change of direction. Aiden froze, dropping his jaw at the sight of the Lizardmen warriors, some armed with spears and morningstars in their webbed hands with bundles of javelins slung across their rigid backs, the larger ones dragging tail barbs behind them as they stumbled in through the undersized door.

A round thorn-covered reptilian monster reared back and launched a javelin. Ben saw it soaring towards them in slow motion. With instincts not of his own, he pushed the wheezing Nico out of the way of the missile's path and then threw his weight upon Sarah, bringing her to the ground and sending Leon's set of keys skidding out of reach.

On the floor, they watched Mara palm-strike Little Danny in the back of his neck. The scrawny waif's knees buckled, and he fell upon all fours with his eyes wide.

"Who let Cormac's kid ou–" Mara was mid-sentence when the javelin pierced through the back of her shoulder, the metal tip embedding into her flesh.

Ben and the others scrambled to their feet as Pythrisse pushed past the other Lizardmen emerging from the small passage. She berated her beastly brethren for trying to kill an inmate. "Adzirick, we need them *alive!*" she hissed, raising the iron barb on her tail and flicking it across the Lizardman's scaly cheek, leaving a gash of cold blood upon his snarling face.

* * *

"*LIZARDMEN!!*" Connor yelled from behind.

Ray pulled away from the pack of inmates trying to break down the barracks door to see the *Kirzakai* warriors spilling out into the cell house on the other side of the staircase.

Inmates screamed and scattered at the sight of the scaly muscle-bound creatures brandishing pikes and ball-and-chain flails. Pythrisse stood in the centre of her troops, rasping orders to quell the rebellion.

Ben, Nico, Sarah and Aiden stood directly in their path, gaping at the reptilian horrors emerging. Ray dropped his mattock and darted towards them from the side. With his incredible speed, he practically knocked his brother over before he dragged Ben by his shirt over to the cafeteria stairway, Nico and Aiden trailing behind with Sarah and Ava supporting the wounded Mara between them.

A new wave of chaos swept across the cell house as the Lizardmen began rounding up the scattering inmates, catching prisoners by the neck with their tails and sweeping their feet out from underneath them.

Casting one final glance over his shoulder before they ducked down into the cafeteria, Ray watched his mattock disappear beneath the inmates' trampling feet.

As the brothers and their friends hurried down the steps, another figure dashed past them towards the stone bench at the front of the mess hall. Ben snapped to attention at their sudden change of atmosphere, acutely aware of the need for caution in the relatively silent cafeteria.

Ray paused at the bottom of the staircase, listening to the hisses emanating from the treasury corridor as more Lizardmen worked to clear the fallen wreckage from the sealed entrance of the cafeteria.

They were trapped.

28 - THEY WON'T FIND ME HERE

Shouts and screams descended from above as the rebellious inmates clashed with Pythrisse and her *Kirzakai* warriors in the cell house. Standing motionless at the foot of the cafeteria's staircase, Ray looked towards the rubble-strewn exit to the treasury corridor. Weaponless, and still wearing the rusty neck brace, he readied himself for combat, waiting for the Lizardmen to break through the wreckage from the other side at any moment.

Ben's attention however, was focused on the opposite end of the room: the stone bench, where a sun-bronzed hand beckoned to them over the top of the counter. Tugging at Ray's green shirt, Ben motioned for the others to follow them towards the front of the cafeteria. They found Jack crouching behind the slab of rock, pressing a finger to his lips.

The two brothers flung themselves down beside him, followed by their friends; Nico, Aiden, Sarah, Mara and Ava.

Mara grimaced as she lay flat on her stomach. Ray's eyes widened at the sight of the javelin protruding from the back of her shoulder. The wooden haft was sticking straight up over the top of the stone bench. He locked eyes with Jack, knowing what they would need to do.

"What were those *things* up there?" Aiden asked no one in particular, his head above the counter, keeping his keen green eyes on the staircase and the blocked corridor exit. "Should we go back for Kenneth, Rashad and Ethan?"

Ray, Jack, and the three girls studied him curiously, but did not answer.

"He just woke up," Ben explained, pitying the confused expression on Aiden's drawn face.

The fair-skinned inmate had been running on autopilot for the past few weeks. His body had recovered from the head injury quick enough, but his mind had taken longer.

Ben turned to Sarah, whispering, "You know this place better than most of us, where should we go?"

"We can – we can…" she trailed off, her eyes brimming with tears as she stared at Mara's shoulder wound. Ben placed a reassuring hand on Sarah's upper arm to refocus her attention as Ray, Jack and Ava tended to the injured girl. With a few deep breaths, she returned his gaze. "We can either go through this door to the kitchen," She indicated the door behind them, "Or, we can escape through the treasury. Whichever way we go, there are elevator shafts that can bring us up to the barracks."

"The kitchen sounds like a good idea," said Ben, not wishing to encounter any more guards.

"But Ray's torc," Nico nudged him from behind. "Maybe he will going to get some shock."

It had not even occurred to Ben that Ray was still wearing his metal collar, and he thought it a miracle as to how they had lasted this long without being sparked. "Okay," he said, "Maybe we can find something in the tool shed to break off his torc."

"Keep quiet, Mara," Jack whispered, holding her down.

Staying low, Ava knelt beside the injured girl and covered her mouth. Mara tore Ava's hand away from her face, squeezing it tightly instead before she nodded up at Ray with a look of both fear and urgency in her eyes.

Ray yanked the javelin out with a quick tug, setting it down with a soft *clack* upon the ground beside her. Mara writhed in silent agony as blood spilled forth in a small fountain. Ava covered her own mouth to stifle a squeal as the wounded girl crushed her hand. Jack ripped his shirt off and tossed it to Ava to hold against Mara's shoulder before ducking below the counter again.

Ray chanced a glance around the cafeteria for signs of anyone else who might have made it down from the cell house, but the sound of the Lizardmen bursting through the far exit's barrier of debris and snaking into the room quickly curbed his curiosity.

Kenneth and Connor will have to take care of themselves, Ray thought to himself as everyone lowered their heads to the floor.

Worried by the rate of Mara's blood loss, Ava placed more pressure on the wound, holding Jack's bundled shirt firmly against her shoulder. Cringing through gritted teeth, Mara managed to bite back a moan of pain.

Straining their ears to hear over the sounds of turmoil descending from the cell house, the inmates crouched with bated breath, staring at one another for minutes on end. Finally, after what seemed like hours, Ben decided that it was only a matter of time before Pythrisse and her warriors would secure the rest of the complex. He moved to stick his head up over the bench, when a snarl hissed from the centre of the room.

In a flash, Sarah pulled his head back down out of sight, their cheeks brushing together. His heart leapt high within his chest. He was unsure whether it was because of her silky brown hair upon his face or the sounds of the reptilian beasts' slithering tails and clawed footsteps as they bounded up the stairs into the chaotic cell house above.

Exhaling slowly, Ray summed up their choices, "So, we go safe through the kitchen and risk me getting sparked later; or, we get this thing off my neck in the tool shed before we head up to the barracks."

Staying low, Jack picked up the javelin, slick with Mara's blood. It was their only weapon. "I'm going for Gremlin," he said, his eyes set with determination. "After that, it's up to you."

Ray nodded, and the eight inmates advanced towards the cafeteria's far exit, Ava and Sarah supporting Mara between them, ensuring that they kept enough pressure on her wound to stem the flow of blood.

They cautiously pressed their backs against the wall, Ray being careful not to scrape his torc. Ben, Nico and the others followed closely behind

Ray and Jack, with Aiden at the rear keeping watch on the staircase. They heard muffled scratches and large objects thudding and clattering in between strained hisses just beyond the doorway.

The others were rapt with dread as Ray peered around the corner to see Gremlin and another Watcher clearing away fallen rocks and rubble from the entrance to the pit. Gremlin seethed with impatience, grumbling with every piece of discarded debris.

On Ray's signal, he and Jack noiselessly stepped out into the corridor. Jack raised the javelin, ready to surprise attack the unsuspecting Watchers. Ben and Nico shadowed their footsteps, the three girls and Aiden sneaking through the doorway behind them.

Jack was poised to strike, when a terrible screeching cry reverberated around the enclosed space from farther up the rubble-strewn corridor.

Ben clapped his hands over his ears at the sound of the head-splitting wail. Looking directly at the source of the horrible sound, he drew back with fright at the unsightly shrieking wraith, Lygia. The sickly green glow of her skin clothed in layers upon layers of black rags was even more disconcerting in the dust-filled corridor. A Watcher stood on either side of the shrill-voiced witch, blocking their escape to the treasury.

Gremlin and the guard beside the stack of rubble whirled around, the short ivory-skinned man squeaking in surprise, dropping a heavy stone on his companion's foot, making him yowl in anguish.

Without a moment's pause, Jack plunged the spearhead into Gremlin's throat, driving it through his neck and skewering him against the piled wreckage. With a look of astonishment riddled across his pointed face, Gremlin gurgled his last breaths in agony, his devilish green eyes clouding over before his head lolled forward.

Ray picked up a discarded rock and knocked the other guard senseless, who had been too busy hopping in pain to draw his shock stick in time.

Lygia's wail subsided, replaced by whistling silence as she pulled a sparker remote from her pocket. "NAUGHTY, *NAUGHTY* CHILDREN!!" she screeched, revealing her fanatical forked tongue between rows of blackened teeth. "After *all* we've done for you! Fed you, clothed you, PUT

A ROOF OVER YOUR HEADS, and *thiss* is how you repay uss!?"

Cackling madly, she thumbed the switch on the sparker, and in an instant, Ray's entire body stiffened at the volts of electricity surging through his torc. Before he could even feel the horrible burning sensation all around his neck, his legs buckled, and he dropped to his knees. He struggled to wrench himself free of the metal collar, but the pain only escalated. He toppled over and fell onto the floor face first.

He heard yelling, it could have been his own. Questions raced through his mind. *Why didn't this happen sooner? Did the wreckage block the signal? How did* she *get a sparker?* His eyes turned upwards and rolled into the back of his skull as if searching for the answers within the dark recesses of his own mind.

Jack, Nico and Aiden charged at the three Watchers while Ben gaped in silent horror at his fallen brother, face down upon the floor thrashing uncontrollably.

Mara shook off Ava's supporting arm, shoving the blonde girl towards the wreckage behind them. "Get Gremlin's keys," she said in a strained voice, leaning against the wall with Sarah keeping pressure on her wound.

Ava gingerly searched the dead man's pockets, watching his face warily as if he would wake up at any moment. As she jangled out his set of keys, the rubble shifted and Gremlin slid to the ground. She screamed in terror and stumbled over the other guard's limp body, falling backwards to land on her elbows. Flipping onto her stomach, she crawled on her hands and knees towards Ray, kneeling beside him and squealing in pain each time she tried a new key on his electrified torc.

Ben started to see spots in his blurring vision as he stared spellbound at his brother's convulsing body. Nearly overcome by queasiness and breaking out in a nervous sweat, he realised that he was about to faint.

Not again, he silently urged himself. *I have to do something.*

Forcing his willpower out of hiding, he ripped his eyes away from Ray and staggered into the tool shed, hoping to find some kind of weapon, but to his dismay, all of the tools were already gone. Breathless, he dashed across to the far end of the room, pulling a minecart from its bay with his clammy hands. He sped back out into the corridor, crashing the metal wagon through the doorway.

One of the Watchers had Nico backed up against the wall, holding him up by his throat as he bludgeoned the Filipino boy with his baton. Aiden was on the ground, his hands alternating between wrestling with Lygia's shock stick stuck in his rib cage and covering his ears from the sickly pale witch's screeching wails. Ben rumbled the minecart down the corridor like rolling thunder, barrelling the pair of guards over.

Splotches of light exploded across Ray's otherwise black vision as he gasped for air through his chattering teeth, feeling as though he was drowning at the bottom of an icy lake. He writhed and kicked until something pressed down between his shoulder blades, pinning him to the floor. His vision turned red. His head felt like it was on the brink of bursting into a thousand electrified pieces.

Ray felt the torc's bolt unlock and heard the metal collar clang as it was thrown against a wall, yet he still convulsed in agony. Head throbbing, mouth foaming and throat dry retching, he looked up to see the blurry green figures of his friends around him, a big solid cube and two thick shaky lines on the ground beneath it, bending this way and that.

Jack turned away from the bloodied and unconscious guard on the other side of the passage, lending a hand to Aiden, who rose with twitches and spasms, but was otherwise unhurt. Ava helped Ray to his feet, slinging his arm around her shoulder as he struggled to regain focus. Ben supported the battered Nico in the same manner.

With Sarah holding up Mara, Jack and Aiden were their only unhindered fighters. Choosing to leave the javelin unceremoniously sticking out of Gremlin's throat, Jack and Aiden picked up a pair of shock sticks from the fallen Watchers and led the way up the slanting corridor into the treasury.

Ava breathed hard underneath Ray's deadweight, his entire body still rigidly numb from the electricity coursing throughout his musculature. Even his vision was reeling in the aftershock, with stars appearing within the rotating walls of the passage like a kaleidoscope.

Jack stopped by one of the workbenches lined up against the wall, the table laden with golden nuggets. He stuffed one into his trousers. "Gotta bribe the NPA with something, right?" he said, before taking another gold rock with a cheeky grin.

"Who's the NPA?" Aiden asked, filling his own trousers.

Nico clucked his tongue, but said nothing.

"See?" Sarah pointed at the square elevator platform idling a few feet away from the minecarts filled with precious metals, "We can take the elevator up to the barracks, and then we –"

She stopped mid-sentence as a stampeding mob of inmates streamed out from the cafeteria behind them, surging up the corridor and into the treasury like a green ocean wave. Ray tripped and stumbled as he and Ava struggled to keep pace with the others.

"We can't hold them off! *RUN!!*" Gavin yelled as the crowd rushed past them to board the elevator.

Before the brothers or their friends could climb onto the packed platform, its taut chains clinked and groaning gears turned to propel the elevator upwards. The overburdened platform was so crowded that at the halfway point in their ascension, the inmates on the outer edges of the square had to climb up to the next level so that they were not crushed against the ceiling.

"Come on, this way!" Ben yelled, pointing towards the hardwood door in the corner of the treasury, the last remaining exit.

Ava steered Ray towards the shimmering wooden rectangle on the opposite side of the room. He stared at the door, and in his swaying delirium, he half-expected Mayor Gaspar and the Sheriff to emerge, as they had done when he had worked pushing minecarts up from the quarry once upon a time.

Ray withdrew his arm from around Ava's shoulders as the others yanked the door open. "I can manage," he said, wavering.

She fell away from his side and came to Sarah's aid instead, who was struggling to hold Mara upright and staunch her wound at the same time. Ben and the others burst through the doorway into a hot passage, coming face to face with a vaguely familiar ascending staircase, a twin set of metal railing tracks embedded in each step leading up to the door at the top. Ben glanced to his left to see the emanating red glow of the steam rooms.

At the sounds of the Lizardmen rasping and hissing farther down the treasury corridor, hot on their heels, the escaping inmates scampered up the steps. Ben threw the door open at the top of the staircase, and they darted into the small sombre room. One lonely wooden table stood underneath a flickering light.

Ray, on the other hand, staggered back towards the laden minecarts along the back wall of the treasury. He threw his bodyweight against one, sending it sailing down the ramp just as the slender brightly-scaled forerunners of their *Kirzakai* pursuers came into view. The metal wagon veered and turned sideways at the top of the incline, tipping over and hurling clumps of rock and dirt at the red-hued reptilian monsters, causing them to lose their footing.

He flipped over a workbench and kicked two more barrows in their direction just to be sure, both of them rolling to a stop a few feet short of the ramp, before he doggedly lurched through the doorway, not even bothering to close the door behind him. The girls screamed at him from the top of the staircase as he placed his hand on the wall to steady himself with each lumbering step. The sound of two metal clashes upon stone followed him up the stairway as the bigger Lizardmen hurled aside his blockade.

Ray stumbled into the room and Ben slammed the door shut behind him, a javelin from the *Kirzakai* warriors splintering through the centre of the door's timber where Ray's head had been just a moment ago. It seemed not all of them were interested in recapturing the prisoners.

Jack threw the wooden table across the room to barricade the door, as though the sole piece of furniture could stop the scaly beasts from breaking the entrance into matchsticks.

They had two exits to choose from, one on either side of the room. Nico wrenched at the handle of the door on the right. It did not budge. He muttered Filipino curses under his breath.

Jack and Aiden whirled around at the sound of the Lizardmen's clawed footsteps climbing up the stairs, wielding their shock sticks like baseball bats on either side of the door.

"Are we there yet?" Mara spluttered with an empty gaze in her eyes, supported by Ava and Sarah who both took in shaky lungfuls of air, frozen at the sight of the javelin's metal barb staring angrily back at them through the door's timber.

"This way," Ray mumbled groggily, still in a daze as he stumbled to the left and opened up the last remaining door.

He took the lead and clumsily navigated their way through the dark and cluttered storage room, the only illumination to guide them provided by the intermittent light of the room behind them. Unseen boxes and shadowy items crashed against the walls as Nico cleared a path for the three girls.

Ben tripped over some dense object, crashing to the floor. He scrambled to his feet and over the scattered obstacles just as the javelin-impaled door at their rear began to shake and shudder with the Lizardmen's powerful impacts, the sounds of timber splitting and cracking under each tremendous blow reverberating throughout the two small rooms.

Still ready to swing at their pursuers, Jack and Aiden backpedalled into the storage room, unable to close the door without plunging them all into darkness.

Ray caught hold of another door handle and threw it open. Light flooded the shadowy storage room as they entered the white ceramic-tiled barracks. He breathed in the cool air, feeling his senses slowly return while he massaged the back of his neck, still throbbing from the torc's electrical shock as they surveyed the room.

Although the typhoon was still raging on outside the floor-to-ceiling glass windows overlooking the rain-whipped cell house roof, the empty dining area had an atmosphere the likes of which they had long forgotten.

The air was refreshing and easy to breathe. Ben coughed at his first inhalation. The chairs and tables in the whitewashed room were made of bamboo, with simple cushions upon each seat. *Cushions!* After countless weeks of sitting on stone block seats in the cafeteria, Ben had never thought that they would seem so foreign to him. He stared down at another elevator platform set in the floor in front of them, the metal piece of decor seeming out of place in such a tranquil environment.

They had almost forgotten their plan to escape until the door set in between the large window panes on the other side of the room thumped thrice with urgency.

"Oi! Open up," Cormac's crude voice came. "They've blocked off the ovva entrance and there's no action to be 'ad down 'ere!"

"Outta the way, Mac, I've got the key here," Leon's unmistakable baritone voice sounded up from the female cell house.

Ray ran past the elevator platform, throwing himself against the door as a set of keys jangled on the other side. "We need to get to the garage," he said to the others, *"Fast!!"*

Glancing to his right, Ray looked through the adjoining passageway connecting to the other side of the barracks where the entrance to the garage was. Stocky inmates held their ground against the guards, some still armed with tools from the pit, others with shock sticks and spears they had wrestled from the Watchers and Lizardmen alike. He spotted Kenneth's fiery red hair amongst them, the Irish prisoner making wide sweeping arcs with his shovel.

"Break the door down, Pop!" Little Danny's reedy voice piped up on the other side of the wooden door. "I wanna see the fight!"

Ray was thrown forward as Cormac and Leon crashed into the door behind him, both of them grunting with exertion. He planted his feet firmly on the floor, bracing against the timber.

Glancing uncertainly at his straining brother and hearing the sounds of fighting echoing from around the corner, Ben turned to Sarah, "Where else can we go?" he asked.

"Down," Mara groaned, the colour in her face draining.

"She's right," said Sarah. "There's a tunnel on the lower level where all of the food and supply deliveries are made, we could go that way."

"Sarah, we don't even know where that tunnel leads!" Ava exclaimed.

"If it's away from here, it's good enough for me!" said Jack, warily staring back through the cluttered storage room, wondering how much longer the door would hold.

"Ray, come on, *let's go!*" Ben urged as he climbed onto the elevator platform with the others.

"What are you doing!?" Ray yelled, still holding off the Watchers with his back against the pounding timber. He jerked his head towards Kenneth and the other inmates, "We need to go *this* way!!"

Just as Ben began to second-guess his decision, a Lizardman plunged through the barricaded door in the other room – Adzirick, the gash from Pythrisse's tail barb still fresh upon his cheek. He narrowed his serpentine eyes at them. The eight inmates could only stare in horror as the reptilian warrior rose up from the ruined timber, untangling himself from the broken door and table and charging towards them.

Thawing from his frozen trance, Jack leapt from the platform, slamming the storage room's door shut and pressing his back against it. The door shook with a heavy impact, throwing him forward momentarily.

"You guys go. I'll find another way out," said Jack, gritting his teeth and digging his heels into the floor. His knuckles turned white from the grip on his shock stick.

"Jack, don't leave us!" Ava pleaded, but there was no time to argue.

Another ram against the cell house door sent Ray staggering forward, the door hanging slightly ajar. Whirling around, he kicked the door shut again and jumped onto the elevator's platform to join the others.

Shooting Jack a mournful glance, Nico mashed the *DOWN* button on the control panel and the metal platform jerked with a rattle as the elevator's gears whirred to life. The air grew hot and humid again as they descended; away from the light, away from the other inmates, away from the surface.

They passed through what appeared to be the kitchen. Two large pots simmered with gruel along the far wall, and a bench with half-prepared gourmet food stood in the middle of the room.

Ray almost vaulted off the elevator at the mouth-watering smell of a good meal, yet Mara weakly tugged at his shirt from behind, the blood loss from her shoulder wound taking its toll.

"Don't do it," she murmured, almost trancelike. "Trust me, it's not worth it."

Ben eyed the gruel pots bubbling away on the far side of the room with disdain. His insides churned at the sight of a cockroach crawling over the edge of one of the cauldrons, soon engulfed by the chunky porridge.

"There's another level below the kitchen," said Sarah, pressing the *DOWN* button again. "That's where the tunnel entrance is."

The elevator ground to a halt in a large storage room filled with dust-coated tables overflowing with discarded belongings. Curtains of spider webs stretched over the stacks of stolen possessions. They began to walk out into the room with caution, yet they stopped in their tracks to listen as one of the barracks' doors creaked open.

"Well, look 'o it is, 'ey?" said Cormac, his crude voice floating down from above. "Got yourself in a bit ovva pickle, sunshine?"

Leon let out a derisive chuckle. "What say we sit back, have a drink and watch what the Lizardmen do to him?"

Jack roared as half of a wooden door along with shattered glass rained down into the elevator shaft, dropping onto the platform where the seven inmates had just been standing. A streak of smoky grey scales and a blue garment flashed by overhead as the *Kirzakai* warriors leapt over the square shaft's gap in pursuit of the fleeing prisoner. All of them grimaced as Cormac, Leon and Little Danny laughed at the selfless inmate's misfortune.

* * *

Ray kicked a table over, sending dust motes flying and causing the others to jump. They all turned to him as he stood above the useless junk.

"Why didn't we just run over to Kenneth and the others?" Ray fumed, flushed with hot anger. "They were fighting in the *next room!* We could've used their help. Now Jack's gone and FOR WHAT!? We're even *farther* away from the garage now. If you wanna keep on taking wrong turns then we may as well just pick up some shovels and walk back out into the pit, because we're not getting outta here like this!!"

Everyone else held their silence, not daring to speak.

Ben gulped nervously. "It – it seemed like the best option at the time," he said, staring down at the floor. "Besides, we still need to get the car keys from Caleb if we want to escape with the truck."

"He was probably in the barracks!" Ray threw up his arms. "This was a stupid idea, Benji. Whatever happens to Jack is on you." Turning away from his brother, Ray put his hands on his hips, looking around at the mess they were in.

"It's my fault," Sarah said softly, standing beside Ben, her doe eyes downcast. "I said we should go this way. I'm sorry."

Ray ignored her. *An apology isn't gonna get us outta here.*

"Stop fighting," Mara groaned weakly. "And you…" she squeezed Ava's shoulder, silent tears tracking down the blonde girl's cheeks at Jack's sacrifice, "Stop crying. Let's just focus on getting outta here, and we'll save the drama for later, okay?"

"Good idea. I don't wanna talk to Benji anymore anyway," Ray said bitterly.

Ben took a deep stinging breath, his brother's harsh tone reminding him of their childhood.

Sarah took his hands into hers. "Ben… You did what you thought was best. Don't be too hard on yourself. And you're right. We won't have a chance of escaping without Caleb's keys to the truck."

Ben smiled at her reassuring words, but he was distracted by something just over her shoulder. There, in the mess of scattered stolen belongings from the table that Ray had kicked over was an item that – unlike everything else in the room – was not completely shrouded in dust.

He moved past Sarah, stooping next to the pile of discarded relics to pick up the familiar leather-bound book. He traced his fingers over the intricately embossed symbol on its front cover. It was his father's journal. In that instant, thoughts of their father's involvement with the quarry, the Lizardmen, and the Faction raced through his mind.

This book will explain everything, he thought to himself.

"Guys, over here!" Aiden called from amongst a cluster of tables in the far corner of the room. He yanked a cowering inmate up by his shirt.

It was Cameron, the minecart pusher with the bent nose. He held his hands up in surrender. "Please, I'm unarmed, just leave me alone."

"What are you doing down here?" Aiden asked menacingly, holding his shock stick to the nervous boy's throat, "Guarding the exit? You gonna turn us over to the Watchers when we leave?"

"N-no, of course not!" Cameron stammered, his voice breaking, expecting the baton's electrical shock at any moment. "I got s-separated from the others. Well, I… When the Lizardmen came into the cell house, Bryson, Levi and I hid with the girls in the cells."

Mara uttered a scornful laugh before wincing at the pain in her shoulder.

"Was Amelia there?" Sarah asked.

Cameron shrugged, "Maybe, I'm not sure. We might have been in different cells. We waited until the Lizardmen went down into the cafeteria before we snuck across to this side of the prison, and then we overpowered a guard and took his keys to get into the barracks. Everyone else wanted to fight the guards, and Bryson and Levi took off, and I just, I just *panicked*, so I came down here. And they won't find me here. They won't find me here…" he mumbled to himself, his eyes tracing back to his hiding spot.

Aiden withdrew the shock stick, and Cameron ducked behind a dust-covered table again. "What should we do with him?"

"Leave him," said Ray, kicking his way through the storage room's trash. "I don't want our backs being covered by a coward."

He strode over to Nico, who silently waited by the only other exit on the far side of the room. Ava and Mara stumbled after Ray through the mess. He looked over the wounded girl, her once dark-featured face now almost pale. Jack's bloodstained shirt covering her wound was soaked through.

"You sure you can keep going?" asked Ray.

Mara straightened up, her eyes burning into his. "Shut up, you're slowing us down."

He smiled at her defiance, holding the door open for the pair of girls. Nico took the lead down the dimly-lit mine tunnel beyond, with Aiden close behind. Ray looked back across the storage room, clenching his teeth at the sight of his brother searching through the junk. "Let's go, Benji!!"

He sighed in exasperation as Ben stood up with a leather-bound book clutched in his hands. Ray moved to one side as Sarah hurried into the tunnel, and then he ran in after her, leaving Ben to catch up.

It was difficult for Ben to take his eyes off their father's journal. He brushed the light film of dust from the covers of the book and tucked it into the waistband of his trousers. He knew Cameron's eyes were still upon him, and he felt the urge to bring the inmate along with them, but he did not want to risk losing the others in the darkness of the tunnel.

* * *

The tunnel twisted and turned this way and that, small light bulbs set in the low ceiling guiding their path. Mara doggedly jogged between Ava and Sarah. Despite her tenacity, the blood lost from her wound weighed down heavily upon her.

Ray passed by the trio of girls, just in case they ran into any trouble up ahead. He jumped over a strange bronze gong embedded into the ground at the last bend before a long stretch, where the tunnel widened, supported by broad beams of roughly hewn timber, reaching far away into the darkness.

Large empty rolling cages were banked on one side of the cavernous tunnel, while a cluster of minecarts – some empty, some filled with dirt, and some broken beyond repair – stood on the other. Nico paused at the edge of the light, holding up his hand in the dim shadows. Aiden knelt on one knee, feeling the ground as he stared out into the darkness.

Ben caught up with the three girls as they ambled over the curious metal gong, and together, they rounded the corner behind Ray, Nico and Aiden, the trio of inmates frozen in place.

"Try to hear," Nico whispered, cupping his ears.

Ben listened intently, but he was unable to hear anything above his own laboured breathing and thumping heartbeat. He attempted to slow his breathing, but it was no use. The blood pumping through his veins pounded in his head.

Then, slightly at first, the earth beneath them began to tremble. Dust fell from the walls around them, and something like steam hissed in the distance. Whatever the sound was, it was homing in on their position. *Fast*.

"I hope that's not coming from the volcano," said Aiden, standing up.

"Move back," Mara urged quietly, hearing the sounds of slithering and scratching echoing along the rock walls, the entire tunnel rumbling now. The others stood paralysed with fear, watching as a great pair of luminous reptilian eyes materialised in the darkness ahead.

"*RUN!!*" Ray yelled, pushing them back the way they came.

Ben backpedalled, unable to tear his gaze away from the looming twin slits. He tripped over a rock and tumbled backwards, but when he stood up again, he found that he was no longer in the tunnel. Instead, he was standing inside a small cave, and a solid wall stood before him where Ray and the others had been just a moment ago.

29 - WE HAVE TO

The inmates sprinted back towards the storage room through the twisting passage, crashing into the shuddering rock walls as they blindly sped around corners. Fuelled by the surge of adrenaline, Mara was able to keep the pace as Ava and Sarah ran abreast with her.

Turning down a long corridor, Ray took a quick head count; Ben was no longer with them. He silently hoped that his brother was somewhere up ahead.

Ray was the last to make it back to the storage room. He slammed the door behind him. Quickly scanning the room, he noted that the elevator platform was still on their level. Icy fingers of fear gripped his insides.

"Where's Benji!?" he asked the others, louder than he had intended.

Dismayed, Sarah shrugged Mara's arm from her shoulder. "He was right behind us," she said, her eyes filling with panic as she glanced around the room.

Catching the full weight of the wounded girl, Ava eased Mara down onto a rickety old table that creaked underneath her. "You don't think he's still in the tunnel, do you?" asked Ava.

Cameron popped his head up from his hiding place behind an overburdened bench in the corner of the room, "Aiden was the first to come back. I haven't seen Ben."

"I will going to look," said Nico, springing back towards the tunnel entrance.

Ray planted his foot against the door, preventing the eager village boy from venturing back into the passage.

"No. He's *my* brother. You stay here with the others. I'll check it out." He opened the door and slipped into the tunnel. Looking back, he said, "If I'm not back in two minutes, start running. We don't know *what* that thing was."

"Ray…" Mara said feebly, her dark facial complexion now whitened to an ashy grey. "Be careful."

The amplified crunching of his footsteps reverberated in the rock-strewn mine tunnel, but they were soon drowned out by the tremors in the tunnel ahead. *Maybe there are other passages branching off this one, or he could have tripped and fell behind*, Ray thought to himself.

He groped along the walls, searching for some hidden recess or niche, all the while keeping a wary eye out for what might appear around the next corner. He found himself thinking that perhaps he had been too hard on his brother earlier for leading them in the wrong direction, and that Ben was simply sulking in a corner somewhere.

Ray swallowed at the thought that finding his brother crying alone in the dark was the best thing he could hope for.

* * *

Tremors shook the natural rock walls and ceiling of the cave as Ben peered around at the small space. It had the same gloomy decor as the tunnel; a cave dug into the rock with just enough height to stand in. A flaming torch and a door were set in the only wall fashioned by hand – human or otherwise.

He felt the smooth rock wall that had appeared where his brother and their friends had been only moments ago. He pounded against it with the flat of his hand, yet the wall was solid.

I must have fallen through some kind of trap door, he thought to himself, massaging his throbbing wrist. "Ray, Nico!" he called. "Sarah!"

Nobody answered.

The small cave rumbled with more intensity, and hisses from the other side grew louder, piercing through the dense rock. Whatever had been in that dark stretch of tunnel was drawing closer.

Ben turned towards the door, yet something caught his eye – the glinting bronze surface of another gong set in the dirt floor, reflecting the dancing flames of the burning torch upon the wall.

Just as he unhooked the blazing rod from its bracket, the quaking from the tunnel outside subsided. He stared into the embers glowing within the metal tip of the torch in the ensuing silence. His eyes darted from the door, to the wall, to the floor.

I have to get back to Ray and the others. We have to escape together. He wheeled upon the gong set in the ground and, in the hopes of attracting the others' attention, he swung the fiery brand down with both hands, its deep metallic clang ricocheting around the cave and vibrating throughout the tunnel.

He turned at the sound of Ray's voice shouting his name, and the solid wall that he had fallen through lifted up on a hinge.

But it was not his brother.

Ben shrieked in dismay, trying to process the monstrous sight emerging before him. A huge scaly head – the size of a boulder – filled his horror-struck vision as the giant terror slithered into the small space with him.

** * **

Ray heard the muffled clash of metal upon metal ringing from somewhere up ahead. "Benji!?" he shouted, racing through the twists and turns of the tunnel. He entered the passage with the bronze gong they had passed earlier, but there was no sign of his brother.

It took a moment for him to realise that the vibrating rumble in the earthen walls had subsided. Dust was no longer falling from the ceiling. For a moment, all Ray could hear was the sound of his own breathing in the shaky silence… until Ben began screaming.

Rushing to his brother's aid, Ray turned the last corner of the corridor and almost stumbled over in shock.

Where there had been a long empty stretch of tunnel before, a huge scaly tentacle now lay, extending through the cave wall into a previously unseen room. He could hear Ben screaming on the other side, but there was nothing he could do.

Kirzakai warriors rasped in Ray's direction as they descended from the twin sets of bony ridges running the length along the top of the twisting tentacle. The forest green Lizardmen looked like younger versions of Ophidirick, with their scales brighter and more uniform in appearance. The wiry-limbed hunchbacked beasts stared back at him with beady black eyes as they began to nock arrows to their shortbows.

"We cannot allow you to esthcape, human," the closest Lizardman hissed, drawing back its bowstring and taking aim.

Ray dropped to his knees, narrowly dodging the arrow as it whistled by overhead and clattered off the rock wall behind him. He rolled across the dusty floor back the way he had come as more arrows studded the ground like a pincushion in his wake.

"Run, Benji! I can't get to you!" he yelled as he scrambled around the corner, gathering up a mound of dirt in his hands. He sprang to his feet and threw his back against the wall, waiting for them to round the corner before spraying them with stones and pebbles.

They blindly staggered after him, hissing and cursing in their strange tongue, afraid to fire another arrow for fear of injuring their own brethren.

Then, something bizarre happened. One by one, their green scales began to turn grey and brown, matching the surrounding earthen walls of the tunnel, their shades darkening according to the light offered by the small bulbs hanging from the ceiling, until only their shimmering outlines remained. The shortbows almost seemed to float in the passage by themselves, arrow shafts stretching back against the bowstrings of their own accord.

Ray kicked himself into motion and darted back in the direction of the storage room, the invisible *Kirzakai* archers firing volleys in his wake. He could only hope that his brother could find another way out of whatever room he had fallen into.

***

The pair of great venomous slits gazed deeply into Ben's panic-stricken eyes. The giant serpent's forked tongue flitted in and out of its reptilian mouth, tasting the fear of its pitiful prey screaming and shrinking against the opposite wall. The enormous snake opened its jaws with a hiss, its narrow eyes widening with glee as it moved to engulf the shivering prisoner within its gaping maw.

Ben's heart hammered within his chest, almost seizing up at the sight of the serpent's jaws extending from floor to ceiling in the small cave, its stalactite-like fangs dripping with venom. Frozen in fear's icy embrace, he could not help but stare at its cavernous unhinged mouth, revealing a leather bridle's weighty bit that seemed like a mere doorstep into the colossal beast's black gullet, the meaty abyss growing larger with every fleeting moment.

Still clutching the burning torch's handle with a white-knuckled grip, Ben snapped himself out of his trance, and in a desperate bid to save himself, he plunged the blazing rod up into the roof of the snake's mouth.

The void of the monster's gaping jaws slammed shut and it threw its skull against the ceiling, writhing and twisting in agony. It seemed as though the entire cave would collapse at any moment as the reptilian horror shook its giant head from side to side, smashing into the walls and raining rocks down from the cave's ceiling.

Ben flattened himself against the back wall, unable to move without being crushed by the serpent's violent thrashing or the rocks falling down from above.

He was searching for a pattern in the monster's wild movements to make a mad dash for the door when, in its throes of pain, the giant snake threw itself against the wall with enough force to bring Ben to his knees.

With a thunderous crack, a massive rock dislodged itself from the cave's roof and came down upon the serpent's head. The beast's skull was crushed beneath the weight of the rock, deflating like a burst balloon with a dull clang resounding in the small space as the snake's fangs pierced the bottom of its own mouth to strike the bronze gong lost beneath it.

Tiny stones and pebbles clattered down upon the boulder that now occupied most of the cave. As the dust settled, Ben tentatively prodded the flattened snake with his shoe. Between his own strained breaths, he could only hear the low hiss of the monster's bubbling venom pooling beneath its self-punctured mouth, corroding through the gong and the dirt floor alike. There could be no doubt that the reptilian horror was dead.

He wormed his way between the wall and the massive rock, and he managed to force the door open just wide enough for himself to slip inside, the sleeve of his green shirt tearing as he squeezed through. Retreating from the cave's grisly scene, he found himself inside yet another strange passage.

* * *

Ray burst through the door into the storage room and slammed it so hard that the wood splintered. Everybody jumped with fright. He threw tables against the door to barricade it against the impending threat of the encroaching Lizardmen. Useless objects and discarded belongings clattered to the floor in shrouds of dust.

Mara was still lying upon the rickety old table with Sarah and Ava trying to staunch the blood from her wound with Nico's shirt.

The bleeding should have stopped by now, Ray thought to himself as his eyes fell upon Jack's once green uniform bundled up on the floor, soaked red with her blood.

Aiden approached him through the mess of tables, keeping his voice barely above a whisper, "I don't know how far we're going, but she's not going anywhere without a ride."

Ray nodded in grim agreement as Mara desperately clung to life.

Now both barefooted and shirtless, Nico was standing at the edge of the elevator platform, peering up at the barracks. He looked around the room before addressing Ray, "Then where did Ben went?"

Ray simply shook his head, his heart panging with regret. The last thing that he had said to his brother was in anger for leading the group astray. He could only blame himself though – he should have taken the lead.

A resounding thump against the door shook everyone back to their senses.

Sarah looked up from Mara's wound, blinking back tears as she realised that Ben was still lost somewhere within the depths of the tunnel, stuck outside with whatever had spewed forth from the darkness.

The makeshift barricade rattled again with another crash against the door, but it held firm. The wiry-limbed archers on the other side were not strong enough to break it down by force.

"Where we will going to go now?" asked Nico.

"We won't make it very far without the truck," said Sarah, wiping her eyes. "We have to go through the garage, and I know the code to unlock the door. I watched Spike key it in while we were cleaning the barracks." Then, breaking out into a fresh sob, she added, "But we can't just leave him behind."

Ray knew that she was talking about Ben. He knew that he should have shown a similar emotional response for his brother, but he also knew that it would serve no purpose. Squaring his jaw, he said, "We stick to the plan. If we don't see him on our way to the garage, then we'll come back for him. We're no good to anybody if we all get caught."

A barrage of arrowheads pierced through the door behind him, the iron barbs embedding themselves into the wood. The inmates glanced at each other uncertainly as the studded arrowheads began to wriggle and squirm like metallic maggots, each of them disappearing with a shallow *thock* as they were plucked out from the other side, leaving behind minuscule holes in the cracked timber.

"You need to leave!" Cameron shouted, rushing over from his hiding place in the corner to reinforce the barricade.

Another volley of arrows against the door punctuated his words, some of the projectiles grazing through the holes in the wood, clattering harmlessly to the storage room's floor.

Ray looked at Mara still lying down on the table. "Can she walk?"

"I don't think she can go on much farther," said Ava, shaking her head sadly.

At this, Mara swung her feet onto the floor, glaring at Ava with renewed vigour. "*She* can still hear you. Have a little more faith, princess," she growled, spitting blood at the floor.

Sarah, still teary-eyed, came to the wounded girl's side and together with Ava they lifted the defiant Mara off the table. Ray, Nico and Aiden moved across to the elevator platform as the *Kirzakai* warriors began to pluck their arrows from the splintered door again.

"Cameron, come on!" Aiden yelled.

The skinny bent-nosed boy gave them the thumbs up as the three girls clambered onto the metal platform. "I'll be fine. Just don't forget to come back for the rest of us," he said with a smile that bent his nose a little further to the left, before starting back towards his hiding spot.

The six inmates nodded in a silent promise as Ray punched the *UP* button on the elevator's control panel. At the same instant that the gears whirred into life and the taut chains clinked, a scaly hand palmed through a weak section of the hole-ridden door.

Cameron had just enough time to turn around, catching the glint of two iron barbs glaring through the gap before his mind slipped into slow-motion. He watched in futility as the pair of arrows sailed into the room, inevitably burying deep into his abdomen. He fell to the floor with one arm outstretched, reaching for the elevator.

Everyone but Mara turned away as a second pair of arrows took aim at the fallen prisoner. She kept her eyes locked with Cameron's until they closed.

* * *

Ben found himself standing at the end of a sweltering dungeon-like

461

corridor. He quickly ducked behind a counter. He had never seen this part of the prison before, so he had no way of knowing who or what to expect. He peered over the countertop, past an array of levers and switches, to see a large room directly ahead, bathed in a fiery red gloom.

He crouched down again, looking back at the door that he had just come through, wishing longingly for it to swing open, with Ray and their friends on the other side.

Ben closed his eyes, summoning his willpower. He had to press on. Nobody was coming to help him now.

On his hands and knees, he crawled out from behind the counter and slowly inched his way forward. He passed by a locked door, its keyhole surrounded by a curious octangular etching. Nearing the large room at the end of the hallway, he rose to his feet with trembling knees and slid his back along the left wall, steadily advancing into the hot chamber.

Cautiously peering around the corner, he saw the source of the red light. Along the opposite wall, a wide metal grate set against the volcanic heat vent cast its flaming glow over the dungeon, emanating the oppressive warmth, the chamber resembling a larger version of the steam rooms. Mounds of dirt had been heaped across the room, each of them indented in varying shapes and sizes. Splintered cattle bones, crushed lobster shells and spiky pineapple skins littered the floor.

This must be where the Lizardmen live, he thought to himself. A pair of arched entrances to adjoining rooms on the far side of the chamber made his breath freeze in the scorching atmosphere. *I hope I'm alone down here.*

Just as the thought crossed his mind, a rattle from behind startled him.

Did that come from the locked room, or the cave?

Ben was not going to wait around to find out. He willed his legs to press onwards into the ominous dungeon, cockroaches scurrying before him as he trod lightly across the waste-strewn floor, taking care not to make any noise. The meshed furnace seemed to follow his progress with a thousand tiny square eyes as he ventured towards the two adjoining rooms.

Thankfully, both rooms were empty, save for the large slabs of rock and stone counters filled with leafy herbs, mortars and pestles, and small metal dishes suspended over thick candles like some sort of medieval chemistry set.

Maybe this is where they make the venom snares.

Ben's thoughts were interrupted by the sound of a door's lock as it *clack*ed open from the passage around the corner.

His mind raced as he looked around the gloomy red chamber.

There would be no escape if he was to slip inside one of the adjoining rooms. Opposite the metal grate however, he was faced with two possible exits on either side of a thin stone wall. On the left side of the partition was a staircase leading upwards and turning to the left. He had his foot upon the first step when he paused, feeling a cool breeze blowing down the dark passageway on the right.

The door creaked open from around the corner, yet he still struggled with indecision.

If he climbed the stairs, he would eventually come across the steam room corridor, as the hotboxes were also connected to the heat vent, and before long, he would arrive at the flight of stairs leading up to the barracks again.

However, if he chose to explore the passage on the right, he would chance either losing himself even farther within the dungeon, or, finding another way up into the barracks, the only place in the entire prison that would be responsible for cool air.

Biting his tongue, Ben ventured down the dark passage just as a pair of footsteps crunched around the corner. Regret of his decision grew with each quiet step forward into the darkness, yet there was no turning back now.

The crimson light behind him was not strong enough to discern where he was going, but any place was better than that eerie red chamber.

He left the warmth of the dimly-lit dungeon as the corridor curved to the right, and he found himself ascending the slight incline of what felt like a stone ramp in the growing void. His sight overcome by the veil of shadow, Ben felt his way along one side of the passage, the air growing cooler with each step.

I must be close, he thought to himself.

Echoes of footsteps following from behind spurred him into a blind run, when suddenly his outstretched hand – guiding him in the darkness – crashed into a solid wall. He skidded to a halt and reared his head back just in time to avoid sprinting headlong into a concussion.

Tiny wisps of light arranged in a small circle shone down upon him from the low ceiling as he felt around in the darkness for the next turn in the passage.

Three walls. It was a dead end.

He turned back to head towards the staircase, when a flashlight's beam shot around the corner, illuminating the narrow passage and shedding light on the escaping prisoner.

"Stop!" came the stern voice of his pursuer.

Shielding his face from the glaring brightness, Ben frantically searched for an escape. With the light at his back, he found three rusty metal rungs set vertically up against one wall. He shifted his gaze upwards to see that the tiny wisps of light above him belonged to a drain, set within an octagonal groove.

He mounted the first rung, but a firm hand caught his shoulder before he could attempt to climb. Ben turned, the pupils of his wide eyes contracting against the torch's sharp beam shining in his face. He threw up his hands to protect his eyes.

"Please…" he moaned meekly.

The flashlight's gleaming aura fell away from his face as a familiar voice issued forth. *"Don't be afraid."*

Ben peeked through the cracks between his fingers. His father's golden medallion shone from the speaker's chest. Caleb's hawkish eyes pierced him as he sank down to the floor.

* * *

Ascending up the elevator shaft, Ray and the others heard the sound of wind howling into the room on the top level. They reached the empty dining area of the barracks, yet no pleasant air-conditioned atmosphere greeted them now, only wind-lashed rain from the typhoon raging on outside.

One of the tall window panes looking out over the roof of the cell houses had been shattered, shards of glass lying scattered across the room. Behind them, all that remained of the door leading into the cluttered storage room beyond was a single wooden plank hinged to the door frame. The rest of the timber lay in pieces among the broken glass on the sodden tiled floor.

Sarah pointed towards the doorway in the corner. "This way will take us to the garage."

The sounds of fighting could still be heard coming through the adjoining corridor.

As they approached the passageway, Mara coughed. "We should head outside and circle back," she said, weakly nodding towards the cell house roof.

Ray nodded, "Good idea. Let's see what we're up against." Shards of glass crunched underfoot as he led them through the broken window. Aiden had to carry Nico, barefoot and shirtless, over the threshold and out into the torrential rain.

Dark storm clouds stretched across the early morning's sky. Only the occasional flashes of lightning could give shape to what was beyond the veil of cascading water.

"Ray, isn't that your cellmate?" asked Ava, pointing towards the far side of the concrete roof.

He squinted, peering into the shadowy distance, trying to catch sight of Connor. Through the downpour, he could just barely make out a pair of inmates on their knees close to the edge of the roof. Two Watchers stood above them, menacing the freshly-caught fugitives with raised shock sticks.

Ray turned to Nico and Aiden. "We're gonna need them if we wanna make it to the garage. Stay close to the wall and outta sight. Keep Mara outta the rain. Try to gauge the situation in the barracks if you can."

"You're so slang, I'm not understand," Nico complained, but Aiden caught on. They huddled next to the hollow-brick wall between the rows of windows on either side of the barracks.

Ray turned and broke into a run to help the pair of inmates on their knees. He had forgotten how good it had felt to run, his leg muscles reawakening. The storm threw stinging needles of rain at his face, but he pushed on, splashing through the water on the concrete as it drained into the iron-barred skylights leading down into the abandoned cells below.

A gaping hole in the roof where the viewing deck had once been seemed to grow as he drew closer, revealing the derivative damage from the ruined cells and crumbled support pillars beneath.

Rapidly closing the distance to the four figures at the edge of the roof, Ray recognised Cormac's leopard-spotted scalp and Leon's shaggy mane, the pair of Watchers standing with their backs turned as they crowed over the bowed heads of Connor and Levi.

Ray launched himself into the air, kicking out with both feet at the guards' backs, bowling them over with cries of indignation. He landed upon his tail bone with a splash. Ignoring the sharp pain, he jumped on top of the bewildered Cormac who lay flat on his stomach trying to push himself up.

Seizing opportunity, Connor wrestled the shock stick away from Leon, thrashing wildly at the Watcher's arms and legs as the man curled up into a defensive ball to shield his face and chest. Levi scrambled away, leaving Ray and Connor to deal with the guards.

Ray rained his fists down upon the back of Cormac's neck and skull. Cormac reached up with one arm in an attempt to protect the back of his head, and Ray instantly recognised the glint of silver gleaming from the guard's hand. He held the crude Watcher's wrist in a vice-grip and wrenched Dana's promise ring from Cormac's stubby finger.

In that moment, Cormac used his free arm to swing his shock stick at Connor, blindsiding him and sending a pulse of electricity up through the base of his spine. The inmate keeled over in agony, dropping Leon's baton with a clatter, one hand shooting towards the ground to catch himself, the other holding the small of his back.

In the blink of an eye, Leon threw Connor aside, picked up the shock stick and landed a powerful blow to Ray's sternum, sending him reeling backwards off Cormac. Winded and on his back upon the edge of the collapsed viewing deck, Ray took a moment to plant the promise ring back on his thumb, forcing it down to the faded tan line, his skin bunching up under the oddly-tight ring.

He kissed the piece of silver jewellery before rolling his upper torso forward in an attempt to get back up, but the pain in his chest was too overwhelming, and he slumped back down again with a wheeze. Before he could roll over onto his side, Cormac jumped on top of the inmate's chest, winding him a second time.

With Ray's arms pinned underneath Cormac's legs, the Watcher leaned forward with a smile, hot foul breath steaming from his crooked yellow teeth. At the first whiff of the horrible stench, Ray coughed and gagged up what little air he had left in his lungs.

"Funny 'ow that 'appens, innit?" Cormac giggled mischievously.

***

Caleb stooped to meet Ben at eye level, the medallion hanging from around his neck glinting in the flashlight's gleam.

"*Don't be afraid*," the Watcher repeated, and with his free hand, Caleb lifted the medallion off his chest, laying the necklace down over the flinching inmate's shoulders.

Ben stared up at him with wary confusion.

"This belonged to your father – my brother – Jacob," said Caleb.

"You? *You're* my uncle!?" Ben exclaimed in disbelief. Caleb nodded. "*You* dropped that note into my cell?" Caleb nodded again. Ben sat up, searching the man's face in the flashlight's sphere of illumination for any signs of insincerity. "Then why did you have me cuffed to the chains rack, asking what was written on that note?" he asked in a more challenging tone.

"I had to put on a show for the others," Caleb responded calmly. "I'm here as a spy for the Faction, you see, and I couldn't afford to blow my cover. But, I kept you on that chains rack as much as I could. It was not until you escaped into town overnight that the others took notice of your light punishments."

"And what about Ray?" asked Ben, "You could've chained him up next to me after the tool shed rebellion, but instead, you sent him to the steam rooms!"

"That would have made my favour upon the pair of you seem far too obvious," he answered. "And besides, I had other intentions for Raymond…"

"Like what?"

"Never mind that now. Didn't Jacob ever teach you never to question a good thing?" Caleb stood, his expression hardening as he offered a hand to help Ben to his feet, "Trust me, or don't trust me, but if we don't move *right now*, you're never going to leave this prison. Understood?"

Ben grew silent, seeing the stern Caleb he had known as a Watcher return in an instant. He grasped the outstretched hand of the man claiming to be his uncle. *What choice do I have?*

"Come on, we have to hurry," said Caleb, pulling him upright. "Where's your brother?"

"We got separated," he stared down the dark passage. "We were in a tunnel and I fell through a wall, and then this huge snake attacked me."

Caleb quickly glanced him over, checking to make sure that he was unscathed. "Come on, I know how to open up that wall's trapdoor," he said, starting back down the corridor.

"Wait!" Ben cried, "The door won't open. It's blocked on the other side by the dead snake. We won't get through that way."

"*You killed a* Colossiboa *by yourself!?*" the former guard asked incredulously.

"More like it killed itself."

Caleb shook his head in disbelief as he reached into his pocket and withdrew a bunch of keys cluttered around an octangular ring.

"Isn't that the Warden's key-ring?" asked Ben, remembering when Kalarish had dropped it at the Warden's feet in the aftermath of the tool shed rebellion.

"He gave it to me after I helped him, Kalarish and Ophidirick escape through the passage you just came from," Caleb replied. "He thinks I'm going to travel to Lungsod to inform Gaspar's guards of the outbreak." He passed the flashlight to Ben and gestured for him to shine it towards the octagonal groove in the ceiling. "This passage exists as a private corridor for him to meet with them," he continued, locking the eight-sided key-ring into place, the keys dangling uselessly. "That tactless Joshua stole this from the Warden to open up the room back there, but he tried this decoy shrapnel instead of the real key, the ring itself, and he set off the alarm that led to his downfall."

"He was my friend!" Ben said suddenly.

"And mine," said Caleb, looking down at him fixedly before turning his flint grey eyes back up to the lock in the ceiling.

Humbled, Ben let his curiosity overcome him. "What was in that room back there?"

"Nothing important," he replied, "Rusty arrowheads, broken swords and shields. Relics of a forgotten battle." He twisted the key and pushed a square hatch open, flooding the passage with light. "We still don't know what the Lizardmen are digging for."

Caleb climbed up the three metal rungs set against the wall, reaching down to offer a hand to help Ben up.

The skinny inmate peered up at him, still hesitant to trust the apparent ex-Watcher. "How did you know it was us?" he asked. "How did you know we were your nephews?"

"A friend travelled by airplane," said Caleb, "He brought a message to Alexia, my contact in Lungsod, advising of Jacob and Joshua's disappearance, and your possible capture and need for protection. I've seen pictures of you and Raymond when you were children, and I thought I had recognised you both when I first saw you, but the message from the Faction made it clear.

The former guard offered his hand again. Satisfied with the answer, Ben accepted his uncle's aid with ease this time, and Caleb pulled him up through the hatch.

* * *

Broken tree branches, leaves and other debris soared over the quarry pit, whipping across the cell house roof with the gale-force wind as Cormac sat on top of Ray. The encumbered prisoner tried to sit up again, even with the callous Watcher's added weight, yet he only managed to catch a brief glimpse of his surroundings before he fell back to the concrete.

Nearby, Connor was lying in a position similar to Ray's, with Leon on top of him, while below, standing on the grassy turf along the side of the building, Levi hacked away at the barbed wire fence with a mattock.

"Levi! Levi, you coward! Help us!" Ray yelled between gasps of air.

"Yes! Levi, you coward, come and help *us!*" Leon barked mockingly, "Come and betray your friends again!" he backhanded Connor across the face with a gruff laugh.

Levi's snivelling voice carried over the surging storm, "Word from the top says you aren't hiring any more Watchers! I'm outta here!"

Cormac grinned, drawing closer to Ray's face. "No one's coming to 'elp you now, sunshine."

As if on cue, a green-clad figure crept up behind the crude Watcher. Relief washed over Ray, thinking that Nico or Aiden had come to their aid. In fact, any one of their fellow inmates would have been a welcome sight.

Except for this one.

"Teach 'im a lesson, Pop!" a reedy voice sounded, Little Danny's peevish face beaming over his father's shoulder in the rain.

"I'm gonna enjoy this…" said Cormac, rearing back his fist with a vile grin on his face.

"NICO! AIDEN!!" Ray yelled with wide eyes. "HELP U–"

SMACK!!

Cormac swung hard with his left fist into Ray's wet cheek, knocking his head sideways. The same meaty *thwack* against wet skin underneath the relentless rain resounded from Leon and Connor, just a few feet away.

Ray rolled his head back to yell up at the dark sky, "LEVI!!"

Cormac cocked back his right fist and brought it down hard upon the inmate's brow. Ray's vision blurred and his head clouded. He did not even feel the next punch, his head simply moved from side to side with each swing. In the corner of his eye, Little Danny eagerly danced and clapped with each wet smack pounding the defenceless inmates.

"Get 'im again, Pop! Teach 'im a lesson!" he cried excitedly, "Told ya you'd be next, Ray! I told ya!"

In his groggy state, Ray knew that help was not coming. *We should have stayed with Jack. We should have run to Kenneth and the others in the barracks.* Another punch knocked his head sideways again. He looked up at the flag that hung over the quarry pit as it whipped around on the pole wildly in the storm's wind.

The flag unfurled for a split second, and Ray saw that all along, what he had thought was an emblem of the sun had actually been the narrow slit of a reptilian eye set within a round iris.

"Like an eye watching us all," Rashad's voice echoed in his ears.

He remembered Rashad's resilience in the tool shed rebellion – it had taken three Watchers to bring the big barrel-chested gorilla of an inmate to the ground.

Drawing inspiration from his former cellmate, Ray summoned his last ounces of strength, lifting his legs up behind the Watcher sitting on top of his chest. In a feat of flexibility that surprised even himself, he managed to raise his feet over Cormac's shoulders, and, digging the heels of his boots into the guard's face, Ray kicked out and thrust down, throwing Cormac backwards and slamming the man's skull against the concrete rooftop.

Little Danny looked at his fallen father with wide eyes, bewildered by the sudden change in the fight. The skinny runt cocked back his own scrawny arm to continue his father's work.

Ray caught the punch and gripped the boy's reed-like arm. Little Danny's baby-face screwed up into an expression of sheer terror as Ray rose to his feet, rain falling in curtains around them.

The bigger inmate took one last look at the boy, brought up in a savage environment and cursed to follow in Cormac's footsteps. And if this was how he would behave as a child bordering on puberty, Ray shuddered to think of what he might become.

He gripped the urchin's stick of an arm with both hands, Little Danny flailing out with his free arm in futility. Shifting his weight on one foot to pull the boy off balance, Ray turned and threw the boy towards the hole in the collapsed viewing deck.

Little Danny tumbled down the pile of rubble, and then fell out of sight into the quarry pit. An impish squeal echoed from the depths below, but it was soon lost amidst the sound of the storm. Ray swallowed, thinking that perhaps he had just crossed some invisible line of morality, but it was already done.

Grunts and groans from nearby instantly brought his thoughts back to Leon, who was still hurling punches at Connor on the concrete.

Clasping his hands together to form a dense club, Ray struck the back of the Watcher's neck with the force of a well-practised mattock swing, sending him sprawling across the Faction inmate.

The battered blonde teen shoved the fallen guard aside and Ray helped him up to his feet. Connor's face was blotched and bloody. As the adrenaline from the fight died down inside him, stinging pain spread across Ray's face, and looking at Connor's fresh welts and bruises made him feel as though he was staring into a mirror.

Ray wiped the rainwater from his eyes, the droplets mixing in with the blood from the cuts in his face. They looked around. There was a gaping hole in the barbed wire fence below on the side of the building where Levi had been just a few moments ago, although they could not see any trace of the snivelling weasel anywhere in the storm now.

"Come on, that's our way out!" Connor urged, running towards the edge of the roof.

Ray ran in a different direction, calling out over the storm, "You go ahead, I'm going back for the others!"

* * *

They were standing in a sandstone-tiled bathroom, and they had just climbed up through the shower floor – another luxury Ben had thought he would never have seen again.

Not bothering to remove the Warden's key-ring from the lock, Caleb kicked the trapdoor shut. "I'm not sure what the situation is out there in the barracks," he said. "We may have to leave Raymond and Jacob's journal behind, as much as I hate the thought of leaving them in this place."

Lifting his shirt, Ben revealed his father's leather-bound journal tucked into the waistband of his trousers. Caleb's stony face cracked into a half-smile, yet soon snapped back to its natural state.

Ben returned the rigid expression, not wishing to leave his brother behind. "We can't just leave him here," he said, fixed to the spot.

"We don't have a choice," said Caleb, opening the bathroom door and cautiously checking the next room. He turned back to Ben, "With the *Kirzakai* warriors taking up guard stations around the complex, we'll never have another shot at breaking you out."

Sullenly, Ben followed Caleb, crossing through a bedroom filled with leafy pot plants and paintings depicting scenes of nature and vast open landscapes. Passing through another door, they emerged into the neatly-arranged Warden's office. Bustling past the armchair and the mahogany desk, Caleb strode across to the other side of the room, opening the door to the barracks just slightly ajar and peering out.

The scuffling and grunts of a brawl sounded from outside as the Watchers continued to struggle to quell the rebellion.

Ben bumped into one of the bookcases as he stared curiously at the brown paper package hanging upon the wall above the water cooler. The oddly-shaped parcel's long barrel and thick handle made it appear to be a rifle, something that they could use, but underneath its packaging, it could have been anything.

Just as he attempted to reach up and take it down, Caleb snapped him out of his trance with an urgent whisper, "Over here." Dropping his arms, Ben sidled up next to his newfound uncle. "As soon as we enter the barracks, we'll take the first right down the corridor leading to the garage. I'll punch the code in." He pulled a set of car keys from his pocket. "There's a pickup truck inside. We'll take it to Lungsod and get some help there."

Caleb gripped Ben's arm in one hand, pressing the car keys against his skin, and he drew his shock stick with the other. Ben's heart pounded in his chest in anticipation. Caleb nudged the door open wider, and they slipped out quietly.

Carnage raged on in the barracks. The Watchers fought to restore order, and the inmates, no longer shackled by the torcs, fought for their freedom.

Ben was surprised to see Jack and Aiden fighting heartily alongside Kenneth, Gavin, Samir, and the rest of the Faction youths. The bigger inmates kept the guards distracted while the smaller escapees made a break for it into the rain still bucketing down upon the concrete rooftop outside. He searched for Ray and the others among the fray.

Pythrisse, Adzirick and a few other Lizardmen stood to one side, their backs against an open heat vent grate set in the wall, the fiery red furnace spewing sulfuric gas into the air. Recaptured prisoners either sat cross-legged or lay unconscious upon the tiled floor at their scaly feet, with Amelia slouched and inert amongst them. The *Kirzakai* warriors loomed over the fallen inmates, ensuring that they did not rise up again as they inhaled the noxious fumes.

The Lizardmen idly surveyed the fight with mild amusement, Watcher against inmate, prisoner against prisoner, in their own twisted reptilian version of a gladiatorial display.

As Ben's uncle pulled him along, Pythrisse's low hiss pierced through the pandemonium. "Caleb, to where do you go?"

* * *

Connor took one final fleeting glance at Ray running back through the rain towards the barracks, from where thin wiry inmates now began to emerge, just one or two at a time, with Bryson taking the lead. Connor waved his hands, calling for the attention of the escaping prisoners and directing them all to safety through the hole in the chain-linked fence below.

Ray returned to the hollow-brick wall where he had left the others. Ava and Sarah gasped at the welts on his face, yet Mara simply stared up at him with the light fading from her eyes, a trickle of blood seeping from her half-open mouth. Nico crouched at the edge of the wall, the barefoot and shirtless Filipino boy soaking wet, peering at the brawl in the barracks through the corner window.

"I've found another way out," said Ray, "But we'll need to go on foot. Where's Aiden?"

"He's buying us time with the others inside," said Ava, as more inmates spilled out from the barracks. "Ray, Mara's not going anywhere on foot," she added, cradling the wounded girl in her arms.

He exhaled, faced with the decision of leaving yet another person behind. "We still don't have Caleb's keys."

"And we still haven't found Ben yet either," said Sarah. "I'm not leaving without him."

"Sarah…" Ava started.

"He *promised* he'd take us with him! We were supposed to leave *together*," Sarah broke out into a fresh sob. "He pr-promised…"

Nico tugged at Ray's shirt, pointing at the barracks window. He said one word. A name. "Ben."

Ray drew closer to the rain-streaked glass, careful not to give away their position. Inside and still rioting, Jack, Kenneth, Aiden and a few other inmates hailing from the Faction held the Watchers at bay with shovels and mattocks and fallen guards' weapons, covering the escape of the smaller fugitives. All of the torcs had been removed, strewn haphazardly across the tiles like hungry bear traps waiting for someone to misplace their footing and break an ankle. The remaining Watchers had given up all hope of using sparker remotes against the unruly prisoners – even sparking the manacles did not seem to affect their zeal for freedom when it was so close at hand.

Ray blinked hard, for through the tempest raging outside, and the chaos reigning within, he caught a glimpse of Caleb holding Ben by the arm, dragging him deeper into the barracks.

* * *

Pythrisse's eyes glowered at Caleb, narrowing her reptilian slits with seething impatience, demanding that her question be answered. Caleb gritted his teeth, preparing to fight off the *Kirzakai* using only his shock stick when inmates began cheering at the sight of Ray charging into the barracks through the rain-lashed glass door on the other side of the room.

Ben's battered and bruised brother sized up the battle on the move. Jack and Aiden were fighting back-to-back, while Kenneth was making wide sweeping arcs with the blade of his shovel. Another inmate stood toe-to-toe with Sheriff Sullivan, the reeking Watcher still covered in filth from the chamber pots that the girls had thrown at him.

Ray dashed across the room, putting all of his weight behind a punch aimed directly at the Sheriff's beer gut, catching him off-guard. The Watcher stumbled backwards, losing his footing over Amelia's slumped figure, his arms pin-wheeling as he fell into the *Kirzakai* spectators.

Nico and the three girls followed Ray as he threw his fists through the frenzy. They were drenched from the torrential rain outside. Mara looked as though she was on her last legs, her head hanging low, supported between Sarah and Ava.

Sarah stooped to clutch at Amelia's hand, but Mara yanked her back upright by her shirt, groaning in agony as she used the wrong arm to pull Sarah back on course with the last of her failing strength.

"She's out cold," said Mara, coughing up blood. "You *need* to leave her behind."

Noticing Ben and Caleb pressing on through the confusion, Pythrisse motioned two Lizardmen forward to apprehend them. Ben would have stopped in his tracks like a deer caught in the headlights if it had not been for Caleb lugging him by the arm into the corridor. His grip on Ben was so tight that the truck key's teeth almost punctured his skin. Caleb cleared the passage in an instant, half-dragging Ben along behind him, and he began punching a code into the garage door's keypad.

Suddenly they were set upon from behind, and Caleb's head crashed into the door before he was wrenched backwards, his hand slipping from Ben's arm. Assuming the worst, Ben turned around slowly, and he was filled with a mix of shock and relief to see Ray wrestling with their uncle on the floor, locking the ex-Watcher in a rear naked chokehold.

"Caleb's on our side!" Ben yelled, transfixed by the swollen red splotches across his brother's face.

Staring up at Ben standing above them wearing their father's medallion, Ray was at a loss for words, but with the Lizardmen advancing up the corridor, he did not argue. He let up on his grip and Caleb sucked in lungfuls of air as Sarah entered in the last sequence of the code.

They piled into the garage; Nico, Ava and Mara narrowly slipping in after them before a dark-featured goateed man – waiting for them inside – slammed the door shut.

"Gassed up and ready to roll, Caleb!" Evander shouted, gritting his teeth and bracing his thickset back against the hardwood door.

The first tremor against the timber shook the walls of the garage, and the drumming sound echoed in the enclosed space. Wooden shelves lined the walls, housing tools and various construction materials.

Sliding off a stack of cartons, a box of galvanised steel nails fell to the concrete floor, the metal needles spraying out like a blast of shrapnel. In another corner, a power drill rattled out of place, landing with a soft thud upon a small heap of fishnets gathered on top of a blue tarpaulin.

In the midst of all the ringing clangour, a big red pickup truck dominated the centre of the garage, large enough to fit all of the escapees. It was all they would need to outrun their pursuers, as well as the other truck in the Watcher outpost at the volcano monitoring station, and, if they could keep their heads down in the vehicle's tray, they might even be able to sneak past the patrols of Gaspar's guards without incident too.

"What's with the change of heart?" Ray asked, getting to his feet and whirling on the two Watchers, "Why are you helping us?"

"You're welcome," Evander said through clenched teeth.

"There's no time to explain," said Caleb, standing up as another wall-shaking thump reverberated around the garage. "You and the villager, grab a shelf and barricade the door," he ordered before disappearing around the side of the pickup truck.

Ray brushed himself off and helped Nico to his feet. Still confused by the guards' sudden betrayal of the Lizardmen, he was more than willing to put as much debris and distance between them and the scaly beasts as possible.

Small bleeping noises resounded from the other side of the door as Ben and the three girls wriggled themselves free from the tangle of bodies. Evander grunted as the next crash threw his upper body off the door, but despite the force of impact, his legs remained firmly rooted in position like a set of tree trunks.

Ray leaned against the side of one of the wooden shelves along the back wall and heaved, while Nico pulled from the other end with all of the compact strength in his wiry body. They strained with exertion, finally building up enough force to scrape the shelf's wooden base across the concrete, a myriad of boxes and tool kits clattering to the floor.

More bleeps sounded through the other side of the door, followed by another heavy crash, sending Evander toppling over as the door opened a fraction. He flipped over onto his backside and kicked it shut from the floor. Scrambling to his feet, the thickset ex-Watcher helped Ray and Nico pull the shelf into position with one hand. They all braced themselves against the rack for extra support, anticipating the next impact.

"Ben…" Sarah called him over with barely a whisper.

Tears welled up in her glistening brown eyes as she looked downwards. He followed her gaze to see Mara lying motionless on the ground, clutching at Sarah's shirt. Ava knelt silently beside her, cradling the dead girl's head in her lap.

He froze with wide-eyed shock. Mara had only ever shown him scorn and contempt, but she had been alive and well only a few hours ago. To see her lifeless body was unnerving. The concept of death was still fairly new to him. Ben had not seen what had become of Ethan, or Joshua, or even his father.

Sarah buried her face into his shoulder, quietly sobbing. Lost for words, he put a comforting arm around her. It was all that he could do.

The pickup door slammed shut behind them, and Ben turned his head to see Caleb standing by the driver's side, patting his pockets, frantically searching for something. "Benjamin!" his uncle yelled, "Focus! Do you have the keys to the truck?"

Sarah pulled away from Ben's embrace, looking up at him with her teary doe eyes as he pondered where the key might be. He tried to retrace their steps in the barracks, but Evander's shout from the makeshift barricade broke his concentration.

"Caleb, starting that truck would be a great idea!"

Caleb worked his jaw, his steely gaze lingering on Ben as he made his reply. "We don't have the keys!"

A cheery voice cut across the silence that followed, piercing through the timber of the heavy door and the wooden shelf. "I think y'all might'a dropped some'n' on ya way out," came the southern drawl of Sheriff Sullivan, followed by the faint sound of a set of keys jingling just out of reach.

Ray banged his fist on a shelf. *Caleb must have dropped the keys when I tackled him.*

Caleb opened the vehicle's door and climbed back into the driver's seat, clenching and unclenching his fists on the steering wheel. "Call the others around to the front of the truck," he said in a measured tone, more to himself than anyone else.

Ben moved around the side of the pickup truck and repeated Caleb's instructions to Ray, Nico and Evander just as the small bleeping sound resumed, emitting from the keypad on the other side of the door. They each exchanged glances before reluctantly releasing their grip on the wooden shelf barring the entrance. The next slam splintered the door's timber, knocking more building supplies off the rack, but the barricade held firm.

Caleb rolled the window down and leaned out the side of the cab as they moved towards the front of the vehicle. "I'm gonna need you to push the truck backwards," he said, shifting gears and releasing the handbrake.

Ray and Evander took up positions in the middle, leaning against the truck's grill, while Ben and Nico each grabbed the outer edges of the bull bar and heaved on the sides.

Ben stopped pushing, straightening up and staring sidelong at his brother, noticing his blotchy red face for the second time. "What happened to your face?" he asked.

"Nothing," Ray grunted over a split lower lip, his face covered in cuts and welts. Caleb honked the horn with impatience, and Ray heaved harder against the truck. Gritting his teeth, he added, "Listen, Benji, about what happened down in the storage room… What I said –"

"You were right," said Ben. "It was my fault, I made a bad decision."

"We've come this far though," said Ray, still trying to offer an apology, "Maybe you made the right choice. Who knows what could've happened if we went any other way?"

Ben heaved and shoved, his shoes simply sliding out beneath him, but with their combined weight, the wheels of the pickup truck slowly began to turn, and they rolled the vehicle back against the makeshift barricade just in time for the next impact.

"We're gonna have to go out on foot," said Caleb, locking the handbrake into position and climbing out of the truck. He and Evander marched to the front of the garage where they unbolted each side of the corrugated roller door.

"I hope you found what you were looking for down there," said Evander.

Caleb stood silent, his stony face downcast as he shook his head. They stooped to the ground and rolled the door up, its metallic acoustic ringing around the garage before it was drowned out by the roaring storm raging on outside.

Gales of wind swept across the dirt road before them, carrying giant coconut leaves and uprooted vegetation with each violent gust. Rain entered the garage to soak the fronts of their trousers. Ben looked over at Nico, only just now realising that he had become shirtless at some point after they had been separated, abandoning the green uniform of the prison.

"There's a Watcher outpost farther down the mountain," said Caleb, turning to the three boys.

"Volcano monitoring station…" said Nico, narrowing his eyes at his own words.

"Right," said Caleb. "Spike and the other Watchers would have sheltered themselves from the storm, which means that their vehicle will still be there and under cover."

Ray walked around the side of the red truck to find Ava and Sarah on their knees beside Mara. "We have to go," he said, "Come on, I'll carry her."

"It's no use," Ava whispered. She looked up at him with tears streaming down her face, "She's gone, Ray."

He swallowed, his boots rooted to the floor, deep in thought as Mara's stilled body etched herself into his retinas. He had barely even known her, and yet he knew that she was one of the strongest women he would ever meet. *I never even asked her where she was from*, he thought bitterly. His focus on defying the guards and escaping had taken precedent over pleasantries.

The angry tempest outside reawakened him, the back of his pants beginning to grow wet again as the rain pelted his heels. With forlorn hope, he dropped to his knees and felt her wrist for a pulse. Her limp hand dangled in his. He set her lifeless limb back down to rest.

"There's nothing we can do for her now, she lost too much blood." Ray rose to his feet. "Come on, we have to go," he said, pulling Sarah up. "If we don't move now, we won't have a chance to later."

Sarah yanked her arm away from his grip and ran to the front of the garage, sobbing.

Ava leaned down over Mara's face, still cradled in her lap. "We made it, Mara. We're free. Thank you, for everything." She set the brave girl's head down gently.

"We shouldn't leave her here," said Sarah, appearing next to Ben and clutching his arm.

She looked back at Mara's lone leaden figure on the concrete floor, fingers of rain driven by the howling wind reaching across the garage for her. Something about the peaceful look on Mara's face made her seem just as innocent and kind and lovely as Sarah.

"I know we shouldn't," said Ben, turning from Sarah's tear-stained cheeks to see his brother reaching underneath the pile of fishnets in the corner. After one final moment of respect, Ray covered Mara's body with the blue tarpaulin. "But we have to."

30 - BACK HOME

They stood at the garage's entrance staring outside in dumbfounded disbelief. The five inmates had almost given up on the fanciful idea of living in a world without walls, yet here they were, gazing out into freedom.

It was the early hours of the morning now, but they had slim chances of seeing the sun today through the thick grey blanket of clouds stretching across the sky.

Needles of rain lanced at their faces as they splashed out onto the muddy dirt road. The landscape before them dropped out of sight as the path took a sharp bend to the right. They ran along the edge of a cliff, with fierce waves crashing against the rocks below, sending up frothing sprays of sea foam. Dark storm clouds hung low over the angry windswept ocean beyond.

The salty sea air followed them down the slope as the squelching road turned away from the edge of the cliff and into the lush green rainforest, bracken blowing and coconuts flying from palm trees as they lurched and swayed violently in the tempest's turbulent winds.

Ray ran ahead with Caleb and Evander. "You still haven't answered my question yet," he yelled over the storm, "Why are you helping us?"

Evander slowed to a jog to let them run ahead, giving them some privacy. Ray glanced back at him occasionally, determined to keep an eye on the other apparent ex-Watcher.

Caleb tensed his jaw as they ran, his flint grey eyes narrowed on the path. "Jacob was my brother," he said. "I'm your uncle."

"But we've never met you," said Ray. "Dad never even told us that he had a brother."

"I was imprisoned during your childhood," said Caleb, still keeping his steely gaze fixated on the road ahead. "When we were young, Jacob and I were both captured and sent to the Quarry Complex. When Jacob escaped, I elected to remain behind and serve as a spy for the Faction, relaying information of the Lizardmen's operations through Alexia – my contact in Lungsod."

"So all along, when you were grilling me about the Faction –"

"It was all an act," said Caleb. "The Lizardmen were watching us through the walls."

Ray remembered the scuttling scratches in the surrounding walls when he had been left alone in the room with the gunmetal grey door.

He skidded to a stop in the muddy road to avoid a falling tree branch. As he caught up to Caleb again, he asked, "How did you know it was us? You knew our faces in the cafeteria the first day we were captured."

"Jacob sent Alexia pictures of you and Benjamin from time to time. I had to destroy them, of course. We couldn't risk the photographs falling into the wrong hands."

"So that's why you burnt that photo when you were interrogating me?"

"Precisely," Caleb replied, "After seeing you and your brother, I searched your belongings, and I found the photo in Jacob's journal. It tied you to Joshua and my contact in the village, so I had to destroy the evidence. But I wanted you to see it first, so that if anything ever happened to me, at least you would know who to look for in Lungsod."

"Hey, Evander!" Ray called over his shoulder, "Are you working for the Faction, too?"

Splashing through the rain, Evander caught up to them. "No, not me," he said. "For a long time, I just wanted to get outta there, but I knew those kids would've suffered without me. I'm thinking if I join the Faction, maybe we can shut that place down for good." He glanced sidelong at

Caleb. "You'll put in a good word for me, right?"

"Of course," said Caleb. He broke his rhythmic breathing with a distracted exhalation. "I only wish that after all these long years, I could have discovered what the Lizardmen were searching for."

* * *

Ben could not resist smiling, tasting the free air once more. Nico ran alongside him with his mouth open and head craned upwards, catching the spears of rain on his tongue.

Though the cascading water falling upon his face stung with each drop, Ben felt the joy of their newfound freedom radiating in a blissful aura around them, and the rain passing through the invisible warmth felt as though it was merely a refreshing shower.

Sarah and Ava kept up with Ben and Nico, their tears in mourning for Mara mingling with the downpour. Their saddened spirits were soon uplifted by the boys whooping with giddy excitement, and their sombre expressions hatched into grateful smiles again, celebrating their escape.

Ben turned back to look at the chain-linked fence surrounding the prison. A hole had been cut into the barbed wire, around the same point in the fence line where he and Nico had once escaped when they had climbed over the barbs with the padded cushion of a mattress.

Other inmates must be on the loose as well, he thought to himself, although he could not see any sign of the fugitives who had escaped from the barracks onto the cell house roof in all the confusion.

He wondered what had become of the prisoners that they had left behind. *Maybe they're being led back to their cells now, or maybe Jack, Kenneth and Aiden are still putting up a fight in the barracks.* They, in addition to Gavin and Samir and the other inmates from the Faction, would not have gone down so easily.

Ben still held onto some hope that they would encounter them along the path ahead. He had not seen Connor since the start of the rebellion. Even the fates of Cameron, Bryson, Levi, and Little Danny remained a

485

mystery to him.

Turning away from the prison as the road slightly curved around to the left, the swaying canopies of leafy foliage broke for a short distance, revealing the peak of the volcano looming up on their right side. The path skirted its vegetation-covered base as they continued jogging down through the mud and rain.

"The volcano," Nico pointed with a smile, although as the girls gasped behind them, he quickly added, "But it's okay, it's not explode in a many year."

"Are you excited to go back home, Nico?" asked Ben.

Nico did not respond at first while their feet squelched through the slosh. "I know my Papa will going to worry for me," he said after some time. "But me, I don't like to going on my home yet."

"Why not?" asked Ava.

"I'm so bored on my village," he said. "I like to *explore*. I like to adventure!" He beamed at his own resolve.

"Do what makes you happy, Nico," said Sarah. "But if it wasn't for the prison and this storm, I don't think I'd ever want to leave. It looks so beautiful here."

* * *

Climbing over a pair of uprooted trees fallen across the path, Ray remembered Joshua's last words after Caleb pushed him from the cell house roof into the depths of the pit. Even though Caleb was claiming to be their uncle, and he had satisfied all of Ray's questions so far, he still harboured a degree of suspicion that the assistance from the two supposed ex-Watchers might have been part of some elaborate plan to extract Joshua's message out of him.

Ray glanced back at Ben, their father's golden medallion hanging from around his neck. Caleb must have given it back to him to earn his trust. *I won't be won over so easily though.*

"Looks like we wouldn't have made it too far in the truck with those fallen trees in the way," said Evander, trying to cheer up his companion, whose hawkish eyes were downcast in thought, fully aware that he had just blown a long-term espionage mission only to return to the Faction empty-handed.

"I assigned those additional duties to you after Joshua's demise," said Caleb, reading the scepticism lining Ray's face. "I had hoped that you might be able to discover more about what the Lizardmen were working towards than what I could."

"Didn't you use Cormac for a while, too?" asked Evander.

"Yes," said Caleb. "I instructed him to move the seized Faction literature to the library, knowing that he would delegate the task to an inmate if he could. I also knew that Ava would help you discover the hidden entrance to the Lizardmen's quarters, as only *she* could have helped Joshua find it in the first place. Did you hear anything of interest while you were down there?"

Caleb glanced sidelong at Ray, studying him expectantly.

Ray recalled eavesdropping on Kalarish and Ophidirick's report to Tyrax concerning the quarry's progress. "All I saw were maps," he lied, choosing to keep Joshua's last words to himself for a while longer – at least until he was sure that they could trust Caleb.

"That is as I had feared," said Caleb. "Now they know the locations of our other three strongholds."

They jogged for a while longer. Evander looked back at Ben and the others lagging far behind, their green uniforms barely visible in the surrounding jungle. Even their faces were obscured by the heavily cascading rain in between the two groups of fleeing fugitives. "You know that's Rico's kid back there, right?"

"I know," said Caleb. "We'll be bringing him and his father with us in the motorboat. Lungsod is no longer safe for either of them if the boy stays here, now that Gaspar's guards have identified him as an inmate. I just hope that Rico can get the boat ready to sail in this storm on such short notice."

* * *

Ray glanced back at them from up ahead. Even with the distance between them, Ben saw for a fleeting moment that his brother's face was still red and swollen. "What happened to Ray?" he asked as they ran farther down the mountain.

"He went to help Connor and Levi while we were on the cell house roof," said Ava. "That's how he came back."

She must have confused Levi with someone else, Ben thought, either that, or he must have misheard her. "So where's Connor now?"

"We saw you're need a help at the barracks," Nico shrugged, "So we didn't left with Connor."

"Lucky these are here," Sarah remarked as they climbed over the two fallen trees in the road. "They won't be able to follow us too easily if they take the truck."

"Do you think they might still be able to get into the garage and follow us?" asked Ava, glancing over her shoulder.

"They might be able to…" Ben started, although upon seeing the terrified expression on her face, he quickly added, "But that rack full of tools and the truck set against the door should be more than enough to hold them back."

"Plus, they have to enter the code every time they try to open the door," Sarah said reassuringly.

"And what's stopping them from just going around?" Ava asked, still unconvinced.

"Yeah, just like us," Nico said with a reminiscent smile, "When we escape and went on my village."

Ben's thoughts led him back to the hole in the chain-linked fence on the side of the prison, and the four of them picked up the pace along the muddy dirt road.

* * *

Reaching the point where the miry brown path turned into wet gravel, Caleb halted, holding up his hand as the wind whipped past while waiting for Ben and the others to catch up. Tiny pebbles crunching underfoot, they approached with their heads down, crouching low at the top of a grassy bank, the volcano monitoring station in sight.

The three steep cliff walls surrounding the small semi-circular glen sheltered the pair of structures from the violent gusts of the typhoon, yet the lush green grass in the basin still swayed to and fro under the pelting rain. The gravel road ran down in a sickle-bend along the tops of two of the rocky bluffs, passing in clear view around the front of the Watcher outpost.

The signal tower wrought of metal stood tall on one side of the glen, overlooking the windswept waves of the ocean, and the double-storey house comprised mainly of concrete with its wooden veranda on the upper level stood strong in the centre of the clearing, yet the satellite dish and antennae on top of the outpost's roof creaked and groaned with the northerly wind coming over the valley.

The house looked as though it had been boarded up against the approaching typhoon. Shutters were closed over the rain-lashed windows. Nothing stirred from within, although they knew that at any moment, the Watcher outpost could burst into life.

Even now, motion-detecting lights were blazing on and off all around the building, set off by palm tree leaves and coconut husks and other detritus being tossed about, borne on the winds of the blustering gale, intermittently bathing the dark glen in pools of pale yellow light.

Beyond the valley, what had once been a beach of powdery white sand was now an iron grey, matching the colour of the concrete road on its border that led into town. Foaming storm surges crashed all along the coast, occasionally raising the water level above the shoreline and spilling across the road into the gardens of the few beach houses bravely facing the angry sea.

"Never liked this place much anyway," said Evander, lying on the grass beside Ray as they scoped out the surrounding area of the Watcher outpost.

"I think we should move quickly," said Ben, looking back over his shoulder, "In case we're being followed."

"It looks like their pickup truck is still in the carport," said Caleb, lying between Ben and Ray, his dark grey eyes piercing through the curtains of rain, scanning the glen for any signs of trouble. "Knowing Spike, the keys are probably still in the ignition."

"Then what're we waiting for?" Ray sprang up and started back towards the gravel path.

"Ray!" Ava shouted with a whisper, "They might see you!"

Evander tried to make a grab at his leg, but to no avail.

Caleb rose to his feet. "They'll be watching the road, but with the boarded-up windows, we might be able to sneak in through the back and start up the engine. They might not even hear the ignition under the cover of the storm."

Evander grinned, "By the time they realise we're here to steal their truck, they'll be staring at their own taillights driving away."

They clambered up onto their feet and followed Caleb down the steep cliff and into the waterlogged basin. They sprinted across the long slippery grass, keeping their backs bent in case a Watcher happened to peer through one of the boarded-up windows. Tripping the erratic motion-detecting lights, they reached the rear of the carport, where the white pickup truck awaited them inside.

Ray shook the water from his hair, his clothes clinging to his skin. He slipped into the driver's cabin with Caleb and Evander, and they shut the doors with soft thuds while the others climbed into the truck's tray as quietly as possible. He wanted to hear every piece of conversation that passed between the former Watchers while they made their escape so that he could be sure of their intentions. Being out of the rain was an added bonus.

Caleb turned the key, the engine ticking idly.

Ben kept his panting breaths shallow in anticipation, being as quiet as possible while glancing back at the dirt path on top of the small cliff to make sure that they were not being followed.

The engine ticked again, but it did not spark.

Nico looked over at Ben with a worried expression.

Meanwhile, the storm wind buffeted the window shutters of the upper level; although it could just as easily have been footsteps stomping around on the wooden floor above. In the back of the vehicle, Ben and the others' silent hope for the former steadily gave way to dreading the latter as they became fully aware of their vulnerability in the open tray.

The screen door crashed against the wall of the upper level, triggering terrified squeals from both Sarah and Ava. Wide-eyed, the girls clapped their hands over their mouths.

"Come on," Caleb muttered under his breath, trying again. "Come on… Come on…"

On Ray's other side, Evander sat in the passenger seat with his eyes closed, pressing his hands against each other and bowing his head, fervently murmuring a silent prayer.

Looking from one man to the other, Ray punched the dashboard.

"COME ON!!"

With another turn of the key, the engine fired up, filling the garage with its rumble. Caleb took his foot off the brake pad and gunned the accelerator, the wheels screeching as they roared out of the carport, soaring over the driveway and landing with a skidding crunch along the wet gravel path, briefly sending Ben and the others airborne before they fell back on their rumps with heavy thuds. The four escapees clung to the sides of the metal tray for dear life.

Muffled by the sound of the engine's revs, Spike and a half-dozen other Watchers yelled in alarm from the outpost's wooden veranda. They ran along the railed walkway of the second level and rushed down the stairs, only to be sprayed with mud and gravel kicked up by the truck's back tyres as the fugitives sped off, the outpost shrinking into the distance behind a thick blue-grey plume of exhaust smoke.

Just as they fishtailed out onto the concrete road, Caleb slammed the brake pad, grinding the vehicle to a screeching halt, sending the four prisoners in the back piling up against the rear window of the driver's cab.

"*What* is he *doing!?*" Ava shrieked.

Wriggling free of the others, Ben scrambled up to look around. Squinting through the curtain of rain, he saw that they were parked up alongside the row of beach houses. Only a short stretch of road ahead laid the intersection where he and Nico had been caught during their last escape attempt.

"Why are we stopping!?" Ray demanded, looking wildly at Caleb as he blared the horn.

"Evander, make room," he said with a clenched jaw, keeping tabs on the rearview mirror, "We're picking up my contact."

Ray was squashed against Caleb by Evander's broad shoulder as the burly ex-Watcher made space on the passenger side. Ray pushed out his elbows against the two men to make some breathing room for himself, and he looked out the window.

The house to their immediate right was strikingly familiar. It was a wonder how the hollow-brick hut was still standing in the violent storm, its decorative bamboo facade long gone as the small house teetered on the wind. The front door flung open with a long-haired brunette woman emerging, shielding her face from the rain with a toned athletic arm.

A flash of lightning gave shape to her slender European features as she stood in the doorway of the hut. Dressed in a black singlet and skinny jeans, she furrowed her eyebrows at the sight of the ex-Watchers and the escaping prisoners staring back at her.

A revelation occurred to Ray: this was the same house and the same woman who had been in the photo that Caleb had burnt in front of him during his interrogation, its flaming image seared into his memory. Ben had a similar realisation, recalling the woman jogging towards the intersection when they had been apprehended by Gaspar's guards.

"Come on, Alexia!" Caleb hollered, punching indents into the steering wheel's horn.

"They're getting closer!" Ava screamed, her eyes transfixed on the Watchers splashing through the rain towards them.

"Go, go, go!" Nico yelled, banging his fist on the side of the truck.

The woman cautiously ventured out into the rain and down her flooded garden path, still oblivious as to what was happening. Evander rolled down the window to beckon her over, and the sounds of the storm and the four prisoners in the back squealing with fright carried into the cab.

Alexia caught sight of the Watchers shortening the distance to the truck and she broke into a run towards the idling vehicle. Evander pulled on the handle and kicked the door out wide for her.

Just as Spike and the Watchers drew their modified pistols to take aim at the inmates in the back of the truck, Sarah pulled Ben down, the launched projectiles flying overhead. One of the venom snares hit Ben's cheek, its sleep-inducing toxins wafting into his nose. He wrenched it off and cast it aside, then, with each hand, he covered Sarah's mouth and his own – Nico and Ava doing the same – each of them fully aware of the snares' tranquillising effects.

Out of nowhere, twin streaks of green flashed by their peripherals, and two more escaping inmates scrambled over the side of the pickup truck and into the tray.

"Space for three more?" asked Connor, settling into the back, his face red with exhaustion as Levi piled in alongside him. The blonde boy from the Faction looked over his shoulder to yell, "Come on, Bryson!!"

The speckled teen was only a few metres behind them, yet he lost his footing as another angry storm surge foamed across the road. Falling to his knees in the rush of the ankle-deep water, he turned in a wide-eyed panic just in time to see a venom snare sailing through the rain, closing around his face like a bat catching its prey. He wrenched at the mask, staggering towards the truck with one hand reaching out.

Alexia jumped into the cab and slammed the door behind her, droplets of water showering the other three. "What's going on!?" she asked, winding the window back up.

"Cover's blown," said Caleb. "We're pulling out, buckle up!" He floored the accelerator pad before she could reach over her shoulder for the seatbelt, the idling truck roaring to life again, launching forward and throwing up caked mud from the tyres in their wake.

Bryson's outstretched hand had come close to reaching Connor's, but not close enough. The truck sped off, leaving the short-lived fugitive to collapse on the road, succumbing to the mask's toxins as the Watchers closed in.

Levi did not even look back at his former cellmate. He merely lay back in the truck's tray, catching his breath in the rain and thanking his lucky stars that it was not him being recaptured, to the combined disappointment of the other five escapees in the back.

They zipped down the road through shallow pools of lingering seawater, the ocean's swollen waves continuing to roll across the shoreline and foam up over the road. Spike and the other Watchers shrank in the distance once again, soon lost behind the curtain of rain.

* * *

Taking the turn slowly to keep control of the vehicle, Caleb pulled left at an intersection, delving into the heart of the small village at the edge of the sea. The windscreen wipers fought the downpour of rain for dominance over the window pane.

Through the barrage of water, Ray could just barely make out what would have been a bustling marketplace on any other day, blue tarpaulins now draped over the abandoned stalls.

Beyond the empty marketplace, storm surges sent huge waves crashing up against the wharf, the tides spilling over the docks and sweeping the closest market stalls out to sea, sacks of food and racks of clothing joining the overturned fishing boats and drifting furniture of former homes in the chaotic surf.

As they navigated their way through the narrow streets and steered around blockades of debris, Ray realised that this was the same village that his father had once brought him and his brother when they were both young. As dark and unclear as his recollections had been, they had seemed much brighter and more peaceful than this place, now overshadowed by the dark storm clouds and the torrential rain swept by the wind battering the shanty homes.

"Did you find out what it is they're looking for?" asked Alexia. Caleb shook his head slowly. Alexia slumped in her seat. "We worked undercover for *too many years* to come up short now."

Caleb kept his eyes fixed on the road ahead, driving slowly to avoid the drifting detritus floating on the flooded streets. With Ray's memories and Caleb's intentions proving true, all but one thing had fallen into place.

"Why did you throw Joshua off the roof?" asked Ray.

Evander glanced sidelong at Caleb, who maintained his silence.

Alexia answered for him. "Joshua was too much of a liability," she said. "Without revealing himself as a Faction spy in the process, it was the only thing that Caleb could do to keep him from telling the Lizardmen the weaknesses of our strongholds… which is *exactly* what happened anyway, because Quartz Hall fell right after he was taken away."

"*Dragonstone,*" said Ray, satisfied with the answer. Caleb, Evander and Alexia stared back at him with perplexed expressions. "*Dragonstone,*" he repeated. "That was Joshua's message. *Find a way to contact your uncle,*" he looked at Caleb, "*Tell him it's the Dragonstone.*"

"I thought that was just a myth," said Alexia, absentmindedly staring out the window.

"Tyrax truly has gone mad…" Caleb muttered.

Evander shrugged at Ray, knowing just as much about *Dragonstone* as he did.

* * *

The fugitives in the back shielded themselves from the rain that was falling harder than ever now, each droplet stinging them like a whipped thorn.

Crouching against the back of the cab with the others, Ben glanced around at the hollow-brick and plywood shacks on either side of the road. Roofs made of corrugated iron and thatched palm tree leaves alike threatened to lift off their foundations. Doors and loose window shutters opened and slammed at the whim of the whirling wind, revealing glimpses of the Filipino families inside huddling together in fear of the furious storm.

Stray dogs yapped and pigs squealed every time the rolling thunder boomed across the sky. The gale blew through several uncovered windows, shattering glass and hurling debris into the houses. Even the truck skidded sideways in the volatile monsoon. Nico hunched over his folded arms, trying not to think about his father and his friends in the village.

"How did you escape?" Ava asked Connor as they rounded another corner, having to yell over the sounds of squalls battering the houses and waves crashing against the shore, "I thought we were the only ones who made it through the garage."

"We found another way out," Connor yelled back, peering into the driver's cabin uncertainly, seeing Caleb and Evander for the first time.

"What happened to your face?" asked Sarah.

Ben leaned forward to see past the others. Connor's face was not red with exhaustion as he had previously thought. Fresh welts and cuts shone across the blonde teen's cheeks and forehead – although strangely enough, Levi's face was untouched.

"Cormac and Leon," said Connor. "We both would've been goners if Ray hadn't shown up when he did. He and I took a beating from the Watchers on the cell house rooftop while this coward…" he gestured towards Levi, "Decided to leave us for dead and cut a hole through the fence."

Levi muttered something incomprehensible to himself, bunching up against the side rail and lowering his head between his knees. Whether it was out of shame or if he just wanted to cover his snivelling face from the rain, Ben could not tell.

"We won the fight eventually," Connor continued, "And I started directing the inmates escaping from the barracks to safety."

"I think that's when Ray came back to us and we saw you and Caleb in the barracks," Sarah spoke softly into Ben's ear.

"From there," said Connor, "We legged it around the volcano, using the trees and the storm as cover in case we were being followed. And we *were* being followed. Somewhere along the way, Bryson, Levi and I got separated from the others, and we heard rasping and hissing… and screams. These Lizardmen, they were different. We couldn't see them, we could only *hear* them. We hid in some bushes for a while, but as soon as the arrows and venom snares started flying, we ran through the jungle until we reached that row of houses, and that's when we heard you guys honking the horn… So, where are we headed?"

All of them looked towards Ben for the answer. Unaware of the plan himself, he knocked on the back window of the cab, and Ray turned in the cramped space to slide it open. Ben drew back at the sight of his brother's blotchy red face and split lower lip up close again. Back in the garage, the lumps and cuts had been fresh and mild, yet upon seeing the damage now, Ray's entire face was swollen.

Perhaps offended by his brother's reaction, Ray looked past Ben to see Connor and Levi huddled with the others in the back. "Good to see you made it, Connor," he said.

Levi looked up from between his knees, supposing Ray would say the same to him. Ray simply stared back at him with a blank expression. It did not take long for the weasel of an inmate to lower his snivelling face between his knees again.

"There's um, there's a b-boat," Ben stammered, still gawking at his brother's face, "A motorboat. The one Uncle Joshua told me about."

"I know," Caleb said from the driver's seat, "We're going to gather up some fuel first. Hopefully our man can get it into working condition on such short notice."

"You sure a boat's a good idea in this storm?" asked Evander.

"It's the only plan I've got," said Caleb.

"There's another option," said Alexia, wriggling upright in her seat. "But it's just as risky."

Caleb caught on to her idea, but glancing up at the rearview mirror to see the two new stowaways that had climbed aboard, he said, "The plane won't be able to carry all of us, we'd be too heavy."

"Well, we *could* ditch Levi," said Ray.

Evander laughed at first, but he was soon put off by Ray's resolve.

* * *

After navigating their way through a few more intersections and being hammered by the rain for what seemed to them like an eternity, the six runaway inmates in the tray breathed a sigh of relief as Caleb pulled the white pickup truck into a petrol station, parking the vehicle undercover. He climbed out of the cab, striding past the fuel pumps and into the store, the place still open for business even in the violent storm.

Alexia turned to face the escapees in the back. "You guys lay low, okay? Your uniforms will give us away." She slid the rear window shut and Ben and the others complied, lying down side by side in the vehicle's rusty tray.

"But still I didn't have my uniform," Nico said as he lied down, his shirt left behind somewhere inside the prison.

Sarah caught hold of Ben's hand, his heart fluttering at her touch. He could have spent an entire day lying there just like that, with the storm's streaming torrents raining down all around them. He smiled. They were on the verge of freedom.

Seeing a police station just across the concrete lot next to the petrol station, Ray ducked down in the cab, remembering that Mayor Gaspar regularly took bribes from the Watchers to keep the Quarry Complex's operations hidden. *I wonder if the officers on their payroll have already been tipped off about the escape*, he thought to himself.

"I thought you and Caleb were just dating," Evander said to Alexia, "I didn't realise you were working for the Faction too."

"We *were* dating. But that was a long time ago," she said with a faraway look in her hazel brown eyes.

"So… you're not dating anyone right now?" he asked. She shot him with a *don't-go-there* glare. "I can't wait to get back to dating," he said quickly. "I can't wait to watch TV again, now that I think about it. Been a long time since I seen a game of football. And a good cheeseburger too. They don't make them over here like they do back home…"

He trailed off as the weight in the rear of the vehicle shifted with a slight groan, and in the silence that followed, they heard the yells of the inmates in the back.

Ben sat bolt upright with the others, shouting, "Come back, Connor!"

Ray, Evander and Alexia piled out of the truck to see the blonde teen dashing through the rain towards the police station in the neighbouring concrete lot. Connor – still relatively new to the Quarry Complex and its operations – had no idea that the local law enforcement was being paid off by the Watchers to keep the prison's existence hidden.

The Faction teen was waving his arms and calling for help as he ran. Ray and Evander hurtled after Connor before he could inadvertently give them away to Gaspar's guards.

"Get down! Get back down in the tray!" Alexia urged the other five escapees still sitting upright above the side railings.

"They're coming!" Ava squealed, directing their attention towards Spike and the other half-dozen Watchers from the outpost – still on foot – rounding a corner in the distance.

Ben looked desperately over at Caleb, who was still buying fuel for the boat inside the store, oblivious to what was happening outside.

Officers in blue emerged from the police station and spotted the green uniforms. A gunshot's *CRACK* rang out over the storm, punctuated by a flash of lightning and a thunderclap, and Ben's head spun around to see Ray, Connor and Evander falling flat upon the ground.

"*RAY!!*" Ben yelled, standing in the tray.

Both Sarah and Ava shrieked in dismay.

Terrified, Sarah clawed at the hem of Ben's shirt, trying to pull him back down to safety. He tore away from her, scrambling out of the truck and running towards his fallen brother. Closing the distance, Ben could see Connor gaping open-mouthed at Evander, both his and the kind man's eyes wide with shock.

"DON'T SHOOT!!" Spike yelled faintly over the storm from farther down the road. "We need them alive!"

Gaspar's guards did not pay attention to Spike's orders, or perhaps they did not understand. Their gunfire continued, bullets pinging off the wet concrete and ricocheting into the row of boarded-up storefronts on the other side of the road. From the small of her back, Alexia whipped out a pistol of her own and returned fire. With a few well-aimed shots, she forced the corrupt policemen to duck behind cover, suppressing their barrage.

Caleb kicked the shop's door open, drawn by the sound of the shootout. Seething at the trio of bodies caught in the crossfire, he hurled one of the red fuel cans at their attackers. Alexia blasted a hole into the plastic canister mid-flight, dousing a few of the officers in petrol. They would not dare to pull another trigger for fear of engulfing themselves in flame.

In the brief reprieve, Ray pushed himself up, yanking Connor to his feet by the scruff of his shirt, and they both darted back towards the pickup truck, keeping their heads down low to avoid any more bullets whistling by.

"What were you thinking!?" Ray yelled. "The Watchers have the police in their back pocket!!"

"I didn't – I don't know…" Connor stammered as they hurtled past Ben.

Evander remained motionless, his body crumpled upon the ground filling Ben's vision as blood trickled from a small hole in his forehead. Ben's feet were rooted to the spot, transfixed by the sight of the fallen ex-Watcher's lifeless body lying in the rain. The gentle guard had always shown a kindness to all of the inmates in the prison. And now, he was dead, brought down by a tiny piece of metal.

"Benji! What are you doing!?" Ray yelled. "Get back in the truck!!"

In his mourning, Ben did not notice the red pickup truck skidding around the corner, scattering Spike and the other Watchers splashing up the road. Sheriff Sullivan, standing in the tray of the vehicle roaring towards them, expertly aimed his modified pistol out from behind the truck's cab and fired a venom snare.

Before Ben could even see the precisely-aimed projectile, the small scented cloth latched onto his face, wrapping around his head, and he fell to his knees as he inhaled the overpowering fumes.

Tyres screeched just a few feet away from where he was struggling and thrashing on the ground, trying to tear the venom snare from his face. A car door slammed, and boots crunched over the wet concrete towards him.

"'ello sunshine, 'ad a fall did ya?" Cormac winked mischievously at the panicked escapee fighting to pull off the scented mask. The vile man bared his yellow teeth in a crude grin.

Ray shoved Connor – still stunned by Evander's sudden death – into Alexia's arms, and ran back to where his brother had fallen, rain-soaked and desperately trying to wrench himself free of the venom snare covering his face.

Cormac stood glowering over Ben, blind to Ray's approach. He was about to pick the boy up and throw him in the back of the red truck when Ray jumped up to deliver a double-kick to the Watcher's back. With a surprised yelp, Cormac toppled over in a heap beside the pickup's big rear wheel.

Still incapacitated, Ben rolled over to see his older brother landing flat on his back with a shallow splash in the gathering floodwaters of the monsoon. He tried to call out, but his voice was muffled by the venom snare.

"Well, look who's come runnin' on back!" Sullivan called out over the storm's rumbling thunder, his fingers fumbling as he hastily worked to load another shot into his modified pistol.

"Shut up and take the shot, Sully!" Leon barked from the driver's seat of the truck.

Although Ray felt a sharp pain shooting up his lower back from the fall, he did not pause in his attack. *Not this time.* Drawing his arms back and over his head, he threw his limbs forward, using the momentum to propel himself back up onto his feet.

Sullivan leaned out from behind the driver's cabin again, taking aim, but Ray leapt up to clock the Watcher across the jaw before he could pull the trigger, knocking the Sheriff's wide-brimmed black hat off his head.

Ray turned back to help Ben when a pair of hands clawed at him from below. He looked down to see two sets of stubby dirt-encrusted fingers locked around his ankles.

"Should've run while you 'ad the chance, sweet'eart," said Cormac.

The Watcher yanked backwards, pulling Ray's legs out from underneath him and sending him face-first into the floodwaters. Spluttering as he pushed himself up and out of the murky depths, Ray looked up to see the barrel of another gun pointing at him. He caught a glimpse of Spike's dark sunglasses before a pungent veil shot out, closing around his face.

"They must have gotten around the barricade in the garage..." Ben thought aloud to himself, inhaling more fumes in his delirious mumbling. *"That pair of fallen trees in the road would have slowed them down, but it didn't stop them..."*

His mind began to cloud. The venom snare was already taking away his better judgement. He reached up to tug at the mask again with numb fingers. His fingertips felt frozen as he fumbled with the snare. The sound of a wet *smack* on skin nearby told him that Ray was still fighting off the Watchers from the truck. *Or the Watchers are fighting off Ray.*

Another figure stood over Ben, shielding him from the rain. A wave of relief washed over him as Nico bent down to help him to his feet. Ben draped a heavy arm over his rescuer's shoulders as they stumbled back towards their friends.

In a blur, Ben looked back over his shoulder to see Ray on his knees, struggling with one hand on a mask of his own, blindly flailing out at his assailants with the other, yet his fist only managed to connect with the side of the red pickup truck. Spike and the other Watchers from the outpost had caught up to them. Ben's outcry was muffled by the snare yet again.

"Throw him in the tray, and get that thing off his face!" Caleb boomed over the storm.

"But what about Ray!?" Ava argued as she and Alexia helped Nico with Ben, pulling him up into the back of the vehicle.

Sarah's face materialised in Ben's dazed vision as he lay down upon his back in the wet metal tray. She rocked back and tugged the mask free of his mouth, tossing it over the side of the truck.

Caleb took a glance at Gaspar's guards and the Watchers regrouping. "It's either Raymond, or it's everyone!" he yelled, climbing back into the driver's cabin with Alexia.

Where are the others? Ray asked himself. *Why isn't anyone coming back for me?*

Cormac's grinning yellow teeth appeared in the apprehended escapee's blurred vision, the Watcher thrusting an unlit shock stick into his sternum. Ray hacked and coughed into the venom snare, wheezing in more of the reeking fumes.

"They're taking him!!" Ava's voice screamed in the distance as Cormac and Spike hauled Ray's struggling body up to Sheriff Sullivan, who tossed him none too gently into a corner of the vehicle's tray beside an unconscious Bryson. Cormac climbed into the passenger side of the pickup truck, and Spike clambered over the back rail of the tray alongside the Sheriff.

"See your friend on the ground there, Caleb!?" Leon barked as he revved the engine, "That's a traitor's death, you'll get yours soon!!"

The escaping inmates ducked their heads down as they heard the *pop, pop, pop* of pistols ringing out from the police station again.

Caleb gunned the engine and they pulled out from the petrol station, their tyres screeching along the wet concrete before they hit the flooded road. Alexia returned fire at the corrupt policemen, hitting a petrol pump as they sped off, causing a deafening explosion in their wake.

Ben watched as the red pickup truck was shrouded behind a mushroom cloud of flames and smoke, burning scraps of metal soaring in all directions.

Ava stared in disbelief, and Connor buried his face in his hands. Levi cowered as low as possible under the tray's railings. Nico and Sarah stayed at Ben's side with grim expressions, his former cellmate shielding him from the rain, and Sarah cradling his head in her lap.

"I think this are not the way for the boat," said Nico, judging by the landmarks of his village as Caleb struggled to steer in the storm's deluge swamping the concrete streets.

"Do you think they're taking us to the plane?" asked Ava.

"Maybe," said Nico, "But I think it will not going to be a good idea, the typhoon so strong now."

* * *

Sullivan stooped to pick up his black hat from the floor of the tray, slapping it against his leg to shake it free of water. He fixed it upon his greying hair again, and then looked down at Ray with a wide grin, his forehead wrinkling as he raised his eyebrows in mockery. "I thought we lost ya there, boy! Glad to have ya back!"

The red pickup truck broke through the destroyed petrol station's plume of smoke, beginning their pursuit of the white pickup truck. Ray rolled with Bryson from one side of the tray to the other with each skidding turn in the wet road, desperately pulling at the foul-smelling mask.

"Won't do ya any good," said the Sheriff. "Ya already inhaled the good stuff! Here, lemme help ya now, I want ya to see your friends' faces when we round 'em up too."

Sullivan stooped down and pulled Ray's venom snare free. Although his body was already enfeebled from its odours, the aching pain of the shock stick's hit to his sternum still lingered, burning through his lungs as he breathed in the clean air.

* * *

Catching sight of the Watchers' truck in the rearview mirror, Caleb began making wild turns through narrow streets and lanes, forcing the six escapees in the back to cling to the rails as they lurched from side to side.

Sarah pressed down on Ben's shoulders so that he would not slide away from her with each sharp bend.

"Where's Ray?" asked Ben, his head lolling in her lap as he looked up into her eyes.

"The Watchers have him now. I'm so sorry, Ben." Her voice was barely a whisper, yet it was clear to him even over the sound of the storm raging on.

He struggled, wanting to tell Caleb to turn back, but the venom snare's fumes had already sapped his strength. He managed to raise his head just slightly to see the red pickup truck still in pursuit, and he silently hoped that the Watchers would catch up so that they could reunite with Ray once they reached their destination.

"NPA, NPA!!" Nico yelled as they neared the toll bridge.

The vehicle mounted the bridge, sending the escapees momentarily airborne. The others gasped in pain as they thudded back inside the pickup truck's metal tray, yet Ben could not feel the impact. He could not feel most of his body. He meekly attempted to raise his head again.

"Relax, lie down," Sarah said in an attempt to soothe him, but he could still hear through her strained voice that she was clearly on edge.

His vision began to blur, and the leaves of the rainforest passing by overhead blotched together into one swaying mass. The typhoon's winds whipped the canopies of palm tree leaves back and forth, giving tidal currents to the green sea of foliage hanging above them.

* * *

Ray remembered all of the people who had made sacrifices to give them a chance to escape; Mara, Evander, and Cameron chiefly among them. He could not let all of it be in vain. He could not let the Watchers recapture his brother and their friends. They had only just met their uncle, and Caleb would surely be executed for his betrayal if they were caught.

He saw Spike and Sullivan aiming their modified pistols over the top of the driver's cabin, and he fought against the nausea in his head and the pain in his chest to sit upright.

Leon slammed the brakes, he and Cormac laughing uproariously at the sight of the NPA toll bridge in the road ahead. Just as the Sheriff pounded the top of the driver's cab, the truck lurched back into motion again. Sullivan maintained his footing, but Spike fell backwards into Ray.

The vehicle's suspension bounced over the crest of the bridge, sparkling rocks falling from the windows of the red truck as it sped through the checkpoint. The assembled NPA soldiers dropped their guns and squabbled amongst themselves for the glittering gems, eager to satisfy their lust for riches as Cormac giggled callously from the passenger seat.

Spike attempted to get back up, but Ray landed a powerful blow across the man's temple, knocking him senseless. Straining in silence, Ray summoned his remaining strength and threw the dazed Watcher over the back rail of the tray, Spike tumbling out onto the road, rolling and skidding in his leather vest.

Ray slowly rose to his feet, fighting off the paralysing effects of the venom snare.

"Oi, Sully!" Cormac yelled, sliding the back window open, "'e's getting up!"

The Sheriff looked around in surprise, but Ray lunged through the open window before the Watcher had any time to react. Halfway through the window, he reached past Cormac's agitated face to grab hold of the steering wheel.

Leon growled at the third hand on the wheel, and he threw an elbow back into Ray's chin. Blows from Sullivan's shock stick cascaded down with the rain on his lower back from behind, while Cormac sparked up his own shock stick, poising to shove it into the inmate's already swollen and welted face.

* * *

"Something's happening in the truck behind us!" Ava shouted with excitement. "Look, Ray's inside the cabin!"

Nico and Connor joined her at the back rail to see what was happening. Ben craned his neck upwards. Sarah lifted his shoulders from the vehicle's tray for him to get a better view.

Sure enough, Ray was halfway inside the driver's cabin with one hand clasping the steering wheel.

Ray took a glimpse of the white pickup truck in front; Ben lying down with their friends gathered around him. The brothers' eyes locked for a brief instant, and with his last ounce of strength, Ray yanked the steering wheel.

The red pickup swerved, its front wheels buckling in the sudden change of direction, and the entire vehicle careened sideways, hurling Sullivan and Bryson from the tray. The inertia sent the rest of Ray's numbed body flying inside the cab as the truck flipped over and rolled, barrelling off the road and into the rainforest, crashing through the jungle's undergrowth.

Ray was thankful that his body had already been desensitised by the venom snare as he flew around in the truck's cab along with the two shouting men. He smiled before he blacked out.

Levi whooped and hollered, alone in his cheer as the wreck disappeared from view.

"Ray!" Ben choked. He fell back into Sarah's lap, slipping into unconsciousness.

EPILOGUE

A weight lifted from Ben's ankle as he lay in the back of the pickup truck. He was staring up at the grey skies looming overhead. The rain had cleared up, leaving vast pools of water across the grassy flatlands surrounding a small concrete airstrip in the storm's wake.

Past the open fields, they were bordered on all sides by lush green rainforest. A lone hangar and a small shed serving as the control tower stood on either side of the dirt road branching off the highway leading to the airstrip. A light aircraft stood at one end of the runway as Alexia busily directed the freed inmates to clear the windswept debris from the concrete.

"Feeling better?" asked Caleb, casting Ben's manacle to the side with a metal clatter.

Ben sat up to massage his foot, yet the sudden movement made him queasy. His head was pounding from the venom snare's after-effects. He leaned over the side of the truck to dry heave.

At the sound of his heaving, Nico jogged over. "Ben will going to be okay?" he asked earnestly.

"He'll be fine," said Caleb. "Help me get him to the plane."

Nico and Caleb each took an arm around their shoulders and they lifted Ben from the truck. He attempted to walk, but his legs were numb with pins and needles. He resigned himself to letting his feet drag across the concrete.

As they ambled towards the small plane, Ben looked over at Sarah, Ava, Connor and Levi clearing the last of the detritus from the runway.

"Where's Ray?" asked Ben. "We stopped and picked him up, right?" he looked over his shoulder at the empty pickup truck.

Nico said nothing.

Caleb clenched his jaw.

Ben struggled, wrenching himself free of their grip. He landed on his backside upon the wet concrete. The fall was painless, his body was still numb. "We have to go back!" he protested.

An engine rev like a gigantic lawnmower erupted from the light aircraft, and its propellers whirred in spinning blurs, with Alexia conducting pre-flight checks in the cockpit.

"There's no time," Caleb spoke over the noise of the engine, "Gaspar's guards could be on us at any moment. I'm taking you to the Faction. You'll be safe there. And once I've made my report, we can coordinate a retaliation attack against the Lizardmen."

"But what about Ray?"

"Nothing can be done for your brother. Right now, my only concern is getting you to safety." Caleb turned on his heel, motioning for Connor and Levi to board the plane.

Sarah and Ava joined Ben while Nico stood off to the side. He felt helpless and trapped, lying on the concrete with leaden limbs.

"Ray's tough," said Ava. "I'm sure he survived the crash. And if he can just hold on for a little while longer, we'll find a way to get him out of that place, along with everyone else we had to leave behind."

Sarah bent down and took his hand. Her voice was soft and understanding, as ever. "Your brother, Mara and Evander sacrificed themselves so that we could make it this far," she said. "I know it's hard to accept right now, and it's hard for me too, but if we turn back, then they would have suffered all for nothing."

Ben blinked back his tears, trying to stay strong in front of his friends. "We shouldn't just leave him back there."

"I know we shouldn't," said Sarah, staring into his watery eyes as Caleb urged them to get inside the airplane. "But we have to."

Nico handed Ben his father's leather-bound journal, having slipped out of his trousers waistband when he had fallen. "I will going to miss my Papa too, but it's okay, we just try to explore now. We will going to go back on here, someday."

Ben stared down at the cover of the book, the Faction symbol embossed across the front. He touched the golden medallion around his neck, his fingers tracing over the intricate carvings divided across the four quarters of the pendant; tiny coins upon balancing scales, a hammer driving a chisel into a pillar, the flames of a fire, and a sword and shield. He stowed his father's journal back into his waistband.

Nico and Sarah helped him to his feet. With his friends supporting him as they boarded the plane, Ben cast one final glance over his shoulder, his eyes fixed with determination at the dirt road leading back into the jungle.

"I'll see you again, Ray. I promise."

* * *

Far away from Ben and the others, a flickering light beyond the veil of his eyelids drew the adolescent to consciousness. Lying upon a hard surface in some dank room, a flashback flitted across the captive's blank vision – an image of his brother and their friends in a white pickup truck racing down a highway, soon lost in the blur of a spinning rainforest.

At least I haven't completely lost it this time, Ray thought to himself.

As soon as the thought crossed his mind, a skull-crushing migraine put his head in a clamp, some imaginary brute twisting and tightening the metal vice around his temples. He fought the urge to gag, sensing others surrounding his prone body. He could hear the laboured breathing of one, and the involuntary hisses of another.

Peering out through a crack in one of his swollen eyelids, Ray found that he was lying upon the splintered remnants of the same wooden bench, underneath the same flickering light, in the same small room that he had woken up in when he had first been brought to the Quarry Complex.

Three silhouettes stood around the room. Ray clenched his fist, wrapping his fingers around his thumb. He would not let them take Dana's promise ring away from him this time.

Spike's voice filled the room as he made his report, "… Blackbeads got most of 'em, the rest are probably lost in the jungle. Gremlin and Evander are both dead, couple of the inmates too. Evander got what he deserved. He was a traitor – him and Caleb. Leon, Mac and Lygia, among others, includin' myself, have all got light injuries. Sully's hurt real bad though."

Ray would have smiled at the news if his facial muscles were not in agony.

"I think we oughta send him back to the swamp," Spike continued. "The people in the town nearby should have the meds he needs."

Ray caught the red-cheeked Warden at the edge of his vision, breathing heavily in his Hawaiian shirt and mopping at his glistening forehead with a sweat-soaked handkerchief.

"I agree," the Warden said in a fluster, "We'll send him back, right away."

Ray opened his eyelid just a fraction wider to distinguish the third figure in the room, yet he could only make out a shadow of orange and purple in the flickering light. A sudden flare of brightness from the overhead bulb forced his eye shut, the abrupt glare dropping a stack of bricks on his skull. He bit his tongue to keep himself from groaning.

"It is clear that the time of human guardianship over the Quarry Complex has pazzed," a soft wicked voice rasped. "Tyrax has decreed that operations shall now fall under my charge."

"And I surrender my charge willingly," said the Warden, audibly relieved at the burden of responsibility now removed from his shoulders. "Although, might I ask, Matron, what is your intention with the labourers who began the disturbance? Punishment no longer seems to be optimal in educating our residents with the preferred behaviour."

"We *could* set an example for the other inmates," Spike suggested. "Throw a couple of their leaders off the roof… startin' with this one."

Spike moved towards Ray, who attempted to bunch his muscles in preparation to strike, yet it was no use. His body was broken from the car crash. The fight had left him.

"Yez," Kalarish hissed. "Yez, we could regain the power of fear we onze held… Yet, it would only be greater failure to wazte zuch talent." The Lizardwoman paced the small room, deep in thought. Ray's fate rested upon her forked tongue. The scratching of her claws upon stone ceased as she reached a decision. "Thiz rebel will be made to zerve the might of the *Kirzakai*. Zend him to the Desert Complex!"

The light flickered out.

THE END

Enjoyed reading The Rauder Brothers & The Lizardmen's Pit?

I'd love to hear your thoughts!
www.facebook.com/SteveHeuzinkveld

Join my semi-occasional newsletter to receive an email when my next book gets published.
https://steve-heuzinkveld.ck.page/newsletter

Can't wait that long?

Follow me on Patreon for **exclusive sneak peeks** of my next book!
www.patreon.com/SteveHeuzinkveld

ACKNOWLEDGEMENTS

First and foremost, I have to thank my beautiful wife, Hariezoy, for supporting and encouraging me every single day, and for giving me the freedom to burn the midnight oil to hit the keyboard every night until the sun comes up.

The concept for this book began way back in 2009, its world constantly changing, characters evolving and subplots shifting. When I first met my wife in 2013, and I told her that I was working on a book, she was the first person to ever believe that I was capable of writing a story. So thank you, Joy, for believing in me, even when I didn't believe in myself.

A big thanks also goes to my Patreon followers, Greg Hyndman, Rupert Lugo, J Sekula and Martin Georgiev. Your support really helped soften the impact when I was hiring professional artists for the book cover design, and they have both done an incredible job!

But more than that, having you guys in my corner was a reminder that there are passionate people out there who really appreciate my work, and it encouraged me to continue focusing on what I love doing – creating compelling characters and stories and sharing them with the world. The world is a better place with people like you!

Thanks to Miguel Firewolf for his amazing artwork on the cover. He worked with me right down to the tiny details like face wrinkles and shading placements, and he was extremely patient with all of my changes. Les from German Creative has done a fantastic job on the cover design as well.

I also want to thank Craig Martelle and Kevin McLaughlin for their expert insight and gems of wisdom in navigating the wild west of the self-publishing industry. I think if I had have known about these two powerhouses twelve years ago, I probably would have completed this book a lot sooner!

And last but not least, thank you. As an independently-published author, this is very often a one-man show, and after the hours upon hours I've invested into this project, it means the world to me that you've taken the time to meet the characters living in my head.

I'd love to put your name here in my future books, right alongside Greg, Rupert, J-man and Martin. Join us on Patreon to speculate on the plot, share fan art and connect with me while I work on bringing more stories to life!

www.patreon.com/SteveHeuzinkveld

Also by Steve Heuzinkveld

Just because the world ended once doesn't mean it won't happen again.

Five years after rogue missiles have ravaged the globe, *Treading On Ashes* follows the intertwining lives of the survivors still struggling to find their place in the new world.

Dess Sheridan resolves to leave the comfort of her rustic log cabin, tormented by the people she left behind while she delves into the dubious death of an old flame.

Living a life of self destruction, what remains of Harlan Reid's moral compass spins out of control when he is offered a mercenary contract to make ends meet.

When the supply of diesel runs dry, Evelyn Royce weighs her family's newfound prosperity against a pack of desperate settlers faced with plunging into darkness.

Meanwhile, an unearthed shadow gathers in the west, murderous marauders raid the farm belt and cutthroat pirates torment the coast as alliances shift in the scramble for safety.

The rich and the reckless, the dutiful and the depraved, all fight for what little remains while *Treading On Ashes*.

Follow the link below for your next adventure!
https://www.amazon.com/dp/B09FXCK1PG/